To Have and to Hold

Also by Fern Michaels
in Thorndike Large Print®

Texas Heat
Texas Rich
Texas Fury
Texas Sunrise

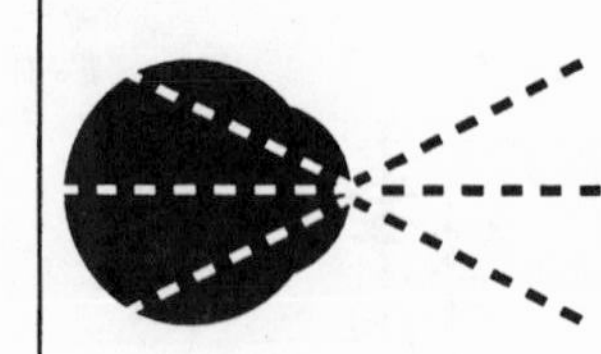

This Large Print Book carries the Seal of Approval of N.A.V.H.

To Have and To Hold

Fern Michaels

Thorndike Press • Thorndike, Maine

Published in 1994 by arrangement with Ballantine Books,
a division of Random House, Inc.

Thorndike Large Print ® Basic Series.

The text of this Large Print edition is unabridged.
Other aspects of the book may vary from the original edition.

Set in 16 pt. News Plantin.

Printed in the United States on acid-free paper.

Library of Congress Cataloging in Publication Data

Michaels, Fern.
To have and to hold / Fern Michaels.
p. cm.
ISBN 0-7862-0336-6 (lg. print : alk. paper)
1. Large type books. I. Title.
[PS3563.I27T59 1995b]
813'.54—dc20

94-34296

To Have and to Hold

PROLOGUE

All during their lovemaking she cried.

And when it was over, she sobbed in his arms.

"Shhh," Patrick whispered. "It's only for a year, honey. I'll be back before you know it."

Kate sobbed harder. She snuggled deeper into the crook of his arm, her nest of comfort and safety.

Patrick nuzzled her neck, inhaling the scent of her hair. Lemon and vanilla, something she splashed on her hair before she dried it. It teased his nostrils. Something to remember. Something to think about while he was away.

Kate was the best thing that ever happened to him. All his friends said so. She was the world's best cook, the world's best mother, the world's best manager, the world's best wife. For one brief second he wondered about the order of Kate's capabilities.

Patrick continued to stroke her hair, crooning familiar words. She always calmed under his touch. It was amazing how well he knew his wife. It had to have something to do with the fact that they'd known each other from childhood. Grown with each other. There were no secrets between them.

She was like a small child, rather like their daughter Betsy now, succumbing to his hypnotic words and gentle stroking. The power he had over his wife never ceased to amaze him. With a word or a look, rarely an explanation, she would do or say whatever he wanted. She was perfect, a shining example of himself.

He thought then about what he was leaving behind. His little family. Other guys worried, but not him. Kate had come to California with him, from Westfield, New Jersey, where they'd both grown up. Kate was his friend, his lover, his wife, and mother to his two little girls. Kate was *his*. When someone loved you with the whole of their heart, you didn't have to worry. Kate would never betray that love.

His fingers plucked at Kate's sleep shirt, so worn and soft it felt like an old friend. He'd given her the shirt himself for her birthday, overlarge, trailing down way past her knees. Even the lettering — USAF TEST PILOT SCHOOL. EDWARDS AFB, CA — was faded. He wondered if she'd ever wear the sexy, slinky gown he'd ordered for her from Frederick's.

Almost perfect, but then no one was perfect.

"Promise me tomorrow, Patrick," Kate whispered.

"All the tomorrows for the rest of our life. I've never broken a promise to you, Kate. Honey, I'm the best of the best, the Air Force says so," he said, with no sense of false modesty. "That means I'm going to go in, do the job I was trained to do, and come home." His voice grew stern. "No more tears, Kate." He felt pleased when she drew in a deep breath, pressing her body even closer. Her skin felt wet, slick against his own.

Patrick craned his neck to see the small clock next to the bed. Eleven minutes till he had to get up. He inched away from her, their skin making a smacking sound. He couldn't get it up again if he tried. "No," he whispered huskily. He brought her closer again, their bodies touching. A deep breath swooshed from his lungs. Sex might be the greatest pastime in the world, but flying had it beat by a mile. He felt a surge of adrenaline when he thought of himself flying *missions* in Southeast Asia. If someone said to him, right this second, What do you love more than anything in the world? his answer would have to be flying.

He was born to fly; all his instructors said so. He said so. A natural-born pilot. Up there he was supreme, one of a kind. Zack Heller, his wingman, was good, but not his equal. As far as he was concerned, he had no equal in the air.

This year away from Kate and the girls was going to be good for all of them. Kate would tend the home fires, and he would finally do what he'd dreamed of doing all his life. Serve his country, get his ticket punched, and come home a fucking hero.

He eyed the Baby Ben, groaned for Kate's benefit, and leapt from the bed. A moment later the shower was pelting his lean body with a vengeance. The force of the water gave him an instant erection, one he massaged with soap and his hand. He closed his eyes and imagined he was driving into his wife, the Frederick's nightgown hiked up around her neck.

He groaned.

When Patrick entered the kitchen fifteen minutes later, Kate was in the tidy room with the fringed place mats on the varnished oak table. She was flipping pancakes in her old chenille robe, her long blond hair brushed and pulled back in a ponytail and tied with a red ribbon. It was the same kind of ribbon she tied in Betsy's and Ellie's hair, but for some reason he didn't think it looked cute. Her eyes were red-rimmed. He could see the quiver in her lips as she turned the pancakes. Blueberry.

He took a seat as Kate placed the griddle cakes in the middle of the strawberry-patterned plate. Then she stepped back and said in a barely audible voice, "Patrick, how is this?" She opened the belt of her robe.

Patrick's eyebrows shot upward as he chewed. In a teasing voice he said, "If you weren't clenching your teeth, I suppose it would look better. I made a mistake, honey. Frederick's isn't for you. Toss it out or give it to Zack's wife." He went back to his pancakes. Kate tied the sash of her robe so tight that she gasped.

"Good breakfast, honey. As always. I'm really going to miss your cooking."

"I'll send you cookies and whatever else I can pack up. The girls love to make cookies." Kate choked back a sob as she dipped the frying pan in the soapy water, swishing it, and then let it fall back into the water, her shoulders shaking.

"Kate, you promised you weren't going to do this," Patrick chided gently.

"I didn't think it was going to be so hard. I miss you already, and you haven't left." Her shoulders continued to shake.

"Is this the memory you want me to take with me?" Patrick demanded, irritation creeping into his voice. Kate heard it.

"No. No, of course not." She forced a smile to her face.

"Guess that's it. I feel free as the breeze. That was a good idea Zack had last night, taking all our gear to the flight terminal in his pickup. Do you want to say good-bye here or at the door?"

"I wish you'd let me go with you. It's not right, saying good-bye like this."

"Yes, it's right. You'll carry on and cry. I don't want to remember a scene like that."

"I promised I wouldn't cry," Kate whimpered.

The edge was back in Patrick's voice. "You're crying now, and you promised not to. Kiss the girls for me." He blew her an airy kiss before he strode from the room.

Kate stood in the kitchen doorway watching her husband as he settled his cap firmly on his head and fired off a snappy salute to the reflection in the mirror. She watched him open the front door, step outside, and then kick it closed with his heel. He didn't miss a step and he didn't look back.

Kate slipped to the floor in a huddle, crying heartbrokenly, over and over, "Just promise me there will be a tomorrow for us, Patrick."

Outside in the crisp, early morning air, Patrick walked to the corner bound by apartment complexes to meet Zack Heller. The moment he saw him, he gave him a thumb's-up salute.

"This is it, Heller!" he called.

"You ready for this, Captain Starr?" Heller asked, a slight catch in his voice.

"I've been ready for this since I saw my first airplane. I think I was three years old. The only thing I can't figure out is why God made me a mere mortal instead of a bird. Man, I was meant to fly. I don't ever want to do anything else. How about you?"

"I'm dedicated, Starr. You're fucking obsessed."

"You got that right. It's my life."

"No, it isn't. That family you left back there is your life."

"Yeah, yeah, but after flying. Hey, I'm *readyyyyy.*"

Patrick tipped his cunt cap to a rakish angle, jammed his hands in his pockets, and started to whistle.

"Off we go, into the wild blue yonder, climbing high, into the sky . . ."

CHAPTER

1

The sewing machine had a sound all its own, the needle jumping up and down through the bright pink felt square. Two pairs of eyes focused on what was almost a finished product. With her head bent to the intricate stitches the needle was making, Kate Starr could still see the telegram on the little table where she'd dropped it earlier, unopened. Patrick had only been gone ten months. She shouldn't be getting a telegram.

It was supposed to be yellow. Everyone said it was yellow.

"Is this going to be the prettiest dress you ever made me, Mom?" Betsy asked.

"Me too, me too! I want one just like it. Betsy and Ellie looked like Mommy," Ellie babbled around the thumb in her mouth. She pointed to a dress draped over the back of

the sofa, her own Christmas dress.

Kate watched as a frown started to build on six-year-old Betsy's face. "Does Daddy want us to all wear the same dress?"

Kate cut the thread and double-knotted it beneath the swirling skirt. "Well . . . yes, I guess so. Daddy . . . always smiled when we paraded in front of him in our mother-daughter outfits. Remember how he always took our picture?" God, her voice sounded so shaky, so . . . fearful. One look into Betsy's eyes told her the child was aware that something she didn't understand was going on.

"I want mine to be different," Betsy said, fighting tears.

"Oh, honey, why?" Kate said, her own eyes misting.

"Want mine different, too," Ellie whined.

Kate stared at the appliqués on the skirt of the dress, refusing even to glance in the direction of the telegram.

Betsy scuffed at the worn carpet. "Daddy isn't here. He won't see us," she said. "I want my dress different."

"Me too. Make it different. Make it like Betsy's," Ellie chortled.

"No! I want mine to be mine. Mommy, don't make hers like mine."

"All right, Betsy. I'll give you a belt buckle and make a bow on the back of Ellie's dress.

Do you want pockets?"

Betsy pointed to the telegram. "What's that?"

"It's a telegram," Kate said, her voice sounding desperate. "A telegram is . . . it's a . . . quick way to send . . . news." Bad news, she should have said. Terrible news. She wanted to cry, to shred the telegram.

"Is the news about Daddy?" Betsy asked, the dress momentarily forgotten. "Maybe Daddy is going to be coming home for Christmas. Open it, Mommy, and see if he is." She marched over to the little table, picked up the telegram and thrust it toward her mother. Kate recoiled, almost toppling the chair she was sitting on.

"Put that back. Now! Do as I say, Betsy," she said in a voice the child had never heard before. Betsy scampered away to obey her mother's orders, then, eyes downcast, scuffed at the carpet.

Kate refused to look at either of her daughters. Instead she bent her head to peer at the stitches she was ripping out. Things were starting to change already, and she hadn't even opened the damn telegram. When a stitch refused to budge with the stitch ripper, Kate yanked at it, ripping the material at the seam. A tear fell on her index finger.

She was losing control, frightening the chil-

dren. I'm not going to open the telegram, she thought. Not now, not ever. "Oh, God, Patrick, you promised me tomorrow, and now I have a telegram," she muttered under her breath.

Kate looked at the appliquéd Santa Claus on the pocket she'd just ripped off Betsy's dress. She had to say something to the child, look at her and not see Patrick reflected in her little face. Patrick always called her a miniature replica of himself. And he said it so proudly. She rummaged in her sewing box for a buckle that would match Betsy's dress. Needle and thread whipped in and out of the soft fabric.

"Want to try this on now, honey?" Kate said in a voice so choked with emotion, Betsy ran to her and put her arms around her in a tight bear hug. Not to be outdone, Ellie wrapped both her arms around her mother's leg.

She needed to be strong. Tough. Little Miss Homemaker, who didn't have the faintest idea how to be strong and tough. All she knew how to do was be a mother and wife. Patrick took care of everything else.

"I think," Kate said quietly, "we're feeling out of sorts because it's almost Christmas and Daddy won't be here to help us open presents. So tonight we're going to write a very

long letter and tell him how much we miss him and how we're going to make Christmas cookies. We have to be brave and . . . and carry on. Daddy will be disappointed if we don't go ahead with things. Now let's see a big smile from everyone." She stretched her own facial muscles into something resembling a smile, then watched the girls scurry off with their dresses. The moment they were out of sight, she crumpled, her eyes again on the telegram.

It had been delivered an hour ago, just as she was getting ready to sit down at the sewing machine. Soon the notification officer would arrive. A chaplain and accompanying officer would probably knock on her door next. "I damn well won't open it!"

The girls were back, prancing back and forth in front of her in their new Christmas dresses. She made all the right comments, smiled, hugged them, and then ordered them to take off the dresses so she could hem them.

There was a glint in Betsy's eyes when she said, "I don't want to wear the matching panties, Mommy. That's baby stuff. I don't like to show off my undies."

"But honey, the pattern calls for matching panties." Suddenly she felt stupid, ignorant. Was it possible Betsy was right and six-year-olds didn't wear matching panties?

"I want mine to match." Ellie giggled, bending over to show her plain white panties.

"She's a show-off," Betsy grumbled. "Boys laugh at you when they see your underwear."

"All right, plain white for you, Betsy, and matching ones for Ellie. We compromised. That means it's fair for everyone."

"Yippeeeee!" Ellie squealed.

Betsy scowled. "When are you going to open your news letter? We're supposed to share. Daddy said so."

"Later, honey. Change your clothes and bring the dresses back so I can hem them. Then you can play Chinese checkers if you want to."

Betsy wasn't about to be put off. "When you open the news letter later, are we going to share it?"

"Yes," Kate said, because there was no other answer that would satisfy her daughter.

Now. She should open it now. But if she did that, she would be breaking a promise to Betsy. There was every possibility the telegram was from Patrick's father or her own parents. But no. She *knew* who'd sent the telegram and she *knew* what it said. THE SECRETARY OF THE AIR FORCE REGRETS TO INFORM YOU . . .

"You wasted your money, Mr. Secretary of the Air Force, because I'm not going to open your hateful telegram," Kate said through clenched teeth.

The girls were squabbling over where to play their game of Chinese checkers. A moment later they were in front of her, demanding that she make the decision for them.

"I have an idea. Why don't you play the first game in Mommy and Daddy's room. Right in the middle of the bed. You can play the second game in the bathtub, and the third game in your own room."

Ellie squealed her delight. Betsy's face indicated it was the stupidest thing she'd ever heard of, but she trotted off behind her sister. Seconds later Kate heard the door to her room close.

She bit down on her lower lip to stop the trembling, and leaned back in the sewing chair she'd upholstered herself. Her position gave her a clear view through the front window.

She thought about her husband then, remembering. As if she could ever forget. Patrick was her life, her reason for being. She knew in her heart that the day God had created her, He'd said to Himself, I'm putting Kate Anders on earth so she can marry Patrick Starr. She'd never told that to anyone, not even Patrick. It was a secret she hugged to herself every day of her life.

She'd known Patrick since grade school, walked behind him and his friends on the way to school, blushing furiously when he turned to look over his shoulder at her. When his friends weren't looking at him, he'd smile and sometimes wink. She'd never told anyone about that, either.

Once in third grade when the teacher had made her head of her relay team, she'd picked Patrick and he'd outright refused to be on her team because his friends heckled him. Later, out in the hallway, he'd hissed at her to never do that again. She'd nodded miserably and then cried like a baby.

On the way home from school that same day, Patrick had rushed to catch up with her and apologized for making her cry. She remembered exactly what he'd said and how he'd said it. "Jeez, Kate, the guys will never let me live that down. Guys don't like that kind of stuff. I don't like to be kidded. I like you. A lot. I'm sorry I made you cry. Don't tell your mother, okay? If you do, she'll tell my dad. Boys aren't supposed to hit girls or make them cry. I'll get a whipping for sure."

Everybody in school knew she *liked* Patrick, and everyone in school, even Patrick's buddies, knew he liked her, too. But it wasn't until they were older, in high school, that they had a real date.

All the girls liked Patrick because he flirted with them, but he smiled at her, his eyes all warm and wet like a puppy's. Once, when she was in seventh grade, he'd touched her hair and said it was like silk. He said she could be his girl if she wanted to, but if she told anyone, then she wasn't his girl. At night she'd added that secret to her growing list, and slept with all of them on a piece of paper under her pillow.

In her teen years every single minute that wasn't used up by school or her family was spent with Patrick. By that time Patrick's friends had paired off with girls, so she was accepted. Patrick was her fella and she was his girl. All the time. If she didn't see him for a day over the weekend, she thought she would die. She knew way back then she could never live without him.

Once she'd been sick in bed with a high fever for three days, which stretched into four and then five. She should have known she was retarding her recovery by being so miserable, not eating or drinking fluids. But she didn't need that kind of nourishment; she needed Patrick, to see him, to hold his hand, to have him smile at her.

She'd waited until the family fell asleep and then crept downstairs, put on her mother's ratty fur coat, and in her slipper socks walked around to Patrick's house and threw a small stone at his window. He'd come downstairs in his pajamas and, outside, had hugged her and kissed her eyes and even her ears. He'd said all kinds of really nice things and then made her go home. She was better the next day. All she thought about for weeks after that were Patrick's kisses, sweet as sugar and warm as summer sunshine.

The kisses had stayed sweet and warm, and then they'd become passionate. Always passionate, even when she was pregnant, right up to the last minute before delivery.

If she lived forever, she would never forget the look of rapture on Patrick's face when he held Betsy for the first time. The doctor, smiling, said father and daughter had *bonded.*

Kate's face closed up when she thought of Ellie's birth. Patrick hadn't bonded with Ellie. He didn't pick her up for two whole weeks, and when he did, he said, "She looks just like you, Kate." How pleased she'd been with that compliment. To her dismay, Patrick said over and over that Betsy was his and Ellie was hers. She wasn't sure even now if Patrick loved Ellie. She'd asked so many times, and Patrick would just look at her and say, "Now that's a stupid question if I ever heard one." He'd never given a straight-out yes or no answer.

A sound from outside jolted her. She wiped her tears away, her eyes fastened on the front window.

She knew who he was the moment she saw the Air Force blue sedan with the gold lettering on the door glide to the curb in front of the building.

Every military wife in the world knew who he was.

She leaped from the chair and bolted for the front door. She slammed the door and double-locked it, her face filled with panic. Her hands clenched into tight fists, the knuckles bone-white. Tears streamed down her cheeks.

How shiny the car was, not a speck of dust on it. The car door inched open, and she saw one brilliantly shined shoe, then another. Feet. Black socks. Two legs, and then the whole of him. How sharp the creases were. Almost as sharp as the ones she made in Patrick's trousers.

Kate glanced toward the little table. She should have opened the telegram. Never!

Dress blues. Spiffy. She knuckled her eyes as she tried to stifle the sobs rearing up in her throat. He squared his shoulders, not the way Patrick did it, all slithery motion, but with a quick little snap that looked ominous. Through her tears she watched him settle his cap squarely on his head. Now he was going to come up the walk.

Kate clutched at her heart. How could it be beating so fast when it was broken, shattered into a dozen pieces?

He was moving. Betsy had counted the steps to the front door once when she was having a race with Ellie: twenty-one. She counted each one, her eyes on the black polished shoes. Ten, eleven . . . Betsy's were a child's steps. This man in his dress uniform and shiny shoes made it in eleven. She should have known it would only be eleven. Why hadn't she known that?

The knock on the door was the loudest sound she'd ever heard in her life. Her heart fluttered in her chest. *Don't open the door. Not now, not ever. If you do, your life will change forever.*

The knock sounded again, louder this time. Kate felt herself start to crumple. Her eyes flew to Patrick's chair, to his picture on the little end table. How handsome he was in his flier's gear. Through her tears she could see the excitement in his face, the endearing, lopsided grin. Her husband, and Ellie's and Betsy's father.

"Mrs. Starr, are you there?"

Of course she was here; what a stupid question. She had two little girls to take care of, where else would she be a half hour before dinner? *Please, God, make him go away*. The clenched fists kneaded her thighs.

"Mrs. Starr, I *must* talk with you. Please open the door."

"Go away," Kate whimpered. *Please, God, make him go away.*

She sensed movement on the other side of the door.

Kate felt her knees buckle. A second later she was crunched against the front door, her eyes level with the kitchen doorknob. She saw his shadow, saw the brass knob turn, saw his creased trousers, his polished shoes.

"Get out of here!" she whimpered as he entered. "You have no right to come into my house. You broke and entered . . . breaking and entering . . . you damn well came into my house uninvited. Now, leave now! That's an order, Major. My husband *was* a captain. Is . . . still is . . . would be . . . you're here . . . leave me alone!" Kate sobbed.

"I can't do that, Mrs. Starr." He approached her, held out his hand to help her to her feet. Kate knocked his hand away and cowered against the door.

"Mrs. Starr," Major Collier said, dropping to one knee so he was eye level with Kate, "the chaplain is on his way. I'm sorry, I thought he would be here. We do our best to arrive together with Mrs. Willard." Mrs. Willard was the wife of Patrick's commanding officer. "There must have been an emergency. . . ." He let his voice trail off. "I know how difficult this is for you. One is never prepared. . . . It's not as though Captain Starr is dead. We don't know that yet. I'm not here to tell you there's been a change in his status. You know how things are done." His voice sounded even lamer than before.

Kate sprang to life. "What are you talking about?" She wiped at her eyes with the sleeve of her shirt. "If Patrick isn't . . . what are you doing here? Why was that telegram delivered?" she said, pointing to the hall table. "I know who you are. You bring messages from the Grim Reaper. Everyone calls you men the big G.R.s How can you do it? *Why* do you do it? Damn you, where is Patrick?"

Nelson Collier flinched. So she hadn't opened the telegram; she didn't know. God damn Air Force.

"Captain Starr's plane was shot down," he told her. "That's all we know. Two of our pilots say they saw him eject. If he ejected, he was alive. He could be anywhere in the jungle, or he could be a prisoner. We just don't know. We try to get the information to the family as soon as we can. Here, let me help you up."

He was taller than she expected, so tall she had to stretch her neck to look up at him. She was aware of everything then, of the radio playing softly in the kitchen, the smell of her meat loaf in the oven, the twinkling lights of the Christmas tree. Patrick wasn't dead. Not confirmed, anyway. Alive somewhere. She had to hang on to that thought. She allowed herself to be led into her tiny kitchen, which sparkled with cleanliness.

"A cup of coffee would taste wonderful, Mrs. Starr."

"All right," Kate said listlessly. She turned off the oven before she measured coffee into the percolator and added water.

"This is a pretty kitchen. My wife would like it," Major Collier said quietly.

"I wallpapered it myself. Patrick . . . said it reminded him of an outdoor garden. It's the ivy pattern on the paper."

"I can see where he would think that, especially with all the plants on the windowsill. Or are they herbs?"

"Both." Placing three green checkered place mats on the table, she watched as Nelson Collier played with the fringe. "I made those, too," she volunteered.

"They're pretty. My wife is partial to green."

"Green was . . . is Patrick's favorite color. Betsy likes green, too. Ellie prefers red. I think I like blue."

"Mrs. Starr, is there anyone you want me to call?"

"No. Most of my friends moved off the base. They went back to their families, and I stayed here. There's been no room at my parents' house since my grandparents moved in. They're quite elderly. Patrick's father lives in a retirement village that doesn't accept children. I decided it would be more economical for us to stay here . . . and wait. How long will it be before you have more information?"

"We'll do the best we can. Things like this take time. There's the other side to deal with."

"So, what you're saying is you don't know. It could take months or even years. And what am I supposed to do in the meantime, Major Collier?"

"Wait. It's all any of us can do. Time, Mrs. Starr, will take care of everything."

"That's not good enough, Major. I want details. I want to know everything. I have a right to know, and so do my children. What's to become of us?" she whispered.

"We take care of our own, Mrs. Starr," Nelson Collier said with an edge to his voice. Hearing a knock, the major looked toward the front door. "That would be Chaplain Rollins," he said. The relief in his voice startled Kate.

Major Collier, with Kate's permission, opened the door. An aide ushered in a tall, graying man dressed in regulation blues. When the men joined her in the kitchen, Kate poured coffee with a steady hand as she suffered through the amenities. She knew the chaplain expected her to fall into his arms for comfort, so she deliberately distanced herself from him, preferring to stand by the stove with her rump pressed against the warm enamel of the oven door.

"Do we pray now?" Kate said bitterly.

"She's in shock, forgive her," she heard Major Collier say, sotto voce.

"Only if you want to, my dear," the chaplain said to her, his voice deep and resonant.

"I don't want to."

"God —"

"Don't talk to me about God, Chaplain. Not now. And you, Major, don't tell me the Air Force takes care of its own. When you walk out this door, I'm by myself with my two children. I know *exactly* how the military works. You'll bombard me for a week or even two weeks, and then I get shuffled into some never-never land, at which point I become a liability. No one wants to deal with heartbroken wives and crying children. I *know* how it works. Each phone call is filtered down to people you have to repeat the story to until you reach the maintenance people. I defy you — do you hear me? — I defy you to prove me wrong!" Kate cried, her blue eyes blazing. She fell apart almost immediately, sobbing into her hands.

This couldn't be happening. It was one of those horrible nightmares she had from time to time when the mail was slow and Patrick's letters didn't arrive. They didn't say Patrick was dead; they said they didn't know. Surely not knowing was better than dead. Dead meant Patrick would never walk through the door again. Never hold her in his arms or kiss her good night. Dead meant she would be a widow, her children fatherless.

At last Nelson Collier stood up. This was the part he hated. "Mrs. Starr," he said, not unkindly, "Captain Starr would want you to be the little soldier he knows you are. This has been a terrible shock. You have to be strong, especially for those two little girls inside. You must keep the home fires burning for your husband."

Kate dropped her hands and stared at him,

incredulous. "That's bullshit, Major, and you know it. I'm not a soldier. My husband is the soldier, and look what happened to him. I'm a wife and a mother. I don't want to be tough, I don't want to . . . I wish you'd leave. I want to be alone with my children."

"We understand, Mrs. Starr," the chaplain said in the voice he reserved for serious sermons. Nelson Collier nodded. "If you need anything, if you want to talk or . . . pray, call me any time of the day or night."

Kate said nothing as she held the door open for their departure. She didn't say good-bye. The dead bolt seemed to move of its own volition.

There were things to do, things that had to be taken care of. She had to set the table, cook the potatoes, cut up the salad greens, slice bread. All the things she did every day according to her schedule. Later, when it was time for her to sit down and knit, she would think about Patrick and prepare what to say to the girls. Tomorrow. Not today. Her eyes filled again as she peeled potatoes. "You promised me tomorrow, Patrick. You promised. I'm holding you to that promise. You're alive, I know it. I know you'll keep your promise."

She was talking to herself, mumbling under her breath. And why shouldn't she? She'd just had the shock of her life. Anything she did now, no matter how strange or bizarre, shouldn't be held against her. *Oh, Patrick, where are you? Are you alive like they said? I didn't ask when it happened. What was I doing at that precise moment you ejected? There has to he a record. Families need to know things like that. Was it yesterday when I was cranky and out of sorts, or the day before, when I had that awful headache? I should have known, felt something. We were always so in tune with one another. Oh, Patrick, what's happening? Why didn't I feel something?*

She rinsed the potatoes a second time before drying off the pot and clamping on the lid. Her movements were sure, deft from years of practice in the kitchen. Mother Earth, was what Patrick called her. Would he ever call her that again? Yes, God, yes. She would accept nothing else.

Kate sniffed, wiped her eyes on her sleeve, and cut the salad greens into tiny pieces so Betsy would have less trouble chewing with her missing front teeth. Ellie liked little pieces, too, and always lined up the tiny pieces of vegetables to make a ring around the plate. At five she knew her colors and alternated the ring with carrots and peppers, chortling as she arranged the bits of tomatoes in the pyramid in the middle. The shredded lettuce was her moat. Every evening they laughed over it. Or she did, as Patrick seemed to tolerate Ellie's ways.

Her chores done for the moment, Kate glanced around, a wild look in her eyes. Now what was she supposed to do? What if . . . what if . . . Eyes burning, she decided to clean the refrigerator. Busy hands didn't allow time for thinking. God, what if he didn't come back? What if he'd been shot when he landed on the ground? Maybe she should call her mother, one of her sisters, somebody who would say, "Don't worry, Patrick's all right. One day when you're least expecting it, he'll walk through the door. Patrick was too vital to die so young. Patrick was a survivor. Hold on to that."

Kate scrubbed industriously, the stainless steel shelves glistening with her efforts. The enamel blinded her. She wished she knew why she had such a fetish about cleanliness. Maybe someday she'd think about that. Patrick thought about it often, chastising her eat-off-the-floor housekeeping. "We never eat off the floor, so what's the point?" he would say. Sometimes he grinned when he said it, and other times he said it sarcastically.

Finally, satisfied with the condition of the refrigerator, she washed the bottles and jars, making sure the lids were on tight. Her eyes raked the ketchup bottle and the butter dish. Her mother always said you could tell a good housekeeper by the way she kept her ketchup bottle and butter dish. Hers were spotless. Patrick always dribbled the ketchup and got little toast crumbs on the butter and the dish. Tears slipped down her cheeks, and this time she didn't stop them. Maybe she needed a really good cry; better to let it out and then get on with it.

She washed the vegetables, the lemons, the cucumbers, the tomatoes, and then dried them with a dish towel. Patrick said she was balmy for doing it. She hated it when he said things like that, so she tried to wait until he wasn't around. But he always knew.

She'd tried so hard to be perfect for Patrick, the perfect wife, the perfect mother, the perfect housekeeper, the perfect lover, the perfect money manager, the perfect *everything*. Patrick said there was no such thing as perfect, and even if there was, he didn't want it. Her ears and cheeks started to burn when she remembered him saying, "Let's have stand-up sex in the kitchen by the sink." The girls were outside in the sandbox, and the kitchen window was open. She'd refused, and Patrick got testy. "What's the big deal? All I do is push up your dress, pull your panties aside, and bingo!" She'd offered to go in the bedroom and lock the door, but Patrick had said to forget it. Instead he'd gone to the bathroom, alone, and she'd known why. She hated it when he masturbated. It was her fault. Her face and ears continued to burn. Patrick was selfish, but then so was she in her own way. Once he'd even whipped out his . . . *his thing,* and done it right in front of her. She'd cried, told him to stop, but he wouldn't. That time, they were in the hall outside the bathroom and the girls were in the tub.

"The past is prologue," she muttered as she dropped the last polished lemon into the fruit bin.

When dinner was finished, Betsy helped clear the table while Ellie shook out the place mats and put them away. Then both children sat down with their crayons and paper. "Remember now," Kate said, "when the big hand is on the three, you have to finish Daddy's picture and get ready for your bath."

It was a ritual the children performed every evening after dinner. On Fridays Kate folded their drawings and mailed them off to Patrick in a separate envelope.

"Mommy, what should I draw tonight?" Betsy asked.

Kate pretended to think. "Draw all of us sitting on your bed. Put a letter in my hand."

"Are you smiling or are you sad?" Betsy asked, her face puckered in a frown.

"I'm smiling. Everyone is smiling."

"What's Ellie doing?"

"Hugging Roseann."

"Can I put a puppy on the bed even if we don't have a puppy? If I put a puppy, will it be a lie?" Betsy asked anxiously.

"No, Betsy, it won't be a lie. It will be a wish. I'll show you how to print the word *wish* on the picture. Daddy will know what it means. A puppy is a good idea."

"Will we ever get a puppy?" Ellie asked wistfully. "If we do, can he sleep on the bed with me? What will we call it, Mommy?"

Kate fought her tears. "That's something for us to think about. Let's all think about a name, and tomorrow after dinner we'll tell each other. The best name gets a lollipop."

"I want a red one. My name will win," Ellie said confidently.

"No sir, I'm the oldest. I know better than you do," Betsy said, petulant.

In order to avoid a squabble she wasn't prepared to deal with at the moment, Kate switched the conversation to the park and the games they would play the following day.

When the girls had finished drawing, Kate beamed her approval at the two pictures and listened patiently as Ellie explained each squiggly line and round circle. She was always amazed at Betsy's drawings. The child had inherited whatever small talent she herself had. She had no difficulty figuring out Betsy's picture. The puppy looked like a puppy, the bed looked like a bed, and even the figures were more than stick lines, rounded out with faces and hair.

"Bath time. Last one in is a smelly fish!"

"Oh, Mommy!" Both girls giggled as they trotted off to the bathroom.

When the girls were in clean pajamas and tucked into bed, Betsy asked the question she'd been dreading all evening. "Who was that man, Mommy?"

"An Air Force major, honey."

"Does he know Daddy?"

"Not really. He knows about him, but he doesn't know him personally."

Satisfied with the answer, Betsy snuggled beneath the covers. "Did we get a letter today?"

"No, sweetie, we didn't, but tonight we're going to read the last two instead of our usual one. I'll read you your last letter and then I'll read you mine, okay?"

"Goody, goody," Ellie said, her eyes closing wearily. A second later she was sound asleep.

"Read mine first, Mommy."

"Okay," Kate said, unfolding the wrinkled

letter the little girl handled several times a day.

" 'Dear Betsy and Ellie —' "

"Daddy always puts me first. Does that mean he likes me the best, or is it because I'm the oldest?"

"What do you think?"

"I'm the oldest," Betsy said, wrinkling her pug nose. Her dark eyes glowed as she waited for her mother to read the letter she already knew by heart, just the way she knew some of the nursery rhymes.

" 'I miss you two little rascals. I hope you're being good for Mommy and doing your chores. I love all the pictures you've been sending me. I have some of them in my plane. I show them to the other guys in my squadron and they say you girls are going to be artists someday.

" 'It's going to be Christmas pretty soon. Be sure to make a present for Mommy. Mommies like presents. When I was little like you, I used to make a present for my mother and she would always give me a big hug and a cookie. I think the hug was better than the cookie.

" 'I love both of you very much. I think about you every day and wonder what you're doing. Be good girls and I will be home soon. Remember now, you have to be extra good or Santa won't leave presents in our house. I heard, and maybe this is a secret, but I'm going to tell you anyway. Santa comes all the way over here to Thailand and leaves us fliers a special present. Isn't that wonderful?

" 'Remember to say your prayers every night. You, Ellie, and Mommy are mine to have and to hold, forever and ever. I send you all my love and kisses. Daddy.' "

"Isn't it a wonderful letter, Mommy?" Betsy said sleepily.

"The best letter in the whole world," Kate said. "Maybe tomorrow we'll get a new one." She looked at the date on the envelope: September 23. She could feel herself start to tremble. "I'll read you my letter tomorrow. Sleep now, honey," she said, bending over to kiss both her daughters.

"Okay, Mommy," Betsy said, drifting off to sleep.

She was alone now, more alone than she'd ever been in her life. She knew what came next on her schedule, what she was supposed to do to fill up the hours until it was time to go to bed. If she deviated now, she would be lost. If she called the chaplain now, she could still do everything and only be off by a few minutes. She wasn't going to sleep anyway, so what difference would it make?

She dialed the number he'd left with her and cleared her throat when the chaplain picked up the phone on the third ring. "Chaplain Rollins, this is . . . Kate Starr. Please, tell me what you know and accept my apologies for . . . this afternoon. I'm sorry if I offended you. . . . I didn't mean to."

"I understand, my dear. Major Collier has all the information, but I'll be glad to tell you what I know. I can come over, if you like."

"No. No, I would rather . . . it's better if I'm alone right now. Talking on the phone isn't . . . it doesn't sound so . . . so final."

"I understand, my dear. . . ."

Kate listened carefully for ten full minutes, hating the sound of the man's voice, hating what he was saying.

"Captain Starr was in a right pull-up when his engine stalled on him. He was already on afterburner. As far as we can tell, he had no options. He ejected behind cloud cover. His wing man didn't actually see him eject. We think he's somewhere in enemy territory, Mrs. Starr."

Enemy territory. In a voice she barely recognized, she asked, "Chaplain, is Patrick . . . what I mean is, would it have been better for him to die than be taken prisoner?"

"We don't know that Captain Starr is a

prisoner, nor do we know he's dead. He could be hiding in the jungle. Unlikely, but it is a possibility. We just don't know."

"When will we know, Chaplain?" Kate asked in the same small voice.

"I can't answer that, Mrs. Starr. We're doing everything possible to update the situation. As soon as we know, you'll know. Search-and-rescue efforts are under way. You must have faith and you must believe. Put your trust in the Almighty and He won't let you down."

Kate's stomach lurched. She wished she'd practiced her religion more faithfully. She went to church on Easter and Christmas and sent the girls to Bible study, but that was it. Praying was something she rarely did, even though the girls prayed every night before going to bed. "Isn't it a little after the fact now?" she muttered.

"Dear girl, it's never after the fact. God doesn't view it like that. Prayer is never frowned on. I don't say you have to go to church to pray. You can pray anywhere, anytime."

Anytime, anywhere. She knew that. "Thank you for talking to me, Chaplain," she said softly, and cradled the receiver.

A moment later she reached for her knitting. Knit one, purl two, *Holy Father* . . .

She stuck with it, knitting and praying for the forty minutes she allotted for knitting on her schedule.

Then Kate threw caution to the winds and repacked her knitting and sketch pad. The hell with the schedule. She was dying inside, so what would knitting and sketching do for her? With that thought, she burst into tears, burying her face in the sofa cushion so as not to wake the girls. Missing in action. Killed in action. Prisoner of war. When would she know Patrick's fate? *Oh, Patrick, where are you, are you safe?*

It was almost one in the morning when Kate crept off the sofa and walked down the hall to her bedroom. She turned on the light and stared at hers and Patrick's room, seeing it through her husband's eyes. Her face full of misery, she walked around the clutter — and that's what it was, clutter. Her crafts, her busywork. Wooden hearts edged in lace, duck plant holders, geese lined up in a row, picture frames with painted hearts with bows and buttons. Every wall, every corner, was filled with *something*. Panic rushed through her when she tried to see something of Patrick's. Yet she'd left everything just as it had been when he'd left.

She lurched, tripping over the lined-up geese, to Patrick's dresser, yanking open the drawers, knowing what she would find, Victorian lace bags filled with shaved cedar shaving. God, even the tassels on the venetian blinds had hearts and ducks on them. She gagged. How many times had Patrick said, "Honey, do we really need all of this?" How many times had he tripped over the parade of geese the way she just had?

She ran to the bathroom, knowing what she would find. The same homey theme of hearts, ducks, and chickens. She'd appliquéd hearts on the shower curtain with the same trailing ribbons, ending in a bouquet of baby ducklings nestled in a wicker basket. The same patterned decals were stuck to the four corners of the bathroom mirror. The bathroom carpet was oversize, latch-hooked three winters ago. She stared at the huge rooster in the center of the carpet and cried anew.

God, why was this bothering her now? *Because you know Patrick hated all this stuff but he put up with it because he loved you.*

In the blink of an eye she was back in the bedroom, pulling and tugging at her dresser drawer. Beneath her slips, bras, and panties was the Frederick's nightgown, wrapped in tissue paper. It was so trashy, so . . . *slutty,* a direct contrast to everything else in the house. She opened a second drawer and withdrew a dimity ankle-length nightgown, neatly ironed and smelling of lemon and vanilla. The neckline was high with a prim satin bow she'd added after she bought it. She had three, pale yellow, pale pink, and pale blue. Demure. Old-fashioned. Ridiculous. She folded the Frederick's nightgown and placed it in the drawer, her eyes filled with tears as she left the bedroom.

In the small living room she looked around. If anything, it was even worse. Every inch of available space was filled with *something*. She could fill the back of a pickup truck with all the junk in the house. Once, in a fit of anger, Patrick had called her crafts "junk" and then later apologized. He was right, it was junk. God, where was the picture of him standing next to his plane with Zack? Her hands were feverish, frenzied, as she yanked at one drawer and then another until she found it. The frame didn't fit the Federal blue of all her crafts, so she'd shoved the picture in a drawer. She'd promised to find a place to hang it. Patrick had looked crushed, but he'd never mentioned it again. *Oh, Patrick, I'm sorry.*

Now when it was too late she was . . . What was she doing? Assuming guilt for her husband's situation? Blaming herself for not being more like the wife he wanted? Blaming herself for being selfish, not caring about what he wanted? All she'd tried to do was make a cozy, warm, happy home. What she *really* had was a cluttered, stifling, sort-of happy home.

Kate sank onto the sofa and reached for one of the pillows to hug against her breast. Dear God, had she done *anything* right all these years? "Our sex life was good," she whimpered. But was it? Patrick liked to experiment, but she didn't. Straight missionary position. She was always satisfied, but was Patrick satisfied? He said he was.

"What's so wrong about going down on me?" he'd asked on his last birthday, when she'd promised to do whatever he wanted and then had reneged on the promise. "Then get on top of me," he'd begged. She hadn't done that either, because she didn't like the way her breasts flopped about and Patrick had wanted to leave the light on. He'd stomped into the bathroom, buck naked, and not only slammed the door, but locked it as well. When he'd come out a while later, his penis dripping semen, he'd shouted, "Are you happy now?" She cried all night into her frilly, embroidered pillow after Patrick had set up camp across the room, and fallen asleep singing the birthday song to himself.

Was it too late to do all this soul-searching? Only if he's dead, she answered herself. But he *couldn't* be dead, he was too vital! She would never believe he was dead. Not Patrick. *Please God, let him come back. I swear I'll be the kind of wife he wants. I'll do whatever he wants. I'll wear trashy clothes and I'll have sex swinging from the chandelier with the lights on if that's what he wants.* She paused, then added, *I'll go back to church, too, and take the girls.* She half expected to hear a clap of thunder, but nothing happened.

God didn't make deals, it was that simple.

Armed with a load of brown grocery bags, Kate attacked the bedroom and bathroom, ripping things off the walls, snatching the shower curtain, kicking at the geese. She lost track of the number of bags she used and the trips she made to the little patio outside the apartment. She was stunned when she finished, at four o'clock, to see how spacious the place really was. She could walk anywhere and not have to dodge or weave her way around things. It was going to take her a long time to patch and paint all the holes in the walls.

Yesterday was gone. Today was here, and tomorrow would arrive soon enough.

Chapter 2

At six-thirty, when it was a bright new day, Kate parted the kitchen curtains. Winter. Her favorite time of the year, but then she said that every year. The truth was, autumn was her favorite time of the year. Autumn back East. She closed her eyes and imagined she could smell burning leaves.

A new day. How was she to think of it? Day one after the news? Day one without Patrick? Day one as head of household? Widow? Alone, with little hope for the future?

Kate clutched the edge of the sink with both hands until her knuckles turned white. How could she go on without Patrick? I don't know how to do anything, she thought. I never worked outside my home. "All I know how to do is keep house, and I botched that up," she said to the sound of the percolator.

Her eyes strayed to the clock on the stove. She had an hour before the girls woke. Thank God it was Saturday and she didn't have to take Betsy to school.

Patrick was smart; everyone said so. A graduate of Texas A&M. Not too many pilots had a Master of Science degree in aerospace engineering. Would that get him through whatever was happening to him now? He was equipped for an emergency: he had his Geneva card, his emergency radio pilot stored under his right arm in a survival vest pocket, and he was in top physical condition. At his last physical he weighed in at 190, the perfect weight for his six-foot-two frame. He had wonderful stamina and endurance. Patrick would survive, but would she be able to say the same? She was already falling apart, unraveling like the yarn on a knitted sleeve.

Maybe she shouldn't tell the girls, at least not yet. Maybe it would be better to wait until she wasn't so raw inside, until she wouldn't burst into tears and frighten them. For now she was all they had, and she had to be their rock. Patrick, she thought, would want it that way. Just pick up the pieces and go on. But on to what?

She ruminated about her situation for a while, and after pouring her third cup of coffee, reached for her Betty Crocker cookbook.

She kept her checkbook and passbook to the savings account in the manila pocket in back. Their savings were meager, less than six hundred dollars in the savings account and one hundred in the checking account. If Patrick didn't return relatively soon, she was going to have some serious problems. Military paperwork constantly got snafued. The voluntary move off the base she was contemplating so she could get a job would cost more, and she'd have to have money for security and utilities deposits. It was unlikely that she could get by without getting a job. And if she did get a job, who would look after the girls? Sitters cost money and she wouldn't be making much to start — providing she even found a job without experience. She knew in her gut Patrick's pay and benefits status was going to be a problem.

"Enough," she muttered, slamming the bankbooks back into the cookbook.

"Help your sister get dressed, Betsy," Kate said an hour later. "I have to take the trash out." It took four trips to the Dumpster behind the apartment building to get rid of all the crafts from her rampage the night before. She wasn't sure how she felt when she entered the kitchen. Exposed, the way the apartment now looked.

"Take my socks off!" Betsy screeched.

"Will not. Mine have the pink bows," Ellie shrilled.

Kate's head throbbed. This was new. The girls rarely squabbled, and if they did, it was usually over in seconds. "Just a minute, let me see the socks," she said, and took a look. "Ellie, these are Betsy's. Here, these are yours," she said, pulling a pair of rolled-up socks from the little girl's drawer.

"She went in my drawer. She's not supposed to do that. You said it was private. I don't go in her drawers," Betsy grumbled.

"You do so. You went in yesterday looking for my letter."

"Because you told me to." To her mother she said, "We were playing school and I told her she had to do show-and-tell. I came in here to get mine and she said to get hers. That's why I went in her drawer."

"You did it!" Ellie cried.

"Shut up." Betsy yanked at the bows on her socks. "I hate these bows. None of the other kids in school have bows on their socks."

"I thought you liked them. They match your hair ribbons," Kate said. God, was this desperate-sounding voice hers?

"I don't want them anymore," Betsy said petulantly.

"Then give them to me," Ellie cried,

snatching the bows Betsy had pulled off. "Now I can have two bows, one on each side. Will you sew them on, Mommy?"

Something was happening here, and she wasn't sure what it was. "All right, later this evening I'll sew them on, if Betsy is sure she doesn't want them."

"I don't. They're stupid. Nancy Davis said they're dumb-looking. She said I wear too many bows and ribbons, and they tease me about the colored buttons *you* sewed on the bottom of my skirt."

"But they look so pretty and colorful," Kate said defensively.

"Sew them on my dress, Mommy," Ellie said happily.

Kate nodded as she stared at Betsy's belligerent face. "I guess that means you want plain things, no ruffles or bows," she said quietly.

"I just want to look like the other girls. I don't want to take those little bags to parties, either. I want to buy a present like everyone else does. If I can't take a bought present, I don't want to go."

"All right, Betsy, you made your point. I'll think about it."

"That's what you always say to Daddy, but you don't think about it. He said so. I heard him say that was just to shut him up."

"Betsy, honey, I'm sorry. I'll try and do better. I promise," Kate said, her voice cracking.

"You always say that, too. You aren't sorry. Sorry means you don't do something again. That's what Daddy said. Ask Ellie, and if she's not pretending to be dumb as Chester Manners, she'll say the same thing." Ellie's head bobbed up and down.

Kate hesitated. "It's not the bows and buttons that are bothering you, although that's part of it. What's wrong, Betsy?"

Betsy looked down at her bare feet, her face full of misery. She bit down on her lower lip, a sure sign that she was about to cry.

"Betsy said Daddy is lost and that man can't find him. Daddies don't get lost, do they, Mommy?" Ellie giggled. "She's just being silly and trying to scare me, isn't that right, Mommy?"

Kate knelt and put her arms around both her daughters. "No, that isn't right, Ellie," she said in a whispery voice. "This is all my fault. I should have told you about Major Collier's visit yesterday, but I . . . had to . . . get used to what he said. I was going to talk to you about it today when we went to the park. You see, something happened to Daddy's plane and he had to . . . leave it, to jump out. You both know what a parachute is. Daddy was wearing his, so he landed safely on the ground. He used his radio to call for help, so now we have to wait for . . . for someone to go and get him, or wait for him to find his way back himself. It might take a little while, so we have to be brave and not worry. Daddy wouldn't want us to worry. We'll think about it and talk about it, but we won't worry. Can we agree to that, the three of us?"

"Does that mean Daddy isn't going to be writing any more letters? Will we still write to him?" Betsy asked tearfully.

"Of course we're going to write. That isn't going to change. Daddy is probably too busy to write. He'll have to find his way out of the jungle."

"Don't they have mailmen in the jungle?" Ellie asked.

"She's acting dumb again, Mommy."

"Do you know for a fact that there's no mail in the jungle, Betsy?" Kate chided gently.

"She said mailmen. Like our mailman. I know the difference," she said testily, her large brown eyes sparking.

"I'll tell you what. Today, after the park, we'll stop at the library. We'll ask the librarian to give us everything she has on Vietnam, and a map, too. If we study it, maybe we'll get a feel for where Daddy is and a better idea of how he's doing. I vote we do that."

"I do, too," Ellie said, raising her hand.

"Betsy?"

"Okay."

"I'm sorry I didn't tell you this last night. I was upset."

"Is that why you threw everything away?" Betsy demanded.

Kate nodded. How wise this little girl was. How like Patrick. "You faked me out last night, didn't you? You weren't really sleeping, were you?"

"I heard you crying. I saw you throw everything in the bags. All that stuff Daddy said was junk. Now he won't know you did it."

"Tonight we'll write him and tell him."

"It's too late. He's lost and they won't deliver his letter," Ellie said, bursting into tears.

"We're going to write it anyway and pray that Daddy receives it. We'll keep writing every day even if we say the same thing over and over. We'll call the Red Cross and ask them for help.

"Now, let's finish dressing, open all the windows, and head for the park. It's going to be a lovely day, the sun is shining, the sky is blue, and we'll have a picnic and play in the park."

"Why can't we buy hot dogs and french fries like everyone else?" Betsy said, pressing her advantage.

"That might be a good idea. It's time we did something different. With relish and mustard, how's that?"

"Oh, goody, real hot dogs. We can write and tell Daddy we had hot dogs. He won't believe us. Will you write it, Mommy, so he truly believes?" Ellie demanded.

"Absolutely," Kate said, forcing a smile to her face. "In fact, we'll have Betsy draw a picture of all of us eating the hot dogs." She tweaked Betsy under the chin. The child grimaced, her facial muscles stretching into something that resembled a smile. She didn't forgive easily. "Happy faces, everyone," Kate said as cheerfully as she could. Finally Betsy grinned, showing the gap between her front teeth.

"Okay, breakfast in ten minutes. Wash your faces, brush your teeth, brush your hair, and bring the rubber bands to the kitchen. Grizzly bear pancakes this morning for Betsy, and puppy dog pancakes for Ellie."

"I'd rather have cornflakes with a banana," Betsy said stubbornly. "You said pancakes are just for grown-ups because they have too much syrup and it rots your teeth. I don't want pancakes."

"Fine, then you can have cornflakes. Ellie and I will have the pancakes," Kate said wearily. *God, what's happening to us?*

An hour later, breakfast finished, Kate led the girls outdoors, jackets in hand. "Listen, instead of going into Bakersfield, let's head for Mojave. It will be something different."

"I'd rather go to the park," Betsy said, nudging her sister.

"Me too," Ellie said.

"Okay. Remember, it was your decision."

"Why do you want to go to the desert? They don't sell hot dogs there," Betsy said, staring straight ahead, her hands folded primly in her lap.

"I'm sure they sell hot dogs there. I wasn't trying to get out of buying them for you. I just thought . . ." She sighed. "Girls, do you think you could be a little more . . . What I mean is, I don't want us to have any bad feelings. I know you feel angry, Betsy, but anger doesn't make things better. Just because I'm a grown-up doesn't mean I don't forget —"

"My teacher says no one knows everything," Betsy volunteered.

"And your teacher is absolutely right. I'm sorry if I . . . I wanted to do everything right. I made a lot of mistakes, I see that now. Families shouldn't squabble. From now on if one of us has something to say, that person should say it. The others will listen. We'll . . . we'll vote. Let's vote now to confirm we're going to vote." Kate giggled in spite of herself. "Aye means yes and nay means no."

"Aye," cried Ellie.

"Aye," Betsy added after a slight pause.

"Okay, the ayes have it. I feel better, how about you?"

"Were the pancakes good?" Betsy asked wistfully.

"See, see, you cut off your nose to spite your face!" Ellie chortled. "Didn't she, Mommy?"

"In a manner of speaking, but you aren't going to say that again. Betsy was making a statement. The next time she'll explain to us if she doesn't want something. Do we agree?"

"Aye," they chorused.

When they reached the park, Kate parked the car and followed the girls to the playground.

"Where's your knitting and your book?" Betsy asked.

"I didn't bring them today. I thought I'd just watch you girls and talk to Della if she's here." Colonel Geary's housekeeper brought the colonel's children to the park every Saturday. The children played well together, considering the Geary children were boys. Kate spotted Della at a far bench and walked over, the girls in tow.

Della Rafella was Mexican, a cherub of a woman whose sweet face was always wreathed in a smile. She loved children, animals, and people. She'd been with the Gearys since the boys were born. Francine Geary, Timmy and Teddy's mother, had left after Teddy's birth "for greener pastures," according to Della. Everyone, she said, knew about Francine Geary and her lust for life, men, and wine. She also said Francine had damaged the colonel's chances of moving up in rank.

Something was wrong today, Kate could feel it as she sat down on the bench next to her friend, her only friend. " 'Morning, Della. It's a lovely day, isn't it?"

"I love sunshine even when it's cold. It's what I miss most about home. Sometimes I think I should go back."

"You could go back for a visit. Goodness, what would the Gearys do without you?" She was stunned to see the woman's eyes fill with tears.

"They don't need me anymore. Colonel Geary is getting married next month, and his . . . his new wife is going to be a mother to the boys. She's going to clean the house and care for them. Colonel Geary is being transferred. I cried myself to sleep last night. I'll have to look for a job now, but I'm forty years old. I can't afford to pay rent and buy food. Housekeeping by the day doesn't pay that well. With room and board, I just manage to get by. I have very little savings, maybe enough to last a month or so."

"Oh, Della, I'm sorry. You can stay with me until you find something. You'll have to sleep on the couch, though. We'd love to have you."

Della's face brightened. "Truly, you would let me stay with you?"

"Truly I would."

"What happens when Captain Starr comes home?" She answered her own question. "By then I should have a job. Did you get a letter this week, Kate?"

"No. I won't be getting any letters for a while." Kate told her about the chaplain and Major Collier's visit, fighting her tears as she spoke.

"This is a terrible thing. Oh, Kate, I'm so sorry," Della said, wrapping Kate in her arms. "Look, let me come and help you. You need me, Kate. At least until Captain Starr comes home."

"Oh, Della, I can't pay you right now. Once Patrick's pay is straightened out it will be different. Besides, I can't bear to stay in base housing. The memories would drive me out of my mind. I'm barely making ends meet now. I'm going to leave base housing and find a job. I really don't know how to do much of anything but keep house. I have no talents, no job qualifications. But I can't go back home. I can't go to my sister, she has three children of her own and a very small house. Patrick's father lives in one of those retirement villages that doesn't allow children. And my parents have their hands full with my grandparents. I've never worked a day in my life. The only money I ever earned was from babysitting, and a little from my sewing. My God, I don't even know how to operate a cash register. I've always stayed home to cook, clean, iron, and take care of the children."

"That's what I do, and it's a full-time job. Really, Kate. Homemaking is very important."

"I wanted to be perfect for Patrick. He's so smart, he can fly a plane, do all those upside-down things pilots do. I just barely managed to get out of high school. What if he doesn't come back, Della? What if I'm a widow? I swear I won't want to live if that happens."

"That's foolish talk. Your husband will come back home. I feel it here." Della thumped her ample bosom. "I don't know when, but he will come back to you and those beautiful little girls."

"All I've been doing is crying and thinking. The girls . . . Betsy sensed something was wrong. This morning she was impossible . . . well, for a little while. Ellie doesn't really understand. I'm going to buy some newspapers on my way home. I told the girls we're going to go to the library. I hate to admit this, but I don't know the first thing about Vietnam. I should know. I should have studied up on it, asked Patrick questions. I don't know why I didn't. It doesn't say much for me. God, Della, how am I going to get through this?"

"One day at a time. I will help. If you allow me to sleep on your sofa and give me food, I will be your housekeeper. I do not require much, a few cents for church on Sunday. For now it is a solution for both of us, if you are agreeable."

"I'm more than agreeable," Kate said, brightening. "It's settled, then, we're a team. I'll help you and you'll help me. Do the boys know you're leaving?"

"Colonel Geary told them last night. Look at them, they're so quiet. First they lose their mother, now me, and they're getting a third mother. Teddy cried all night. Timmy said he's going to run away. The colonel whacked his bottom and made him do thirty push-ups. It is sad, is it not? Little children should not have to suffer."

"When is your last day with the Gearys?" Kate asked.

"Next Friday."

Kate nodded. "I'll drive down and pick you up after school. Oh, Della, I'm so glad things worked out this way! When God closes one door, He truly does open another. Now, let's go get the children some hot dogs. It's my treat. Sodas too." She stood up and began walking with Della toward the hot dog vendor, then stopped. "What's her name?"

"Whose name?" Della asked.

"The soon-to-be Mrs. Geary."

"Tiffany Wexelworth," Della said, breaking into her first smile of the day.

Kate burst out laughing. "May they live happily ever after."

Kate spent the following week in a state bordering on hysteria. For hours on end she'd read everything she could on Southeast Asia. She tried making up stories for the girls about the people and the strange land she was coming to despise, but Betsy and Ellie both balked after the third session, at which point she made up stories about a frog and a rabbit, which threw them into fits of giggles. While they colored or played school, she pored over the want ads and apartments for rent. Twice each day she called Della to report on the want ads, and if an apartment appeared promising, Della would check it out and report back on her success or failure.

By the end of the week she knew nothing more about her husband's situation. She bristled when she was told about the "government keep quiet policy" and demanded to know *exactly* what "keeping quiet" meant. Captain Bill Percy, her caseworker, who was cadaver thin with bulging eyes, told her the Air Force felt the communists treated prisoners in a humane and civilized way. "I believe our men are treated well," he said authoritatively. She didn't believe it for a minute and insisted on knowing if her husband was a prisoner. Percy looked her in the eye and said, "I don't know, Mrs. Starr," to which she replied, "Bullshit!" She blushed furiously but held her ground.

In his report, which grew thicker by the day, Percy wrote, "Possible troublemaker."

On Thursday, the day before she was to pick up Della, she called the casualty assistance representative for the fourth time to find out when she could expect to receive her husband's pay. There was no return call. For the last five months her checks had been late. One month she received two at the same time. Another time she'd missed an entire pay period. She was now a month behind and when she spoke repeatedly to the finance officer all he would say was he was looking into the matter. She then called her insurance agent to see if she could borrow on the family's insurance policy. With the paperwork involved, she was told the process would take four to six weeks. "We can starve in four to six weeks!" she screamed into the phone before she broke the connection. No one at the insurance office called her back. She then called the finance officer and complained again.

On Friday, Della's last day at the Gearys', Kate picked up Betsy from school and drove to Bakersfield, where the housekeeper tearfully climbed into the car with a suitcase an two paper bags full of her belongings. Sh leaned over to peck Kate on the cheek befo stretching around to chuck the girls un the chin. "I'm here now to take care of I will be a mother hen and you three be my chicks. It is agreed?" she asked.

"Absolutely. I've always wanted to be a chick. Patrick . . . Patrick always said I was his slick chick," Kate said with half a smile.

"Daddy said we were his chicklets," Betsy gurgled. "Chicklets are chewing gum, did you know that, Della?"

"No!" Della said in mock horror. Betsy and Ellie bobbed their heads up and down. "Well, if your daddy said you were his chicklets, he must have meant you were sweet and tasty."

"Is everything all right, Della?" Kate asked, her eyes on the road.

"It was sad. The boys cried, I cried. I'm starting a new life now. I cannot dwell on sadness, nor should you, Kate. I think I found an apartment. I called the owner last evening and he said we could come to look at it at four o'clock. Are you sure, Kate, that giving up housing on the base is the right thing to do? He said it needs work. It's by the California state college. There are three bedrooms — two, actually, and one oversized closet the man said could double as a tiny bedroom. If you like it and think you can afford it, I will sleep there."

"How much is the rent?" Kate asked anxiously. "Yes, moving is right for us. I need to get a job, a life. There's nothing for me at the base."

"He said it is negotiable, which makes me think it'll be a real dump. But we will do what we must to get by until Captain Starr returns. Soap and water plus a little paint can work miracles."

Kate brushed at the tears filling her eyes. "I can't believe this is happening," she whispered. "I have so much to tell you, but we'll discuss it later. I don't want the girls to get upset."

Della nodded. "I bought the paper this morning thinking you wouldn't have a chance to pick one up. Do you think you could be a receptionist? There are several girl Friday jobs listed."

"I don't know. I've never worked on the outside. But I can learn," Kate added firmly.

Twenty minutes later, after following Della's directions, Kate stopped the car in front of a run-down building with a FOR RENT sign in a front yard that was more of a trash dump than a yard. She cringed at the sight. "I guess this is it." Neither woman made a move to get out of the car. A man as unkempt as the front yard appeared out of nowhere and sauntered over to them, hitching up his pants as he went along.

"Afternoon, ladies," he said, tipping a

imaginary hat. "Come along, it isn't as bad on the inside as it is outside. If you decide to take the apartment, I'll have the trash hauled away." He gave his pants a second hitch as he shrugged his light flannel shirt into place over his skinny shoulders. Despite his youthful manner, Kate could see he wasn't a young man; he might have been sixty. "Donald Abbott," he said, holding the door open for Della. "I do like a woman with meat on her bones," he said, and winked at Kate.

"I do not like scrawny men." Della gave him a sour look.

"You look like a good cook. The stove in the apartment is almost new. The oven works. Everything works. Even the shower."

"That's a relief," Kate said tartly. "Is this neighborhood safe?"

"Of course it's safe," Abbott said testily. "Families live here. Poor families. They all help one another. Being poor doesn't mean the neighborhood isn't safe. Miss Della told me over the phone you had two little girls. If it wasn't safe, I wouldn't have given her the address." He hitched up his pants again as he marched behind Kate up the front walkway.

Fifteen minutes later, her heart thumping in her chest, Kate said, "Providing you clean this place, and providing the rent is right, I'll take the apartment. One hundred and ten dollars," she said firmly.

"One hundred and fifty dollars, and I'll let you have the wringer washer in the cellar. It works. Laundry tubs included. There's no Laundromat close by. I'll pay the water bill."

Kate weighed Abbott's words. Two showers a day for her and Della, a filled tub for the girls each day, and laundry water, not to mention trips to the Laundromat if she could find one . . . "One hundred and twenty-five with the washer and no water bill. It's all I can afford, so I can't counteroffer again. Oh, the rooms need painting. If you give us the paint, we can do it ourselves. It's your decision, Mr. Abbott."

It was a terrible apartment, Kate thought. She wasn't sure if paint and curtains would improve it. Maybe she could find the same green-and-white wallpaper and redo the ancient kitchen. "New linoleum in the kitchen," Kate blurted. God, she was really considering moving here!

"You strike a hard deal, little lady," Abbott said, extending his hand. "Consider yourself my new tenant. Rent is due the first of the month. I normally ask for a month's security, but you look to me like you're strapped right now. You can pay me ten dollars a month toward the security."

Thank you, God. "That will be just fine, Mr. Abbott. We'll move in the first of February. Do you need a deposit now, or is my word good enough?"

"Five dollars will hold it. It would help if I knew your name. This pretty lady, too," Abbott said smiling at Della.

"I'm Kate Starr and this is Della Rafella. My girls are Betsy and Ellie."

"Is there a Mr. Starr?"

"Is that any of your business?" Della snapped.

"Yes, there is a Mr. Starr, but he —"

"Jumped out of his plane and he's lost," Ellie chirped.

"I see," Abbott said. "Listen, you don't have to give me a deposit now. February first when you move in will be fine with me. My boy was killed in the Korean War." He shuffled off, his shoulders slumped.

"It's going to be fine," Kate said in the car on the ride back to the desert. "We'll make that apartment a showplace, you wait and see."

Della blessed herself. "They say God watches over fools and foolish women. I don't have any bad feelings about it, Kate. I might even be able to find some baby-sitting jobs to help out, and Ellie will have someone to play with."

"I made some decisions this week, Della. I have to have a . . . I don't know what to call it, an agenda maybe — maybe that's the wrong word — but I honestly believe Patrick will come back. I don't know when. Until he does, I'll cope rationally with the uncertainty. I'm going to stay as busy as I can and do whatever I can for Patrick, even if it's just writing letters every day that pile up someplace I've never heard of. I'll keep Patrick alive for the girls. He is alive, Della, I know he is. For now I have to be patient because I have no other choice, and when my patience wears thin, I'll . . . do whatever I have to do. What do you think?" she said breathlessly, a catch in her voice.

"Are we really going to move into that dump?" Betsy demanded from the backseat.

Kate's heart fluttered. "It just looks like a dump, Betsy. It isn't really. We are going to have such fun fixing it up. You girls can pick out the color paint you want for your room and you can help paint. When it's all done, we'll take pictures and send them to Daddy. He's going to be so proud of you."

"Pink and red," Ellie said.

"If you paint pink and red, the room will be hot-looking and you'll sweat," Betsy said.

"I think we should paint it yellow so on a cold rainy day it will seem sunny. My teacher said yellow is a sunny color. Isn't that right, Mommy?"

"Yes, yellow is a sunny color, but pink and red are kind of cozy. Maybe we can think about doing the walls different colors or making new bedspreads. It's something for all of us to think about and plan."

"Okay," Ellie said agreeably.

"What are we having for dinner?" Betsy asked.

Kate could feel the child's eyes boring into the back of her neck. She was about to say macaroni and cheese but changed her mind at the last second. "Hamburgers and french fries."

"Yippee!" Betsy squealed.

"Yeah, yippee!" Ellie seconded her sister.

Oh, Patrick, where are you?

Betsy squeezed her eyes shut. She should have been asleep a long time ago. She opened her eyes to see her sister roll over.

"Ellie," she whispered, "are you asleep?"

"You woke me up," the little girl whined. Her thumb went into her mouth immediately. "Now I'm scared. Can I have the night-light, Betsy? Can I sleep with you?"

Betsy hated the night-light, it made scary

pictures on the wall. "Okay, but you have to be real quiet. Mommy gets mad when you sleep with me. And you better not wet the bed," she hissed.

"I promise," Ellie said, snuggling into the narrow bed with her sister. "I know a secret," she whispered.

Betsy wiggled on her side of the bed to make more room for herself. "I know lots of secrets."

"My secret is about Mommy. Is your secret about Mommy?" Ellie asked sleepily.

Betsy's heart thudded in her chest. She wiggled some more. "If you tell me your secret, I'll let Daddy hug you first when he comes home. That will be a promise. I'll even make a big red X on your tablet so you won't forget." Her voice was anxious when she said, "Tell me the secret."

"Mommy said a bad word today. I heard her. You were in school. I'm going to tell Daddy when he isn't lost anymore."

"If you do that, you'll be a tattletale. Daddy doesn't like it when we tell on someone."

"He does so."

"He does not. I'm the oldest, I know. He told me so. When you're the oldest, you know more. I go to school. What's the secret, Ellie?"

"Mommy said a bad word. She was looking

in the book for her money and she only had three. She said the bad word and then she started to cry. That's the secret. It's a good secret, isn't it, Betsy?"

"Do you mean the cookbook?"

"It's like the checkerboard. In the pocket." Ellie started to cry, sniffling into her blanket. "Mommy doesn't have enough money, that's why she said the bad word. Maybe we won't have any breakfast tomorrow. Will we starve, Betsy?"

"No," Betsy mumbled.

"Daddy's not here. Mommy is doing everything different. We are so going to starve." She was sobbing now, clutching her sister's arm for comfort.

"We can eat berries and roots like the rabbits do. Miss Roland read us a story like that. People don't starve."

"When is Daddy not going to be lost anymore, Betsy? I want him to come home. Everyone but us has a daddy."

"We do so have a daddy. He isn't here, that's all. Don't you ever say that again. If you do, I won't like you."

"Jackie Rosen's dog got lost and they didn't find him. He's lost forever and ever," Ellie said mournfully.

"That's different. Jackie's dog was dumb. Daddy isn't dumb."

"I bet you're the smartest sister in the whole world. I love you lots and lots, Betsy. Tell me a story about Daddy. A nice story. I don't want to hear a sad story. I don't like sad stories. Maybe the Easter bunny will bring Daddy home. Is it stupid to wish for that?"

"No, it's not stupid. I wish it, too. Did Mommy cry hard and have to blow her nose or did she have tears in her eyes?" Betsy asked in a choked voice.

"She put her head down on the table and made funny noises. After she said the bad word. Tell me the story, Betsy."

"Once upon a time there was a little baby named Ellie. . . ."

When Betsy was sure her sister was asleep, she crept from the bed. On tiptoes she walked over to the dresser, opened the drawer quietly, and withdrew her bank. She knew exactly how much money she had: $5.12. She had two one-dollar bills and the rest was in change. Ellie had the same amount in her bank. With the handle of her comb she fished inside the bank until she was able to pull out the dollar bills. Then she did the same thing with Ellie's bank. She rocked back on her heels for a moment as she stared at the bills in her hand. She was stealing Ellie's money. That wasn't right.

She crawled over to her desk and reached for her tablet and pencil. She wrote $2.00 and printed her name. She was borrowing the money to give Mommy. When she opened the cookbook tomorrow, she'd think the Good Fairy had left the money. Ellie wouldn't have to worry about starving and eating roots and berries.

Betsy wanted to cry. Everything was different now. When Daddy was home, things were good. Everyone was happy. Now, everyone was grouchy and grumpy and nobody smiled. At that moment, she settled a thought in her mind. Daddies made a big difference. When a daddy didn't live in the house and take care of things, it went wrong. Mommies didn't know how to do things daddies did. There was always money in the back of the cookbook when Daddy was here. He was going to be proud of her when she told him she put money in the pocket to help Mommy. He'd hug and kiss her and say she did the right thing.

Careful not to make any noise, Betsy walked down the hall to the kitchen. She stood on her tiptoes to reach for the Betty Crocker cookbook. She carried it over to the counter under the night-light and looked into the back. Ellie was right. Three one-dollar bills were folded neatly. With chubby hands she smoothed out the four bills in her hand, laid them on top, and then folded them again. Now they wouldn't starve.

When her daddy came home, she'd tell him Mommy tried to do her best. She cried, then, as she made her way back to her room and crawled into Ellie's bed. She popped out a minute and pulled the covers up to her sister's chin. She bent over to kiss her cheek and whispered, "We aren't going to starve. I'll take care of you, Ellie, just like I promised Daddy. If Mommy can't do it, I can do it. I made a promise and I'm going to keep it."

She buried her face in Ellie's pillow and cried. "I want you to come home, Daddy. I love you very much. Please, God, this is Betsy Starr talking. Send my daddy home, don't let him be lost anymore."

She slept then, her pillow damp with tears that continued to seep from her eyes even in sleep.

Ground Hog Day turned out to be a beautiful, warm, sunshiny day just the way Kate had promised the girls it would be. "The day of the big move" was how she'd referred to the date. Tears sliding down her cheeks, she walked through the apartment one last time, reliving memories of she and Patrick together. When Patrick returned, they'd come back together and ask the new tenants if they would permit a walk-through.

She was in what Patrick called her "garden kitchen." Her eyes strayed to the phone, which had been disconnected just an hour ago.

Telephones were the lifeline to the outside world, to the military, to news of Patrick. When her new phone was installed on Monday, she would have to start the calls all over again and leave her new number. She knew in her heart her situation would be set back weeks, maybe even months, by something as innocuous as a changed phone number.

During the night, as she'd struggled for sleep, she'd realized she had to change her personal deadline for her husband's return. It simply wasn't going to happen in a matter of weeks or months, as she'd first thought. At some point during her restless night she'd extended his return to a year, possibly two. She'd cried then, begging God to hear her prayers, to return Patrick to her safe and sound.

Her eyes still on the kitchen wall phone, she remembered in agonizing detail the last conversation she'd had with Bill Percy. She'd badgered him relentlessly to tell her how the military could keep records of Patrick.

"If he isn't listed as a prisoner of war, how

can he be returned? If those people shot him, will there be a record? Admit to me that Patrick is on his own. I don't want to hear excuses and lame explanations. How long is this war going to last?" She'd been furious and disgusted when Percy couldn't give her the answers. As a parting salvo, she'd shouted, "If you can't give me answers, then I'll have to find someone who will." And as she was hanging up the phone, she'd heard him say in a rock-hard voice, "Mrs. Starr, you will endanger your husband's well-being if you start trouble. You must remain calm and let us do what we're trained to do." To which she'd replied, "Bullshit!" She'd found that the word no longer embarrassed her as it once had.

Kate wiped at her misty eyes. She couldn't fall apart now. She was on her own and she had to hold things together. It was almost a joke. What did she know about things like this? She was a mother, a housewife. Patrick had always taken care of things.

She needed a plan. Two plans. Plan A would work for Patrick's return and Plan B would be . . . would be a means to live her life without Patrick. "I'll learn. I'll learn," she muttered, locking the door, then sliding the key under the mat for the next tenant.

The girls were settled in the car, and Della

was waiting on the sidewalk. Her eyes spewing sparks, Kate exploded, the volley of words startling the housekeeper. "I am *pissed off*, Della! *They* should have moved me. *Paid* for this move. They don't care. No orders. My husband is missing in action and they say they have no orders, so my move is my move, but they won't release Patrick's pay for me to pay the rent here. I can't *believe* it!"

"Never mind, Kate," Della said comfortingly, ushering her behind the steering wheel. "Let's just head for our new home. I can't wait to see if our new landlord worked a few miracles on that ratty house. I'm just glad we'll get there before the furniture. I loaded all the cleaning supplies in the trunk just in case."

"I don't know what I'd do without you," Kate said, leaning over to hug her.

Church bells were tolling the noon hour when Kate stopped the car in front of her new home. She was relieved to see that the pile of trash was gone and the yard was neatly raked. Grass seed had been planted, and fragile threads of green could be seen waving in the slight breeze. Even the beautiful olive tree had been pruned and clipped. Kate could feel her spirits lifting.

Inside, her jaw dropped before she uttered a squeal of pure delight. All the walls were

a pristine white. Light fixtures had been replaced, and there was a new floor covering in the kitchen. "Look, Della, it isn't linoleum, it's floor tile. No cracks, and there's even a border. Ohhh, look how clean this refrigerator is, and the stove positively gleams. Shelf paper! Good Lord, there's wax on the venetian blinds. I can smell it."

"The bathroom has been regrouted. It's so clean and sparkling, you need sunglasses," Della said happily. "The parquet floor is beautiful. And look at that fireplace! It will be wonderful on chilly evenings. We can even have dinner in front of it."

"Mommy, our bedroom is white," Ellie whined.

"Two walls are pink," Betsy said.

"I'm sure there's a reason for the pink walls. Mr. Abbott was trying to be nice to us, so he painted the rooms so we wouldn't have to do it. I think for now we should just appreciate it, and later, if he gives his permission, we can repaint it."

Ellie said, "Okay."

Betsy sulked.

"There's nothing for us to do," Della s examining the oversize closet that was t her room.

"I think you should share my room, This is too tiny. We can use it for st

"No. Your room is your room. When Captain Starr comes home, he might be upset if he knew I shared what should be his space. This is fine for me. All I'll be doing is sleeping in it. Now it's settled, I don't want to hear another word."

Kate gave in, just the way she always gave in when someone else made a decision that affected her. "I wonder if he'll ever see this room," she mused.

"Of course he will. Never, ever think negative. If you don't think and act positive, the girls will sense it."

"But what if he doesn't come back?" Kate whimpered.

"He will come back. I don't know when, but he will. I hear the moving truck," she cried excitedly. "Take charge, Kate."

"All right, girls," Kate said, dabbing at her eyes. "Forward, march!"

It was five o'clock when the last dishes had been washed and placed in the sparkling white cabinets. At six o'clock the sheets were on all the beds. At six-thirty Della served up hamburgers and french fries and then did the dishes. At seven-thirty the last of the girls' clothing had been placed in the drawers and hung in the closets. By eight-thirty the girls had had their baths and were sound asleep in their beds.

When Kate returned to the living room, Della had a small fire going and the coffeepot was full and waiting. "We deserve this," she said happily as she placed Fig Newtons on the saucer along with the cup.

"Oh, Della, this is so nice. Thank you. Thank you so much for everything," Kate said, flopping against the soft cushions of the worn sofa.

"How are the little ones?"

"Sound asleep. Betsy is . . . anxious. We're off our routine. We didn't write Patrick today, so she wanted to know if that meant we were starting to forget him. We had this routine . . . God, Della, I had every minute of the day accounted for. Now when I think back to those ten months Patrick was gone . . . it seems so . . . so cruel. I had those girls jumping through hoops. Now this. I just know Betsy isn't going to like her new school. She adored her teachers."

Della let loose with a string of Spanish, then switched to English. "Today is a new day, a new beginning for all of us. What we do from here on in is what's important. Drink your coffee. Did I tell you I brought some packets of flower seeds with me, a dozen or so? They came in the cereal boxes and I saved them. Tomorrow while you go through the papers, the girls and I will plant them. This little house will look like a rainbow surrounds it when the flowers bloom."

"That's nice," Kate said sleepily. "You know, next month is Patrick's birthday."

"I'll bake a cake," Della said.

"Double chocolate fudge with real frosting, and colored sprinkles for the girls. Candles, all colors. And a present. One with a big red bow. We'll keep it in the closet until . . . he gets back."

"Wonderful! Now why don't you take your shower first. I'll clean up, damper the fire, and get ready for bed. Everything is going to be fine, Kate, I promise."

Kate believed her. Della was wonderful, the next best thing to a mother. Maybe even better. Her mother had rarely hugged her or praised her; she'd always seemed too busy. Della was a hugger, and she always seemed to say the right words. "Thank you, God, for Della," she said aloud.

That night, for the first time since Patrick left, Kate slept deeply and soundly.

She awakened the next morning to the smell of coffee and frying bacon and hurried to the kitchen. There, seated at the table, was Donald Abbott, and in front of him was a plate of scrambled eggs and bacon. She could hear the girls in the backyard. Della was smiling. And Kate herself smiled when she beheld her landlord in a smartly tailored dark suit, a snowy white shirt, and flowered tie. His black shoes gleamed with polish, and his gray hair had been neatly barbered.

"Morning, Mrs. Starr. I just stopped by after church to see if everything was to your satisfaction and to collect the rent."

Kate sat down across from him. "Mr. Abbott, everything is fine. I can't thank you enough for . . . for everything. I am so pleased. We didn't have to do anything but move in. When I get a job and things are better for me, I'll pay you more rent. I promise. The military has everything mixed up right now, and it will probably be a while before things get straightened out. You've been very good to us. I think you're a very nice man."

"Thank you, ma'am, I am. Guess you thought I was a bit disheveled when you saw me last. I was, but I was working on some property a ways from here. I was in my work clothes.

"And listen, if the military is giving you a problem, you go straight to the top. You call Washington, D.C., and get hold of the general in charge of Air Force personnel and tell him what your problem is. I'd recommend you start with your caseworker, and if you don't get any results, call Washington. I had to do that when my son . . . I had to do that."

"Thank you for the advice, Mr. Abbott."

"That was a real good breakfast, Miss Della," Abbott said when he'd finished eating. "I'll be going now."

"Let me get the rent for you," Kate said.

"Do you need a receipt?"

"I guess not," Kate said.

"That's good. I like it when people trust each other. Nice little girls you have there," Abbott said, pointing to Betsy and Ellie. "They told me they're making a rainbow around the house for their daddy so when he gets back he can see it from his airplane."

"They said that?" Kate said in awe.

"That's exactly what they said. Guess I won't be seeing you till next month. If there's any problem, call me. Miss Della has the number."

"Why don't you come for dinner next Saturday, Donald," Della said. "I'll make some real Mexican food and you can tell me how you like it." Kate's eyebrows shot upward, as did Abbott's.

"I'll be here," he said, then left the house. Kate waited for him to hitch up his pants, which he did when he got to the bottom of the back steps. She smiled. Della smiled, a merry glint in her eyes.

"He looks like he could use some fattening up. He's going to lose his pants one of these days. I wouldn't want the girls to see his drawers if that happened. After all, he is our landlord. We have to be nice to him."

"I agree," Kate said. "I take that to mean he's a widower."

"Yes. He likes us, I can tell."

"Can you now?" Kate teased.

"Get on with you, finish unpacking your clothes. I'll wash up here and help the girls. Get the Sunday papers for yourself. Don't worry about a thing. I think, and this is just my opinion, Kate, but I do believe Donald is going to be a surrogate grandfather to those two little girls, and it's going to be the best thing in the world for them."

"That would be really nice. Do they like him?"

"Ellie does for sure. Betsy was a little reserved. I heard him tell her he had a bicycle he was going to spruce up and did she know anyone who needed one. She told him she was someone and would be glad to take it. He kind of chuckled over that. I think he's looking for a family, Kate, and if you have a mind to share yours with him, he'd be eternally grateful."

"We didn't make a mistake coming here, did we, Della?"

Della shook her head. "Some things are meant to be. Just accept them."

"I think Patrick would approve of all this. No, no, no, I know he would. I can almost hear him say, 'good choice, Kate.' "

It was Sunday, a day of rest for Kate.

Tomorrow her life would continue, but down a different road.

CHAPTER 3

It was December 1971, a year since Patrick had ejected from his plane; twenty-one months since he'd left their little apartment in the desert. And still there was no concrete news of her husband's whereabouts. He was still listed as Missing. Kate still called Bill Percy every day, and every day he said the same thing: "Everything is being done that can be done. We haven't forgotten about your husband. Be patient, Mrs. Starr, and for your own sake, don't stir up a hornet's nest that you can't control."

Her language was stronger these days, she'd found, born of anger, frustration, and despair. "Fuck you and don't hand me that fucking bullshit! I want to know. You keep telling me the government is doing things, but you won't tell me what things. I have a right to know. I'm going to call the newspapers and I'm writing a letter to President Nixon."

To which Percy replied with an edge to his voice: "Please don't do that."

The conversation usually ended at that point with Kate slamming down the phone.

She'd prayed for Patrick's return for Christmas, realizing she was praying for the impossible. The government said he wasn't a prisoner, so how could he be returned? Still listed as Missing, he would literally have to call someone to come and get him, or simply walk out of the jungle and say, "Here I am, come and get me."

Kate now belonged to various support groups and had signed on as a member of the League of Families. She continued to read everything she could, stuffed envelopes, and did mailing for her various groups. It was neither rewarding nor fulfilling. She cried more, lost weight, grew gaunt and irritable with the girls, and with Della as well. She still hadn't found a job that paid her a decent amount of money. She suspected her sallow complexion and look of desperation turned off personnel interviewers. Her part-time job in a used-book store allowed her to stay in the back room pricing and cataloging books. There was little interaction with the other employees, who were out front dealing with the public. She found it easy to withdraw into her shell, and sometimes didn't speak to anyone at all during her four-hour shift. She always cried when she deposited her pitiful check each Friday.

She was tired all the time, and at Della's insistence was taking megadoses of vitamins, which did nothing for her energy level. Going to school at night, taking secretarial courses again at Della's and Donald Abbott's insistence, and studying in the morning, left her drained.

Christmas was upon them before Kate realized it. It was Della and Donald who put up the Christmas tree, Della and Donald who wrapped presents for the girls, Della who baked the Christmas cookies while she kept to her bed, refusing to go to work or to class. She was neglecting the girls but seemed unable to help herself. She lost more weight, grew more gaunt. More than once Della had to drag her from bed and push her into the shower.

From somewhere in the apartment she could hear the sound of Christmas carols being played. And the sound of whispers. Or was that in her mind? she wondered. Lately she wasn't sure of anything. Maybe if she lay there long enough, she'd die. She was so tired, so weary. *Patrick, where are you?*

You promised me tomorrow, and tomorrow is here. She buried her face in the pillow, sobs racking her thin shoulders.

Outside in the hallway, the two little girls whispered to one another.

"I just want to see her. Maybe if we sneak in, she'll wake up. I won't make a sound, I promise, Betsy," Ellie pleaded.

"She doesn't want to see us. Santa Claus is coming tonight, and she didn't make Christmas cookies. We can't go in, Della said so."

"I don't care," Ellie whined. "Please, Betsy, just a peep. I'll hold your hand. Will she still be in bed when the Easter Bunny comes? That's a long time, isn't it?"

"A lot of days," Betsy said flatly. "Promise you won't tell Della and Donald, okay? We'll just look at her. You have to promise, Ellie."

Ellie danced from one foot to the other. "I promise," she said.

Betsy licked her lips. Daddy had told her that only lazybones lay in bed for no good reason. The little girl's heart fluttered in her chest as she led her sister to her mother's bed. She wished the blinds were open so she could see her mother better. She felt frightened suddenly, wishing she hadn't come in here. Ellie's hand was wet in hers.

They tiptoed to the edge of the bed, and

Betsy stared down at the stranger there. Her hand moved on its own volition. The bedside lamp came on, all rosy and pink. Her eyes bulged when she saw her mother up close. She backed up a step and then another, dragging Ellie with her. Her mother wasn't playing lazybones. Lazybones leaped out of the bed when the light came on, and then giggled and laughed. Lazybones was a game. She knew instinctively, as only a child could know, that her well-being and that of her sister was on shaky ground.

"What's wrong with Mommy's hair?" Ellie whispered.

"That's how hair gets when you don't wash it," Betsy said quietly.

"It smells funny in here," Ellie said.

"I know," Betsy said.

"If Mommy stays in here *forever*, does that mean we don't have a mother anymore? We don't have a daddy. If we cry, will she hug us and get up?" Ellie sobbed.

Tears rolled down Betsy's cheeks. She didn't know how to answer her sister. What if her mother died in bed because she didn't wash her hair or take a shower? What if Daddy never came home? She squeezed her eyes shut. She was supposed to be a big girl and not cry unless she was really hurt. Daddy said so. She hurt now so bad she didn't know what to do.

Her feet moved, closer, until she was at the edge of her mother's bed. She dropped to her knees, one hand on the mattress for support, the other clutching her sister. "Mommy," she whispered. When there was no response, she whispered again, her face inches from her mother.

"Is she dead, Betsy?" Ellie blubbered. "I want her to hug me."

"You promised to be quiet," Betsy hissed.

"I don't care. Make her wake up."

Betsy felt frightened now that she was so close to her mother. Maybe she was dead. When you were dead, you didn't move, and then you went to heaven, where all the dead people were. She wanted her daddy, more than she wanted Christmas presents, more than the big turkey, more than the Christmas tree. Daddy could carry Mommy out of bed. Her daddy could do anything.

Her hand shot out to touch her mother's shoulder. She reared back when Kate's eyes snapped open. "I'm sorry . . . Mommy, I wanted you to wake up," Betsy cried. "Are you going to die? Ellie wants you to hug her. Are you being a lazybones?" She wanted to run, not look at this person who was supposed to be her mother. Daddy wouldn't like it that Mommy looked so terrible.

Kate stared at her cowering daughters, unable to comprehend what they were doing in her room. She had no idea what time it was or even what day it was.

"Santa Claus is coming tonight," Ellie sobbed.

Kate saw Patrick through a haze. A handsome, sturdy little boy with a rusty bike he rode everywhere. "Oh, Patrick," she crooned, "God made you an angel."

"Are you going to die?" Ellie whimpered.

Betsy waited for her mother's answer. Her mother wouldn't lie about dying. She heard her sister repeat the question. She thought her heart would blow out of her chest until, in a funny-sounding voice, her mother said, "I don't think so."

"Oh, goody," Ellie cried happily.

Betsy ran from the room, giddy with relief. God wasn't going to make them orphans. "If You made us orphans, Daddy wouldn't know where to find us," she whispered. "I knew You wouldn't do that on Christmas."

In her room, Kate crushed her face into the pillow. The day before Christmas. She dozed then, dreaming about a little boy with the face of an angel on a rusty bike, his wings flapping in the breeze as he careened past her house.

Patrick.

* * *

Kate woke with a pounding headache, knowing it was still the day before Christmas because she could hear the girls singing "Jingle Bells." Ellie was babbling about Santa coming down the chimney. She had to get up, take part in whatever was going on outside her room. She managed to pull on her robe and stagger to the kitchen, where Della, Donald, and the girls looked at her with wide, staring eyes. Della shooed the girls into the living room with fat sugar cookies in the shape of Christmas trees.

"I'm glad you're up, Kate," Della said sternly. "I have something to say to you. I'm sorry it's today, it being Christmas Eve and all. I'm leaving the day after Christmas. Donald here, well, he's asked me to be his bride, and I've . . . accepted."

If Kate had been looking anywhere but at Della, she would have seen the look of shocked surprise on her landlord's face. "But . . . you never said anything about leaving," she cried. "I can't . . . what will the girls do without you?" Her heart was pounding as fiercely as her head.

"I'm just your housekeeper, Kate. You're their mother. Somewhere along the way, you forgot that. They need you, not me. This is Christmas, and you didn't lift a finger to help, didn't care enough for those little girls to make any kind of effort. They're going to remember this. If you can't take care of them, Social Services will place them in foster homes. How will you explain that to your husband when he gets back? He left you in charge of his daughters, trusting you to keep . . . his home for him until he returned. Instead you lie in bed, refuse to eat, and leave it to me to do everything. I can't do it anymore. I'm getting to be an old woman, in case you hadn't noticed. Donald has promised to make life easy for me."

"That's a selfish attitude," Kate mumbled.

"Perhaps you should look in the mirror and see who the selfish one is. You haven't even paid the bills. Do you know the electric company is shutting off our electricity the day after Christmas? There's no more wood for the fireplace, and Donald has been buying our food. And it won't do any good to cry. I've had enough of your tears and your whining. Your husband would be so disappointed in the way you're acting."

Kate's shoulders shook and tears rolled down her cheeks. She wiped her eyes on the sleeve of her robe. "I have a terrible headache," she cried. "I had this dream . . . it was awful . . . I was a child back in Westfield, and Patrick had just moved in around the corner with his family. He . . . he had his old, rusty bike and he was pedaling it past my house. In my dream . . . he was leaning over my bed, but I was me, like I am now. He said he was an orphan or something like that. I wanted to put my arms around him, but I couldn't move. His voice was funny, like he was trying to cry. Patrick never cried. He was so proud of that. I can't comprehend that, Della. Never crying, I mean. I cry all the time. It's such a release. Men . . . men should cry, too. God, my head is killing me."

"You always have a headache, and if it isn't a headache, your stomach is bothering you or you have cramps or you're coming down with a virus. You drink black coffee by the gallon, smoke cigarettes you can't afford to buy, and you don't eat. No wonder you're sick all the time. . . . I'll stay through Christmas because I can't let those little girls be disappointed again. All week they've been making presents for you. What did you do for them?" Della turned back to the stove and winked slyly at Donald, whose eyes were bugging out of his head.

"The first Christmas wasn't so bad," Kate said hesitantly. "We had Patrick's letters and we knew he'd be home for this Christmas. He isn't here. . . ."

"But you are. You have to make the best

of it. I'm tired of your whining. Now I know where Ellie gets it. Betsy is like her father. It's not right of you to make Betsy responsible for Ellie. You're messing up their lives," Della said quietly.

Kate squared her shoulders. "It's true. You're right. . . . Has Donald really been buying our food?" She turned to stare at him, and Donald met her questioning gaze with pity in his eyes. "Do you love Della?"

Donald's Adam's apple bobbed up and down in his stringy neck. He hadn't been expecting the question, but now that it was put to him, he answered honestly. "She's a fine woman, and the man who gets her is one lucky man. And to answer your question: yes, I do."

"How could I not know that?" Kate asked, puzzled.

"Because you shut us all out of your life, that's how," Della said, not unkindly.

"I'm sorry. Do the girls hate me?"

"Oh, Kate, of course not, but they don't understand. They need to talk to you, need to have you hug them. They're so vulnerable. Betsy is having some problems in school, and Ellie is . . . Ellie is starting to lie . . . a lot. They need you, Kate."

Kate didn't trust herself to speak, so she merely nodded.

"There's a lot of mail, Kate. You haven't looked at it in over a month."

Kate nodded again.

"I could use some help with this turkey. I wanted to make bread today. I promised Betsy I'd make it for her. Donald is going to string some Christmas lights around the front door. I can still make a late breakfast for you, if you like, before I get started."

"Yes. Yes, I would. Eggs and bacon and some juice, but first I want to take a shower. I'll help with the turkey. The bread, too. I want to be the one to punch down the dough."

Della drew in her breath. Donald's eyes rolled heavenward. "When you wash your hair, why don't you pile it high on your head with a ribbon. Betsy made this for you a few days ago," Della said, taking a messy red string bow with curled edges from one of the kitchen drawers. Put it in your pocket for now, you can't mess it up any more than it is already. Toward the end she got frustrated and said it didn't matter because you weren't going to get up anyway."

"Oh, God," Kate said. "What's happened to me, Della?"

Della let loose with a long stream of Spanish, switching to English the way she usually did when she got to the punch line. "The devil got hold of you, and you didn't shake him loose, that's what happened." Her voice was triumphant as she helped Kate up from the chair.

Kate turned to Della and said, "The devil my ass, it's the goddamn military and government. Come to think of it, they're probably in cahoots with the devil."

Della clucked her tongue in disapproval at Kate's language. Donald chuckled.

"I think it worked," Della said softly the moment Kate was out of earshot. "I know I'm a fine, wonderful human being, but were you telling the truth when you said you loved me? And why would someone as fine as myself want a skinny old buzzard like you?"

Donald scratched at his straggly beard. "Well, you're fat, and I don't see anyone better than me banging at this here door. I'm a kind, generous man, have money in the bank, and receive a nice pension. I fixed this place up for *you*. I didn't have to do that. I take you to bingo and give you my card when I win and you don't. I go to church and pass the collection plate. I am an upstanding man, Miss Della. When do you want to marry me, now that you compromised me?"

"Why I —"

"Don't be coy with me now. I put a

straightforward question to you and I expect the same kind of answer. Admit it, you've never been asked before and you don't know how to respond."

"I suppose I could do worse. Swear to me you'll take care of me and this little family. I don't ever want to be out on the street without a home. I would have been if not for Kate."

Donald threw his hands in the air. "Look at me, woman," he blustered. "Who in the goddamn hell has been taking care of all of you since Kate got the miseries? Well then, I rest my case. When's it to be?"

"June," Della said sourly. "We'll tell Kate you got cold feet and postponed it till June. That way we'll all save face and she won't be the wiser. We really shook her out of whatever she was in. You'd best be getting on with your light stringing, Donald. And make sure you string them all the way across the roof and put some of those little twinkling ones on the Joshua tree."

"You nag, Della."

"And don't forget to do the red arrows. Ellie is going to cry all day and night if you don't get those arrows in place. Can you believe that little tyke worrying about Santa knowing she moved? She's terrified he won't know she's in this house. Red arrows, Donald, or it won't be Christmas for that little girl."

"I made them in my workshop yesterday. All I have to do is line them up. Painted them last night."

When the kitchen door closed behind him, Della danced a jig. Kate was coming out of her bad spell, and she had a proposal of marriage from a man who had his own house as well as Social Security. Christmas truly was a time for miracles.

It was dark, but not scary dark, Betsy thought as she crawled out from under the covers. She tiptoed to the doorway, careful not to wake her sister. She poked her head out the door, her breath hot little gasps. Santa had left the tree lights burning the way he always did. She was in the middle of the short hallway when she stopped, thought about it, and decided she didn't believe in Santa Claus. She turned on her heel to return to her room. Quietly, in the dark, she felt along the edge for her father's picture. She hugged it to her breast as she made her way back to the living room.

The tree was so beautiful she wanted to cry. She felt herself taking deep breaths to savor the spicy pine scent.

This was her moment, hers and her dad's.

She dropped to her knees in front of the fir and let her eyes rake the presents that circled the tree. "Merry Christmas, Daddy," she whispered. "This one is for you, and so is this one. Ellie's is the one with the green ribbon. I tied red on mine because you like red. This flat one," she murmured, picking up the tablet-size package, "is the one I made in school for you. Ellie's school present is the one with the macaroni glued to the top. I know what it is, but I promised not to tell. I didn't even tell Mommy. I have to look for Mommy's present to you. We're going to put them in the closet and give them to you when you get home. The whole shelf is for you. Our Easter baskets are there, too. Mommy says if the shelf gets full, we'll ask Donald to build another one. I can't find it, Daddy," she whispered. "Mommy wouldn't forget. It must be in the back, behind the others." She rummaged some more but was unable to find a present for her father with her mother's handwriting on the Christmas tag. A tear splashed on her hand. She wiped at her eyes with her pajama sleeve.

Betsy reached for Patrick's picture and hugged it to her chest. "I know I'm not supposed to cry, but I don't feel like a big girl this morning. I miss you. Mommy's sick and looks different. Ellie said she smells *pee-uey.*"

Words rushed out of her mouth, some of them garbled, all of them full of fear and anger.

"Miss Rolands read us a story before school was out. Everybody in the class cried but me. It was about an orphan who didn't have anyone to love her at Christmas. She was dressed in rags and she was hungry. The only thing she had to keep her warm was a puppy she found who was as hungry as she was. She was little, like Ellie, and she lost her mommy and daddy. This kind man was on his way home and he saw her and the puppy. He had real big arms and he picked up Martha and the puppy and took them home and gave them hot cocoa and a real big jelly sandwich. He put cocoa in a dish for the puppy and meat in a dish. The mommy came into the room and sat down with the little girl, and the puppy climbed on her lap. She hugged and kissed the little girl. The puppy, too. She let the puppy lick her face. She didn't care about germs. She cared about the little girl and her dog. When everyone was nice and warm and not hungry anymore, the lady and the man took them upstairs and gave them a bath and put them to bed. They hugged and kissed them and sat by the bed all night while they slept. Martha wasn't an orphan anymore. When I go back to school,

I have to know what the moral of the story is. That was our homework."

Chubby fingers traced the outline of Patrick's face as her tears rolled down. "I love you, Daddy. Merry Christmas."

Kate stood in the kitchen doorway, her eyes glued to her daughter. She had to move, go to her firstborn, kiss her and hug her close and tell her she was loved, but she waited a moment too long. Her father's picture clutched in her hands, the little girl ran to her room. "My God," Kate whispered, "what have I done to this child?"

Kate ran down the hall to her daughter's room and opened the door. Betsy was curled beneath the covers. "Betsy," she whispered in a choked voice. "Betsy, honey . . ." She dropped to her knees and let the tears flow. The little girl didn't move. Kate reached out a hand, drew it back. The moment was gone. Part of Betsy was gone, too; she could feel it.

"Merry Christmas, honey," she whispered.

Chapter 4

He didn't know if it was night or day, sunny or rainy. He no longer knew what month it was, much less the day. He did know he was in a space no bigger than a coffin. He could stand or sit, but he couldn't lie down. He couldn't stretch his legs out in front of him, either.

Captain Patrick Starr wiggled his toes. They worked, but he no longer had toenails. Or fingernails. He was no longer sure if his hip was broken or just fractured; not that it made any difference. For a long time he'd had to lean into the coffin corner with the homemade splint some faceless person had strapped on him.

Crippled. Was it better than being dead? A man could live without toenails and fingernails and with a limp. His tongue slid across his broken teeth with their sharp edges. Teeth could be fixed. Movie stars always had their teeth capped. Kate had beautiful teeth, an ear-to-ear smile that showed them off to perfection. Kate wouldn't care if he had caps on his teeth.

Patrick shifted his position slightly before he urinated all over himself. Once he'd had a slop bucket, but it was gone now. He reeked of himself, but the smell seemed to be less nauseous than before. With his broken nose, he couldn't seem to smell much of anything.

He didn't want to cry, but he did, tears rolling down his cheeks. He didn't bother to wipe them away, they felt good. No one could take tears away unless they punched out his eyes, which was a daily threat. God Almighty, if his sense of smell was gone, as well as the hearing in his left ear, what would he become if they really carried through with their threat to punch out his eyes? He wouldn't be able to see Kate again or hear the girls laugh. He'd never be able to smell Kate's meat loaf or the Thanksgiving turkey. The Christmas tree might as well be artificial. Worst of all, he wouldn't be able to smell Kate's hair, that warm, sweet vanilla-lemon smell that was always with her.

If . . . if he ever got out of here, he was going to be a gawdamn fucking vegetable.

What would Kate say and do when they delivered him to her doorstep, a broken, beaten man with no sight, no sense of smell, and very little hearing? The girls would be scared out of their wits. "You bastards! You gawdamn fucking bastards!" For a moment he thought he'd shouted the words, but he hadn't. The words were less than a whimper.

He continued to cry, more from pain than anything else, as he struggled to his feet to lean into his corner. He felt rather than heard movement near his feet. His good leg shot out and then stamped down. With his good ear he heard a weak squeal and knew he'd smashed one of his roommates, a scrawny rat that had less energy than he had.

Patrick tried to grind himself into his corner when he saw the heavy metal door open, throwing blinding light into his coffin. His arms shot up to cover his eyes. At the same time, he felt a metal prod gouge him in the pit of his stomach. He knew what *that* meant. He was to stagger out into the light, where they would question him and then beat him.

For one wild, crazy moment he thought he saw Kate ladling potato salad onto his plate at the Fourth of July picnic. She was smiling at him, knowing how much he liked her potato salad because she sprinkled little bits of crisp bacon over the top, just for him. By

God, he wanted that potato salad more than anything in the world. He did his best to square his shoulders, to walk as straight as he could. He stared into the blinding light and jerked away from the metal pole gouging him in the ribs.

He was a weasel, Patrick decided, this man who constantly interrogated him, speaking perfect English. Once he'd said he was a graduate of UCLA. Then he'd rattled off what he knew of Patrick's credentials.

Back then, when he still believed in things like the Geneva Convention rules, he'd stood his ground and given name, rank, and serial number. After his second — or was it his third — beating, he'd realized the rules didn't apply here in this godforsaken country. He'd shown some spirit, though, calling his interrogator a cocksucking UCLA reject.

Patrick looked around, trying to identify the structure he was in. It seemed different from the last one, but he did recognize the crude table with rows of torture equipment. He tried not to look at the syringes and the small vials of clear liquid. He did his best to steel himself against the man standing in front of him, did his best to meet his level stare, and felt that he'd succeeded. The only thing he couldn't match was the man's evil smile. He waited for his nod, said what he'd routinely been saying: "Fuck you, you son of a bitch!" He saw the arm rise, saw the club with the spiked prongs, a second before his mind retreated to Westfield, New Jersey.

The wind was whipping his hair backward as he pedaled his bike down the sidewalk, the red, white, and blue crepe paper he'd intertwined between the spokes making *thwack*ing, sputtering sounds. He was new in Westfield, but already he had three good friends and a speaking acquaintance with a blond-haired girl named Kate who lived around the corner. He was riding next to her in the Decoration Day parade. His bike number was six and hers was seven. He had to remember not to pedal fast so she could keep up with him.

His heart beat extra fast when he saw her coming down the driveway on her bike. He reared up on his Schwinn, letting the front tire hit the ground with a thud. He was pulling a roll of crepe paper from his hip pocket when she smiled at him. "You need streamers on your handlebars," he said shyly.

He felt himself jolt sideways on his bike when Kate said, "Do you have enough left over to tie some on my handlebars?"

Did he? "I have a whole roll." He fell off the bike, shook his head to clear it. "You have to rip the streamers. If you do, they make more noise. All the guys are doing it."

"It looks pretty," Kate said.

"Yours looks pretty, mine looks . . . nifty."

"Is that because you're eight years old?"

"Yeah. Boys don't do stuff that looks pretty."

He was on the ground again, tripping over his own feet. Kate was off her bike in a second, reaching down to help him up. She smiled shyly before she climbed back on her bike. Her saddle shoes were so blindingly white he couldn't see past them.

"Let's ride fast, real fast," he muttered, confused by the whiteness of Kate's shoes.

"I'll try to keep up," Kate said, hunching over the handlebars.

They rode down the street, around the corner, passing strolling couples, children, and dogs, all headed to the fairgrounds. They rode through a cloudburst, shrieking with laughter, the crepe paper *thwack*ing and sputtering, the streamers billowing upward and outward.

Patrick braked and was off his bike in a second. "I have a quarter," he said proudly.

"I have ten cents." Kate giggled. "I'm going to spend a nickel on cotton candy and save the other nickel. The hamburgers and weenies are free. I'm going to eat three of each."

"Go on, I can't eat three, and I'm eight," Patrick said.

"Can so," Kate said huffily. "Wanna make a bet?"

"For money?" Patrick said in awe.

"Sure. The nickel I'm saving. Two ears of corn, too, and maybe a slice of watermelon. I like to eat."

"You'll throw up."

"How do you know that?" Kate demanded.

"Because I know. My dad doesn't eat that much. You shouldn't say something like that unless you can really do it. If you say it and don't do it, then it's a lie. It's like a promise. If you break a promise, it's a lie."

"No, it isn't. It's a mistake."

"It's a lie," Patrick said adamantly. "It's a sin to lie."

"I didn't mean all at one time," Kate said, chagrined. "We have all day. So there, Patrick Starr."

"Then it won't be a lie. What time do you have to be home?"

"When the streetlights go on. Seven-thirty, I guess. What time do you have to be home?"

"Eight o'clock. I'll ride home with you."

"Okay."

"If I win the sack race, I'll give you my prize.

"Why?"

"Because you're a girl. Boys don't want stuffed animals and those jiggers on poles and strings. Boys are supposed to give them to girls. You're a girl."

"It will be my first present from a boy," Kate said happily.

"Don't you go saying that, Kate. It's a prize, not a present. That makes it different. Don't you go telling anyone, either."

"Is it supposed to be a secret? I don't know if I can keep a secret."

"Shoot, yes, it's a secret, and you better not tell anyone, either. If you do, I won't be your friend anymore."

"Okay, I won't tell. Do you have any secrets, Patrick?"

"Shoot, yes. Guys always have secrets. Wanna hear one?"

"I thought you said you couldn't tell a secret," Kate said sourly.

"This one I can tell because it's only about me, not another person. Someday," he said, drawing out his words, a dreamy look on his face, "I'm gonna fly an airplane. When I fly over your house, you have to run out in the yard, and I'll tip my wings so you'll know it's me."

"Ooohhhh," Kate said, her eyes round. "That's a great secret."

"Do you have a secret you want to share?"

"Someday I want to be a mother. The best mother in the whole world."

Disgust showed on Patrick's face. "All girls get to be mothers. Don't you want to be *something special?*"

"Being the best mother in the whole world is special. That's all I want to be. Don't you think that's good enough?" Kate said, grinding the toe of her saddle shoe into the fairground dirt.

"That means you don't have any imagination," Patrick said with a grimace.

"Then what do you think I should be?"

"A movie star. That's special. When you grow up, you'll be real pretty. You can be my girl."

"Honest, Patrick?"

"Don't you go telling anyone I said that. Yeah, honest."

"Ooohhh. I promise. How old will we be?"

"Fifteen."

"Will you take me to the prom?"

"Sure."

"Will you give me a corsage?"

"Sure, those little white flowers that grow like bells on a stem. They smell real pretty."

"Ooohhh," Kate said.

Patrick reached for Kate's hand.

When they dragged Patrick back to the cell, his face bloody and torn, all he could see were two children walking hand in hand into the fairgrounds.

His Kate, from that day on.

No matter what they did to him, they could never take Kate away from him.

He cuddled into his corner, his good arm wrapped around his broken left arm, his wife's name on his lips. "I promise you tomorrow, Kate . . . somehow, some way. I promise. I never lied to you, Kate," he whimpered.

CHAPTER 5

It was April 1973, nearly two and a half years since Nelson Collier's appearance at her kitchen door, and Kate did not know any more about Patrick than she did on that day.

She wasn't exactly the old Kate, but thought of herself as the new improved, better version of Kate Starr. She had put some of her weight back on, the shadows beneath her eyes were gone, and her backbone was stiff with resolve. She'd given up her job at the bookstore and applied for a position as a part-time secretary at an architectural firm. She was typing fifty words a minute without mistakes, and taking dictation. On occasion when the architects needed renderings of a building before work commenced, Kate did them for extra money. She loved her job because she had her mornings free to be with Ellie and to keep up her volunteer work with the League of Families and commiserate with other wives in the same position. Gradually she'd weaned the girls and herself from their daily letter writing to Patrick, simply because it was too sad for all of them. They wrote one letter each week on Sunday afternoon.

When April showers gave way to the bright spring flowers of May that the girls had planted around the house, three letters without a return address arrived in Kate's mailbox. Inside each was a check made out to her for four hundred dollars, drawn on the Wells Fargo Bank. She had no idea who they were from or what the checks were for. Her name was spelled correctly, and the envelopes carried the proper address. The single sheets of paper without letterhead read: FOR SERVICES RENDERED. PATRICK STARR $400. The total was twelve hundred dollars. The dates on the envelopes were all the same, which meant they'd been mailed the same day. The dates on the three sheets of paper were March 1, April 1, and May 1.

For one brief moment Kate thought her head would explode. Patrick was alive and doing something top secret for the government. What else could "services rendered" mean? March, April, and May meant the present. Twelve hundred dollars had to be all the money in the world. She could splurge and get a haircut and finally pay Della for having helped her at a crucial time. The girls could get new shoes, and she could buy some art supplies. Or — her thrifty nature intervening — she could invest the money if it was truly hers. Maybe she would keep some of it, pay Della, and invest the rest.

Her address book within easy reach, Kate called several of the women in her group and asked if they'd ever gotten such unexplained checks. Only one of the women, Bethany Warren, admitted she had. Bethany belonged to the group but always opposed "going public" for news of their husbands. That was fine for Bethany, Kate thought, because her husband was listed as POW, not Missing.

"I don't understand," Kate said quietly. "Who's responsible for these checks? Why am I getting them now after all this time? Does it mean he's alive? Please, Bethany, I need to know," Kate pleaded.

"My situation is different from yours, Kate. I have five children and I can't make it on Michael's pay. I think you should call your contact and talk to him. If you like, we can meet for coffee later in the week." This last was said so fearfully, Kate found herself starting to tremble.

"I'd like that. Friday after work, Mabel's Café."

"Kate," Bethany said hesitantly, "don't cash those checks until you're sure it's what you want to do. What I mean is, you're getting by and you have a housekeeper and a job that might lead to something better that pays a decent salary. I'll see you Friday."

More puzzled than ever, Kate called Bill Percy and asked to set up an appointment. He said he'd stop by later in the evening on his way back to the desert. "Ten or so," he said briskly. She tucked the checks, envelope, and papers into the back of her Betty Crocker cookbook.

It was important, but what was really important at the moment was sewing a satin pocket for the tooth fairy. Yesterday she'd gone to the bank and asked for a shiny new quarter, compliments of the tooth fairy. By bedtime Ellie would lose her first tooth. When Kate finished the satin pocket pillow, she stuck it in her drawer. Ellie would be so happy. She had to take pictures of the girl to send Patrick.

Today was Kate's day off because she worked alternate Saturdays. Della and Donald were taking Ellie to the zoo. They'd offered to wait until Betsy got out of school, but the little girl said she hated to smell the animals, which meant Kate was free until it was time to pick her up. She had phone calls to make, letters to write, lists to make.

I'm doing what I can, Patrick. I'm doing my best. I got lost there for a little while, but I'm on track now.

She had a cheap vinyl briefcase that was ripped at the corner from all her clippings, notebooks, and magazines. Her pens, pencils, and writing paper were secure in a separate side pocket. As always, she read through the articles, skimming over the hateful parts, the parts that offered little hope, and going on to whatever was more positive. There wasn't much. She wept, allowed herself a small amount of time to grieve before she tackled her sixth letter to the President of the United States. She ended this one by saying, "President Nixon, my daughters and myself deserve to know what is being done to bring my husband home. We don't understand how Patrick can still be listed as Missing two and a half years after he ejected over enemy territory." She signed the letter "Captain Patrick Starr's wife, Kate Starr." Later that afternoon, when both girls returned home, she'd have them sign the letter, too.

Next she wrote to the Departments of State and Defense, demanding answers that were long overdue. Her third letter was to the Air

Force, to every general on the list she'd gotten from the library. In this one she wrote, "Doesn't anyone care about the families left behind? Don't we deserve something better than evasive answers? What am I to tell my daughters? Please, send someone here to talk to me and the support group we've founded. Don't neglect us any longer. Your motto has always been 'The Air Force takes care of its own.' Give me a date and a time when this will occur." Again she signed the letter, "Captain Patrick Starr's wife, Kate Starr." The girls would sign these letters, too.

I know you're going to come back, Patrick. My heart would tell me if you were dead. I know they want me to believe you are, but I won't believe it, not ever. I pray for you every day. A day doesn't go by that we don't speak of you. The girls kiss your picture good-night. I do the same. I know God will keep you safe.

The urge to smash something was so great, Kate clenched her fists. What good would it do? She was doing so much better these days at controlling her anger. Always think positively, turn every disadvantage into an advantage; it was Patrick's personal motto.

The hours rushed by, and before she knew it, the girls were sound asleep, and Bill Percy was due to arrive. She felt positive now; she'd mail her letters later. She wondered why she felt so confident, so *up*. She'd written the same letters before and there had been no answer. What made things different now? It was the checks, she decided, the strange envelopes, and Bethany's response to her questions.

Five minutes into her meeting with Bill Percy, Kate realized that she'd never really liked the man. It wasn't that he had cold eyes — he had evasive eyes. His voice wasn't compassionate, it was irritable. He accepted her plum tea, the fat sugar cookies Della had baked, and suffered through the amenities, and then sat back and waited.

"It's been two and a half years, Bill." They were on a first-name basis now, but she knew it didn't mean a thing. "There must be some small bit of news. How much longer is this war going to go on? If you don't have something positive to tell me, I'm going to go to the newspapers and beg, plead, get down on my knees, whatever it takes to get answers. The other wives feel the same way. We deserve better than this."

"You are receiving Captain Starr's pay, aren't you, Kate?"

"Yes, but it took almost four months. I had to threaten to call Washington, and then I got an answer in three hours. You should have helped me. What have you done for me, Bill? I have this feeling you don't even like me."

"That's not true. I think you're overwrought. I want you to think about something. If we list your husband as dead, you get a pension. It would not be substantial. Leave things alone now. When we have firm evidence of anything, you'll be the first to know. Everything that can be done is being done. Don't make waves, Kate."

"That sounds like a threat." His forced laugh sent chills up Kate's spine. "Then tell me what that 'everything' is. Spell it out for me and the other wives. We have rights, too. It's been two and a half years, for God's sake!" Kate's eyes sent sparks in Percy's direction. She wondered how people like Percy were picked as "contacts" for wives and families. She stared at him, at his slicked-back sandy hair, at his bulging hazel eyes. She just knew he hated the angry red pimple on his right cheekbone. He'd cut himself shaving, too, she noticed. Maybe he was just supposed to be strange-looking, which he was. He had uneven teeth and never smiled. Maybe it was his ears, she thought. They seemed to be too small for his long, narrow face. Whatever it was, she didn't like him or his long skinny fingers drumming on the table impatiently.

"I know it's a long time. I pass every query

you make to the right people. Listen to me, Kate, you cannot stir up any trouble. Do you realize that if you start trouble, the communists will get wind of it and the prisoners could be mistreated? You must remain calm and in control. We are doing everything possible. When we know something, you'll know something. Now tell me why you needed to talk to me in such a hurry."

"I'm not falling for this again, Bill. I'm going to do whatever I can to get news of my husband, and I'm encouraging the wives to do the same thing. Today I wrote a letter to the President, to the State Department, to all the generals I could find in the Air Force directory. And I'm ready to take on the media if I have to. And yes, I called you for a reason." She had the checks and envelopes out of the cookbook before Percy could blink. "Just what in the damn hell are these for? I think I have an idea, but I want to hear you say it."

"I have no idea, Kate."

"Was Patrick involved in some kind of . . . of covert operation, the kind spy novelists write about? This is guilt money, isn't it — hush money. I don't want it, I want my husband, dead or alive. I want to know, I need to know. So, take this — this whatever it is, and give it back. I want you to know, though, I made copies of everything this afternoon, and they're in a safe place. I don't think I'll be calling you again, Bill, so they can assign you to some other poor wife. Take some advice from me and sharpen up your bedside manner."

"Listen, Kate, you're tired, it's late —"

"Yes, it's late, but I'm not tired. What I am is disappointed and disgusted with the system."

"Kate, don't violate the 'keep quiet policy,' as you refer to it."

"Good night, Bill," Kate said, holding the door open for him. The checks and papers were secure in his calfskin briefcase, she noticed. He looked back once, seemed about to say something, and then thought better of it. "I think I just scored a point for my side," Kate muttered to herself.

It was a lovely night, the sky star-spangled. She found the North Star and made a wish, not for herself, but for Patrick. *Keep him safe and out of harm's way.*

Reluctant to go back indoors, Kate strolled down the walkway to the gnarled old Joshua tree. With the help of one of the neighbors, Donald had fixed a swing for the girls from the lowest branch. She sat down gingerly. This was normal. The meeting inside had not been normal. *Oh, Patrick, where are you? I'm doing my best, but I don't think it's enough. God, how I need you.*

Kate was right: her efforts weren't enough. The meeting with Bethany was a farce. The older woman was so fearful, all she did was cry and bemoan her fate the way Kate had done months earlier. "I don't want them to list Michael as dead. If they do that, I'll have to go to his pension, the extra money stops, and I won't be able to survive. If you keep up what you're doing, you're going to endanger all of us. I think you should stop, Kate."

"Stop what?" Kate said in disgust. "No one answers my letters. Don't you understand, no one cares! So what is it that I'm doing that's so wrong? I gave back the money. I'm not obligated to anyone. And who is this *they* you're so worried about? Look, I'm sorry, I know how hard it is. Your husband has been missing longer than mine. I marvel at your stamina. I fell apart there for a while. I'm working now. I'm thinking of going to college. I realize I can't depend on anyone but myself. I want the life Patrick promised my girls. Since he isn't here to provide it, I have to step in and do it for him. I won't let them declare him dead, I can promise you that. Let them take away our benefits.

I'll survive, and so will my children."

"I'm not going back to the group," Bethany said quietly.

"That's your choice," Kate said just as quietly.

"You and all the others have to be aware of what you're doing. If just one of our husbands is killed or tortured because of what you're doing, will you be able to live with that?"

"No, of course not. I want to know what happened to *my* husband. I have a right to know. If he's dead, I have the right to bury him. If he's a prisoner, I have the right to know that, too. This whole thing is wrong. It's been wrong from the beginning. Don't judge me or the others, Bethany. Sometimes you have to . . . to stand up and be counted. Thanks for talking with me. If you ever want to come back or just hang out for a while, call."

Kate was in the parking lot when Bethany caught up to her. "Did you really give back the money?"

"Yes. At least I gave it to Bill Percy. What he does with it is his problem. It felt good, too. I don't like him. I think he's . . . an insignificant piece of snot. Actually, I dismissed him. He hasn't done one thing to ease my worry, or said one thing to give me hope of any kind. I have enough negatives in my life, I don't need him adding more. So, he's out of my life."

Bethany's eyebrows shot upward. "Who will you talk to?"

"Anyone who will listen. Take care of yourself."

"You do the same."

Kate pulled out of Big Bob's parking lot, trying to remember what she'd had to eat. Nothing, just coffee. Bethany had eaten two hamburgers and a huge stack of french fries, yet she'd let Kate pay the bill. Kate wondered how that had happened. Years of tidying up, she supposed. She'd just automatically picked it up because it didn't belong on the table. In the scheme of things, it really didn't matter.

And so Kate's life went on. She attended her local support meetings, journeyed once to an important League of Families meeting, and came home with renewed faith. She was working full-time now and going to school at night. Half her business courses at the community college she attended were being taken care of by the architectural firm she worked for. She was making a life for herself, one step at a time. She thought of it as building a house, brick by brick. Each and every night when she said her prayers, she blessed Della and Donald for all their help, and then she prayed for the safe return of her husband and the well-being of her daughters. She never asked for anything for herself.

Time's pace accelerated, and before Kate knew it, another year had passed. It was January 23, 1974, and she had a pounding headache, an exam at six o'clock, and a full day at the office. Three months and she'd be finished with school. Patrick was going to be so pleased. Then again, maybe he wouldn't be proud of her. He might be annoyed. She swallowed three aspirin.

"I was just thinking, Della, that Patrick would be proud of me when I graduate. I wasn't sure at first. Once I mentioned taking some night classes, and he didn't seem to like the idea. He would have liked me to go out to work, but school . . . for some reason, he wasn't keen on the idea."

Della grimaced. "Maybe he didn't want you to be as smart as he is. Maybe he would have viewed that as a threat."

Kate forced a laugh. "Just because you're an old married woman now doesn't make you *that* intuitive." She felt instantly ashamed because she'd thought the same thing. "I could never hope to be as smart as Patrick, even if I went to school night and day. He's got such a technical mind. He's so smart he amazes me. I used to hear him talking to some of the men, and he sounded like he came from another planet."

"Ah, yes, but does he have common sense? From what you've told me, he lacked that. Don't let his education take away from your own. I'm proud of you, and so is Donald."

"I couldn't have done it without you, Della. If you hadn't threatened to leave that Christmas, I'd still be lying in bed sucking my thumb."

"Since we're in such a complimentary mood, let me say that if it wasn't for you, I never would have met Donald and I wouldn't be married today. He's helped me with my English a lot. I can write it pretty good now. And he's learning a bit of Spanish, too. I owe you more than I can ever repay, Kate. But most important, I've come to love Betsy and Ellie and you and think of all of you as my own. My family. Donald feels the same way. You're our family, and like he says, we pull together."

Kate wrapped the plump woman in her arms. "I will be eternally grateful to you and Donald," she murmured, her eyes misty.

"Get on with you or you'll be late. I have to listen to Ellie's spelling words before I drop her off at school."

"I'll see you tonight. I'll probably be home early, since I just have to take the exam. Thanks for offering to help out. I might make it by dinner if you don't serve till seven. What's on the menu?"

"Hot Mexican chili."

Kate grinned. "My tongue is burning already. Have a good day, Della."

During the day, Kate took six more aspirin, received several compliments from her boss, and studied for her exam during her lunch hour while she nibbled on an apple. When she left the office at five-fifteen, she took two more aspirin.

On the ride to the college she ran possible test questions over and over in her mind while she listened to the news on the radio. Her headache disappeared like magic the moment she heard the news commentator say, "President Nixon will address the nation this evening." He went on to speculate as to what the President would say. Kate knew in her gut what he was going to say, had prayed for it faithfully.

Her mind sharp and clear, Kate sailed through the exam and finished at exactly six-thirty. She rushed to the parking lot and drove home in a frenzy of excitement. "Did you hear the news?" she cried when she entered the kitchen.

"Kate, don't get your hopes up," Donald cautioned.

"Things are finally going to move!" In her excitement she failed to see the worried look Donald and Della exchanged. The girls were hyper, picking at their salad and chili.

"Can we stay up?" Betsy pleaded.

"Will they talk about Daddy?" Ellie queried. "I'll hold his picture when they talk to us. Is that okay, Mommy?"

"Of course it's okay. Finish your dinner, take your bath, and we'll have a nice fire while we wait for the program. Maybe hot cocoa with marshmallows. I feel so good about this. I mean, I feel really good. You're going to stay to see the program, aren't you?" she asked Donald. Though they were married, the Abbotts often took their meals with Kate and the children. Della cleaned up and Donald took her for a walk. They always ended with an ice cream cone on their walk home, to their own little cottage less than two blocks from Kate's apartment.

"Of course we're staying," Donald said. "I'll take the trash out and bring in some firewood. I'll have a blaze going as soon as the tykes are ready." To Betsy he said, "I think I finally figured out how we can get smoke to come out of your volcano for your school project. I set everything up down in the basement while you were in school. Now move your tushie so you can take a look at it," he said fondly.

Bless your heart, Donald, Kate told him silently, her eyes warm as she watched him with her children. Thank you, God, for allowing these wonderful people to come into our lives. Then, uninvited, a nasty thought crept in. Patrick would call Della and Donald intruders. He'd say he appreciated their help and then turn to her and say something like, What's in it for them? She pushed the thought back into the recesses of her mind.

Ellie started to cry. "I didn't get an A today."

"What did you get, Ellie? Did you spell 'bear' wrong?"

Ellie hung her head, tears dripping down her cheeks. "Uh huh. I didn't get a star, I got a rainbow."

"Spell 'bear' for me now," Kate said, smiling.

"B-E-A-R. Bear."

"That's good, honey. Now you'll never spell it wrong again. Sometimes you have to do something wrong before you can do it right. A rainbow is good. I love rainbows. Remember the time you and Betsy planted a rainbow of flowers around the house? All the neighbors said how beautiful it was, and we even sent Daddy a picture of it. Scoot now, into the bathroom."

"You fibbed to her, Mommy," Betsy said. "Everyone in school knows rainbow stickers aren't as good as gold stars. You . . ." She thought for just the right word. "You mollified her."

"So I did." Kate's voice was sharper than she intended. "Everyone can't be number one. Everyone can't get an A."

"Daddy said you can do whatever you want to do if you want to do it bad enough. I want to get all A's so he'll be proud of me. Ellie doesn't care. Ellie's sloppy. I never get rainbows," she said loftily. "I don't like rainbows."

"Then it's your loss, Betsy. Do not make fun of your sister. She's doing the best she can."

Betsy always had to have the last word, just like her father. "She's not doing her best, and when Daddy comes home, he'll know it. I'm going to tell him. Ellie's a baby. You even treat her like a baby."

"I don't want to hear any more talk like this, Betsy. You need to be kinder to your sister."

"She needs a good slap," Betsy said, stomping out of the room.

Kate threw her hands in the air. "Now what do I do?"

"Nothing," Donald and Della said in unison. Della added, "She's upset because Friday is the student-father breakfast, and of course she doesn't have a father to take. Donald offered to stand in for Captain Starr, but she refused. Said it was cheating, and he was too old to pretend to be her father. Maybe you shouldn't make her go to school on Friday, Kate."

"She said that?"

"Lately she's been saying a lot of things like that," Donald said. "The children at school talk about their fathers a lot and what they do with them on the weekend, that kind of thing. She does love her father. Ellie just sails along. Actually, even though Ellie is younger, I think she has a better grasp on everything."

"Well, we'll just see about that," Kate said, and headed down the hall to the girls' bedroom. She was angry now because her headache was back. When she closed the bedroom door, she could hear Ellie splashing in the tub.

Betsy's face was sullen. She was sitting stiffly on the side of the bed. "Are we going to have one of *those* talks?"

"Yes, we are. For starters I'd like to say

it's been a very long time since I've seen a smile on your face. You're being very fresh to your sister, and I do not care for your belligerent attitude. Worst of all, you've been unkind to Donald and Della. I need to remind you that without them we might be sleeping in the park in a tent. Donald is helping you with your school project, taking time out of his day to make things better for you. He doesn't want to be your father, he just wants to stand in your father's place for you until your daddy gets home. I think that's wonderful. I expect, and will settle for nothing less than, your full cooperation in this matter. You will go to breakfast and you will take Donald and you will have a smile on your face, and from now on your attitude had better change. It has not been easy for any of us, but we're all trying to live normally. I would appreciate your help. Don't make me resort to other measures, measures neither of us will like. Now, let's see a smile."

"My friends will laugh at me. Donald is too old to pretend to be my father," Betsy stormed.

"If your friends laugh at you, then they aren't your friends. I would assume by now you've explained to all of them about your dad. Donald is not going to pretend to be your father. He's going to be his stand-in.

Your teacher will explain that to the class. I can call her and have a talk with her if you like."

"No, I don't want you to talk to the teacher, I'm not a baby." Suddenly she was a little girl again, throwing her arms around her mother and sobbing. "What if Daddy doesn't come home and Donald dies because he's old? Then who's going to stand in for *him?*"

"Don't talk like that, Betsy. Your daddy is going to come home. I don't know when, but he will. He promised me. Your dad never broke a promise. He promised you, too. We can't ever give up hope, even when things get dark and it gets harder and harder to believe. We have to keep going. I won't ever give up hope. I can't make you believe, only you can do that. Now, what's your decision?"

"Okay," Betsy said, blowing her nose. "But it was your decision. You said so when you first came in here. I was going to do it anyway. I don't want to hurt Donald's feelings. It scares me, Mommy."

"What scares you, baby?"

"What if I forget Daddy? I like it when Donald hugs me and sings those silly songs. I like it that he's helping me with my project. What if I start to like him more? What if he dies and leaves me with no one to hug me and sing to me?"

"Oh, Betsy, you will never forget your daddy, I won't allow you to forget. It's okay to love Donald, Daddy would approve. And Donald isn't going to die. He has Della to take care of him. You don't think for a minute she's going to let anything happen to him, do you? Not on your life. Now, let me tell you what I *think* you should do. I think you should find Donald. If he's outside, put on your coat and find him. Give him one of those big hugs that make your ribs ache, and tell him you would be honored to take him to the father-daughter breakfast. If you don't really feel that way in your heart, then I won't expect you to do it. I'm going in the bathroom to wash Ellie's hair. You sit here and think about it for a few minutes, okay? Let's see that famous Betsy smile Daddy said was as bright as sunshine."

"I don't have to think about it. I'm going to do it. Right now. Thanks, Mommy."

"My pleasure. That's what mommies are for."

Betsy ran down to the basement, words trembling from her mouth like a waterfall. "Donald, Donald, I need you to go to the breakfast with me. Mommy explained how you'd be Daddy's stand-in. Will you go with me?" Behind her back she crossed her fingers, waiting for Donald's reply.

Donald pretended to think. "Do you have to wear a sign that says I'm a stand-in?"

"No. Everyone knows about my daddy. I'm going to say you're sort of my grandfather. How old are you, Donald?" she asked fearfully.

"Old enough to be your grandfather, that's for sure." Donald chuckled. "I like the idea of acting the part of a grandfather. Is there anything special I need to do besides get all spruced up?"

"Nope. Just walk beside me and sit next to me when we eat. You have to get up and say your name after I introduce you. How old do you have to be to die?" she blurted.

Taken aback, Donald shifted the glasses on the bridge of his nose. Something important was being said here, and he needed to pay attention. "Honey, you can die at any age. Babies die sometimes. Youngsters in high school die. Young men in war. It would be nice to think only old people like me die after we lived our life, but it doesn't work that way. Is there a reason you want to know?"

"I don't want to be an orphan. I'm used to you now. I have *real* grandparents, but they don't bother with me and Ellie. Daddy's father is *really* old. Mommy says he can't remember things, and my other grandparents are too busy with my great-grandparents. Everybody forgot about us but you and Della. I don't want anything to happen to you. Sometimes I get scared."

Donald took a deep breath before he picked her up and set her on his knee. "Honey, it's okay to be scared. I get scared sometimes, too. So does Della. Your mom has been scared for a long time. But we have to live our lives, pray and hope for the best. We're a family now, and family members take care of each other."

Betsy snuggled into the crook of Donald's arm. "When my daddy comes home, will you still stay with us? I wouldn't want you to leave. I love you. I love Della. I don't want to miss you and Della the way I miss Daddy. I don't want to do it two times. Promise me you won't die, Donald. Please promise," Betsy said tearfully.

"Honey, I can't promise something like that. No one knows when they're going to die. Only God knows that. But I'm not going to die right now, that's for sure. I'll probably be hanging around until you get out of college. That's a pretty long time, if you ask me. By then," he said cheerfully, "you'll be pretty darn sick and tired of me hanging around."

"No, I won't. I always want you to be

here. My daddy is going to love you and Della. I betcha he gives you a present for taking care of us. What kind of present do you think it will be, Donald?"

Donald laughed. "A big red wheelbarrow."

"A shiny one," Betsy chirped.

"With big green tires," Donald said.

"And we'll put a horn on the handle. I'm going to write Daddy a letter this weekend and tell him all about Christmas, and I'll tell him about the wheelbarrow."

"That's a mighty good idea, little lady," Donald said, hugging the little girl.

"Mommy's all better now. Donald, can you keep a secret?"

"I'm the best secret keeper in the whole world," Donald said, his face solemn.

"Alice Baker told me when you die they put you in a box and close it. Then they put the box in a hole in the ground and cover it up with dirt. You can't get out. You can't ever wake up again, and you turn to bones. People plant flowers over the hole and then they put up a statue of an angel that has your name on it. Alice is so smart she gets all A's. She's the teacher's pet, too. She said her grandmother died and that's what happened to her. Is that true?"

Donald's jaw dropped. Then, instead of answering her question, he asked one of his own. "Is that what's been worrying you?"

"Uh-huh. Mommy wouldn't get out of bed. She started to look funny and she didn't smile or laugh. I don't know how to be an orphan. I don't want to be an orphan. Ellie will cry all the time if that happens. Daddy said I was supposed to look after her. If . . . I wouldn't be able to do that if we were orphans."

"Well, you don't have to worry about that. Your mother is going to be just fine. She wasn't feeling like herself for a while back then, but she's okay now. Now you have to promise me you aren't going to worry about things like that anymore. The minute you start to worry, you come to me and we'll talk about it. When you talk about things, it helps and it doesn't seem so bad. I bet you even feel better now."

Betsy smiled before she wrapped her arms around his neck and squeezed him as tight as she could. "I love you, Donald. I love you almost as much as I love my daddy. I have to love him more because he's . . . he's . . . personal."

"I understand." Donald chuckled. "Now that we have all that serious stuff out of the way, let's get down to the real important things like getting this volcano to belch smoke."

"Is it going to be the best project in class?"

"Pretty darn close, Betsy, pretty darn close."

"I love you, Donald, I really do."

Later, when they were settled in front of the television, Della said, "That man is walking on air. I couldn't see his face for his smile. I don't want to know what you said to Betsy, but whatever it was, she seems to be her old self. I've never seen Donald so happy. He truly *wants* to go to the breakfast. He polished his shoes and he's getting a haircut tomorrow. He wants me to take his picture when they walk out of the house."

"Betsy's afraid that Donald will die because he's 'old,' " Kate said to her, "and there won't be anyone to hug her or sing to her. That's all it was, Della. She loves him and is afraid she might start to love him more than she loves her daddy. Explain that to Donald later, okay?"

"There'll be no living with him if I do. He's already like some prancing peacock, but I'll do it because he's such a good man. Kate, we are one lucky family."

"I know. Another minute here and we'll both be slobbering. Another crisis has passed. May they all be solved so easily."

"Time for the cocoa," Donald said, joining

them. "It's almost nine o'clock."

"Call the girls in and let's toast some marshmallows."

Della pointed to the hearth, where long sticks and bags of marshmallows were waiting. "Donald got them ready."

Kate bowed her head and said a prayer as President Nixon's face flashed on the screen.

"Did you hear that?" she said ten minutes later. "We're going to sign a peace treaty on January twenty-seventh. That's just four days from now. The first group of POWs will be home in two weeks. Two weeks, Della! By March they'll all be home. Patrick will be home then, won't he? God, he has to be with them!"

"Kate, Captain Starr isn't listed as a POW," Donald said quietly. "He's listed as Missing."

"He's missing over there. If he's in hiding in the . . . jungle or something, he'll come out. Are you saying he won't . . . that he won't be with the POWs?"

"I'm saying I don't know," Donald said.

"I'm not going to work or to class tomorrow. I'm going to call everyone in the world if I have to. He's there, he has to come home with the others. He just has to."

Captain Patrick Starr did not come out in

the first group, the second group, or the third group. When President Nixon said, "There are no more prisoners in Vietnam," two things happened. Kate collapsed, and eight-year-old Betsy verbally attacked her mother.

"You lied! You said Daddy was coming home!" she screeched. "You lied to me. You're a liar. Daddy hates liars!"

Della and Donald closed in protectively and coddled the little family that was torn apart once again. It was Donald who insisted a therapist be called in for both Kate and Betsy. With gentle pushing and prodding from Della, Donald, and the therapist, Kate was able to finish the semester and graduate with honors. Her job was put on hold until, as her boss put it, she got her shit together.

CHAPTER 6

It was early, that gray time of morning when the night relinquished its hold on the day. Soon the sun would creep to the horizon, and according to the weatherman, the day would be sunny and golden — perfect for an outdoor birthday party.

Kate shuddered beneath her warm flannel robe and sipped her lukewarm coffee. This year she'd hoped to avoid celebrating Patrick's birthday, but the girls wouldn't allow it, so today was going to be like the other nine birthdays they'd celebrated in the past. Of course "celebrated" was hardly the right word. They all cried, Donald and Della, herself and the girls. Tears rolling down their cheeks, they thumbed through the well-worn photo album, reread all the tattered letters, and then toasted Patrick with tall, frosty glasses of root beer. Those last few minutes of the party, signaling an end to the ritual until next year, were the best for Kate.

Ten years. Five hundred twenty weeks. Three thousand, six hundred, and fifty days. When Betsy had given her the numbers last night, she'd stared blankly at the paper, wanting to make some comment that would ease the misery in her oldest daughter's eyes, but the words wouldn't surface. All she'd managed was, "Ten years is a very long time. I don't think Daddy wants us to live on memories. We have to get on with our lives. That doesn't mean I'm giving up or that I will stop believing he'll return someday. It means I'm being realistic, and you must be, too. It's not healthy for us to live in the past."

Then, seeing the stubborn set of Betsy's shoulders, she'd sighed and added, "We'll have the party today, but this is the last one. It is simply too painful for me to go through the anxiety each year as we prepare. It can't be good for you or Ellie, either."

A tear dripped into Kate's coffee mug. From the Joshua tree she heard a bird chirp its morning greeting. "Good morning," she said softly. Suddenly it was important to see the bird that chirped its greeting to her every morning. In her bare feet she ran down the porch steps and around to the front of the house. She knew the nest was high in the tree, and for one crazy moment she thought about climbing up. She might have attempted it, too, if she hadn't heard Della's chattering voice and turned to see her friends coming down the sidewalk. She waited as Della pushed Donald's wheelchair onto the walkway, feeling silly now that she'd almost given in to her impulse.

"Kate, you look like you're thinking about climbing old Josh here," Donald said, gesturing to the tree. "My boy did it on several occasions and broke his collarbone and then his ankle. That nest has been there for years. If there was one thing I could always count on in those lonely days after his death, it was those birds singing to me in the morning. Right cheerful sound, but now Della's voice is all I need. You need to find another voice, Kate. And the sooner the better."

Kate smiled. Donald and Della could always wash away her anxiety. She bent over to kiss Donald's weathered cheek. "I'm working on it." She winked at Della, then ruffled the springy tufts of white hair that protruded from Donald's Mets baseball cap. "Is today a good day, Donald?"

The old man flexed his hands, trying to unbend his crippled fingers. "The hot wax helps some. The pills help a little. Della's kisses help the most," he said, chuckling.

"The flowers are so pretty this morning. I think we had some rain during the night," Della said cheerfully. "I'm always amazed at this garden or border or whatever it is Betsy calls it. Just the other day I was talking to a lady at the grocery store, and somehow or other this garden came up in conversation. She said she brings people by just to look at it. She said it was a *whole* rainbow. Betsy's sixteen — I would have thought by now she'd have outgrown this garden."

"Never! She works so hard on it. And each year she uses her allowance to add more seeds. I think the colors are more vibrant this year, don't you? All so she can preserve her . . . father's rainbow." Kate sighed. "Still, Dr. Tennison says it's all right for her to be doing this. Enough of this talk — let's go in and have breakfast. I opt for waffles and blueberries. Donald, what's your choice?"

"Whatever this fine woman makes is okay with me. I'd eat sawdust if she put it on my plate." He would, too, Kate thought fondly as she led the way inside.

"Have you made a decision yet about this evening?" Della asked slyly, her back to Kate.

"Yes, I'm going. I . . . I haven't told the

girls yet. I can't believe I'm such a coward, but do you know, I actually called Dr. Tennison to ask if it was okay to go to dinner with a man. Betsy is going to throw a fit. I can't believe I forgot it was Patrick's birthday when I made the date," Kate said, her eyes wild. "Charlie is . . . he's very nice . . . but it's not serious or anything like that —" She broke off and clutched Della's arm. "Oh, God, what if Betsy carries on? What will I do? Maybe this wasn't such a good idea after all."

"Keep this up and you'll talk yourself right out of it," Della said sourly. "You need to have a life of your own. And you need to stop going to bed at eight-thirty at night."

"Listen to her, Kate," Donald said. "She always makes good sense. I say you should go. We'll be here to baby-sit and to wait up for you just like parents."

"What are you going to wear?" asked the ever-practical Della. "Where are you having dinner?"

"I thought I'd wear my navy-blue and white, and I said I'd like to go to Stefano's. I did mention the Jade Garden, but Charlie said he was partial to Italian food, so it's Stefano's. It's simply a dinner invitation, nothing more. Charlie isn't my type. We're friends, nothing more."

"Time —"

"No, Della, time will not change anything. Patrick is — was — is the only man I'll ever love. No amount of dinner dates is going to change that."

Della snorted, a very unladylike sound. She turned, hands on her ample hips. "You are much too pretty, much too vital, to tie yourself to a memory. A ghost. That's what Patrick is now, Kate. It's time to give life a chance. If you don't start getting out and about, you're going to die on the vine."

Kate sat down at the table with a fresh cup of coffee. "I know you're right," she said, sighing. "It's just that I feel so disloyal, so . . . sneaky. If Patrick comes back and finds out, what will that make me in his eyes?"

"Kate, it is unlikely Patrick will come back. It's been ten years. You have to face reality. Hoping is one thing, living on that hope is something else. If Patrick does come back, you'll deal with it then. How many waffles?" Della asked briskly.

Kate smiled. "Three."

"Four for me," Donald spoke up.

"All right, Della, I'll tell them at breakfast," Kate said. Della nodded. Donald reached over to pat her hand.

"Morning, Mom," Ellie said, bounding into the kitchen and leaning over to kiss her mother. "Oh, waffles! I'll have six, Della. What are you going to tell us at breakfast?" She took her place at the table next to Donald and without missing a beat said, "And you're looking dapper and sexy this morning, Donald."

"I know," Donald said seriously. "Women just flock to me. But I'm a one-woman man."

"See that it stays that way," Della groused. She slipped four waffles on his plate and drizzled warm butter and syrup on top.

Ellie cut up the waffles for him. "Nobody answered my question," she said.

How pretty she is, Kate thought.

Ellie would be fifteen in another few months. Lively and outgoing, she had laughing blue eyes and a smile that stretched from ear to ear. She wore her hair in a high, pulled-back ponytail that swished when she walked. She claimed to be irresistible to the opposite sex, and Kate had to believe her, given the endless parade of boys who stopped by on a regular basis. Ellie was a B student at school, whereas Betsy was a straight A student. There was very little that Ellie took seriously except Betsy's garden.

"Tell us what?" she said now for the third time.

"I was going to wait till Betsy came down, but if you absolutely must know now," Kate said lightly, "I'll tell you. I have a dinner date this evening."

"Jeez! With who? Is he good-looking? Do we know him? Where'd you meet him? What time will you be home?"

"His name is Charlie Clark. He's a friend. I met him at work. We're going to Stefano's, and I'll be home early. Della and Donald will stay here until I get back. Any more questions?"

"Yeah. Does this mean the party is off?"

"We're going to do it at two o'clock."

"Aw, Mom, the gang is going roller-skating this afternoon. Look, I thought we agreed not to do the party thing anymore. Can I skip it? Please, Mom."

Kate wondered why she hadn't expected this. She shrugged. "It's your decision, Ellie. But Betsy will be disappointed."

"Well, I'm sorry, but I can't help it. It's the way I feel. Look, I hope I'm wrong and he does walk through the door someday. For Betsy's sake. But I can hardly remember what he looks like. I know you're doing the party for Betsy. But you know what? It's time Betsy grew up and became realistic. You coddle her too much. Scratch this party and let's get on with it."

"Betsy needs —"

"No, Mom, Betsy doesn't need this. It's

just her way of getting attention. You give in to her on everything. She has no friends. She keeps writing those stupid letters she never mails. All she talks about is when Dad comes home and the things *they're* going to do. It doesn't help to keep having these parties."

"Just this one last —"

"No. Not for me. You said the same thing last year and the year before that. I absolutely refuse to do it anymore. What's the point?"

Kate sighed. "All right, Ellie, I understand how and why you feel the way you do. I want you to go with your friends today and enjoy yourself. After this party there won't be any more. Now eat your breakfast."

"Mom," Ellie said, picking up her fork, "can I have my own room and my own phone if I pay for it with my baby-sitting money?"

Kate smiled. Nothing kept Ellie down for long. "Donald and I have already been discussing how we can make room for you. He's suggested we take out the linen closet and the hall closet and take three feet from Betsy's room. It'll be a small room, though. Very small. And when you show me you have enough money for the phone installation and enough for three months of bills, we'll discuss giving you your own phone."

"Thanks, Mom. Donald, you're the best.

You, too, Della," Ellie said, getting up and planting kisses on all three of them. "I don't care how small the room is. All I need is a bed and my dresser. And a door with a lock so nosy Betsy can't sneak up on me. Can you do that, Donald?"

"You drive a hard deal, little girl," Donald said, flashing his widest grin. "A door with a lock. A girl needs her privacy, Della says."

"I wish we had a rec room," Ellie said from the doorway.

"Don't push it, Ellie," Kate said.

"What's she whining about now?" Betsy said, brushing her way past her sister. She was dressed, her hair combed, her teeth brushed. Her bed would be made, her half of the room tidy. She took being a military brat seriously.

"She wants her own room. Donald has agreed to knock out the closets and take three feet from your room. It shouldn't be too much of a job. Would you like some waffles, Betsy?"

"Two will be fine. When are you baking the cake, Mother?"

"I'm not. I have a lot of work to catch up on. I had to bring it home this weekend, so we moved the party up to two o'clock. Ellie won't be here. I bought some cupcakes and the root beer. I won't be here for dinner this evening. I'm having dinner with a friend."

"Did you at least get a card?" Betsy asked snidely.

"No, as a matter of fact, I didn't. I'm not buying cards anymore, or presents. I'm willing to toast your father's birthday this one last time, but it's been ten years, Betsy. Time to let go."

Betsy fixed her narrow gaze on Della and Donald. "Do you feel the same way as Mother?" They both nodded. "Is your dinner date with a man?" Betsy said to her mother.

"Yes, but he's a friend, nothing more."

"I can see how this would be a good time for something like that," Betsy said. "Well, you're all wrong. Dad is coming back. He promised, and he's never broken a promise to me."

"Betsy, we haven't heard a thing in ten years. We need to get on with our lives. Do you want to keep going to Dr. Tennison for the rest of your life?"

"I'm not going anymore, and I want to become a Catholic. Catholic people pray to Saint Jude for helpless and hopeless causes. You can't stop me."

"I won't try," Kate said sadly. "However, I wouldn't close the door with Dr. Tennison."

"Well, I am. I only went to please you. All he does is talk about how we have to look at the world realistically. I know what he's going to say before he says it. I think we should forget the party since everyone is so opposed to it. I'll have my own out in the garden. Don't worry about me, Mother, I have things under control."

Kate stared across the table at her daughter. Where Ellie was pretty and wholesome, Betsy was downright beautiful, with big warm brown eyes and thick lashes. Her dark hair, so like Patrick's, was curly, falling in lustrous waves about her shoulders. And she was so much like Patrick, it was scary at times.

"If that's what you want," Kate said quietly.

Betsy pushed her plate away. "The waffles were good, Della." On her feet, she towered over Kate. "I hope you have a miserable time this evening. You're cheating on Daddy, and that makes you a tramp."

"Young lady," Kate said, reaching for her arm, "don't you *ever*, ever talk to me like that again. You apologize to me now or you will find yourself sitting in this kitchen until you do."

Betsy's eyes ricocheted around the kitchen, took in Della's stunned expression, the disappointed look on Donald's face, the anger on her mother's face. "I'm sorry," she said, and ran from the room.

Kate sighed wearily. "I suppose this all is my fault," she said. "In the beginning I tried to keep him alive for all of us with the letters, the gifts, the parties. I let it get out of hand."

"Then why isn't Ellie reacting the same way," Donald said quietly. "It's not your fault."

"Then how did she get like this? For God's sake, there's only a year and a half between them! Betsy took this all so seriously, yet Ellie . . ."

"It's not your fault, Kate," Della said firmly. "You can't do more than you've already done. The rest is up to Betsy. If you give in to her and keep on with this nonsense, you'll make yourself sick."

"My God, Della, she called me a tramp. Me, her mother."

"She didn't mean it. You have to put it out of your mind. Tomorrow when she's had time to think things over, she'll come to you and give you a real apology."

"No, she won't. This to her is the ultimate betrayal. And the funny thing is, it's simply a dinner with a friend who just happens to be a male. I guess I'll just have to live with it."

"Guess so." Della smiled.

"She is a smart woman," Donald said cheerfully. "If I wasn't all crippled up with this dad-blang arthritis, I'd waltz you two fine-looking ladies around the room."

"And we'd both be tripping over our feet. Patrick didn't like to dance, so I never learned. In the scheme of things it didn't seem important. One of these days I just might take lessons." She was relieved to see smiles on her friends' faces. If she was lucky, she could go about her business and not think about Betsy's stinging remark.

Oh, Patrick, I tried so hard. I want to believe, but it seems so hopeless. I can't believe you'd want us to mourn and grieve forever. I'll never marry again, that much I do promise. We both agreed to that, remember? Where are you? Do you think of us? Are you alive, Patrick?

The sun was high in the sky when Betsy, freshly showered for the second time in the day, stepped into the garden, carrying her gift-wrapped present on a tray along with a glass of root beer and a cake she'd picked up at the bakery, topped with ten candles. Her first trip out she'd carried her portable phonograph, writing tablet, and a pen and lap blanket.

Tears pooled in her eyes when she spread the blanket. Her hands were trembling and she felt light-headed. She hadn't expected her mother's declaration. Sooner or later she knew Ellie would balk, but her mother . . .

Tears dripped down her cheeks when she placed her gift, a complete desk set and a card, on the corner of the blanket. She sat down squaw fashion. Her fingers itched to turn on the phonograph to play the birthday song. She wiped her eyes, feeling suddenly silly and childish. Were they right? Was she wrong?

"I don't seem to belong here anymore, Daddy," she murmured. "Dr. Tennison says I'm holding on too tight. He thinks I'm not stable, that I can't handle life without you in the background. He's wrong. I can. I *know* you're going to come home. I know it. When you know something, feel it like I do, you can't buckle under and say what they want you to say. Mom's right, though, ten years is a very long time. Sometimes I feel myself almost giving up, and then I remember your promise.

"I've tried so hard to be the kind of daughter who will make you proud when you do come home. I make the honor roll each period. I'm a straight A student. I keep my room neat and tidy because I know how neat you like things. I don't know what else to do anymore except to pray and hope. That will never change.

"Mom is . . . Mom has a date this evening. She said it's not a real date, just a friendship thing. She's never really lied to us before. This is . . . I think this is the first step for both Mom and Ellie in letting go. That's what Dr. Tennison calls it, letting go. I'm not ready to do that, Dad, I don't think I'll ever be ready.

"I can't wait to leave here, to be on my own. I think I feel like you did when you left. You told me it was going to be a big wonderful adventure and something you dreamed of all your life. That's how I feel. So, Dad," she said, turning on the phonograph, "happy birthday."

Betsy drank her root beer in two gulps. She blew out the ten candles she'd lighted, licked at the frosting with her finger. When the song was finished, she bundled up the record player, the gift, and the blanket and glass, and carried them into the house. She threw the cake in the trash. "I won't forget," she whispered.

CHAPTER 7

Kate wondered if it was possible for the mirror to lie. She leaned closer to stare at herself with clinical interest. Lately she hadn't paid much attention to her looks, preferring simply to wash her face, cream it, and leave it alone. It was Ellie, who adored makeup, who'd taught her how to enhance her best features. Now she applied eye shadow, dabbed at the tips of her thick lashes, and rubbed a dot of rouge on her cheekbones. She finished with a glistening coral lipstick that somehow, mysteriously, Ellie said, made her eyes sparkle. She wore earrings, too, tiny pearl drops that seemed to bring a warm glow to her cheeks, a glow that had nothing to do with the rouge.

A month ago she'd gotten a fashionable haircut and had preened when the beautician, a man, said, "Do you have any idea how many women would kill for curly hair like yours?" Then he'd gone on to say she looked like a woman of the eighties, whatever that meant.

She was twirling under a spritz of cologne when Betsy entered the room. "Mom, I'm sorry. I don't know what made me carry on like that. I won't do it again. Is that the perfume Ellie and I gave you for Christmas?"

"No, this is something I picked up at Conrad's last month. They were giving out samples and I decided to buy a bottle. I like to alternate." She didn't want to tell Betsy that the scent the girls had bought her reminded her of the vanilla and lemon she used to douse herself with. For one second her husband's face flashed before her.

"Do you like it, Betsy?"

"I can't get over how you look," Betsy said, her eyes narrowing slightly. "Is that a new dress you're wearing?"

"As a matter of fact it is. I'm going to wear it to the company dinner next week. The salesgirl said it looked good on me. Do you think so, honey?" Kate asked anxiously.

Again Betsy avoided answering directly. "If this is just a dinner with a *friend,* why don't you wear your seersucker suit and that white piqué blouse? I think you have too much perfume on, too. You never used to dress this way."

"What way is that?"

"Sexy. You look sexy," Betsy mumbled.

"You sure do," Ellie chirped from the open doorway. She whistled softly. "If Charlie Clark is just a friend, maybe he'll introduce you to someone who . . . you know, will be more than a friend."

"You are absolutely disgusting, Ellie," Betsy snapped. "Mother is married. Married women don't fool around."

"Get off your high horse, Betsy. I was teasing Mom. But you never know. What are you going to do if he wants to kiss you good night? You have my permission," Ellie said, sticking her tongue out at her sister.

"You really do condone this, don't you?" Betsy spat at her sister.

"Can't you send her away to some special school where they have kids just like her, Mom?" Ellie said. "She's not real. She's like a stupid cop. She monitors all of us, and you know what? She *writes* it all down so she can tell Daddy if he ever comes home."

"You sneak, you read my diary. You miserable little sneak!" Betsy shrilled.

"Get off it, sister dear, I did no such thing. Is it my fault you talk in your sleep? You gonna blame that on me, too? Listen, I can't wait to get out of that room and into one of my own. Why don't you go weed your flowers or plant yourself six feet down. You'd make wonderful fertilizer." Ellie turned to her mother. "Don't let her make you feel guilty, Mom. She thrives on that because she's stupid. You look real pretty, and Charlie Clark, whoever he is, is one lucky guy to be taking you to dinner. Be home by twelve," she trilled, to her sister's horror.

"Twelve! If you're leaving at six . . ." Betsy trailed off. Her eyes flashed dangerously.

Kate's heart fluttered. She had to do something about this child of hers. Lord, where had she gone wrong? "Betsy, you have to stop taking everything so seriously. Ellie needles you and you fall for it every single time. Sweetheart, I'm sorry about today, but I just don't want to be depressed anymore. I want sunshine in my life. I don't want to upset you, Betsy, but I must get on with my life. I will always love your father, that will never change. But we can't live in the past, it simply isn't healthy."

"He is coming back, Mother," Betsy said quietly.

"I pray that he does, but until I see him walk through the door, I can't live my life on hope. I plan to involve myself in several groups and organizations, make friends and go out more. I'm even thinking about starting my own business. And I could use a little more support from you."

"I know Dad is coming back. What's he going to think when he finds out how you've changed? When he sees the way Ellie decks herself out and the way she's chasing boys? What is he going to think?"

Kate straightened her shoulders. "I don't know what he would think, and right now I don't care. When and if he appears we'll deal with it, but not before."

"You're not the same anymore," Betsy said coldly.

"No, I guess I'm not, but I would like you to think about something. If your father does come back, he's not going to be the same man you remember. He'll be changed, too. You've changed, so has Ellie. You're seventeen, ready for college. He has no idea what you're like now. If he's alive, he's thinking of you and Ellie as his *little* girls. Please, don't keep blinding yourself to facts."

"You have an answer for everything, don't you?" Betsy snapped.

Kate sighed. She felt like taking off her clothes and crawling into bed. Betsy always managed to make her feel ashamed and guilty.

"If I did have the answers to everything, I'd damn well package them and sell them at a discount. Every time I make advances in my life, you somehow try to make me slide backward. I wish . . ."

Betsy's eyes flashed. "What, Mother? That it was time for me to leave for college?"

God in heaven, that's exactly what she was thinking. "I don't care to discuss this anymore, Betsy. And the next time we're in each other's company, I damn well better hear a change in your voice and see a smile on your face or you won't be going away to school, you'll be attending the community college. You think about that this evening. You're *dismissed.*"

Alone, Kate sank to the edge of the bed. She'd handled Betsy all wrong. Why was Ellie so . . . so normal, and Betsy so . . . *Patrick, where the hell are you? Why am I being forced to go through this? She's just like you. I don't know what to do for her, what to say to her. We go over the same things, day after day, and we manage to slide backward each time. I hate to say this, but I don't like our daughter very much these days. She was right, I can't wait till she leaves for school. I'm sorry, Patrick, that I'm not doing a better job. I try so hard. This dinner tonight means nothing, I'm not being disloyal. I'm not cheating on you. Our daughter called me a tramp. Oh, Patrick, where are you?*

"Mom, your . . . friend is here. Oooooh, he's a . . . *hunk,*" Ellie hissed from the doorway. "He told me to call him Charlie." She rolled her eyes and gave a thumb's-up salute. Kate laughed. "Remember, in by midnight, and don't do any of those awful things you tell me not to do when I go out. C'mon, get going!" She hugged her, a silly smile on her face.

Kate laughed. "Okay, okay!" Her eyes thanked her daughter.

When the front door had closed behind her mother, Ellie stalked down the hall to the bedroom she shared with her sister. She bounded into the room and grabbed hold of Betsy's hair. "You are a miserable, stinking bitch and I hate your stinking guts. You take all the life out of Mom. You just damn well suck it right out of her. Would it have killed you to be nice to her, to have gone downstairs to meet that guy? You know what?" she said, yanking at Betsy's curly hair. "I hope Dad does come back, because I'm going to tell him what you've done to this family. God, I can't wait till you leave. Promise me you won't come back for the holidays." She gave her sister's hair another vicious yank. "Della said to tell you dinner is ready. I for one hope you choke on your food." She stormed out of the room, slamming the door behind her.

Betsy stared at the closed door, her expression blank. From under her pillow she withdrew her diary and a banana. She dated the pages and wrote, "Happy Birthday, Daddy."

CHAPTER 8

"Comrade." The single word speared through Patrick's body. He really was in Russia. How he'd gotten here, he had no idea. He remembered being shoved onto a plane, remembered the prick of a needle. And now this. This, he decided a moment later, was worse than being in Vietnam. He'd always hated the cold.

They were speaking to him in English. He responded by giving his name, rank and serial number. Then he said, "The rules of the Geneva —"

He was on the floor, clutching his ribs and screaming in agony. He thought about punctured lungs, shattered spleens, before he blacked out. When he came to, he felt something hanging over his eyes. Tentatively he reached up and felt a needle-thin icicle hanging from his eyebrow. He started to shake with pain and cold, welcomed the sight of the needle and the oblivion it would bring. They weren't ready for the needle yet; first they would torment and torture him. His battered ribs were just a teaser.

He retreated to a warmer, safer place, a place where he was free to do whatever he wanted, and what he wanted to do this very minute was climb into an airplane and fly into the heavens.

"I have enough," he said happily. "Forty dollars, enough for both of us for an hour. I know it's just a crop duster, but it has wings, and the pilot said he'd let me take the controls. If you don't want to go, Kate, I can fly for two hours."

"Oh, Patrick, you saved so long for this, you go. I'll stay here and watch. I brought a book with me to read. I'll wave to you when you get up in the air."

He didn't mean for his voice to sound so relieved when he said, "Are you sure? This was supposed to be our day. We talked about it for months. Are you just being nice?"

"Sure I'm being nice." Kate giggled. "You'll have two whole hours, Patrick. I brought three dollars with me. After you land, we can go get some hamburgers and french fries and you can tell me all about it, how it felt. I'll like that better. Besides, I might get sick up high. Remember everything so you can tell me about it."

Later, when they were snug in a booth in the Linden soda parlor, he said, "It was everything I thought it would be."

"Did you feel like a bird? Weren't you afraid?" Kate asked.

"Heck no, I wasn't afraid. I felt better than a bird. You know what, Kate? I felt like God. Just like God. Listen, we have to hurry or my father will beat the bejesus out of me. If either one of our parents ever finds out we rode our bikes this far, we'll never be allowed to leave the house again."

He pedaled faster, right down to the swimming hole, where it was warm and sunny; a paper sack full of egg salad sandwiches for him and the guys. Kate might show up, so he'd brought one for her, too. All his buddies knew Kate was his girl. Well, sort of his girl. Bill Duke had a girl, too, and so did Buck Inhabinet.

He was on his bike again, pedaling and finishing the last of his egg salad sandwich, the best sandwich he'd ever eaten. He'd put little seeds in it, the ones his mother used to use. It put zip into the egg salad. He tossed away the wax paper, braked his bike, and pedaled backward to pick up the paper and stuff it into his pocket.

Kate was ahead of him; he could see her saddle shoes sparkling in the sun. Bill and Buck were bringing up the rear.

Without knowing how he got there, he was suddenly at the senior prom, awkwardly trying to lead Kate on the dance floor.

"Oooooh, isn't the gym beautiful, Patrick?"

"Sure is. Boy, do you smell good. You smell like those flowers in front of your house."

Kate giggled. "That's because I stuck some of them down my . . . bra."

"Will you let me look later?"

"No!"

He groaned. "Come on, Kate, you let me feel you sometimes."

"Feeling is different than looking. The answer is no, Patrick."

"Let's get some soda pop and go outside. Bob has some cigarettes. We're all going to smoke."

"Well, I'm not. You shouldn't, either."

"Why not?"

"Don't do what everyone else does. I like you because you aren't a copycat. You're special."

"What makes me special?"

"You're going to be a pilot someday. That makes you special. You're real smart, the smartest boy in the whole school. In the yearbook they said you would be the most successful. I believe that."

He preened. "They said that because it's true. I'm going to fly all over the world, and when I come home, you'll meet me at the door and have a big chocolate cake waiting in the middle of the table. Lots and lots of frosting. You'll always wait for me, won't you, Kate?"

"That's a silly question. Of course I'll wait for you. I'm going to be the best wife and mother in the whole world."

"It's important to be the best. Mothers and wives don't have to be the best. Just men. You know what I mean."

He was pedaling again, faster than ever. He wanted to be the first to arrive at O'Malley's barn for the last hayride of the season. His plan was to hide in the straw in the wagon and whoop and shout when the others arrived to wonder where he was. He wasn't going to be a kid anymore after tonight. He propped up his bike out of sight and headed for the wagon. The fresh straw felt warm and prickly and smelled earthy. He inhaled deeply, lay down in the straw and thought about Kate.

Kate was warm and soft and smelled good. Kate smiled all the time, did what he wanted when he wanted. Except she wouldn't have sex with him.

Kate was part of his life, would always be part of his life. She was his. Everyone said so. For a moment he wondered what would happen if he told the guys he wanted to give her back. Their eyes would bug out of their heads. You didn't give someone like Kate back. And who would he give her back to, Din Radson? No, Kate was his forever and ever. They were going to get married someday and have lots of little Kates and Patricks.

He looked back over his shoulder and then at the sterile corridor he was standing in. He looked around wildly, expecting to see Bill and Buck. Kate, where was Kate? He had to find Kate, ask her what was going on. He shivered. He'd never been so cold in his life.

"Captain Starr, is this your daughter?" He was shaking, shivering, unable to get warm. He could barely see the paper his interrogator was holding up in front of him. He couldn't even nod, his neck was too cold to move. He was numb. Where was he?

Then he remembered.

The voice sounded as cold as he felt. He listened to the words, tried to make sense of them.

"She's dead. Your family was killed in an

auto crash. You have no family anymore. You are going to live and die here. You will never return to your home, so you might as well tell us what we want to know."

Kate had promised she would always wait for him. Kate never broke a promise. They were trying to wear him down. How damn stupid they were. Didn't they know all they had to do was give him one of their needles and he'd spill his guts? He muttered his name, rank, and his serial number.

The blow caught him over the left ear. He felt something pop inside his head. "Fuck you!"

"I hate it when you swear like that, Patrick," Kate said. "Now, are we going to the park or not? It's such a beautiful day, not a cloud in the sky. I packed some sandwiches. . . ."

CHAPTER 9

The months whizzed by, and before Kate knew it, it was time for Betsy to leave for college. Her two trunks had been sent ahead the week before, and all that was left to do now was carry her two large suitcases to the car and drive her to the airport. The good-byes were going to be awful, Kate thought. I'm going to cry like a ninny, the way I did the day I took her to kindergarten.

They were all lined up on the front porch, Della, Donald in his wheelchair, Ellie and two of her friends. "What's taking her so long?" Kate muttered.

"She's probably primping," Donald said, smiling. Kate didn't respond, and a moment later the screen door banged open just as a taxi pulled to the curb, horn blaring.

Kate felt a rush of panic. "Why is that taxi here?"

"I called it, Mother," Betsy said quietly. "I think it's best this way. You're going to get all emotional and embarrass me, and I don't want that. I'll be fine. Don't worry about me."

"But . . . we agreed. . . . I planned on driving. . . . Oh, why did you do this, Betsy?"

"I told you: I think it's best."

There were no hugs, no kisses. With an airy wave, Betsy marched across the porch and down the steps, suitcases in hand. She didn't look back, didn't wave a second time.

"I'll write and phone once a week," Kate called after her.

"Don't hurry back!" Ellie shrilled.

"Ellie!"

"Sorry, Mom. It just slipped out." Ellie grinned. "See you later. I'm going over to the football field and watch all the guys. I have cheerleader practice at three-thirty, so I might be late getting home for dinner."

Kate sank down on the front steps and glanced up at Della, eyes bright with tears. "I don't believe Betsy did that. It was agreed I would take her to the airport. I would have cried, but I wouldn't have made a fool of myself or embarrassed her. And a taxi! It's just the way Patrick left me. My God, what am I doing wrong?"

Della sat down and cradled Kate in her arms. "This is one more thing you have to get through, Kate. Come on, get up now and come into the kitchen with me and Donald. We're going to have coffee and a slice of my pineapple upside-down cake, and then Donald is going to go over your business plan with you. That child is going to be just fine, Kate. This might be the best thing for her, getting off on her own. She'll be in New York, attending a large university, and she'll make friends. When she comes home for Christmas, she'll be totally different. She'll be forced to interact with the other students. And don't forget she'll have a roommate. Trust me, everything is going to be fine," Della crooned.

"Enough!" Donald roared. "I thought we were going to have coffee and cake!"

"We are," Kate said shakily. "I'm all right now. And I want an extra large slice of cake. Do you realize, Della, Ellie will be going off to college next September if she takes two courses next summer? I'll be completely alone then."

"I don't want to hear talk like that," Donald said gruffly. "As long as we're here, you won't be alone. We're a family, and don't you ever forget it."

"Oh, Donald, thank you. Every day of my life I thank God for sending you and Della into my life. I owe you so much."

"You don't owe us anything. Without you, I would never have met or married Della. I wouldn't have my new family. I think we're pretty much even. Now, can we have the damn cake?"

"Yes, sir!" Kate said, saluting smartly.

Dinner that evening was a lively affair, but it was a forced liveliness. The tension was broken at last when Ellie said, "So, okay, I miss her sour puss staring across the table from me. I'm going to miss her hogging the bathroom, too. I might even write her a letter and tell her so." Kate smiled, which was what Ellie had been angling for. "Now, Mom, let's get to business. I'll help Della with the dishes so you and Donald can talk. But I'll be listening. Remember now, I know numbers and I'm going to be a CPA one of these days. *If* I pass the exam."

"You'll be the best CPA in the state of California," Donald said loyally.

Kate spread her papers out on the kitchen table. "This is my business plan," she began. "These are all the papers from the Small Business Administration. There are two possible locations I'm interested in renting if the SBA gives me the loan. The rent is reasonable on both offices. One is smaller than the other, but if my business grows, then I might need a larger one. I've checked out three used office furniture places, and their things are reasonably priced. I've also been in touch with a print shop and know where to get mailing lists for a good price. And my boss said he'd refer his associates to me if they want renderings. What do you think, Donald?" Kate asked anxiously.

"What I think, Missy Kate, is you have a good thing going here. You're just the type of person the SBA likes to help, and having Captain Starr in the background won't hurt you at all. The loan payments are going to be tough for the first year, until you build your clientele. You'll have to use some of the loan to make the payments, but you can pay that back to yourself later on. You lowballed everything. Lenders like to see that. It's when you get in over your head that they turn you down."

"I just did what you told me. Ellie worked up the numbers. If you two think this is okay, then I'm mailing everything off Monday morning. Until I hear from the SBA, I'm going to see if I can line up some customers. I have enough money put aside to buy one mailing list. I can have a modest printing done. If they turn me down, I'll work out of the house. When the weather is nice, I can move my drafting table out onto the back porch. Keep your fingers crossed, everyone."

"Architectural Renderings by Kate Starr," Ellie said, dancing around the kitchen. "A crisp black-and-white sign done in script will look soooo nice, Mom. Are you going to write 'Before' and 'After' on the sign?"

"No. The clients know that I do one drawing of their project before it gets started and then I do the finished product. It's understood. Listen, Ellie, we're going to be living on a shoestring for a very long time. I want to build this business so if I do make a profit, I'll be putting it back into the business."

"Don't worry about me, Mom. I start my part-time job at the supermarket the last week in September, but I can handle cheerleading, school, and the job. Dates only on Saturday night. No problem there." She giggled.

"Okay, as long as you have it all straight," Kate said.

"Will there be enough money for tuition?" Ellie asked anxiously.

"There will be enough. That's my problem, not yours. Your dad and I took out endowment policies when you and Betsy were born. It will get you through at least two years if you work for your spending money like Betsy is going to do. By then the business should be making a profit and things will be easier. If the business doesn't work, I'll get a job and take out college loans."

It was mid-December before Kate received word that the SBA had approved her loan. Euphoric, she set about renting office space and furnishing it. She wanted to open her doors January second. "This is going to be such a wonderful Christmas!" she said happily to Della and Donald as all three sat together in the kitchen. "We'll get this tall, fragrant tree and decorate it. We'll bake and cook, buy presents, not costly ones, just little mementos. Betsy will be home, and we'll be a complete family again. I can't believe how blessed I am. I'm just sorry Patrick isn't here to enjoy it with us."

"You could invite that nice Charlie Clark," Donald said out of the corner of his mouth.

"No, I can't. He's getting married in February. I told you he was just a friend. All we ever talked about was his lady and Patrick. Evan Carpenter was the same, and so was Douglas Withers. Just friends."

"Someday," Della said sourly.

"No, Della, not someday. I'm not like that. Until the United States government tells me Patrick is dead, I am still married. He is still MIA. Besides, I haven't met anyone who even remotely interests me. I have two daughters to put through college and a business to get off the ground. There's no room in my life for a man."

"If you say so," Della said.

Kate laughed. "I say so."

Unfortunately, Kate's happiness was short-lived. Later that evening, during dinner, she received a call from Betsy.

"How are you, honey?" she cried, pleased. "I hear you have snow in New York. . . . Yes, everyone is here, we're having dinner. I have wonderful news. . . . Oh, *you* have wonderful news. All right, let's hear it!" Everyone stopped eating to watch Kate.

"She's not coming home for Christmas," Della and Ellie muttered at the same time.

"I knew it," Donald mumbled.

"If you're sure that's what you want to do, Betsy. I'm afraid money is a little tight right now. I can send you fifty dollars, but — No, I'm not a skinflint! I told you money is tight right now. I sent your allowance out the first of the month. It was short because I had to buy your plane ticket. I don't know if you can get your money back for it. Just remember, Betsy, if you do turn it in, that's January and February's allowance. . . . I'm sorry you feel that way. I doubt very much if you'll starve, since I paid for your room and board. . . .

Yes, Betsy, Merry Christmas to you, too.

"Betsy won't be home for Christmas," Kate said flatly when she returned to the table. "She's going to Boston to spend the holidays with her roommate's family. She said her roommate's father was a pilot in Vietnam and managed to return in one piece and said he'd met Patrick at one point. It's understandable why she wants to go."

"Oh, well, Easter is just three or four months away," Ellie said, digging into her apple pie. "Then there's spring break." The minute she was finished she excused herself, but not before she gave her mother a big hug. Only Della saw the tears glistening in the girl's eyes.

Kate carried her plate to the sink. She whirled around. "Look, you two, it's okay. I think I knew Betsy wasn't going to be home for Christmas. She won't be home for Easter, either."

"You didn't get a chance to tell her about the loan and —"

"I'll write her a letter after Christmas or in January. She isn't very interested in what I do these days. If you two want to go home, I can clean up here."

"If you carry in the wood, Kate," Donald said, "I'll build you a nice fire before we leave. There's still a few things I can do on my own, and making a fire is one of them."

Kate bent over to kiss his weathered cheek. "I don't think I've told you lately how much I love you and how grateful I am for all your support and help. I'm sorry I don't say it more often, Donald. I wish there were something I could do for you, something meaningful."

"Make a success of that business. We got you to this place in time. The rest is up to you. Give it all you got, Kate. We'll keep things going here for Ellie."

Tears slipped down Kate's cheeks. "He's not coming back, is he, Donald?"

"I'm afraid not, Kate. As much as I hate to say this, I think you should press the government to give you answers one way or the other. Make a stink, a real one, whose smell will go all the way to Washington. If you tell me what to do, I'll do it. You start the ball rolling, and I'll keep it rolling. I think this family has waited long enough for news of Captain Starr."

"You know what? I think you're right," Kate said grimly.

"Atta girl! We'll make them shudder in their boots. And that's a promise."

"Donald, there are days when I can't remember what Patrick looks like. I have to haul out his picture. Then I feel guilty. Other days I don't think about him at all. I feel like I'm letting him down, that I'm not doing my part."

"Would you like us to stay with you this evening, Kate?" Della asked.

"No, you two have done enough for me. I'm fine. Really."

"You make it sound like we live miles away. We're only around the corner," Della muttered. "You look peaked to me. Maybe you're coming down with something, it is the flu season."

"I'm fine. I wanted this Christmas to be . . . oh, I don't know, special in some way. Starting the new business, you know, doing something on my own. With your help of course," Kate added hastily.

"Hold on here," Donald said briskly. "You did this all on your own. All we did was listen and support you. Don't you go thanking us for something you did yourself. Don't you ever take away from your abilities."

Kate smiled tiredly. "Patrick would be stunned if he knew what I've been doing. I don't think he ever thought I had the brains to do anything but be a wife and mother. That used to bother me. He is . . . was so smart. I always felt inferior. I wanted so desperately to be part of what he did, to at least understand what he was all about, but when

I'd ask him to tell me about his day or the missions, he'd start to talk, then remember it was me asking the questions, and he'd kind of smile this . . . quirky smile, and say, 'Kate, you'd never in a million years understand this stuff. Make bread or sew some curtains, that's what you do best.' He was right, I wouldn't have understood, but the next day I would have looked up all the words, tried to find out more so I could talk to him on an intelligent level. But he wouldn't give me a chance. I gave in too easily. I guess it was better for me at the time to bake bread and sew curtains. What really hurt was that he thought I was stupid. He didn't have to say the words out loud, I could tell by the way he acted."

"It doesn't matter what he believed, Kate," Donald said. "You proved you are a woman who can make it on her own. Della and I are so proud of you we could bust, and if the captain was here now, he would be, too. You've climbed a mountain to get to this place. You're going to make a success of this business. Betsy will come back to the fold when she gets all this anger and hurt out of her system. Until she does, you go on with your life and hope for the best." Donald grunted. "Didn't know I was so long-winded."

"I keep telling you you're a windbag," Della said fondly as she tweaked her husband's ear.

"I love you two, you know that," Kate said tearfully.

After Kate and Della had brought in wood and Donald had gotten a cozy fire going in the hearth, Della and Donald said their good-byes and Kate settled herself in front of the cheerful blaze. How much she owed Donald and Della, she mused. Probably her life, and the lives of her children. She paid Della a pittance to cook their meals and keep up with the house. With the low rent Donald charged, she'd been able to put money aside for Betsy's tuition. Still, it wasn't enough. Earlier in the summer she'd been sitting at the kitchen table going over her finances, trying to figure out where she could juggle, whom not to pay so Betsy could go to the school of her choice, when Donald and Della had joined her in the kitchen. Donald had a bankbook in his hand and handed it over. All the deposits were the same, her monthly rent for years. His voice gruff, jerky, he'd said, "Della and I don't have much use for this. It's just sitting here drawing interest. I have my pension and the rental from two other houses, so it would please us if you used this for Betsy's college."

"We want to do this, Kate," Della had

added. "We feel like we're the girls' grandparents, and grandparents always help out. It's not a loan, we're giving it to you. If you have trouble with that, we can call it a loan and you can pay us back when you're rich and successful." God, she'd cried that day — no, howled like a banshee would be more like it.

Later she'd thought about her parents back in New Jersey. She'd asked them for a loan and had been turned down cold. Business wasn't good, they had the grandparents to take care of. She'd hung up the phone and cried some more. They'd seen her only once in ten years. They never wrote, never called. Gradually she'd stopped calling and writing, too.

Kate marched out to the kitchen to look for her address book. She always kept it in the cabinet with the tea bags and coffee. She reached for it and flipped it to Bill Percy's number, not caring that it was ten o'clock at night. She identified herself, went through the amenities, then charged ahead, drawing a deep breath as she did so.

"I'd like an update, Bill, on my husband's situation. It's been eleven years. Surely the government is willing to say *something*. If Patrick is dead, I want to know that so I can hold a service. I need to know. I'm not the same weak-kneed person I was when you and I last met. I've got a backbone now, and it's stiff, Bill. With resolve."

"You sound like Elizabeth, Kate. I think you two are working at cross purposes here."

"Elizabeth who? What are you talking about?" Kate said irritably, certain Percy was going to give her the brush-off, as he had in the past.

"Come now, Kate," he said snidely. "Elizabeth Starr, your daughter. Are you saying you don't know about her involvement in all the groups she's joined since going East?"

"No, I don't know what she's involved in. But if she is, what of it? At least she's *doing* something. Something you and your superiors should be doing, getting me and others like me news of our husbands. Now, I want some answers, and I want them now, damn you!"

"Would you like me to make up something just to make you happy? I can't do that, Kate."

"Then declare my husband dead or tell me he's POW. And don't you ever insult my intelligence by telling me there are no POWs over there anymore. I know there are."

"Kate, it's ten minutes past ten. There's nothing I can do at this hour. We're coming up on to Christmas. A lot of the . . . officers have taken leave for the holidays. I'll get back to you in a day or so."

"I'll give you a day or so, but no longer. And you'd better come back to me with *news . . . information,* something concrete."

"I'll do my best," Percy said quietly.

"Your best isn't going to do it this time, Bill. This time you're going to have to actually *do* something. Good night, Bill, and . . . Merry Christmas."

Kate had no idea if the airman returned her greeting or not as she hung up the phone. Now Betsy's trip to Boston made a little more sense. An overwhelming sense of relief washed over her. The Bill Percys of the world wouldn't be able to slough off Betsy, she simply wouldn't allow it. Which doesn't say much for me, Kate thought.

Grim-faced, she got out her writing paper and a pen and composed a letter to the President of the United States and one to the editor-in-chief of the *New York Times.* Both would be ready to mail when Percy got back to her on Friday.

She had just finished and was settling in on the couch when Ellie came in at eleven o'clock.

"How's it going, Mom?" she asked, curling up on the floor at her mother's feet. Kate told her. "Wow, I bet Betsy gets some results. Nobody shuts that girl up. In this instance it might be good for her, for us, too. Do you believe Dad is still alive, Mom?"

"Part of me believes it, part of me doesn't. If your father was alive, I think we would have heard something by now. I know you don't believe it. You always were the realistic one."

"If he did come back, I wonder what he'd be like? How would he react to us? We're all grown up now. And look at you, Mom, you're a smart dresser these days, you're fashionable and worldly, too. You have a job and are going into business for yourself. You went back to school, got a degree. He wouldn't know what to make of you." Ellie giggled.

"I don't think he'd like this new person I am," Kate said sadly.

"Aw, Mom, now you sound like Betsy. He'd be so proud of you he'd just bust. Are you really going to type up those letters and mail them out?"

"With copies to everyone I can think of. It's damn well time I received an answer I can live with. We need to lay your father to rest. It's that simple."

"We can do that, Mom. We can have a private service, buy a plot in a cemetery, put up a stone and visit. You never did go through Dad's things. Those two metal boxes are still in the cellar. Maybe what we could do — what we *should* do — is bury those. On Sundays we can take flowers, or when you feel the need to talk to Dad, you can have a place to visit. If you think it's a good idea, I'm for it."

"Betsy will never agree."

"But the way I look at it, she's outnumbered. It'll be private, just us. No one else needs to know."

"What if . . . if by some miracle your father does come back? What do we do then?" Kate asked.

"Then we take down the stone, dig up the boxes and . . . and say Betsy made us do it," Ellie said, breaking into a fit of hysterical laughter.

Kate smiled in spite of herself.

"I think Dad would understand," Ellie said. "Look, you don't have to decide now, but the new year would be a good time to . . . to make a new beginning. Maybe . . . maybe we could do it between Christmas and New Year's. We can start fresh then. Think about it, okay?"

"Sure. Now I think you should be in bed, young lady, tomorrow is a school day."

"Would you like me to make you a cup of tea before I go upstairs?"

"No, I'm fine. I'll be up soon. Ellie, did you ever . . . feel like I neglected you, that

I didn't do my best? Do you think I should have done more where your father is concerned?"

"No, to all your questions," Ellie said, hugging her mother.

"Betsy does."

"Betsy expected you to be her slave, as well as her mother and father. If she had her way, she would have had you grow a telephone out of the side of your head and single-handedly take on the U.S. government and the entire Air Force. Mom, you did your best. Someday Betsy will understand that. And if that day never comes, we'll live with it. 'Night, Mom."

"Good night, Ellie, sleep tight."

Alone, Kate added another log to the fire, then curled back up on the couch. How many lonely nights she'd sat like this, dreaming and hoping for the impossible. And on most of those nights, she'd cried herself to sleep. Memories were wonderful, but they could also be one's undoing. It was time to lock up those memories. Ellie was right, the new year would be a perfect time for a new start on life.

There was one decision she had to make before she could contemplate Ellie's plan. She had to make the decision to give up Patrick's pay and file for his insurance. She'd need a lawyer for that. It wouldn't do any good to declare Patrick dead and continue to take his monthly pay. Either she was going to do it right or not at all. Numbers swam behind her weary eyelids. The government would fight her, that much she knew. Therefore she couldn't count on her husband's insurance. She'd truly be on her own. If I have to, I can get a job working evenings as a waitress, she told herself. I can do whatever I have to do to make a clean start.

When Kate, Donald, and Della entered the house on Friday evening at six-thirty, the phone was ringing. Kate knew it was Bill Percy before she picked up the receiver.

"What do you have for me, Bill?"

Percy cleared his throat. "There is no news, Kate. Captain Starr cannot be declared dead until we have some sort of evidence from the Vietnamese government. Their position is the same, there are no POWs in Vietnam."

"Patrick isn't a POW, he's an MIA. Where is my husband, Bill? You sent him over there, so it's up to you to find him. For eleven years you've been feeding me the same stale, sorry line, and I'm sick and tired of it. I gave you my husband, and now you're telling me you can't find him, that there are no records. Well, I'm telling you I want something.

I'm mailing a letter to the President, to everyone in the world if I have to. I want to know what happened to my children's father, to my husband. All you're concerned with is your top-secret crap and the lies you tell us. It is so hard for me to believe how shabbily you've treated me and the girls. It isn't fair. We're in limbo. You're ruining our lives, can't you see that?"

"Kate, when I have news, I'll call you. Have a nice Christmas."

"You son of a bitch!" Kate's hand flew to her mouth and she turned to face her friends. "I'm sorry, I never swore like that in my life. He makes me so . . . so angry. He thinks he has me over a barrel, that I won't do anything. He actually told me to have a nice Christmas. I'd like to drop a ten-ton rock right on his head!"

"Now calm down, Kate, you knew he was going to say what he did," Donald said soothingly.

"I hoped, Donald. God, how I hoped," Kate said sadly. "I thought if I threatened, there would be some small kernel of information. But no one cares. Why is that?"

"I don't know. Tomorrow, mail your letters. I called the church, and the service is scheduled for December twenty-seventh at ten o'clock. Della and I picked out a nice plot and ordered the stone. I know a handyman who will come over in the morning and transport the boxes of personal effects to the cemetery. Are you going to open them?"

"I don't think I can do that, Donald. No, no, I'm not. I don't want to make this any harder on Ellie than it is. I called an attorney recommended to me by my old boss and he's going to open the office and see me tomorrow. He's a Vietnam vet. He said he wouldn't charge me, do you believe that? He said . . . he said he'd be honored to attend Patrick's service and speak if I wanted him to. I said yes, knowing I would choke up. Somebody has to say something, not some strange minister Patrick didn't know. I think it's the right thing to do. At least it seemed like it at the time. What do you think?"

"I think you did right," Donald said. Della nodded agreement.

"Then it's settled. Nicholas Mancuso will speak at Patrick's service. He's nice, you'll like him. He said all the right things, said he knew how I felt, said he knew how guys like Percy operated, and he said — and this is a direct quote — 'Don't believe their bullshit, some of our guys are still over there.' He was wearing an MIA bracelet like we all wear. He made me feel good, and said the burial will shake them up."

"Ellie's working late," Della said. "I probably shouldn't tell you this, but the child has been putting in extra hours so she can get you something nice for Christmas. Now don't you let on you know or be cross with her for working the extra hours."

"Okay, Della. I don't suppose there's any mail from Betsy. I wonder if she'll send us a card?"

"I'm sorry, Kate, no. Just the usual mail."

Kate mailed her letters the following morning. She had no great hopes or expectations that either the President of the United States or the awesome *New York Times* would respond.

She managed to get through the days until Christmas, although she felt high-strung, irritable, and moody. She cried a lot as she packed up the things Patrick had left behind. She was doing, by her own choice, what millions of people did when a loved one passed on.

"Maybe . . . maybe this is all wrong, Della," she said with a catch in her voice. "Surely it won't hurt if I put all these things in the cellar. I never go down there, I won't have to see them, but I'll know they're there. It won't be over then. I'll still be Kate Starr, wife of Captain Starr MIA. Am I really doing the right thing?"

"If you want to get on with your life, you're doing the right thing. Does it feel right or wrong?" Della asked quietly.

Kate kicked the box sitting at her feet. "It feels right *and* wrong. My God, what if by some miracle Patrick does come back? How will I ever explain? He'll . . . Lord, I don't know what he would think. . . ." Her shoulders squared imperceptibly. "I guess it's too late to worry about that now."

Della patted Kate's shoulder. "You used the right word a minute ago. It would be a miracle if Patrick came back, and miracles are pretty hard to come by these days. Donald and I both think you're being brave and realistic. For you it's right. You go upstairs and get dressed. I'll transfer these things to that old trunk Donald had in the cellar. They're due to be picked up any minute now."

Kate needed no second urging. Upstairs, Ellie was putting the finishing touches to her hair. "How do I look, Mom?"

"You look nice, Ellie. Your father would . . . he would be so . . . Oh, I can't think straight this morning," Kate said distractedly. "Come into my room and talk to me while I get dressed."

Ellie watched as her mother slipped on a deep brown wool dress with a flared skirt.

She cinched it at the waist with a gold and brown braided belt that Ellie had braided for her mother at the YWCA day camp when she was ten or so. Kate brushed her hair, added a slash of lipstick and a smear of rouge across her cheekbones. She finished off with a bright orange scarf around her neck. "We have to remember, this is not exactly a funeral, but a service. Or is it a funeral?" Kate asked jerkily.

"I suppose it's a little of both. We are burying something — all that remains of Dad."

Kate removed the orange scarf. "That's how I think of it. Yes, that's a good way for us to think of it. When we come home, it will . . . it will be all over. We can cry for a few days. We're going to cry, Ellie, at least I will. Then on New Year's we'll . . . we'll get up and . . . go on. I don't know how we'll feel that morning . . . probably sad and . . . probably guilty. For some reason I always feel guilty when I think about your father. I don't know why that is. Do you?"

Ellie shook her head. "If I had to take a guess, I'd say it's because you're still alive and Dad isn't. Time to go, Mom." She took her mother's arm.

"Betsy is never going to forgive me for this," Kate said tightly. "Or you for going along with it."

"I know that. Do I look worried? I wrote her a letter last week. Don't get nervous, it was a nice letter. I explained how I felt and how I thought you felt. I did kind of ream her out for not giving us an address or telephone number where we could reach her. Her going away for Christmas was unforgivable."

"Ellie, you do understand that I'm giving up your father's pay by doing this? It's going to be hard for us to manage, and I can't keep taking from Della and Donald."

"Don't worry about it. I can live on baked beans and toast if I have to. I'll be working full-time this summer, and I can go to the community college if I have to. None of that's important to me. What's important is that what we're doing is going to affect the rest of our lives. Now wipe that grim look off your face or Della will start to cry, and when Della cries, we need towels," Ellie said, striving for a light tone.

"I paid cash for the cemetery plot. They wanted me to buy two, you know, for when I . . . I had to say no, I didn't have the money. My God, imagine not having enough money to bury yourself." Kate stopped at the bottom of the steps and looked at her daughter. "That's not important, either, is it?"

"Not in the least. I'm kind of glad you didn't take the plot on time payments."

A smile tugged at the corners of Kate's mouth.

When they reached the cemetery, Kate was stunned to see a crowd of people around the spot she'd chosen for Patrick's service. The minister was there in his clerical garb, along with a host of men dressed in suits and ties. The only person she recognized was Nick Mancuso. The others, she decided, must be friends coming to . . . what? Pay their respects? Gawk at these unorthodox proceedings? No. She raised her eyes and met those of a man standing at the outer rim of the half circle. Even from this distance she could see the tears in his eyes. No, never to gawk, only to pay their respects. She could feel moisture build behind her own eyelids.

Della pushed Donald's chair over the spiky grass, and Ellie walked alongside her, her arm linked with hers. Kate acknowledged each man and thanked them for coming.

The service began.

Fifteen minutes later it was over. As the vets filed past Kate they handed her a white flower. She nodded her thanks, tears streaming down her cheeks. Nick Mancuso was the last to hand her his flower. "I don't think this was wrong, Kate. I know how hard it is for you. I'll talk to you in a few days," he said, and drifted away.

"I should thank the minister," Kate murmured to Della as the crowd dispersed.

"He's already gone, Kate," Della told her. "I think this was uncomfortable for him. It doesn't matter. Who's that man standing over by the angel stone? I saw him taking pictures before."

"I have no idea. I assume he's one of Mr. Mancuso's people. Why don't you three go back to the car. I need a few minutes here alone. I'm okay, don't worry about me, I can handle this. I just need a few moments of private time."

"Mom, I don't think —"

"I need you to help me push Donald's chair," Della said to Ellie. "The ground is too rough here."

"Go along, honey. It's all right," Kate said soothingly.

Kate stared at Donald's old battered trunk and the two gun-metal gray boxes the Air Force had sent on that she'd never opened. She was dry-eyed now, almost angry. She started to shiver, felt her knees weaken when she felt a presence next to her. She raised defiant eyes to stare at the stranger who had been taking pictures. She stared at him for a full minute before she shrugged off his arm.

He was young, twenty-eight or so, with summer-blue eyes and a thatch of unruly curls crowning the top of his head. Freckles marched across the bridge of his nose and cheekbones, ending at his dark hairline. She just knew he hated the freckles and his curly hair. She sensed his tallness, his thinness, when her eyes returned to the three trunks in front of her. "I need to say good-bye alone. I appreciate your coming here, but you should have left with the others. Please, I don't want to be rude, I just need to say good — good-bye alone."

His voice was deep, soothing. "I'm sorry, Mrs. Starr, I didn't mean to intrude. I thought you were going . . . to faint." She nodded, sensed him moving backward. And then she forgot him entirely.

Kate moved forward to place the white flowers on top of the gray metal trunks. What should she say, how should she say it? "I love you, Patrick. I'll always love you." But was that true? Would she always love him? She squeezed her eyes shut and willed his face to appear. Satisfied with the vision behind her closed lids, Kate whispered, "Good-bye, Patrick."

She turned, stumbled, and would have fallen if the man behind her hadn't reached for her arm. "Easy does it, Mrs. Starr."

"Thank you, Mister . . ."

"Stewart. Gustav Stewart. My friends call me Gus. I'm from the *New York Times*, Mrs. Starr. Your letter was turned over to me. I'd like to talk with you and your daughter. I know this probably isn't the best time, but I flew here at my own expense, and I have to get back to work. I'd like to do a human-interest story on Captain Starr and your family." He was leading her back to the car, and she was following him like a lost puppy.

"Human interest!" she yelped when they reached the car.

Stewart held up both hands. "Whoa, it's not what you think. When *I* say human interest, I mean to make the world aware of what happened to Captain Starr and your family. This . . . service is, to my knowledge, the first of its kind. I think people need to know about this. I'm a good reporter, Mrs. Starr. I'd like you to trust me. I'll even show you the article before I turn it in, in case there's anything you object to or want to change. You did write to us. Did you have something else in mind?" There was such compassion in the reporter's eyes, Kate wanted to cry.

"I don't know what I meant, what I expected. I had to do something. No one was helping me, I didn't know what else to do. I don't think I really thought beyond mailing the letter. I guess I assumed your paper would research the MIAs and speak to the wives. Give us recognition. Eleven years is a long time to be told the same thing. We don't know anything. It's not just me, Mr. Stewart, there are other wives out there in the same place. We gave up our husbands, and now we're like pariahs. Look, if you want, come back to the house with me. We can talk where it's warm over a cup of coffee. Follow us."

It was nine o'clock when Gus Stewart left the Starr house. He felt as if he were carrying a hundred-pound burden on his shoulders. In his gut he carried an even heavier weight. He would do the story, but would it get printed? He'd been given this assignment because he was young, a cub reporter, and none of the pros wanted it. He hadn't lied when he'd told Kate he was a good reporter. His eyes and ears were tuned to the world seven days a week. All the way home on the red-eye his stomach churned. If he handled this just right, it might turn out to be something really big. It wasn't going to be something he dashed off to meet a deadline, either. He had names now, other leads, copies of letters, and he'd get more. He might get an entire feature article and really do some good for the MIAs.

He'd even work on it on his own time if it would help. It wasn't going to be the Pulitzer he dreamed of, but damn close.

He liked Kate Starr, really liked her. No matter what, he was going to stay in touch with her. Jesus, imagine burying a guy's belongings because there was nothing else left. What was it she'd said? "For now, this is acceptable. We have a place to go, a place to mourn, a place where we're able to say good-bye."

In his opinion, Kate Starr was a hell of a woman. He couldn't help but wonder if she would be able to handle the fallout if the story got printed. His stomach started to churn again. He grinned in the darkened plane. Kate Starr, he thought, was probably capable of handling anything.

Gus scrunched himself into his window seat. Kate's last words were, "I have a right to know." That's what he was going to call his feature story. Only he would change it to read, *"They Have a Right to Know,"* meaning all the wives of the missing MIAs. And he would feature Kate Starr and her family in the article.

Unfortunately, it didn't work out that way for Gus Stewart or Kate Starr. None of the other wives were as brave as Kate; they feared the loss of their husbands' pay if they went public and broke the "keep quiet" policy they'd adhered to in the past. They did talk freely and willingly, but in confidence, always ending with, "This is off the record, please don't print what I'm saying."

Gus grew frustrated, angry at the military and the government. He finally began to realize how Kate and the other wives felt. Everywhere he turned he was stonewalled. When he finally called Kate on a late June afternoon to tell her the story had been killed for the third time, she showed no surprise.

"I'm sorry, Gus. I know you worked hard. In a way, you can't blame the wives. A lot of them don't have a Della and a Donald like I do. We tried, that's the important thing. If you ever find yourself in my neighborhood, stop by and I'll take you to dinner."

"You can afford dinner out?" Gus joked.

"A hot dog from a street vendor, maybe a bottle of soda pop."

"How's business? Any regrets?"

"Business is great. I'm making my bills and have a little left over every month. I don't have enough hours in the day. I've been thinking of hiring some part-time help. I've had to turn down three jobs in L.A. because I can't be away from the office. Then there are days when I sit here sucking my thumb and hoping a job will come in."

He didn't want to hang up. It didn't sound like she wanted to, either. "How's Della and Donald?"

"Donald is in pain a lot of the time. Della fusses over him something fierce. They still come over every day."

"And Ellie?"

"Ellie's working full-time for the supermarket, doing the bookkeeping. We have her scheduled for West Chester University in Pennsylvania in the fall. They have a very good accounting department. If my business keeps going the way it has been, tuition won't be a problem."

"You're working seven days a week, aren't you?" Gus challenged.

"Now where did you hear that?"

Gus chuckled. "I just guessed."

"It's the only way I can get ahead. Della makes it easy for me. I've had to get glasses, though. Ellie says I look like an owl."

Gus laughed. "Kate, I really am sorry about the article. I'm not quitting on you. If there's ever an opportunity, or if things change, I'll be right there with it. I just wish there was more I could do."

"You tried. That's more than anyone else was willing to do."

"Call me sometime, okay?" Gus said gruffly.

"You bet. We're friends, aren't we?"

"Yes, yes, we are. I'm going to hold you to that dinner, now."

"I'll start saving now." Kate laughed. " 'Bye, Gus."

" 'Bye, Kate."

CHAPTER 10

It was seven years before Kate saw Gus Stewart again, and then it was by pure accident.

The airport was noisy, crowded with hordes of travelers following tour guides with feathers in their hats for easy identification.

As she entered the rest room on the concourse, Kate wondered — and not for the first time — what she was doing back in her home state of New Jersey. She could just as easily have vacationed at home in bed or in the garden with a book. But, no, that was too easy; she had to come back here and torture herself.

She made a face at herself in the mirror as she applied lipstick, washed her hands, and brushed her hair. She looked nice, moderately professional in a crisp blue-and-white seersucker suit that wasn't exactly crisp at this point. She grimaced at herself again, then straightened the strap of her handbag and marched back out to the concourse.

Her plan was to rent a car, drive to Westfield, cruise past the house she'd grown up in, maybe knock on the door to see who now lived in the house since her parents retired to Florida. Then she'd drive by Patrick's old house, maybe knock on that door. She'd drive through town, go past the church, stop at the library, maybe go in the school and look at her high school class picture on the wall, check out Patrick's picture, too. Then she'd get on the parkway and head for Toms River to check out Patrick's father's house, which had been left to her last year when her father-in-law died. She'd wanted to sell that house, but the attorneys had said that without Patrick's death certificate she couldn't. She should think about renting it, though, to help pay the taxes.

Kate glanced around the concourse to get her bearings and then heard her name being called — not over the loudspeaker, but close at hand. She turned.

"Kate! Kate Starr!"

For a moment she couldn't remember his name, and then it came to her. "Gus! How nice to see you again. What are you doing here? It must be, what, seven years? You look well."

"Ten pounds heavier." Gus laughed. "What are *you* doing here? Too much air traffic over Kennedy, so our pilot landed here. I'll take a ground shuttle into the city. God, it's good to see you. Listen, are you making connections or do you have to be somewhere at a certain time? If not, let's head for the nearest bar and get a drink. I could use a sandwich. I couldn't figure out what it was they served for lunch on the plane, so I passed on it."

"My time is my own. I could use a drink. Only one, though, I'm driving."

"They'll hold your bags if you checked them. Car rental companies are good about late arrivals. See," he said, throwing his hands in the air, "it's all taken care of. Let's dine in this . . . this whatever it is." He motioned to a public room that had a bar with a brass railing along the sides.

Settled, with menus in their hands, Gus leaned across the table. "Kate, it's so good to see you. How's everything going? You look great."

Kate could feel a warm flush creep up her cheeks. He's flirting with me, she thought, stunned. Seven years ago he'd looked boyishly young. Now he looked mature and . . . *sexy.*

"You look pretty good yourself," she blurted. "I'd kill for your eyelashes and those summer-blue eyes —" God, *she* was flirting. Actually flirting! With a *younger* man. A delicious thrill coursed through her.

"Bet you're beating off the architects with a stick, huh?"

"Hardly." Kate laughed ruefully. "I really have no time for a social life. Occasionally I have a business lunch or dinner, but that's it. I'm trying real hard to make a success of my business. What free time I do have, I help Della. Donald isn't well, and he takes a lot of care. He's crippled with arthritis and he's in constant pain, but he still manages to smile. He's eighty-two. I can't believe it. Where have the years gone?" she said breathlessly.

The waitress hovered. "Kate, what will you have?" Gus asked.

"A pastrami on rye with lots of mustard, and a Michelob."

"Make that two," Gus said, handing over the menus.

"How's Ellie?"

Kate preened. "She finally passed the last part of the CPA exam in the fall of last year. She's a bona fide CPA, and I was her first client. Well, Architectural Renderings was her first client. I'm so proud of her."

Gus laughed. "I can tell. Are you still living in the same place with that beautiful garden?"

"No, unfortunately. Three years ago a developer wanted to buy most of the area, three or four entire streets. Everyone sold but Donald. He held out to the last minute to drive up the price, and got a fortune — and I mean a fortune — for the house I rented, his house, and that other little rental property he owned. The four of us lived in an apartment for over a year while he had a house built for us. It's so beautiful, all redwood and glass and very modern. He had a guest house built on the lot, which I thought Ellie and I would live in, but he wouldn't hear of it. So we live in the big house and he and Della live in the cottage. We have a swimming pool, a cabana, and a three-car garage." He was so easy to talk to, Kate thought. "Oh, oh, wait, we even have a Sundance hot tub. It's for Donald. We got this . . . contraption that lifts him out of the wheelchair and puts him in the tub, clothes and all. He loves it, and it really helps his arthritis."

"I like hot tubs. They have one at the gym where I work out. Do you ever go in it?"

"Once or twice. By the time we get Donald in and out, we're too tired to go in ourselves."

The waitress poured their beer. Gus held

his glass aloft. "What should we drink to?"

Kate pretended to think. "Chance meetings? Friendship? Airports? Or all of the above?"

Gus nodded. Glasses clinked. The sandwiches arrived, warm and full of oozing, spicy, brown mustard.

"Now this is good," Gus said, munching happily.

He's nice, Kate thought. I like him. "Tell me about you," she said, her eyes watering from the tangy mustard.

"Well, I haven't written my Pulitzer yet. I will someday, you know. I've covered some good stories, gotten my share of bylines. The pay isn't going to get me a hot tub on my patio on Forty-ninth Street. My mother said if you can buy one good suit a year, pay your rent, feed yourself, and give in the collection box every Sunday, you have nothing to complain about."

"A wise woman," Kate said, smiling. She wondered what it would be like to have a male friend, one she could call on the phone at any time and just talk.

"How's your other daughter, Betsy?"

Kate laid down her sandwich. "I rarely talk to her. She went on to get her master's and doctorate. She teaches now at Villanova University. I see her once a year and she calls every so often. She's never forgiven me for that . . . 'funeral' we had. I understand she's very active in several Vietnam organizations. She doesn't talk to me about what she does. What little information I have I get from Ellie, who gets it from a friend of Betsy's." She hesitated. "You know, what really bothered me most about leaving our home was Betsy's garden. Do you remember that glorious rainbow of flowers she planted around the house? I tried to duplicate that garden a hundred times over the past three years, with no luck. Ellie says Betsy planted them with love and a pure heart, and that's why God made them grow for her. I took pictures from a neighbor's roof before we left and had it enlarged. It's hanging over the mantel now. I think that's my only regret at this point in my life." Kate picked up her sandwich and bit into it.

"Where are you going when you leave here?" Gus asked. "How about us having dinner?"

"We're eating now." Kate laughed. "I was going to Westfield and stir up some old memories, but since I met you, I think I'll just get on the parkway and head for Toms River. I'd like to get settled in before dark." She went on to tell him about her father-in-law's house. "Thanks for the invitation, though.

This monstrous sandwich will hold me over until tomorrow morning."

"I love the beach, the sun, blue skies," Gus said wistfully.

"Melanomas . . . tsk, tsk," Kate said, clucking her tongue.

"I wear a number-fifteen sun block. I manage to get down to Point Pleasant three or four times during the summer. I've always been a beach person."

Kate knew he was hinting for an invitation. Should she or shouldn't she? *Definitely not. Absolutely not.* "Maybe you could come down this weekend. Saturday morning, Sunday if you prefer. I can make dinner or lunch." *Breakfast. Definitely not. Absolutely not.* "Or if you get an early start, breakfast."

"Hell yes, I'll come. Thanks for inviting me. Hey, have you ever been to Atlantic City?"

"No, never. I'm not a gambler."

"Me, either, I work too hard for my money. But it's a good way to spend a Saturday night."

"With or without a date?" Kate asked, and could have bitten off her tongue.

"A couple of friends. They think they're going to strike it rich. I watch."

"Don't you have a girlfriend?" Kate asked. She felt her ears grow warm. What in the world was the matter with her? He was a puppy, a warm, endearing puppy. Thirty-one at the most. There was at least fourteen years' difference in their ages.

"I have dates from time to time, but there isn't anyone serious in my life. Like you, I have very little spare time. I'm usually working on a story or doing my Big Brother bit at the Y. Is that a frown building on your face? Look, I come with references. I'm not a stranger, we met before. Kids and dogs like me. Old people think I'm nice. I have a decent job. I don't smoke or drink. Well, hardly ever." He grinned when Kate lit one of her stress relievers and offered him one, which he took with no hesitation. "Terrible habit."

"The worst. But if you look at it as a stress reliever, and taking a drink as an attitude adjuster, it doesn't seem so bad. This is the first vacation I've had in five years."

"That's not good," he said. "Everyone needs a break, even if it's to go to a hotel for the weekend. I make sure I take mine every year. I come back full of spit and vinegar. Shame on you," he teased.

"It's not that easy when you're in business for yourself. You have to stay on top of things. I have two assistants now and I moved into a larger office space. I'm still spread pretty thin, though. I wouldn't exactly say I'm in demand, but I've built up a good business reputation and my prices are fair. Believe it or not, I turn down work if I feel I can't give it one hundred percent. I have money in the bank, I repaid Della and Donald, I managed to put Betsy and Ellie both through college and still paid for Betsy's master's and doctorate," Kate said proudly.

"And I knew you when you were sweating Ellie's tuition. You should be proud."

"I am, but I could never have done it on my own. Every day of my life I thank God for those two."

The waitress ambled over with the check in her hand. Gus handed her a twenty-dollar bill. "I think she's trying to tell us she needs this table."

Kate looked up to see a line of people at the entrance. "I think you're right, and I hope you're right about our baggage being safe. I'd hate to think I'm going to be walking on the beach in this suit and high heels."

"Not to worry. I'd lend you a pair of skivvies and a T-shirt," Gus said, picking up her carryall. Kate stumbled, certain her face was as red as the carpet she was walking on.

Kate found her bag sitting with six others at the end of the carousel. "I guess I'll see you on Saturday, Gus. Thanks for lunch, I really enjoyed it."

"My pleasure." Gus grinned. "See you," he said, kissing her lightly on the cheek before loping off to catch his shuttle bus.

Kate smiled the whole time she was checking out the Lincoln Town Car she'd rented. She was still smiling when she signed her name and picked up her keys. Then a whirlwind of motion behind her made her turn. In all her life she'd never seen anyone so frazzled: curly hair standing at attention, shirt dragged halfway down his arm with the weight of his suit bags, eyes full of . . . was it terror?

"What's wrong?" Kate asked anxiously.

"You forgot to give me the damn address!" Gus sputtered, sweat rolling down his face.

"Oh. You didn't ask," Kate said lamely. "I'll write it down."

"Jesus, no, don't write it down. If you write it down, that means I have to put all this stuff down, and I'll never be able to harness myself again. Just tell me what it is."

Kate laughed. "It's Eighty-eight Rosemont Road."

Gus trundled off, his bags flapping against his knees as he muttered over and over, "Eighty-eight Rosemont Road."

Kate alternated between smiling and giggling as she drove the rental car down the service road and out through the toll booth onto the New Jersey Turnpike.

What kind of clothes had she brought? For the life of her she couldn't remember. Well, she could always go to the mall and buy some new things. What did a forty-four-year-old woman wear on the beach with a man who was at least fourteen years younger? She wasn't exactly ugly, but she wasn't going to be any match for the young beach bunnies with their golden tans and string bikinis. She groaned, feeling every one of her forty-four years.

Maybe they'd run on the beach. Running was good. Would her thighs jiggle? Running was not good. Sweatpants, thin cotton ones. A baggy overblouse, again thin cotton. She wouldn't look so white and . . . slightly overweight. Maybe she'd pick up one of those Indian cotton mumu things women wore on the beach. Those things covered *everything*.

God, what if Gus made . . . advances? How would she handle that? Was she jumping the gun here? She did have an active imagination. He was just coming for the day. Just to get out of the city and . . . and just enough for the day. There was nothing wrong with two people walking on the beach, eating together, talking together, having a drink together. So what if he was about thirty and she was forty-four? He knew how old she was. He knew everything there was to know about her. Ellie would say, "Oooh, he issssss delicious." Kate broke into a peal of laughter when she drove the car into the driveway.

Saturday was only a day away.

CHAPTER 11

It was a tidy little four-room house in a retirement village. Patrick's father had always been a tidy man, much like Patrick. The furniture was old, shabby, from a long-ago era. Tears pricked Kate's eyes when she ran her hand over the back of the sofa. How many times she and Patrick had cuddled and necked in the corner. It had to be fifty years old at least, yet it wasn't junk, nor was it an antique. It was just old, shabby, and full of stains.

In many ways the box of a house was a memorial to Patrick. His pictures were everywhere. Kate wished now she'd done more, but the elder Starr had been a private person and not one to show interest or love for anyone. She'd done her best, sending cards, small gifts on Father's Day, his birthday, and

Christmas. She'd sent the girls' school pictures faithfully, even though he never responded.

She felt like an intruder as she walked through the house. It was hers now. Maybe she shouldn't rent it. What in the world would she do with all of her father-in-law's belongings? Send them off to California? Store them in the basement or the garage until she died herself and the girls had to go through her things? Better to leave the house empty, pay the taxes and insurance, and thank God she was able to do it.

She busied herself then, unpacking, washing the linens for the bed, and dusting. She ran the dishes she thought she would need through the dishwasher. It was eleven o'clock when she pushed the upright Hoover vacuum cleaner back into the closet.

Kate scanned her appearance in the bathroom mirror. She looked presentable enough to go to Pizza Hut for her dinner and to the 7-Eleven for her breakfast. She ate, showered, and was in bed by twelve-thirty, but she couldn't sleep. The street outside bathed the front bedroom in a yellowish glow even though the white shade was drawn to the sill. Patrick's picture glared at her from the dresser. She got up, turned the photograph facedown, and got back into bed. Still she couldn't sleep. She got up again and slid the picture into the top drawer of the dresser. When she got back into bed, she fell asleep instantly and slept soundly, awakening at six o'clock to the sound of birds chirping.

Good Lord, what was she to do with herself all day? At eight o'clock she could go next door and ask to use the phone to call the telephone company to turn on the phone. She could call Della and Ellie and talk to them, call her office and talk to the receptionist. She could go shopping or walk on the beach, but that meant she'd have to get in the car and drive. "You are lazy, Kate Starr," she muttered as she poured coffee into an earthenware mug.

Patrick had sat at this table for his meals from the time he was old enough to eat with the family until he left for college. The top of the table was badly scarred and gouged. She'd eaten at this same table several times when Patrick had invited her to their old house in Westfield. It was a memory now. How sad that there were no male Starrs to carry on the name. She'd been so sure Ellie was going to be a boy by the way she'd carried her. She'd even managed to convince Patrick of it. How clearly she remembered his look of disappointment at the hospital when he'd learned otherwise. Maybe that was why Betsy was his favorite. Maybe a lot of things, she thought sadly.

"I wonder," she said aloud, "what it would be like to kiss another man." She propped her chin into the palm of her hand as she tried to remember what it felt like when Patrick kissed her. It must have been wonderful because the sex was good, at times. She always enjoyed the pillow talk, but Patrick was usually asleep in seconds, and when she chastised him, he'd say, "Honey, it's a compliment to you. It was great and you wore me out." A memory, nothing more.

"I'm beginning to wonder, Patrick, if I ever liked you. I know I was in love with you, but I don't think I liked you," Kate mumbled as she drained her coffee. "And it's taken me eighteen years to figure that out." It was a mistake to come here; she should have stayed in California, gone to the library for rest and relaxation. She didn't need these trips down Memory Lane. That was all behind her.

In the bathroom she pulled on a pair of jeans that were snug around the waist and a Banana Republic T-shirt. She slid her sockless feet into a pair of Keds. There was something she could do; she could go back to Westfield, buy some flowers, and visit the cemetery where her father-in-law was buried.

She'd stop at the first phone booth she came to and call the phone company. This way she wouldn't have to bother the neighbors.

The word *pilgrimage* flew into Kate's mind when she pulled to the curb in front of her old house. She tossed the word away immediately. She was merely a lookie-look, checking out the old neighborhood. The house looked shabby and run-down, grass growing between the cracks in the driveway. The lawn was brown in some spots, bare in others. One of the front windows was cracked, and the paint on the front door was peeling. There didn't seem to be any curtains on the second-floor windows. She didn't feel anything when she drove around the corner to Patrick's old house. She stared at it, thought about Patrick running down the front steps to meet her on the sidewalk under the maple tree. He'd kissed her a hundred times under that maple tree. The sidewalk was cracked now where the roots protruded. She remembered how they used to huddle under the umbrellalike branches where the sidewalk was perfectly flat.

Kate drove away and didn't look back.

For lunch she ordered a double cheeseburger and a large order of fries at a Burger King. She told herself she needed the fat to fortify herself for the trip to the cemetery.

Then she smoked two cigarettes, sipped a lukewarm cherry Coke, and tried not to think. It was a futile exercise. At last, tires squealing in the parking lot, she pulled out onto the road.

The cemetery was small, quiet, and peaceful. Meandering brick paths wound through the closely cropped grass. Kate knew where the Starr plot was because she'd come here with Patrick to visit his mother's grave when they were both teenagers. They'd sat together on the grass, and she'd held his hand while he cried. He missed her terribly, he'd said, and his father was too busy with his own grief to pay any attention to him. Patrick Starr, Sr., had not been a demonstrative parent in any way. He'd been a stern man, an unyielding man.

"God rest your soul, Mr. Starr," Kate said, laying the bouquet of pink-and-white Shasta daisies near the headstone. Halfway down the brick path she turned and went back. She bent down and undid the wire holding the flowers together at the stem. She picked out seven of the prettiest flowers and laid them beneath the stone that read CHARLOTTE STARR. WIFE. MOTHER. Suddenly she noticed the extra plot. She'd never seen it before, or had never paid attention to it. Why had the Starrs bought it? she wondered. Did some families always have an extra? Whom were they planning to . . . She stiffened. *Maybe Patrick is supposed to be buried here. Oh, God!*

Kate struggled to her feet, stepping on her shoelace. She ran then, the lace slapping at the brick path.

She crawled into the car, her breathing ragged. A fly buzzed past her nose, exiting the window on the passenger side. With trembling hands she lit a cigarette, choking and sputtering on the smoke when she inhaled. She was shaking. Sweat beaded up on her forehead and rolled down into her eyes. Did she have the guts, the strength, to have Patrick's belongings dug up and brought here? Did it matter? She tossed the half-smoked cigarette out the window and fired up a second one.

Nervously she leaned out the car window and looked upward, certain Patrick's parents were there watching her, waiting for her decision. They belonged together, they were family. How many plots had she bought when she'd decided to bury Patrick's things? One? Two? She couldn't remember. If she'd just bought one, then there wasn't room for her when she . . . when she . . . If she moved her husband's things, who would lie next to her when her time came? *Some damn stranger, that's who. Oh, God, oh God.*

She tossed out the second cigarette. The fly was back, buzzing around her head. She swatted at it, missed. "Shit!"

She stuck her head back out the window and yelled, "Okay, okay, I'll give him back . . . *his things*. Maybe I'll have the two boxes the government sent on dug up and shipped back here for . . . for you. I'll keep the trunk I had buried left there so Ellie and I can . . . have a place to visit. That's fair. Yes, that's fair." A cloud rolled by and then another, until there was nothing to see but the summer-blue sky, as blue as Gus Stewart's eyes.

Kate arrived back at the house a little before four o'clock. She turned on the radio, the television, the stove, the oven, and the toaster oven. A minute later she turned them all off. It was something to do. If there had been anything to eat in the house besides puffed rice, she would have eaten it. She always ate when she was under stress. She made a pot of coffee, and while it perked, she called Ellie at her office.

"Honey, listen to me and don't say anything until I'm finished, okay?"

"Sure, Mom," Ellie agreed in her sweet voice.

Kate explained about her day, ending with, "I don't know if it's the right thing to do, so I'm going with my instincts and doing it. Will you make the calls for me, arrange to ship the trunks so they're here by Monday? I'll see if I can find someone on this end to pick them up. Maybe Gus will do it for me."

"Gus who?" Ellie asked instantly.

Kate explained again, saying, "He's coming down tomorrow. He likes the Jersey shore."

Ellie laughed. "What's that I hear in your voice, Mom?"

"Nervousness. Look, don't be getting ideas, Ellie. How is Donald?"

"The same. Della is so worried. He's not eating. I spent an hour last night coaxing him just to eat a little soup. He hates being fed, Mom. He told me he feels like he's losing his dignity, and he absolutely hates that . . . that *thing* Della put on him. Don't worry, though, we're taking real good care of him."

"I know, I know, I hate being such a worrier, but that's the way I am."

"If you want to worry, then worry about what you're going to wear tomorrow for your date. And it is a date, Mom, no matter what you say."

"Ellie, it's not a date. It's a . . . what it is is . . . it is not a date," Kate said, flustered by her daughter's laughter. "For heaven's sake, Ellie, he's only thirty or so! I'm a forty-four-year-old woman."

"Uh-huh," Ellie drawled. "So what are you going to wear?"

"The same thing I'm wearing right now, jeans and a shirt. It's not a date. I don't want you telling Della and Donald, either," Kate said sourly. "I'll never hear the end of it."

"A chance meeting in an airport. I bet they made a movie like that with Ingrid Bergman or somebody," Ellie said dramatically. " 'Bye, Mom, I'll call you when it's all wrapped up on this end."

"Thanks, honey, I'll talk to you later."

"Mom, remember that movie *From Here to Eternity* with Frank Sinatra? You know, where that couple, I can't remember their names, made love on the beach. Well, don't do that, you know how you hate getting sand in your bathing suit."

"Ellie!" Kate sputtered, her cheeks flaming. "I didn't even bring a bathing suit. . . ." But she was talking to a pinging receiver.

Now, why in the world had she ever mentioned Gus Stewart? *Because,* a niggling voice drawled, *you wanted to* . . . What?

"This is stupid," she muttered. Damn stupid. It's not a date. I don't date. Furthermore, I would never date a man that much younger than I am. Good God, do you think I want people to call me a cradle snatcher? "It's not a date!" she wailed.

CHAPTER 12

Kate was sitting on the front stoop waiting for Gus, coffee cup in hand. Dark glasses shaded her eyes from the sun as she watched couples stroll by in sneakers and pedal pushers, their arms linked either in cozy companionship or to hold one another upright. Kate smiled. The retirement park was a busy one, she reflected as an oldster wearing green-and-white-plaid pants and a nifty white blazer pedaled by on a three-wheel trike, his golf clubs in a wire grocery basket hooked onto the back of his wheels. She couldn't help but wonder if Patrick's dour father had participated in the activities provided for the retirement village. She doubted it.

Kate heard people exiting the house next door and glanced in that direction. Her view was obscured at first by an overlarge azalea bush. Then her hands flew to her mouth when she saw her neighbors, three couples, hit the sidewalk dressed in western garb. There was a hoedown at the community center, and obviously they were on their way to participate. How wonderful that these retirees were so active, she mused, thinking about Donald and Della and how they'd devoted their lives to her and her family. How much they missed out on by not joining in things designed for their retirement years. "It's by our choice, Kate," Donald always said. "You go to *those places* when your family doesn't want to be bothered with you. We *have* a family, and we take care of them, and we don't have time for such things."

Family was what made the world go 'round.

The street was suddenly quiet again. Kate wished she knew how her father-in-law had passed his time. The last time she'd been here, she'd checked out the community center and had been amazed at the activities. Every hour of the day could be filled if one was so inclined. It bothered her to think that Patrick's father might have spent all his time indoors with the television set. She had to wonder why he'd never invited her or the girls to visit. She gave up further thought when a dark blue Ford Escort wheeled into her driveway. Her guest had arrived.

Kate's breath exploded in a loud *swoosh* sound when Gus climbed from the car. He wore tattered denim shorts and deck shoes. Hairy legs, just like Patrick's. As muscular, too. His oversize T-shirt, stretched out at the neck and hanging crookedly at the hem, announced HARD ROCK CAFE, the burgundy lettering faded to a dull rust color. On his head he wore a Mets baseball cap, and the zippered bag he slung over his shoulders read NIKE in bold white letters. "You are a regular walking advertisement," she said.

"All true," Gus replied, sweeping off his cap and bowing low. "I like being down-and-out comfortable. You make me feel that way, Kate Starr."

Her cheekbones felt warm, and she laughed self-consciously. "Would you like a cup of coffee?"

"Love it. Or would you like to go out to breakfast? Brunch?"

Kate thought about it, then shook her head, remembering her midnight trip to the Shop Rite. She had eggs, Canadian bacon, raisin English muffins, freshly squeezed orange juice, frozen home fries, just-right cantaloupes, and plum jam. "I'll make breakfast," she said.

"Good." Gus smacked his hands together and followed her into the house. "There's something about a kitchen that appeals to the kid in me. My apartment has this counter that's supposed to be my kitchen. I eat standing up, no room for chairs."

Kid. He was hardly more than a kid now. "That sounds terrible," Kate said. "We have a marvelous kitchen back home. Every appliance known to man. A center island, pretty tile, cedar beams, and lots and lots of green plants. It's the nicest room in the house. Our table is long and sort of low with benches we can move so Donald can sit at the table with us. At least he used to. Now Della feeds him separately and he has to wear a bib and —" Kate began to choke up.

Gus's hands shot into the air. "None of that now. Today is my day, yours too. We are going to have fun, lady, just as soon as you feed me. Then," he said, grinning wickedly, "we are going to scoot out and leave the dishes in the sink. What'ya think of that?" He leered at her.

Kate's tongue felt thick. She slapped the succulent Canadian bacon into the frying pan. What . . . what are we — are you planning?"

"I thought we'd drive to Point Pleasant, hit the beach for an hour or so, and then take in the boardwalk. I'm game for some rides, but none of those spinning things. I get dizzy. We can gorge on greasy killer food that always smells so good, play a little bingo, I'll win you some stuffed animals . . . you know, all that great kid stuff."

Kid stuff. She'd never really done any of those things growing up. She and Patrick. "It does sound like fun."

"Sounds like? Trust me, you'll have the time of your life. I am the oldest kid I know," he said proudly. "It's that very quality that endears me to the opposite sex. Women can't wait to get their hands on me. They want to coddle me and cuddle me."

Kate laughed in spite of herself. "I'll keep it in mind."

"I wish you would."

Kate whirled at the tone of his voice. He wasn't bantering now. Confused, she turned back to the eggs she was whipping to a golden froth. "Do me a favor, Gus, in the garage there's a shelf with paper goods on it. Will you get it for me so I can drain this bacon?"

"Sure."

He was gone so long, Kate walked into the garage to see what he was doing. When she spotted him, her breathing seemed to stop. "No!" she shouted. "No, don't touch *that!*"

Gus recoiled as if bitten by a cobra, his arm stretched out in front of him.

"That's — that's —"

"Patrick's bike," Gus said softly. "His father brought it with him when he moved here, eh?"

"Yes . . . I saw it the first time I came here. I couldn't . . . I wanted to touch it. . . . He rode me on the handlebars. . . . The tires are flat."

"I can fix them, Kate, if you want me to," Gus said. "I can get a patch kit and pump them full of air. Hell, I can sand off the rust, too."

"Patrick loved that bike. He delivered papers on it, rode it all over the place, and later, when he got older, he hooked a basket on the back and delivered groceries. He rode it in every parade the town had. He painted it every year. Every year he changed the color. One year he painted it yellow with black stripes. I told him it looked like a long bumble bee. You should have heard him laugh. He called the bike 'B.B.' after that." She started to cry but waved Gus away when he offered her a strip of the paper towel he was holding in his hand.

"Let's go inside, Gus."

"So," Gus said lightly, when they were back in the kitchen, "what did you do yesterday amid the seniors?"

"This place hops, I can tell you that, but I didn't have time to hop, so I went up to

Westfield." She told him about her trip and the decision she'd made. She was okay, Gus was making things feel better.

"Jeez. That must have been tough on you."

Kate nodded. "The trunks arrive tomorrow at four o'clock. We're going to have a twilight service. The caretaker of the cemetery is doing it all. I found a minister the caretaker recommended who agreed to say a few words. I'm leaving Monday morning."

"So soon? I thought you were going to stay the week. You said you were staying a week."

It sounds like he's accusing me of something, Kate thought. "Donald isn't doing well. He doesn't want to eat anymore. Ellie said Della thinks he may have had a small stroke. He's being checked over now. I have to get home."

"Kate, I'm really sorry. My being so flip, that doesn't mean anything. I get like that when I'm around a woman I like. Right away I start to think I have to be witty and charming and . . . and all that stuff so she'll like me. I don't handle women well, or they don't handle me well. Christ, how I hate that bar scene and what you have to do to get out socially. I was probably meant to be a hermit living off the land or some damn thing."

Kate slid the eggs onto the plate, placed the perfectly browned toast alongside the bacon. She set the plate in front of Gus, and one for herself across the table, and sat down. She was stunned when he said grace. Later she would think about what he'd just said.

"You are a good cook," Gus remarked, wolfing down his food, as Kate began to eat. "I always eat fast," he added apologetically. "I come from a family of eleven kids, and you needed a long arm or you went hungry. I was the youngest. God, I wish my mother could live in a place like this. She has this apartment in Brooklyn that's not too swift. She won't come to live with any of us. We grew up on welfare, and my mother did housework on the side. My old man took off after I was born. You'd like my mother, she's like your Della."

Don't do it, Kate. Don't get involved. Absolutely not. "I'm looking for a tenant for this house," she said, looking up. "It's mine, but it isn't mine. I can't sell it. If your mother is interested and can pay the yearly taxes and utilities, she can live here. As you can see, the furniture isn't much, but neither are the taxes, just a few hundred a year. There seems to be a lot to do here for retirees. Do you think she'd be interested? I'd feel a lot better if I knew someone were living here and taking care of the place."

Gus stopped eating to stare at her. "Are

you kidding me, Kate Starr? What I mean is, is that a firm offer or something you just threw out?"

"I'm serious, if that's what you mean. Why is it when you try to do something nice, it immediately becomes suspect?" she said defensively.

"I'm a New Yorker," Gus said by way of explanation. "If you fall down on the street, they walk over you or around you. No one wants to get involved. I wouldn't do that, but I've seen it happen. I didn't mean to offend you."

"I guess I'm touchy these days. I don't know what would have happened to me and the girls without Della and Donald. I do try to give back when I can."

"Want to hear something sad, Kate?" At her nod, he said, "I never lived in a house. We always lived in an apartment in triple-decker bunk beds, six of us to a room. The girls' room had five, but you know what I mean. If you really mean it, I'd like to use your phone to call my mother."

"Go ahead." God, what was she doing? Something good for someone. Her family would approve. A smile built on her face as she listened to Gus's end of the conversation.

"Ma, you there?" he bellowed. "Ma, listen,

have I got a surprise for you. I found a house for you in Toms River. . . . No, no, Ma, it's in New Jersey, down at the shore. It has . . ." Kate held up four fingers. "Four rooms, a front stoop, and a back one. You can put your rocker on the back porch. Grass, Ma, real honest-to-God grass and flowers that grow in the ground, not in pots."

"Bingo and activities," Kate whispered.

"Bingo, Ma. Probably every day. All kinds of things to do. I can come down for the weekend and mow the grass and rake the leaves. There's two trees, big ones, shaped like umbrellas. . . . I don't know what kind, Ma, green, and they have brown trunks. You interested? You can move in next weekend. . . . You can afford the rent, Ma, it's free." Gus's voice changed, softened. "Sometimes, Ma, people, nice people, really do things for other people. It belongs to a friend of mine, a very good friend of mine. All you have to do is pay the light bill. . . . Ma, I said the *place* was free, I didn't say the light bill was free." To Kate he whispered, "I'll pay the taxes and heating bill." Listening, he smiled into the phone. "Yes, you can bring your own pillows and blankets and the Depression glass and your Coney Island lamp. The pictures, too. You can bring whatever you want. There's room for your sewing machine." He looked at Kate, who nodded. "Okay, Ma, you call everyone and start packing."

Kate smiled. It felt good, right.

"It was the bingo that did it," Gus said happily as he hung up. "How do I say thanks?"

"You just did. I don't think my father-in-law was happy here. He was such a private person, and so lonely. I don't think he knew how to get involved, or else he didn't want to make the effort. It's so easy to sit in front of the television set."

"He must have loved his son very much, his pictures are everywhere."

"If he did, he never showed it, never said the words to Patrick."

"I think this might be a good time for us to dump these dishes and get moving," Gus said lightly.

"I think you're right," Kate said. "Listen, why do we have to put the dishes in the sink? Why don't we just . . . leave them?"

"That's a hell of a good idea. After you, madame," he said, bowing low.

They laughed and giggled, kibbitzed and joked, all the way to the beach. God, he was so nice, so comfortable to be with.

"I have never seen so much . . . *skin* in one place in my life. I think half the suits on this beach should be outlawed. I don't care if that makes me sound like a prude or not," Kate said when a young girl of seventeen or so strolled by in two pieces of string and little else.

"This might surprise you, Kate, but I agree. Personally speaking, I like a full suit. To me, it's sexier."

"Hmmmm," was all Kate said.

A bronze Adonis strolled by in a stop-sign-colored Speedo suit. "Nice buns," Kate said, and giggled. The look on Gus's face chased the giggle back down her throat. "They should be outlawed, too," she said virtuously.

"The guy probably takes steroids and never worked a day in his life. I have pretty nice buns myself."

"Oh, yeah," was all Kate could think of to say.

"I'm in my prime, you know."

Kate said "Oh, yeah" again. "Exactly how old are you?" she asked cautiously.

"How old do you think I am?" Gus asked carefully.

Kate hedged. "If I knew, I wouldn't have asked. At a guess, twenty-nine, maybe thirty." God, he was so young.

"Thirty-one on my last birthday."

"And when was that?"

"Two weeks ago," Gus said sheepishly.

Here it comes, he's going to ask how old I am. She waited. When he didn't ask, she blurted, "I'm forty-four. I'll be forty-five next month."

"Oh, yeah," Gus said. "Well, guess what? I already knew that. You told me your age when I wrote that article that never got published. Does that bother you?" he asked curiously.

Kate avoided his gaze. "Sometimes. Forty-five is just five years from fifty. That's the halfway mark. There are times when I feel like I haven't really lived, just existed. I missed a lot. One of these days Ellie or Betsy is going to make me a grandmother. I don't know how I'll handle that. By the same token, I have experienced things other people only read about. I guess it evens out in the end."

"I can't wait to reach forty," Gus said. "I expect this instant wisdom, instant fame, instant riches, instant everything. My Pulitzer. Hey, do you like horror flicks?"

Kate blinked. "I love them."

"Good, let's rent my favorite, *Invasion of the Body Snatchers*."

"I like that one, too. Della chews her fingernails when we watch it. There's no VCR at the house."

"We can rent one."

"Are you going to get married when you reach forty?"

"If I meet her on my fortieth birthday, I might. Being a bachelor has its good points. According to *Cosmopolitan*, I'm in demand. Still, I'm pretty careful. And I'm all for safe sex. What's your feeling? This AIDS thing is scary. It's enough to make a person want to go for monkhood. I know a girl at the paper who went to a nunnery — you know, one of those places where you give up all your rights, and wear black, and don't even think about sex."

"Oh, yeah," Kate said. "Listen, I think we should talk about something else."

"Why? What'd I say? Oh, you mean because I asked you your opinion. It goes with being a reporter. All I do all day long is ask questions. I guess that means you don't get out and about much."

"Is it important for you to know that?"

"Well, hell yes, it is. I like you, Kate Starr. When you like someone, you want to know everything about them. I've made you uncomfortable again. I'm sorry. Come on, let's pick up and head back. We'll pick up a couple of videos, a VCR, some popcorn, and while you're cooking dinner I'll hook it all up."

Relieved that the conversation was taking a new turn, Kate smiled agreement. "It was a wonderful day, Gus, I'm glad you came to visit."

On the boardwalk, while Kate was tying her sneakers, Gus said, "You're a very pretty woman, Kate. You got just the right amount of sun today. The color becomes you. I'm not being fresh, and this is not a come-on of any kind. This is just a guess on my part, but I don't think you've gotten your share of compliments over the years. Was your husband complimentary?"

"Not really. He criticized real good, though," Kate said briskly.

Gus slipped his feet into his Dock-siders, and they made a last run down the boardwalk to pick up the tacky prizes they'd won earlier.

He was nice, Kate thought. Very nice. Real. A "what you see is what you get" kind of person. She liked that. *But he was only thirty-one.*

She had no idea what time it was when the last horror video ended. Earlier she'd taken off her watch to do the dishes, and there was no clock in the living room. Gus, she noticed, wasn't wearing a watch. She wondered why and was about to ask when he said, "According to the clock on the VCR it's one-thirty. Good thing we don't have to get up with the chickens. Hey, let's go for a walk in our bare feet."

That had to be the silliest thing she'd ever heard of. *Absolutely not.* "Okay," she said airily.

"Atta girl. I knew you were my kind of woman," Gus said, reaching down to pull her to her feet.

His kind of woman. What did that mean, exactly? She wanted to ask. The word *foreplay* rushed to mind, and she cringed. The word *seduction* ripped through her when Gus took her hand in his. She tripped, stubbing her big toe. She bore the pain in silence and hobbled along.

The night was warm, soothingly soft, with only the star-spangled sky for light. The sodium vapor lamp at the end of the street wasn't working. She should tell someone. The seniors needed light; they paid for it.

"This is the kind of night poets write about," Gus said lazily. "Look at that moon. It's a perfect crescent. I like moonlight. You?"

"Oh, yes. Moonlight is so romantic." The moment the words were out of her mouth she winced. Her toe throbbed. Her stomach started to churn, and she wasn't sure why. "Are you paying attention to the way we're walking? We could get lost." What an incredibly stupid thing to say.

"Hardly. I used to be a Boy Scout. All

you have to do is look for the North Star, and wallah —"

"Really."

"No. I was teasing. I've been looking at the signposts, and we only turned one corner. Trust me, I'll get you back safe and sound."

Kate wondered if he realized her hand was clammy. "Do you ever wish on a star?" she asked wistfully.

"Every chance I get. In New York we have so much pollution, we don't see too many stars. How about you?"

"When Patrick was shot down I did. I wigged out there for a while. I started reading astrology books, wishing on stars. You name it, I did it. I probably should have prayed, but I thought God was punishing me for something. It was a very bad time for me. I wasn't strong enough. There was no one to guide me, to help me mentally. Donald and Della did what they could, but I was stubborn as a mule. Thank God I got myself together."

"And now?" Gus said quietly.

"Emotionally I'm in a good place. Legally I'm in a terrible place. Nick Mancuso, my lawyer, told me I could divorce Patrick, but I could never bring myself to do that. Holding that . . . funeral service wasn't legal. I did it for me. I need to lay Patrick to rest in my mind. I know he's never coming back. There was no one in my life that . . . What I mean is, a divorce wasn't something I gave any serious thought to."

"Don't you want to remarry, to have a life outside your work?" Gus asked quietly.

"Maybe someday."

"Your girls are grown, it seems such a shame for you to be alone at this point in time. You lost the best years of your life, Kate. I don't mean that literally. But think about it. You could have had a second family . . . ah, you know what I'm trying to say."

"But I do have a family, I have Della and Donald. Ellie is in my life every day. Besides, I have this terrible guilt where Patrick is concerned. I also have this vision of God striking me dead if I do something like getting divorced. I really expected to feel His wrath when I buried Patrick's things. I got a little brave when nothing happened." She paused. "Why are we talking about this?"

"I guess I want to know what kind of guy Captain Starr was."

"I never talk about Patrick," Kate mumbled.

"Why is that?"

"Because when I talk about him, I feel guilty that I'm alive and he isn't. He was the vital one, the intelligent one. He was so smart, Gus. I always felt so inferior. He contributed. I existed."

"What kind of thinking is that?" Gus demanded, coming to a standstill.

"Patrick said it often enough, so I believed it. Patrick was selfish. There are givers and takers. I was the giver and Patrick was the taker. I had this narrow little existence. Patrick insulated me, or I insulated myself. I think the proudest moment in my life was when I got my degree. Do you want to hear a secret?"

"Hell yes," Gus said, his eyes round with interest.

"The day I graduated, I kept my cap and gown an extra day. That night, around four in the morning — actually, it was morning — I drove back to the college and out to the commencement field and . . . and I put on the cap and gown and walked the whole length of the field. Then I sat in the chair I sat in during the exercise and . . . went through the business of accepting my diploma all over again, walked back to my chair, sat down, and when it was over in my mind, I threw up my hat and screamed at the top of my lungs, 'Now, Patrick, who's the dumb bunny?' Then I wailed like a banshee. I guess it was a stupid thing to do. God, why did I tell you that?"

"Because you needed to say it aloud. You trust me and feel comfortable with me. We're friends. If you're starting to regret telling me, how about I tell you one of my innermost secrets so we'll be even. Let's sit here on the curb. Want a cigarette?"

Kate was certain she was going to hear something startling, something revealing, something that would endear her even more to this strange young man. She hugged her knees and waited.

Gus blew a perfect smoke ring. "Remember I told you my old man skipped out on us? Well, I'd been working at the paper for about a year when I decided I was going to find the bastard. My mother never once said a bad word about him. Each of us kids had our own secret story about him, but the bottom line was he walked out on us. With the help of a friend, I used the *Times* resources to track him down. It took two years, but I found the son of a bitch. He changed his name, has a new family. He lives in . . . on an estate. You should see the house. It must have forty rooms. He's got a butler, maids, governesses for the kids. A pool in the back, tennis courts, belongs to the country club. The bastard has it all. His wife is half his age, wears diamonds to play tennis, rubs Evian water on her body when she sits in the sun. He's got a six-car garage and it isn't empty. Two Rollses, a Benz, a Jag, a Porsche, and a Lamborghini. He's got a yacht he keeps down here at the shore. Do you want to know the name of it? Well, the goddamn name of it is the *Matilda.* Matilda is my mother's name. He's a building contractor with underworld ties. It's all in the investigator's report."

Kate squeezed his hand and inched closer to him. He was staring across the dark street, barely aware of her. "How awful," she whispered.

"Thousands of dollars were billed to the paper. I felt really bad about that and was going to 'fess up and make arrangements to pay it back somehow. Instead I hit on a better idea. I drove up to Connecticut, to this palatial estate, one evening. The investigative report said Mr. Ronald Wedster — that's his new name — always spent Thursday evenings at home. It took a couple of months to screw up my courage to go there, but I did it. Bold as you please, I walked up to the front door and rang the bell. I wore a suit and a tie. Do you believe that? Anyway, I handed my business card to his snooty butler and was told to sit on this little spindly bench and wait. I waited for thirty goddamn minutes. It took him that long to get over the shock that I was there. When he finally came out to see me, I wanted to kill him. He had the coldest damn eyes I'd ever seen. The funny thing was, he was dressed in a suit and tie, too. I never figured that out. He said, 'What do you want?' "

"Oh, God, Gus, what did you say?" Kate whispered.

"I said," Gus said, clearing his throat, " 'I want what you have.' I didn't mean to say that. I wanted to say something about Mom and my brothers and sisters, but I didn't. I knew in that one split second that he'd used those thirty minutes to make a few calls, check me out. No one fucks with the *New York Times.* I found him, you see, so he had to pay attention. If I found him, other people could find him."

"Then what?"

"Then the son of a bitch said, 'How much?' "

"Oh, my God," Kate said.

"I said, 'Fifty thousand a month. Deposit it on the first day of every month at Chase Manhattan. The up-front payment is five hundred thousand, payable *now.*' He wrote the check on the spot. He did ask a question, though."

"What?" Kate squeezed his hand.

"He said, 'What does this buy me?' "

"And you said . . ."

"I said," Gus said hoarsely, " 'It doesn't buy you a goddamn fucking thing,' and he said, 'That's what I thought, you are your mother's son,' at which point I decked him. What do you think about *that* secret?"

"My goodness," was all Kate could think of to say.

"I never told my brothers or sisters or my mother. I never spent any of the money. It's sitting in the bank. The deposits are made once a month, right on the first day of the month. I did take out enough to pay back the *Times*, but that was it. It's all invested. There's a lot of money in the bank. Close to four million dollars. I don't know what to do with it. This last year I've been dicking around with the idea of parceling it out to the others, but I can't come up with a story about where it came from. I don't want any of them, especially my mother, to know about him. It would kill her. Guess you think I'm not a very nice person, huh?"

"On the contrary. I think you are a very nice person. You did what you had to do. Why don't you look at it as child support, college expenses, birthday, Christmas, and graduation gifts? That would certainly eat a lot of it."

"I've taken money for my silence. What

does that make me?"

"The question should be, what does that make your father?"

"I knew I liked you for a reason. You always say the right thing. You're a hell of a lady, Kate Starr. Come on, I think we should be getting back. And I think that's a security car coming in our direction."

A second later Kate was on her feet. Once again her hand was in his. She wasn't sure who reached for whom. How strange that she was the one who felt comforted.

Back home, Kate locked the doors. "There's only one bathroom. You can have the room on the right. I made it up this morning. I'll clean up the kitchen while you use the bathroom."

"I'll help," Gus offered.

"I'm just going to soak the dishes."

"You're sure?"

Kate nodded.

"Kate, does my secret change your opinion of me?"

She smiled. "Not one little bit."

"It kind of makes us conspirators, doesn't it?"

"Yes. Your secret is safe with me."

"And yours with me."

Now what? Kate wondered, her heart fluttering wildly in her chest. Now what, indeed?

Later, in the dim hallway, Gus beckoned her with his index finger. “C’mere,” he said.

Trancelike, she moved toward him. When she was standing next to him, she realized how tall he was, towering over her so he had to tilt her chin with the tips of his fingers so he could look into her eyes. He was going to kiss her, and she didn’t want to stop him. Her eyes closed of their own accord as she waited. His lips, when they touched hers, were soft, giving as well as taking, persuading her gently to respond. She could feel his arms cradle her against him. He felt strong, and she felt safe and natural in his embrace. His fingers touching her face were tender, trailing whispery shadows over her cheekbones. Having him kiss her felt like the most natural thing in the world. It was a kiss. A tender gesture, tempting an answer but demanding none.

“Good night, Kate Starr. Sleep well,” he whispered against her hair. And then he was gone, a door separating them. For one incredible second she wanted to turn the knob on the door, but she didn’t.

On the other side of the door Gus waited, sensing her indecision. He felt like applauding her when he heard the door to her room open and then close. Instead he groaned.

How good Kate felt in his arms. The kiss

had been just what he'd expected, too. But it wasn't time for anything else. She was still too vulnerable, yet strong in so many ways. He liked it that she had confided in him. They were friends now, open and up front with one another. One step at a time, Stewart, he admonished himself. No game playing here. Games were for children, and more often than not they hurt rather than gave pleasure. Slow and easy, he cautioned himself. You like Kate Starr too much to ever step over the line she's drawn. When and if the time was right, Kate will have to be the one to cross it, because she wanted to.

It was a spartan room, Gus thought as he shed his clothes. Was this considered the spare room, a room for Patrick Starr to sleep in if he ever came to visit? There was just the single bed with a navy-blue spread. Where would Kate and the girls have slept? Out of curiosity he lifted the sheets to check the mattress. It looked new to him, the covering shiny, the threads of the quilting intact. Was Patrick Starr as strange as his father? Kate said he didn't compliment, preferring to criticize. He wished he'd known Kate Starr when she was young, and then he wished he was her age. When he laid his head on the firm pillow, he muttered, "I think I'm falling in love with you, Kate. I really think I am."

* * *

Kate was frying bacon and talking on the phone when Gus walked into the kitchen next morning, fresh from the shower. She pointed to the coffeepot and the glass of orange juice she'd poured for him. He listened to her conversation because he had no other choice.

"I'll be leaving at noon tomorrow. Don't worry if you can't pick me up at the airport, I can catch a cab. You're sure now that there's no change in Donald. . . . Ellie, I hate to say this, but doctors don't know everything. What does Della say? Della is with him twenty-four hours a day." She listened carefully as her daughter spoke. "I agree with Della, Donald has had enough poking and prodding. Give him a hug and kiss for me. Gus and I are going to Atlantic City for the afternoon. It's only an hour and twenty minutes from here. . . . Yes, Ellie, I will play one slot for each of you and bring home your winnings in silver dollars. . . . Ellie, they didn't . . . there wasn't anything in the paper today about, you know, digging up the trunk, was there . . . ? That's right, I forgot about the time difference. Well, if there is, there's nothing we can do about it anyway. I'd just prefer . . . God, when is this going to be over?"

"Tomorrow morning," Gus said, mouthing

the words silently. Kate favored him with a dazzling smile. He felt light-headed when he sat down at the table. He wanted to kiss her again. He mouthed the words and grinned when her eyebrows shot upward. He almost laughed aloud when she dropped the spatula. Her face was pink when she bent down to pick it up. His own felt flushed.

" 'Bye, honey," Kate said, and hung up. She turned to him.

"So, how would you like your eggs — over easy, sunnyside up, or scrambled?" she asked briskly. No fooling around this morning, he thought. It must have something to do with talking to her daughter. He felt pleased with his observation.

"Over easy. I like to dunk."

"Me too," Kate said. "I like two cups of coffee when I have eggs. One for dunking the toast with the egg yolk, and a cup for drinking."

"Me too, but I wasn't going to say anything," Gus said happily. "My mother said only slobs eat like that." Kate laughed and poured out four cups of coffee.

They dunked and munched as they grinned at one another over their plates.

"Are we leaving the dishes today, too?" Kate giggled.

"Damn right. Let's get this show on the

road. Wait a minute," he said, fishing in his wallet for money. "I'm going to need enough for gas and tolls." He left a ten-dollar bill on the table. "I have forty dollars left. Kick me if I go past thirty-nine bucks."

"Okay," Kate said, and checked her own purse. "I need money for a taxi and buying some magazines, and I like to keep some change in my wallet. That gives me fifty-three dollars." She laid a twenty-dollar bill on the table next to Gus's ten. "Has it occurred to you," she said impishly, "that with all the money you have in that New York bank, and my healthy bank account, we could take A.C. by storm?"

"We are high rollers. Ninety-two bucks between us. Let's make a bet — are we going to be winners or losers today?"

"Winners!" Kate said enthusiastically.

"I agree. How big?"

Kate giggled. "I say we come home with double our money."

"I say we come home with three hundred twelve dollars, and I hope you're the big winner because you owe me dinner. Remember that promise you made, how long ago, seven years?"

"What I said was a hot dog and a soda pop. I didn't forget." God, was it a sin to be happy?

"You can take me to the Lobster Shanty if you win. Deal?"

"Deal." Kate smiled.

"I have to leave here by seven, Kate. There will be miles of traffic for me going home. You look sad," he said, pleased at the crestfallen look on her face.

"I guess I am. I'm missing you already. This has been such a nice weekend. I can't remember when I've enjoyed myself more."

"I can come to California to visit you. Not often, but if you invite me, I'll come."

"I'd like that, Gus, I really would." The smile was back on her face and in her eyes. "Consider yourself invited. You have an open invitation." She reached for his arm, and together they left the house, each wearing a wide smile that rivaled the sun.

CHAPTER 13

The stream of postcards, letters, and Hallmark greeting cards during the following months was constant. Kate's voice sizzled over the long-distance wire to the tune of three to four hundred dollars a month. She and Gus were friends, staying in touch on a daily, sometimes twice-daily, basis. There simply weren't enough hours in the day for either of them to make the three-thousand-mile trip to visit. On recommendations from previous customers, Kate found herself traveling to San Francisco, Sacramento, Los Angeles, and Nevada to quote prices and secure more work than she could handle. A second office in Los Angeles was being considered. On the East Coast, Gus Stewart was up to his hips in a crime investigation that threatened, according to the FBI, to go on forever.

"This friendship is costing me a great deal of money," Kate muttered as she scanned her latest phone bill. "Good Lord, I couldn't possibly have talked $533.12 worth in one month!" She looked around uneasily, to see if anyone had heard her comment. Della was busy folding laundry and Ellie was swimming her daily laps. Donald was propped up in the hospital bed in the family room so he could see out into the garden.

In the four months since her visit to New Jersey, Donald's health had deteriorated alarmingly. Della steadfastly refused to sign him into a nursing home and insisted on taking care of him herself. At Kate's insistence he had been moved to her house so she and Ellie could spell Della. A home health aide came in at nine in the evening and sat with Donald through the long night.

Della looked up from the pile of sheets she'd just folded. "He knew me for a little while today, Kate. He looked right at me and said, 'You're getting skinny, old girl.' "

"He's right," Kate said worriedly. "We need more help. We're both so tired we can hardly stand up. I know you want to be the one to do for him, I do too, but we have to be realistic. If we wear ourselves down, we won't be any good to Donald. I'm as worried about you as I am about him. None of us has the energy to eat anymore. Look at us! We're skin and bones. I haven't been to the office in three weeks. I'd breathe my own life into Donald if I could, you know that, Della. If it came right down to it, I think I'd give my life for that man. But he wouldn't want this, and we both know it. Decisions are called for here, and you and I have to make them."

"But, Kate, he knew me today," Della said, her dark eyes filling with tears.

"And he knew me two days ago," Kate said quietly. "Look at him, Della, at all those tubes and machines. If he were able to, he would rip them all out. Donald had such dignity. I think we should let him go. We're being selfish. We have to think about Donald, not ourselves," Kate said, wiping her eyes.

"Kate, I wouldn't know what to do without him. How will I get through the days? You and Ellie don't need me, but he does." Della sobbed into a tissue.

"If I ever, ever, hear you say a thing like that again, I'll — I'll smack you. Do you hear me?" Kate shrilled. "I'm going to forget you said that. Now you . . . go wash your face and make some coffee. We're going to talk when Ellie comes in. We're going to — to do what's best for Donald. Go on, Della."

Tears dripped down Kate's cheeks when

she walked over to Donald's bed. Her dearest friend in the whole world couldn't breathe without his oxygen mask, couldn't pee without the catheter, and because he couldn't eat, was receiving glucose and other nutrients through his veins. His hands and feet were so crippled, his fingers and toes were curled backward. When they washed him, they dribbled warm water over his hands and feet. Just yesterday she'd seen Della blow-drying his feet, which were blue with cold. Her eyes fell on the neatly stacked pile of diapers with their sticky tabs.

She reached for Donald's crippled hand, careful not to put any undue pressure on it. "The first time I saw you, Donald, I thought you were a derelict. I'm sorry for that awful thought. I've never known a kinder, more gentle, generous man in my life. For years I've wanted to do something for you, something that would bring a smile to your face, something to make you happy. I wish your son and daughter were here. I know God put you on this earth to take care of us. I believe that with all my heart. So, Donald dear, I think I finally figured out what it is I can do for you. Della won't be able to do it, but I think I can. I'm going to send you to that . . . that place where your son and daughter are waiting for you. I bet your son will be wearing his army uniform, and I bet when he sees you, he's going to snap off a salute that will create a breeze."

"Coffee's ready, Kate," Della said quietly as she entered. "Black and strong, just the way you like it." She fussed with the sheet blanket, brushed at Donald's sparse hair, tweaking a stray away from his ear. She continued to smooth the wrinkles on the blanket until Kate led her into the kitchen.

"Who's watching Donald?" Ellie asked anxiously from the deck.

"He's sleeping," Della said.

"He's comatose, Della."

"I'll sit with him," Ellie said, reaching for a cup. "I'll tell him a story the way he used to tell them to us. Sometimes he smiles. I know — like babies, it's gas. But I don't understand how it can be gas when he doesn't eat. I prefer to think I'm amusing him. I don't care how it sounds."

Della sobbed quietly into the dish towel. Kate blew her nose.

"Della, this is what I think. . . ."

A long time later Della nodded. "You need to get back to the office. Ellie has to get on with her life."

"Della, I don't give a hoot about the office. I can close up shop right now and not look back. Ellie feels the same way. Donald is what's important. You're important. If we lose it all, so what? We were poor once before and we survived."

"Yes, but only because of Donald. Without him we couldn't have made it."

"That's debatable," Kate said briskly. "Now we're both going to think about what I just said, and tomorrow morning the three of us are going to make a decision, and then we are going to act on that decision. You know I'm right, Della. You sit with Donald and I'll make us something for dinner."

"Not tomato soup again," Della pleaded.

"No, hot dogs with lots of mustard and relish. I'll do them on the grill. And some of that macaroni and cheese that comes in a box." Della shuddered. Kate smiled wanly.

"You look like you could use a friend, Mom, or at the very least, a massage," Ellie said. "I'm going to clean the bathrooms. Why don't you call your friend Gus?"

"That sounds like a good idea. Are you sure you don't mind doing the bathrooms?"

"Mom, I live here. Della has her hands full. You're going to make dinner. Do you think I'm going to just watch both of you? Leave the salad for me. Everything's going to be okay."

"No, it isn't."

"I meant with us. Go on, call your friend.

Did anyone wash towels today?"

"Della has been doing Donald's laundry. I was going to do them after dinner," Kate said wearily.

"I'll do them. Want me to turn on the grill?"

Kate nodded. She reached for the phone to dial Gus's number. He sounded so pleased to hear from her that she felt better almost immediately. They talked for forty minutes, and twice Gus managed to make her laugh. "You're doing the right thing, Kate," he said before he said good-bye. "My turn next time."

"Why did I cook this if no one is going to eat?" Kate grumbled half an hour later as she pushed her plate to the center of the table. "None of us can afford to lose much more weight."

"Who's going to call Betsy?" Ellie asked.

"I will, in a little while. I tried calling her the past several days, but there's been no answer. I'll try again around nine. Now, let's get to it."

Della nodded miserably. Ellie said, "I feel it's the right thing to do. Did you call Donald's doctor? He knows about his living will, doesn't he?"

"Yes to both your questions," Kate said quietly.

"When?" was all Ellie said.

"Dawn. When the sun comes up. Donald always liked to see the sun come up. He said new days were meant for many things, journeys, loving, and just plain old living."

Ellie's eyes were wild. "Are we . . . are we going to . . . keep a vigil? We aren't going to go to bed, are we?"

Kate shook her head.

"I think he knows," Della said. "His breathing's changed. It's like he's fighting something, but he can't wake up fully. He knows. . . ."

At nine o'clock Kate walked into the kitchen to call her daughter. She let the phone ring twelve times before she hung up. She hated her daughter at that moment. She stomped her way back to the family room, her eyes murderous.

At midnight Donald opened his eyes, looked around, and said clearly and distinctly, "It's nasturtiums. That's why we couldn't make a rainbow of flowers. We forgot the nasturtiums." They crowded around the bed, happy smiles on their faces. "Where's my honey button?" he said, again so clearly that Kate blinked.

"I'm here, Donald," Della said. "Did you hear that, Kate? He called me his honey button. Oh, Donald," she said, smothering his face with kisses moist with her tears.

Kate clutched at her daughter, her eyes wild. "My God," she whispered, "we were going to . . . we almost —"

"Shhh, Mom, this isn't what you think. Donald is trying to make things right for us the way he always did, before . . . before he goes. Listen, his voice is weaker, less distinct."

Kate strained to hear what he was saying. "Take some of the money and do good . . . go back to Mexico and help your family. Promise me, Della."

Della threw herself across her husband's wasted body. "I'll do whatever you want, Donald. I promise." When there was no response, she started to shake her husband, but he was in another place, far from the cocoon of sleep he'd crawled from. Kate and Ellie led her over to the chair.

"Even now he thinks of us," Della wept, "never himself."

"That's why we have to do it, Della," Kate said. "Stay with her Ellie, I have to do something."

She was a madwoman when she entered the kitchen and punched out her daughter's telephone number. She didn't care what time of the night it was. Her eyes narrowed when she heard her daughter's sleep-filled voice.

"Turn on the light, Betsy, and wake up. Listen to me. Are you listening . . . ?" she asked coldly. "Good. Donald is dying. We plan to remove — Yes, we're going to do it at dawn. He's lapsed into a coma. I want you here. . . . What do you mean you can't make it? You *will* damn well make it! You are a miserable, ungrateful snot, and I'm ashamed to say you're my daughter. Get dressed, Betsy, and be here by morning. I don't care if you have to crawl. You be here! Without Donald you wouldn't be sleeping in that comfortable bed of yours. I will send the state police for you if you don't come under your own power. I mean it!" Kate slammed down the phone, her shoulders shaking.

"Whoah," Ellie said from the doorway. "I didn't think you had it in you, Mom."

"You'd be surprised at what I have in me," Kate said tightly. "I meant it, too. I'll send the state police to bring her here."

"Be real, Mom," Ellie said, not unkindly. "They can't *make* her come."

"She'll come, won't she, Ellie?"

"No, she won't."

"What happened to her? My God, is it my fault? I did my best."

"You know that, I know that, but Betsy . . . Betsy wanted the dream to go on.

She was Dad's favorite. Miss Princess Betsy. It was all make-believe. We had to do what we did, go through that fantasy period of believing Dad would come back, in order to go on with our lives. Betsy wanted to stay in that fantasy world. She wanted to keep on playing make-believe, but you wouldn't let her. She isn't a forgiving person. Personally, I think she's warped."

"I will never forgive her if she doesn't come," Kate said.

"Yes, you will. You're a mother. Mothers forgive all their children's sins. Mothers love unconditionally. It's supposed to be that way."

"Not this mother," Kate said grimly.

Ellie stared at her mother, knowing she meant exactly what she said. "On the other hand, there are some mothers who don't . . . who aren't like that."

"Number me among that group, Ellie. I cannot believe that girl is my child. I cannot believe she has 'something more important to do.' Where did she get the nerve, the goddamn *nerve,* to say that to me?"

"I'm going to make some coffee," Ellie said. "Remember how Donald used to say if you drank too much coffee you'd grow hair on your chest? I lived in fear of that. I used to check all the time to be sure. I knew he was making it up, but I checked anyway. I'm really going to miss him, Mom." Ellie threw herself into her mother's arms.

"Me too, honey."

"When the sun comes up and we . . . do it, how long will it be?" Ellie blubbered.

"Not long. Donald's ready to go. Whatever that was — his last words — I believe it was his way of telling us it's okay. I had this talk with him this afternoon. I think he wasn't certain . . . he's counting on us."

"I'll bring the coffee in when it's ready," Ellie said, blowing her nose.

Ellie measured out coffee, filled the pot, and plugged it in. Anger rushed through her, anger at her sister for the way she treated everyone. She tiptoed down the hall to her mother's office, closed the door, and called her sister. Her voice was a growling hiss when she heard Betsy's voice.

"I just wanted to go on record as saying I think you are a first-class bitch — the most selfish, self-centered person I have ever had the misfortune of knowing. All you do is take up air other people need to breathe, people like Donald. Mom's right, you are an ungrateful snot. There's not one good, nice, decent thing about you. As far as I'm concerned, I don't even have a sister. . . . Well, *say* something, you miserable bitch!"

"Good-bye."

Ellie's jaw dropped, and she raised her eyes. "I'm sorry, God, but it needed to be done. Can't you straighten her out? So, sometime in the future I'll write her a note and . . . No, I won't. I meant everything I said. Every word."

Betsy Starr stood in her pristine kitchen and looked around wildly. She clenched and unclenched her hands as she tried to fight the tears she knew were going to drown her if she ever *really* let go.

She started to make coffee, then gave up on the idea when she couldn't remember how much coffee the machine required. She reached for the jar holding the tea bags, dropped it, watched the glass scatter all over her white tile floor. In order to get to the refrigerator for a beer or soda pop, she'd have to walk over the glass slivers or clean them up. Too much effort.

She backed out of the kitchen, found herself in a corner, where she cowered, arms wrapped around her chest. She pressed into the corner, her heart pumping so loudly she could hear it between her sobbing breaths.

This wasn't supposed to happen. Never, ever. Donald was supposed to live forever.

No, no, that wasn't true. He'd said he would still be around until she got out of college. The problem was, she hadn't been around. Not because she didn't care, but because she did care. Too much. "That's my problem, I care too much, and I don't want anyone to know, and I don't know why that is!" she said, sobbing.

She thought about her mother's words, her sister's phone call. She sobbed harder. A picture of a shiny red wheelbarrow flashed in front of her eyes. "Oh, Donald, I'm so sorry. I know it wasn't *my* promise to you, but I promised you for my dad. I should have bought it for you. I meant to do that the first Christmas when I went away to college, but I had this opportunity to meet . . . I'm sorry Donald. I love you . . . still love you . . . will always love you. More than I could ever say, more than I could ever show you."

She blew her nose in the hem of her nightgown. She'd so wanted to ask her mother about Donald, but that was another one of her problems: when she needed to talk, to show how she felt, she couldn't. Family was supposed to understand that. Her father, according to her mother, was supposed to have had the same problem.

She wished she were more open, more outgoing, like Ellie. She'd tried when she was younger, but it was such an effort, and people looked at her strangely when she tried to copy her younger sister's ways. She was a serious, solemn, studious person. Just like her father.

What it all came down to was, she felt things too deeply. She loved too much. And she didn't know how to handle those feelings. Ellie was forever calling her an emotional cripple. "I am," she sobbed.

Her life flashed in front of her, all negative. She howled her misery as she stumbled her way back to her bedroom. She dropped to her knees and fumbled under the bed for her suitcase. She threw in clothes any old way, stepped into her slippers, searched for her raincoat, the long military-style one that would cover her nightgown. She found her purse, her car keys, and trudged out to the carport.

She turned on the windshield wipers before she realized her tears were the reason she couldn't see. She drove around for two hours, looking for a store that was open so she could buy a shiny red wheelbarrow. After the fact. *It's too late. It's always too late, Betsy Starr.*

She continued to drive until she found herself in front of St. Angela's Church. She ran up the steps and tried to open the door, but it wouldn't budge. Churches shouldn't be locked. People needed to pray. It shouldn't matter what time of the day or night it was. "I need to go in here!" she shouted, kicking at the door again and again. She shouted over and over, "I need to go in here, damn you! Can't you hear? I need to go inside."

She felt a hand on her shoulder and whirled around.

"What is it, child?"

"Oh, Father, I need . . . I tried to find this red . . . he promised me he'd live till I graduated. . . . I need to talk. My father is . . . I need help, Father. Please help me. . . ."

Kate was dozing on her chair at five o'clock when the front doorbell rang. No one moved. "It must be Betsy," Kate said coolly.

"Maybe the priest decided to come early," Della said.

"Or the doctor," Ellie said.

"I'll get it," Kate said. "There are a few things I want to say to my daughter in private."

She turned on the hall light before she opened the heavy oak door. She wanted to see her daughter's face clearly. She could feel her shoulders tighten with the tension she felt. She saw the whole of him at once, saw the concern, the anguish, in his eyes. She fell into his arms, glad it wasn't her daughter standing in the open door.

"I had to come," was all he said.

"I'm glad you did," she said.

"Are you all right?"

"I am now," she said. "What about your crime story?"

"Let them all kill themselves. The public doesn't need to read about more blood and gore. It wasn't important to me."

"Will they fire you?"

Gus laughed. "There was no contest. Besides, I know this guy in Los Angeles, and he said I could come to work for him anytime. You forget, I'm a rich man. I'll tell you about it later. What's important now is you."

"I'm glad you're here, Gus. You're my best friend. I don't know how that happened," Kate said, puzzled by her own statement.

"You took the time to get to know me. My sterling character started to shine through and you saw it. I knew you'd make a good friend the first moment I saw you. I'm just sorry it took us so long to meet again. Now, what can I do?" he said briskly.

Kate shrugged helplessly. "What color are nasturtiums?"

"Blue? Bluish purple?" He didn't think the question odd at all.

"I wonder if it's one of those flowers that

come in all colors? I rather think it does. You know, enough different colors so if planted right they'd look like a rainbow. We have to get some," Kate said simply.

Hell, yes, a whole truckload if she said so. He'd plant them, too. Whatever she wanted.

"It's getting light out," Ellie said, getting up from her chair.

"Ellie, this is Gus Stewart. Gus, this is Ellie, all grown up."

Ellie's hand shot out. They smiled at one another. "Ah," Ellie said, rubbing the back of her neck, "the reason for the high phone bills. They are not tax deductible, you know."

Gus smiled again. He likes her, Kate thought, but then he'd liked her seven years ago. He'd said she was open and a "what you see is what you get" kind of person.

"It's going to be full light in a few minutes," Ellie said.

"I know," Kate replied, moving toward Donald's hospital bed. Tears filled her eyes when she saw Della holding his crippled hand. She was weeping quietly.

"It was so hard for her. She told me once that Donald was the only man in the whole of her life who ever told her he loved her. She hasn't been able to let go. For weeks now Donald has been drifting in and out of consciousness. Yesterday he lapsed into . . .

She knows it's the end, and she's feeling so very guilty because she didn't do what he wanted. He left a living will. He didn't want any of this. His eyes . . . he used to plead with me with his eyes after his last stroke. I couldn't make Della . . . He was her husband. . . ."

Ellie said, "We didn't discuss who was going to —"

"I know," Kate said. "I . . . I'll do it. I should have insisted. I should have done something more. . . ."

"I'll do it," Gus said. Kate sagged against him with relief until she remembered her promise to Donald.

"No. I *have* to do it."

Kate moved then, with an efficiency born of desperation. Ellie and Gus watched her as she moved the oxygen mask, disconnected the catheter, set aside the heart monitor. It was hard, but she pried Della's hand loose. "You have to get his clothes, Della." To Ellie she said, "Get the basin and make sure the water is warm. Ivory soap, Ellie, and a soft towel." Her voice strengthened and grew strong.

All the while she worked, washing and drying Donald's wasted body, Kate talked. "I'm working as fast as I can, Donald. I'm sorry it's taking me so long, but I had to think of Della, too. We're spiffing you up," she said, sprinkling Johnson's baby powder on the frail, heaving chest. She quickly pulled on a freshly ironed undershirt and then struggled to get his limp arms through the sparkling white shirt with French cuffs. Her movements were sure, deft, as though she'd been practicing for this very thing. She removed the oversize diaper, washed him. Out of the corner of her eye she saw Della reach for a diaper. "No!" The word exploded from her mouth like a gunshot. "He is not going to meet his son and daughter wearing a diaper. Get his shorts, Della, and get them *now!*"

The boxers shorts were crisp, freshly ironed, pale blue in color. Kate struggled with them and then with the trousers. "I need a belt," she said, tucking the snowy white shirt into the waistband. She was huffing and puffing with her efforts. "Cuff links," she said hoarsely. "Now the paisley tie. Damn you, Della, get the tie! Hurry up," she cried. "Oh, God, I don't know how to tie a tie! Donald likes Windsor knots."

"I'll do it," Gus said, stepping forward. As he struggled with the tie, he could feel the tortured breaths of the man beneath him. His chest heaved, bucked with the effort to breathe without the oxygen mask.

The moment Gus was finished, he stepped aside. Kate straightened the points of the shirt collar, tugged at the jacket, buttoned the vest and then the jacket. Without having to be told, Gus pulled socks onto Donald's crippled feet. His eyes were frantic when he searched the room for shoes, knowing it would be impossible to get them on his feet. He looked at Kate helplessly.

"He's going in his stocking feet," she said. "His son will be so glad to see him, he won't look at his feet."

The room grew so quiet, Kate looked around to see what had caused the sudden silence. Her own chest heaved in grief when she realized Donald's chest was still. "Goodbye, old friend," she whispered. She turned and fell into Gus's arms. "I kept my promise. It was all I could do for him. I hope he understands. . . . I bet he's *up there* already . . . walking around in his stocking feet. He's probably showing Bobby his paisley tie and telling him how much it cost."

"Della is —"

"Sit with her, Ellie. I have calls to make. The service is going to be this afternoon, if I can arrange it. Someone from the funeral home will be here as soon as I call Mr. Muldoon. Donald . . . Donald picked out his own casket a year ago. He knew Della wouldn't be able to do it. You should have seen him picking and choosing, punching at those pillows, fingering the satin coverlet. Della was at the dentist when I took him there. It was the worst hour of my life. He . . . got a big kick out of it, took care of every last detail. He counted on me to . . . to make sure Della did what he wanted, but I couldn't — she wouldn't listen. She thought if she took care of him, cleaned him and sat with him, it was all right to keep him alive even when it wasn't what he wanted." She straightened, blew her nose. "We should have coffee or tea or something. I need to call . . . somebody and take all these things before we get back from the cemetery. I have a . . . a list."

"I could do that for you, Kate. What about the priest or minister?"

"Donald didn't want anything religious at the end. He said he didn't want anyone paving the way for him. God was either going to accept him on his own or reject him. He agreed to *one* prayer at the cemetery. Keep it short and sweet, he said."

"I'm sorry I didn't know him better."

"I'm sorry, too, Gus. He was a wonderful person. He could always make you feel better by saying just the right thing. Della is going to be lost without him."

"Time . . ." Gus said lamely.

"No. Della will grieve the rest of her life. I know her so well. She'll do what Donald wanted, she'll go back to Mexico, help some of the poor families, stay for a while, and then she'll come back here and . . . and wait till it's time to join Donald. And who am I to say she shouldn't do that?"

"I always thought the will to live was so strong," Gus muttered.

"I used to think that, too, back in the beginning, when Patrick was lost to me. I don't think that way anymore."

"Did Donald just have one son?"

"Yes. He had a daughter, but she was killed when she was eighteen. On a bus that was hit by a car. She was going to church. Her name was Lucia."

"Jesus."

"Everything is going to change now. Della is going to leave. When she comes back — *if* she comes back — it won't be the same. I want to hang on to her, but I have to let her go. Ellie is going to move. It's time for her to go out on her own. She's been talking for a while about going to Los Angeles. She needs to have a life of her own, and I accept that. But what in the world will I do with this big, fancy house?"

"You don't have to think about that now, Kate. Why don't you take a shower, put on some clean clothes, and I'll make some coffee and make these calls for you."

Kate nodded. "I'm forgetting something. Damn. There's something I need to do," she said vaguely.

"It'll come to you," Gus said, measuring coffee into the little metal basket. "If you don't dwell on it, it surfaces."

"I suppose you're right. You're a reporter, you should know."

Kate was about to step into the shower when she remembered. She pulled on a bright, lemon-colored terry robe and ran barefoot into the kitchen. "I remembered. I was going to call a greenhouse and ask them to deliver nasturtiums and all those other flowers so we could plant a . . . a flower bed."

"Kate, it's September."

"So?"

"Won't they die at this time of year?"

Kate thought about it. "I don't care. I want to plant them now. They have them in the greenhouse in little plastic things. I don't care what it costs. All colors. Enough to ring the house. See if they can deliver them this afternoon. I want to start planting them when we . . . when we get back. I need to do this, Gus."

"That's fine, Kate, but who are you doing it for? Betsy?"

"What does Betsy have to do with this? Betsy isn't here. She couldn't be bothered. She's never been to this house. I'm doing it for Donald. It was one of the last things he said to me. He came up from that deep, dark place he was in just to . . . It's for Donald. How he loved that other garden. When he looks down, I want him to see it. I don't care, I don't care," Kate said, holding up both arms. "I'm doing it." Her face was so full of determination, Gus could only nod.

"I'll call. How many plants should I order?"

"Enough to plant a ring around the garden. A lot."

"Yes, but what's a lot? Hundreds? Thousands? It's going to cost, Kate."

"Thousands, and I don't care what it costs. Ohhhh, Donald is going to be so pleased."

"Kate . . ."

She heard the worry in his voice. "I'm not *losing it,* Gus. But if you think I am, then humor me," she said with a smile in her voice.

That was exactly what he was thinking, but only for a minute. He waved her away, reaching for the phone at the same time.

When they returned from the cemetery they walked in a huddle, close together as though for warmth, their eyes on the ground.

Gus saw the truck first. Finnegan's Greenhouse. "Thank God," he muttered. "This is what we're going to do, ladies," he said, taking charge, and marching them inside the house. "We are going to change our clothes, have a sandwich and some ice tea, and then we are going to garden." He looked around the huge family room as he spoke. Everything was gone, the carpet vacuumed, the indentations from the hospital bed picked out. It looked like any other room. Even the sickroom smell was gone. The sliding doors to the deck were open, creating a warm, light breeze.

"What is it we're going to do?" Della asked in a daze.

"We're planting flowers," Ellie said lightly. "The way I see it, we might be done two weeks from next Thursday if we get a move on." She led Della from the room without a backward glance.

"I don't know how to thank you, Gus," Kate said, reaching up to kiss him on the cheek.

Suddenly he was embarrassed. He wanted to say, Just love me, just tell me you care about me. But he was afraid to say the words, afraid she would withdraw from him, send him away. "I'll think of something," he said. "Ellie's wrong, we're going to finish this project tonight, if we have to plant by moonlight. I called the placement counselor at the community college, and a dozen or so students will be arriving shortly to help us."

Kate kissed him again, her eyes bright with unshed tears. "I like raw onion on my liverwurst," she said.

"Oh, God! Don't tell me, let me guess, with a dab of tangy mustard?"

"More than a dab. I like to smear the whole slice of onion with it."

"Me too," Gus said in awe.

"Skip the iced tea, I like beer with my liverwurst. So do Ellie and Della."

"Jesus," Gus said.

Kate grinned. "And I like mustard and butter on my bagels."

"I don't believe this. If I searched the whole world over, I couldn't have found anyone with tastes so like mine. I think we were meant for each other." Gus drew a deep breath, expecting her to back off, to run and say something that would squelch any hopes he had of a more meaningful relationship.

"Do you think so?" Kate asked seriously.

"Yeah, I do," was all he could think of to say.

"Imagine that," was all Kate could say.

Gus literally danced a jig in the kitchen as he smeared honey mustard with a bite to it over the large slices of sweet white onion. The rye was only a day old and still fresh, the liverwurst slices stuck together. He made a mess of the meat, then finally gave up and pressed the onion firmly into the liverwurst. Hopefully no one would look beneath the top slice of bread.

It had been a hell of a day so far, yet it was one of the best days of his life. He had so much to tell Kate, things he hadn't wanted to discuss with her over the phone or put on paper. Things that were important to him, and maybe to her, too. He wondered if he was wrong to feel as if he belonged here, to want to be a part of this small family. If it was wrong, someone would enlighten him soon enough.

"Soup's on!" he bellowed.

They ate and drank, two beers apiece. Gus showed his approval by cleaning off the table. "I hate to be the one to mention this, but our planting crew has arrived, I can hear them. Let's order in for dinner. Kentucky Fried. Mashed potatoes, coleslaw. My treat," he said magnanimously.

"You are a kind, generous man, Gus Stewart," Ellie said with a devilish grin on her face.

"Tell that to your mother," Gus grumbled.

"She already knows. She's the one who told me." Ellie winked. "She told Della, too." Kate blushed furiously.

They worked and worked, and then they continued to work, with a ten-minute break on the hour. They took turns handing out iced tea, beer, and cold water. The only ones to complain about aching backs and sore knees were the college kids, who slaved to the tunes of Bruce Springsteen and Rod Stewart, who Gus said was no relation, thank God.

"What time is it?" Kate asked, taking a swig from her beer.

"Three-thirty in the morning," Gus said wearily. "I had no idea gardening was so tiring. My back hurts so bad I don't know if I'll ever be able to stand up again. How about you, Kate?"

"We're all pretty tired. Don't forget, we really didn't get any sleep to speak of the night before. We can use the hot tub when we're done. That should ease some of the ache."

"I'll drown," Gus groaned.

Kate grinned. "I'll save you."

"Because I'm worthwhile or because you

don't want me drowning on your property?"

"Both. I haven't thanked you, have I?"

"Several times." She didn't want him to drown, she'd save him. She'd wrap her arms around his neck and then he'd kiss her and they'd swim off into the sunset or sunrise, whichever happened first.

"Penny for your thoughts," Kate said quietly.

He told her his thoughts.

"We have a wonderful friendship. Anything more would spoil it," Kate said, her bottle drained.

"Will our friendship ever change?" Gus asked seriously.

A lump settled in her throat. "I don't know, Gus. What I do know is I don't want to lose you as a friend. You've become very important to me, very dear to me. I'm not ready for anything else. I can't promise more than that."

He was important to her, dear to her. "For now," he said.

"For now." Kate smiled.

"I can accept that. For now."

Kate's stomach muscles contracted. If this man walked out of her life, she would miss him terribly. I would grieve, she thought.

"A penny for *your* thoughts," Gus said.

She told him.

Gus strutted. She cared about him. She just didn't know how much. Yet.

Before they resumed their planting, Gus pierced her with his summer-blue eyes. "I'm not falling in love with you, Kate, I am *in love* with you." Kate felt her knees start to buckle. Gus reached for and eased her down on the ground.

Across the garden, Ellie nudged Della. "I don't think either one of us has to worry about Mom. That guy is gonna take real good care of her. If she lets him. You don't think she'll do something dumb and let him get away, do you?" Ellie asked anxiously.

Della shook her head. "Your mother's no fool. She may be a little mixed up in her mind when it comes to love and marriage. She may have buried your father's belongings and for a while thought of herself as a widow, but there's another part to your mother, that obsessive loyalty she has to Captain Starr. Then there's your sister. Your mother is going to be forced to make some hard decisions soon."

"You mean do it or get off the pot, that kind of thing?"

"Yes, that kind of thing. Why are we doing this, Ellie?"

"You mean planting the flowers?"

"Yes, why are we doing this?"

"Because Mom has it in her head that Donald is going to wake up in the morning in the Hereafter, look down, and see this . . . whatever the damn hell it is. I thought you understood. It's not for Betsy, it's for Donald. She told you, Della, I heard her," Ellie said gently.

"I guess I didn't hear her. I was so wrapped up in my grief, I didn't hear much of anything. I can't even remember what was said at the cemetery. I'm going home, Ellie," the older woman said sadly.

Ellie jabbed at the dark brown earth. "When will you be back?" She could feel her stomach start to churn. Della was like a second mother to her.

"I don't think I'll be coming back."

The plant in Ellie's hand lost its petals as she squashed it with her thumb and index finger. She looked at it, stuck it in the ground, and said, "This one is going to die."

"Everything dies sooner or later," Della said.

"I don't understand. Why don't you think you'll come back? What will Mom do without you? What will you do without Mom? You've been together so long, you're my other mother, Della," Ellie said, wiping the tears forming in her eyes.

Della pointed to Gus. "You said it yourself.

He'll look out for her. You're moving to Los Angeles. Donald's gone. He told me to take the money and go home. I have many family members I haven't seen in a long time. I can make their lives easier with the money Donald left me. There's no place at the cemetery for me. I saw it with my own eyes. Donald's first wife is buried there. And it's supposed to be that way. The family, they belong together. That's why Donald said I should go back to Mexico. That's why he . . . he paid me off."

"Oh, no, Della, you mustn't think like that! That wasn't what Donald meant. I don't think Mom knew anything about his first wife. Donald never talked about her, and Mom isn't one to ask questions. You never talk about her, either."

"That's because I didn't know. I thought . . . she left him when the children were young. He never talked about her to me. I didn't know she was dead or buried there with his son and daughter. He should have told me. I had a right to know. I thought I was going to be buried with him."

"Oh, Della," Ellie said, taking the older woman in her arms. "We can buy another plot next to theirs. You can still be buried there."

"No I can't! They're a family. I don't belong there," Della cried. "The last words out of Donald's mouth were to tell me to go back where I came from. So I'm going. One should always grant a dying person's last wish. Your mother is planting these flowers, and I am going back to Mexico."

Out of her depth, Ellie said, "I think you need to talk to Mom about this. Nothing is either black or white, you know." Soothingly, she added, "We won't be able to get along without you."

"I'm seventy-three years old, Ellie, an old woman. I'm not much good for anything anymore. Your mother thinks she fooled me. At first she had someone come in to do the heavy work, then the work that wasn't too heavy, and finally someone to do the light work. One lady irons and does laundry. A different lady to clean the windows, someone cleans the pool, someone else does everything."

"Mom was trying to make it easy for you, Della. You had all you could do to take care of Donald. It was her way of helping, paying you and Donald back for all the care you've given us over the years. Please don't break her heart. If you want to go back to Mexico for a visit, go, but come back."

"I cannot, my sweet Ellie. I made a mess of things. I didn't do the one thing Donald wanted me to do. I couldn't let him go. I was selfish. I was wrong. I don't want to talk about this anymore. It's going to be light soon, so we must work now to finish, for your mother's sake. I understand what she's trying to do now. And you must understand what it is I must do. Don't cry, Ellie, you'll soak the plants and they will die."

"I don't care," Ellie blubbered.

"I care, so stop," Della said.

Ellie reacted to the authoritative voice she remembered from her younger days. "You're a meanie," she said, as she had when she was little.

"Among other things," Della replied.

"You're going to break Mom's heart," Ellie said stubbornly.

"Enough already. If her heart breaks, that man will mend it for her. Look at them. He loves her very much. I see this. Do not concern yourself with her heart."

The stubbornness stayed in Ellie's voice. "You don't know *everything,* Della."

"This is true, *almost* everything. Dig."

"What about *my* heart?"

"You're young, you'll mend. Dig!"

What seemed like a long time later, Kate said, "In another twenty minutes or so it's going to be light. We still have a quarter of the way to go. I was so certain we'd be done. The kids have worked hard. You were right, Gus, it was an impossible, foolish task. What's the use?" She rocked back on her heels. "We might as well quit now. Everyone is dog-tired. Tell everyone to stop, Gus, I simply don't have the energy."

"You're quitting!" Gus said, stupefied.

"Yes."

"Then tell them yourself," he said, continuing with his planting. "I never much liked quitters."

"To each his own," Kate snapped. A moment later she was on her feet, shouting for the others to stop and listen. When she had their attention, she said, "The sun will be coming up shortly, so we're going to stop. I really appreciate your efforts here, work- ing through the night and all. I had hoped by some . . . *miracle* we could finish. I just want to thank you all. If you give me a few minutes to wash my hands, I'll pay you. I'll even treat you all to breakfast if you're not too tired to eat."

She watched as one student left the group and stepped forward, a young man with weary eyes, wearing a straggly gray USC sweatshirt. "Ma'am, would you mind telling us why you're doing this?" he asked.

Half a dozen responses flew to Kate's mind, but she knew none of them would satisfy the young man in front of her. They had worked hard and diligently, she told him with tears in her eyes.

The young man looked at the others and then at the grayish dark sky. "If we move the flats according to color, we can finish it. After the sun comes up we can continue planting. The object here is to plant a rainbow. I don't think the plants actually have to be in the ground. From *up there* it will look complete. Move! Move! We have about eight minutes."

In her life Kate never saw such a concentrated effort. She heard shouts of, "More pink, I need a blue, purple, no, no, yellow goes here, the pink there, hurry, faster, more purple, the red goes at the end. Move! Move! Three minutes, more blue, the daisies go there, two minutes, it's almost up, come on, Beasley, you're on the goddamn track team, move it! That's it, one more minute . . . all purple here. Thirty seconds, you got it!"

"Oh, my God!" Kate said, smiling through her tears.

"I'll be damned," Gus said.

"It's beautiful," Ellie said in awe.

"Heavenly," Della said.

"Guys, we do good work," said the kid in the USC shirt. To Kate he said, "Now what?" He looked uncomfortable when he added, "Shouldn't you sort of point, say something, you know, maybe a prayer?"

Kate licked her dry lips. Her tongue felt swollen and thick. She raised her eyes, palms upward. "Hey, Donald," she shouted as loud as she could. "This is for you! For your son, Bobby! For your daughter, Lucia!"

"And now I'm going to make breakfast for everyone," Della said. "Ellie, you will go to the store to buy eggs and bacon."

"Thank you, thank you so much," Kate said, walking among the boys to shake their hands. "If you want to go for a swim, go ahead. We'll make breakfast. This is going to be a long break, and you each get a bonus."

Kate's eyes were moist but full of stars when she looked at Gus. "I never would have thought about lining up the flats, would you?"

"Nope. I'd have kept on digging and planting, though. That kid homed in on it right away. And we're older and supposed to be smarter."

"That's why we send them to college." Kate laughed. "It looks so pretty. I can just see Donald's face. It was worth it, every single backbreaking minute of it. I can use some coffee, how about you?"

"You aren't mad at me for calling you a quitter?"

"Why should I be mad? It was the truth. I would have quit. All my life I've been a quitter. When things get hard or I don't want to deal with them, I crawl into a shell and blank everything out. No, I'm not mad."

Later, coffee cups in hand, the kids' voices echoing up from the pool, Kate said, "What are you going to do, Gus?"

"I have options," he said carefully.

"The *Times* is no shabby paper. Can you rethink . . . Your family is all back there. By the way, did you ever tell them about, you know, the house in Connecticut?"

"Actually, no. I got an attack of conscience and went back to Stamford. I was going to give the goddamn money back, but the house was empty. I checked around and found out the old man sold out his half of the business to his partner and took off. The guy handed me an envelope. He said my old man said I'd show up sooner or later and he was to give it to me. I expected a letter telling me why he left us. Maybe an 'I'm sorry' kind of letter. Maybe he'd asked about Ma or the others. There was no letter, no note. I wanted to bawl. Hell, I did bawl in the car."

"What was in the envelope?"

"The deed to that fancy eight-million-dollar estate. I guess there was a note of sorts. Scrawled across the front of the deed, in pencil, it said, 'You said you want what I have. Here it is. If you're reading this, it means you came here to give back the money, and that makes you a fool.' "

"Why didn't you say something to me? When did this happen?"

Gus shrugged. "A couple of months ago. I did feel like a fool. I didn't know what to do, so I called a family meeting. Jesus, you should have heard them. They called me every name in the damn book. In the end it had nothing to do with the money. They wanted to see him. They said they had as much right as I did and I took that right away. My mother's eyes were so sad. I disappointed her. In time they might forgive me, but I doubt it. I divvied up the money, sent them all checks. But none of 'em cashed them. My mother refused to take a cent. So for all intents and purposes I still have the damn money, and now I have that . . . Mafia-looking estate. Oh, I lied. I didn't get fired. I don't even know why I said that. So, being a quitter isn't half as bad as what I am. I guess I was hoping you'd feel sorry for me and ask me to stay out here. The only thing left back there for me is a few friends. My family hangs up on me if I call. I can't stand to see the hurt in my mother's face, so I don't go there anymore."

"Oh, Gus, I'm sorry. Life is never easy, is it?"

"I guess it would be pretty boring if it was."

"I'm sure your family will soften in time. Family is so wonderful. You'll pull together."

"I told them what he was like, about his flashy new wife, the big estate, and how arrogant he was. They all refused to believe he didn't ask about them. Even my mother wanted to know what he said about her. I lied to her, told her he said he hoped she was well. She fucking smiled at me when I said that, and then she got this awful look on her face. I swear to God I thought she was going to tell me to invite him for dinner. Instead she said, 'Gustav, you did a terrible thing.' Then she gave me a whack on the side of the head that made me sore for a week."

"You found him once, so you can find him again. Your brothers and sisters have all that money now. They can look for him, too," Kate said, sounding desperate.

"Don't you think my old man is thinking exactly what you just said? No, he's gone.

With his obvious connections, I'd say he's in Europe or someplace in Argentina. He doesn't want to be found. I'm not sure why. I blew it."

"I still think time will heal the wounds. You said you were a close family. Sooner or later they'll come around to understanding and forgiving you. You have to go back, Gus. You have to be there when that time comes. You'll hate yourself if you don't."

"I know."

"Just so you know." Kate smiled and reached for his hand.

CHAPTER 14

It was downright cold, Kate thought when she climbed behind the wheel of her newly leased Mercedes 560 SL. She was wearing a white wool coat with a champagne-colored cashmere scarf. She looked exactly like what she was, a highly successful businesswoman whose bank balance was the picture of health. The last year and a half since Donald's death had been the busiest of her life. When she'd found herself without Della and Donald, she panicked, throwing herself into her work, often staying at the office overnight. She now had branches in Los Angeles and San Diego and was contemplating a third in San Francisco.

She was on her way to Los Angeles to spend a few days with Ellie and to monitor business at the second location. And to do some shopping on Rodeo Drive.

"If I was happy, I'd have it all," Kate muttered as she slid a tape into the tape deck. Roy Orbison's clear voice relaxed her almost immediately. She fired up a cigarette and thought about Gus. She always thought about Gus when she was relaxed or about to fall asleep. She even thought about him when she woke in the morning or was in the shower. She dreamed about him, fantasized, but never acted on the dreams or fantasies.

Gus was upset with her. He'd invited her East for the holidays, but she'd declined, saying she always spent Christmas with Ellie and that maybe Della would come back. She'd been so rattled with his invitation that she hadn't thought to invite him to spend the holidays with her until later, and then she'd known he would think of it as an afterthought on her part. Sometimes she couldn't do anything right, especially when it came to Gus. Their friendship — because that's how she thought of it — had progressed to the point where she knew that if she didn't make a move, the whole thing would fall apart. It bothered her that she couldn't make a . . . What was it Gus wanted? A promise, a definite time when things would change. Commitment. The word scared the hell out if her. Commitment meant she would have to make love with Gus. In her mind and heart she was capable, but her body . . . her body was fearful. Her age was like a lighted beacon that sent shivers of fear down her spine. He was thirty-two now, going on thirty-three. She was forty-six going on forty-seven. The numbers didn't change. In three more years she'd be fifty. She'd be half a century old. She'd go through menopause. She'd start to drip sweat and get cranky; her skin would get dry and her face would turn beet-red with the hot flashes. It would be a nightmare. Her skin would lose its elasticity. Her hair would probably start to get thin on the top, her earlobes would wrinkle, and the lines around her eyes and mouth would deepen. Her rear end would droop, the skin around her knees would start to wrinkle, veins would show. And she'd just read something recently in one of the women's magazines that said facial hair was a problem at menopause.

She had three years until the nightmare became a reality. Maybe longer, since it wasn't engraved in stone that menopause started precisely at fifty. Three years to *do something*. She was entitled. She deserved to do something. The life she'd led for the past nineteen years wasn't natural. Always when she came to this part in her thinking she drew back, refused to think about being involved with *someone* in a sexual, romantic way. Gus was too young for her. She'd seen him with Ellie, teasing her, laughing with her, kibbitzing. Ellie or someone Ellie's age was more suitable for him. No matter what she did, no matter how she dressed, no matter how she thought, those fourteen years would always be there. When she was sixty Gus would be forty-six. When she was sixty-five and ready for Social Security, Gus would be fifty-one. There was no way he could catch up. Her hair would be gray and frizzy, she'd probably have a partial plate in her mouth, her fingernails would have ridges and her toenails would be yellow and ugly. Gus would be in his prime. Men in their fifties were always mature, worldly, and distinguished. She should know, she dealt with them on a daily basis — successful businessmen with wives and families and mistresses on the side.

She was an old maid, a dried-up old maid. And there was no excuse for it.

Kate's thoughts stayed with her all the way into Los Angeles. She drove straight to Olive Garden, where Ellie was taking her to lunch. "It's three blocks from the Big Eight firm I work for," Ellie had said last night. "I only have an hour for lunch, so if you get there first, order for me. Ziti will be fine. Oil and vinegar on my salad."

"Mom, you look like . . . a million bucks," Ellie now chortled happily. "I've never seen you look this good. Is there a new man in your life?"

Kate flushed. "No," she said, more sharply than she intended.

"New hairdo — and may I say it is fashionable. If I'm not mistaken, that's Sun Glitz in your hair, and I know a Chanel suit when I see one. And a Chanel bag. Come on, Mom, what's the scoop?" Ellie teased.

Her face warm, Kate said, "There *is* no scoop."

"Then what's with the trip to Rodeo Drive *to shop?*"

"Christmas is only a few weeks away. If I don't shop, there won't be any presents under the tree."

Ellie waited until the waitress had placed their wine spritzers in front of them before she spoke. "Mom," she said, leaning across the table, "I need to talk to you about something. How upset would you be if I . . . went to Denver with Pete for Christmas? He wants me to meet his parents. It's serious, Mom. I think he's going to give me an engagement ring. I want to go, but I don't want to leave you alone. If Della were here, I wouldn't feel so bad. . . . Jeez, Mom, you aren't going to cry, are you? If you cry, you're going to slop up your makeup and ruin the effect of that suit and the Glitz in your hair."

"God forbid," Kate said, dabbing at her eyes. "Oh, Ellie, of course it's okay for you to go. I'm crying because you're getting engaged. I like Pete, he's a great guy. I'm so happy for you, darling, really happy." She reached across the table to squeeze her daughter's hand.

"Pete reminds me of Gus, Mom. He's got the same laid-back attitude, the same warm, crinkly grin. He cares passionately about everything, animals, the environment. For an accountant, he's not boring at all. He wants us to open our own office at some point in the future. Nylander and Nylander. Has a ring to it, don't you think?"

"Definitely," Kate said.

"That means you're going to be loose for the holidays. That's going to bother me, Mom."

"Maybe I'll take a vacation and go see Della. Won't that be a surprise? I wish she'd write more often. God, Ellie, I can't tell you how much I miss her. I write once a week. She calls me from a store once a month. She sounds awful. All her spirit seems to be gone. I begged her to come back. I threatened to get a cat and told her it would be her replacement. She didn't even chuckle."

"Listen, Mom," Ellie said between mouthfuls of her salad, "on the off chance you wouldn't be upset about me going to Denver, I took the liberty of looking into a vacation for you. Before you say no, listen and then make up your mind. The travel agent said she could start you out from San Diego. You could have three days — two, or more if you want, with Della, and from there a trip to Hawaii. A tour trip so you wouldn't be alone. People your age. Men and women. You'll visit all the islands and have private accommodations. On Kona you'll be staying in a grass hut on a lagoon. It looks wonderful. You'll make friends, meet people, eat, put on some weight, get a tan, and come back full of vinegar. You need a vacation. I can make all the arrangements, all you'll have to do is get on the plane. I wish I could give you the trip as a present, but I can't afford it. What do you say?"

"Do you need my answer right this minute?" Kate said, flustered.

"Yes, Mom, I do. This is the holiday season. I'll need a check, too."

"Okay, I'll do it. Ellie, honey, do you need money?" The checkbook was in her hand.

"No. I'm fine. I didn't even charge Christmas presents this year. I paid cash and only bought things made in the U.S.A. Pete is real big on buying only American."

"Are you sure? Would you rather have gifts or money for Christmas?"

Ellie laughed. "I like to open presents, and I like money, too. I'll leave it up to you, Mom. Hmmmm, I can't wait to dig into this ziti, but first I have to call the travel agent. I'll drop off the check after work. Mom, you're going to have a great time. Now you can really shop Rodeo Drive. Go for the flash — on you it'll look great! I'll be right back."

Ellie sprinted like a young colt out to the foyer of the restaurant. She used her calling card, her blunt nails tapping on the hard metal tray beneath the phone.

"Gus Stewart, what can I do for you?"

Ellie giggled. "It's not what you can do for me, it's what I can do for you. It's a done deed, Gus. She agreed and is writing out the check as we speak. I don't think I'd let her see you until the plane is in the air."

"Thanks, Ellie, and Merry Christmas. I owe you."

"Damn right. Make sure my wedding present is a handsome one."

"You got it! Listen, you aren't upset over this, are you?" Gus asked anxiously.

"Hardly. I think you're the best thing that ever happened to Mom. If you can get her past that age thing, you'll both be real happy. Merry Christmas, Gus."

Ellie was breathless when she sat down at the table. "Everything will be mailed to you, Mom. All you gotta do is get yourself to the airport and do some shopping. Look for exquisite, Mom, and get one really knock-'em-dead outfit."

"You sound like you're plotting a seduction," Kate said sourly. She was already regretting her decision to make the trip.

"Mom, if I give you the money, will you pick up something for Della for me? By the time I get it, wrap it, and mail it out, it won't get there till after Christmas. You're going to see her, and it would save me a lot of worry."

"Certainly. Della is the hardest person in the world to shop for. However, I have my present all paid for and wrapped up," Kate said smugly.

Ellie fanned her mouth, string cheese dripping down her chin. "Jeez, this is hot. What'd you get her?"

"Drink some cold water," Kate said in the motherly voice she rarely got to use these days. "I had an aerial photograph made of the rainbow this summer. I got it enlarged, and it came out just beautiful. I hope she likes it. I also got her a shawl; it's got every color of the rainbow on it, fringe, too. That's what I wrapped the picture in."

"You are creative." Ellie handed over twenty-five dollars to her mother. "I know this kind of limits your choice, but do the best you can, and don't you dare add anything to it. If you do, it won't be the same. Della doesn't care about price tags."

"Have you seen or talked to your sister?" Kate asked carefully.

"You mean since Donald's funeral? Once. I ran into her in the drugstore. Can you beat that? Dr. Starr, as she likes to be called these days, now has a political science degree. She fancies herself an authority on Southeast Asian affairs. She was with a very . . . radical-looking individual. She looked great. She asked about you. She didn't mention Donald or Della. I told her about Della. This is all by the antacid section. I asked her if she had a job, and she said, 'I expected you to say something like that.' End of quote. She was dressed well. She's collecting donations from private individuals for a group of mercenary types to go on into Laos. Seems there's been some kind of sighting, and she thinks Dad might be one of the POWs in the picture that's been flashed around. She's nuts, Mom."

"Obsessed," Kate said quietly.

"No, Mom, nuts. You have to be nuts to

give up your family. She doesn't care about us. She made me so damn mad, I told her about the rainbow, and I don't think she heard a word I said. I told her to drop dead and left."

"Ellie, you didn't!" Kate cried.

"Yeah, I did. I'm not sorry, either. Lord, look at the time. I gotta go. You're paying, right?" She flashed a grin, hugged her mother, and was gone a second later.

Kate finished her coffee, smoked a cigarette, and paid the bill. "Rodeo Drive, here I come," she muttered as she steered the car into traffic.

Kate whizzed from store to store, buying anything and everything that struck her fancy. Each time she returned her platinum American Express card to her wallet, she wondered if it would go through a meltdown process. She had Ellie's gifts wrapped and shipped direct to her apartment, bearing DO NOT OPEN TILL XMAS stamped on each one. She did the same to Betsy's presents and wondered if her daughter would accept them or if she would send a Christmas card in return. When she sent out her Christmas cards, she would enclose a check for both Ellie and Betsy.

On the drive home, munching a bagel she'd bought earlier, she thought about all the things she'd purchased for herself for her sudden vacation. She giggled when she remembered how she'd told the clerk, "I'll take this in every color" or "I'll take two of those, three of those, and I'll take this with me." She'd spent a bloody fortune. A case of fine wine shipped to Gus, gifts from Gucci for her office staff, gifts for everyone she knew. The United Parcel man was going to need a truck just for her purchases. But she felt really good about her day, and made a mental note to go shopping more often. She'd come a long way from the days when she used to sew her own clothes, decorating them with frills and geegaws. She winced when she remembered what she called her "artsy days."

It was late by the time Kate got home. This was the part she hated the most, coming home to a dark, cold house with no fragrant smell to greet her. She usually turned on the television, the radio, and every light in the house the minute she walked in. Then she made coffee, listened to her messages, snacked on whatever was in the refrigerator, curled up on the sofa and called Gus.

The packages she'd brought home with her were scattered all over the den floor. She could hardly wait to tell Gus about her day. She heard the machine come on and, disappointed, left her name and the time she called. She frowned when she realized he might be out on a date. He hadn't actually *said* he dated, but he was a young, virile man. The thought perturbed her. She tried his number again at eleven-thirty before she crawled into bed. This time she didn't leave a message. Her face burned when she thought of him in bed with a *younger* woman whose skin was soft and slick. She had no strings on Gus. He could do as he pleased, just as she could do as she pleased. Only she didn't please.

Her dreams were invaded by a handsome pilot spraying bullets into her rainbow garden, which was dormant for the winter. "Run, Gus, run. He wants to kill you!" she shouted. She was running, too, dragging a huge trash bag full of gaily wrapped Christmas presents. The rat-a-tat sound of the bullets slapping into the ground around her running feet woke her. She was breathing hard, her chest heaving with the effort. She fell back against the pillow, her mind in turmoil as she tried to fathom the dream. It was raining out, the fat drops slamming against the window with the force of the wind. Patrick was the pilot, of course. He wanted to kill Gus because she was contemplating *something*. She'd been trying in the dream to protect Gus. Why? What did that bag of

Christmas presents mean? All those gifts from earlier days that she and the girls had wrapped so lovingly and never had a chance to give.

Kate was awake now. "Damn!" She hadn't dreamed about Patrick for years, and she rarely thought of him these days. She must have dreamed about him now because of Ellie's news of Betsy. She squeezed her eyes shut and tried to picture Patrick. She used every trick she knew to conjure up his image, but it wouldn't surface. Instead, Gus's crazy features flashed behind her closed lids. He had such a gentle smile, such caring eyes. His touch was gentle, too. Her eyes snapped open when she remembered her last phone call with no answer on the other end of the line. Her hand snaked out from under the covers to snatch the clock. Good Lord, it was nine o'clock! Noon in New York. Gus should have called her by now. Unless he didn't go back to his apartment last night. In the past he'd always returned her phone calls.

Kate leaped from the bed. She would not think about this. By the time she showered, dressed, and made coffee, she had fixed in her mind an image of the girl she thought Gus had spent the evening with. She was twenty-six, maybe twenty-eight, a professional, wearing a crisp suit with a crisp white

blouse and a single strand of pearls. She wore Bally shoes, had a French manicure, a casual wash-and-wear hairstyle. She was shapely, looked good in *anything*. She was beautiful and witty. She drove a firecracker-red Porsche, had long, shapely legs, and wore spike-heeled shoes. She carried a briefcase, and was so experienced in bed that men, Gus in particular, became addicted to her charms after only one night. Her name was . . . was Gennifer with a G, not a J. G set her above all the other Jennifers in the Big Apple.
"Shit!" Kate said succinctly.

She stomped about the kitchen in search of food. The withered wrinkled apples in the fruit bowl had been sitting there for a month. The bread in the refrigerator had mold on it, as did the cheese. The lone cucumber in the vegetable bin was a slimy mass of yellow, putrid-looking seeds and skin. The bag of Oreo cookies was full of tiny bugs, and so was the box of Ritz crackers. God, how long had she had this stuff? Obviously she had to go to the grocery store, and there was no better time than right now. She would take the day off, too — go to the store, fill her car with groceries, come home, put them away, and then cook. Maybe she'd even bake a pie. Then she would sit down and eat everything. She wasn't going to call the office, either. And for sure she wasn't going to answer the phone. Maybe she'd make some fudge, with marshmallow fluff, peanut butter, and real nuts. A banana cream pie. A roast chicken with stuffing. She could eat all week. Maybe a pot of spaghetti. She could freeze everything into portions. She'd eat the whole pie through and most of the fudge. Let Gennifer What's-her-name eat the bean sprouts and yogurt. *She* wasn't trying to trap anyone, she didn't need to stay needle-thin. She was a real woman, one who liked to eat.

"Oh, shit!" she muttered as she yanked on her raincoat. "Shit, shit, shit!"

CHAPTER 15

When Kate returned home from the market with eleven bags of groceries, she could hear the phone ringing. "Ring, damn you, see if I care," she muttered as she started to put away her groceries. Earlier she'd disconnected the answering machine. She was being silly, stupid. And so *very* jealous. As she slammed boxes of cereal and rice into the cabinet any old way, she kept muttering over and over, "Gennifer with a G, Gennifer with a G." The faceless, nameless person was rapidly taking on an identity in her mind, and with each hour she grew more beautiful, more sophisticated, more upscale. Now she was model-thin, incredibly beautiful, with full, pouting lips and a mane of hair that was just curly enough, had just enough body to it, so she could toss her head and have it fly around like a moving nimbus.

Her groceries tucked away, Kate banged the frying pan on the stove to brown the chopped meat for the spaghetti. Her mind attacked Gus when the phone shrilled. He was with Gennifer with a G, a sappy look on his face. Gennifer with a G would stretch like a cat, the nipples in her breasts taut beneath the thin sheet. "C'mere, love," she'd purr. "I know what you want. We have time, love." Yes, yes, she'd call him something stupid like "love." Gennifer with a G would surely say, "We have time for a little . . . nookie. . . ." No, she wouldn't say that. She'd say, "Oooohhh, make love to me again." And still wearing the same sappy look, Gustav Stewart would oblige. Twice. But was Gennifer with a G exhausted? Not on your life. She'd get up, stretch, making Gus aware of her high, firm breasts, her perfectly flat belly, her perfectly proportioned rear end. He'd groan and maybe moan, bury his head in the pillow and say, "Let's do it again. Soon. Real soon." Gennifer with a G would toss her mane of hair, wink slyly and say, "It all depends, love, on what you have to offer." At which point he'd rear up and say, "How does an eight-million dollar estate in Connecticut and four million in the bank sit with you?" She'd give her tush a seductive wiggle and say, "If you're telling me the truth, love, just fine. This body, all one-hundred-ten pounds, is yours."

"You son of a bitch!" Kate screeched as the onions started to burn. She scraped at them with a vengeance. "You said you were dividing the money up, you said you didn't want the estate. You bastard! You stinking, lousy bastard!"

The phone shrilled. Kate shut the stove off. The man hadn't been born she would trust now. First Patrick and now Gus. "I always harbored a secret fear that at some time in our life Patrick would be unfaithful, but I never thought you would, Gus," she whimpered. She flung open the refrigerator and reached for one of the bottles of wine she'd put in earlier. Supermarket wine. And she'd sent a whole case of 1924 Mouton Rothschild to *him* for Christmas. "Well, we'll just see about *that!* Gennifer with a G is not going to drink wine I paid for, either."

Her purse was still on the kitchen table, filled with all the receipts from yesterday's shopping. Kate rifled through them until she found the one she wanted. On the verge of tears, she tapped out the phone number, identified herself, gave her order number, and screamed into the phone, "Cancel that order! Credit my account. Buy your own goddamn wine, Miss Gennifer with a G!"

Kate poured white zinfandel into a water glass and drank greedily. In her life she'd never had a drink of wine at eleven o'clock in the morning. "Well, there's a first time for everything," she muttered as she tripped from room to room, removing telephone wires from the jacks.

At twelve-thirty she finished the wine, went to the bathroom, and was sick. She brushed her teeth, tottered back out to the kitchen, and uncorked a second bottle of zinfandel. At two o'clock she tried to march into the bathroom and was sick before she reached the door. "Oh, shit!" she muttered as she puked. "Now who's going to clean this up? Delllllllaaaa! . . . Ah, the hell with it."

On her way back to the kitchen, she looked over her shoulder at the mess she'd left by the bathroom door. In true Scarlett fashion she said, "I'll think about that tomorrow. Then again, maybe I won't. Maybe I'll never use that bathroom again. Oh, Della, I miss you. I'm drunk, Patrick. You should see me. I puked my guts out. Twice!" she said triumphantly. "Gennifer with a G would never throw up, never lose control. Who give's a good rat's ass? Do you hear me, Patrick? I'm using dirty language and I'm drunk. It's pissifying. I learned these words from Ellie and her friends. What do you think of me now, Patrick?"

She should make coffee. She was cooking, wasn't she? The mess on the stove smelled good. The array of bottles, cans, and packages on the counter confused her. Maybe she should just throw it all away and start over. "Waste not, want not," she said, giggling. Later, when she felt . . . different, she'd figure out what to do with all the stuff. Now she needed coffee. Any fool could make coffee, even Gus.

She started to cry as she measured coffee into the wire basket, spilling half on the counter and half on the floor. She tried a second and third time before she got enough into the basket. She slopped water all over the package of spaghetti, stared at it for a minute, and then shrugged. "Who cares? I don't." She giggled again as she staggered over to one of the oak chairs and sprawled on it in a very unladylike pose. "I'm drunk, I'm drunk, I'm drunk," she mumbled in a singsong voice. Her stomach heaved threateningly. "I hate you, Patrick, for going off and leaving me. I hate Gus Stewart for being so unfaithful. But I *love* you, Della," she cried. "What's wrong with me that you all left me?" She dropped her head into her hands and cried for her loss. She was wailing, beating her fists on the kitchen table, when the front doorbell rang. "Go away!" she cried. "I didn't invite you, whoever you are. Leave me alone." The bell continued to ring, the coffee continued to perk. "Shut up, I have a headache," she muttered. There was instant silence; the doorbell stopped ringing and the percolator offered up its last plop. "I need a cat!"

Kate's eyes focused on the two wine bottles and the mess on the counter. My God, was it five o'clock already? "Who cares what time it is. It's just another day, another hour," she said as she poured out coffee into a giant-size cup. Who the hell was going to drink all this coffee? "Guess I am, since there's no one else here and I don't have a cat. God, I need a cat," she said, her eyes welling with tears of self-pity. Maybe Ellie would get her one, a tabby with yellow stripes and big eyes. She'd call it Betsy II.

She reached behind her to a bank of light switches and flicked on all six. The kitchen blazed with light. The floodlights on the deck and in the yard made her blink. The back doorbell rang. Kate looked at the sliding glass doors and saw two policemen peering in at her. "Go away, I gave at the office!" she shouted. The doorbell rang again.

"Mrs. Starr, will you open the door? We

need to talk to you."

"Why?" Kate said craftily.

"Please, it will only take a minute."

"Did I do something wrong?"

"No, we just need to talk with you. Your phone doesn't seem to be working."

"Well, la-de-da. Since when is that the policeeee's business?" she said, slurring her words. "Go away."

"We're going to stay here until you open the door."

Kate thought about the words. "You will. Even if I go to bed?"

"Yes."

"If I give you a check, will you go away?"

"If you open the door first to hand it to us."

"Oh, no, I'll slide it under the door. Come back tomorrow."

"Mrs. Starr, if you don't open the door, we'll break it."

"Then you'll pay for it," Kate said spiritedly. "That's . . . that's breaking and entering. This is my castle, you can't do that." She turned her back on the policemen and started to drink her coffee.

The back doorbell rang again. "Ellie sent us," one of the officers said. "We're friends. Now will you open the door?"

"She's such a sweet child. Did she give

you the tickets to bring all the way here?"

"Mrs. Starr, open the door."

"I can't find the lock. It won't open. Guess I can't let you in," Kate said, sashaying back to the table. "Just leave the tickets on the deck. I'll call somebody to open the door tomorrow."

"Mrs. Starr, go around to the front door and open it. You can open the front door, can't you?"

"Do I have to sign for the tickets? This is such a bother." She staggered to the front door. The moment the door was open, the two officers each reached for one of Kate's arms and led her backward. "Mrs. Starr, I'm Officer Archer and this is my partner, Officer Enright. Your daughter called us, she was worried about you. Then your office called us, and then a man named Gustav Stewart called us."

Kate drew herself up haughtily, shaking off the officers. "You lied, you don't have the tickets. I don't care if the President of the United States called you. I don't want you here. You should be out catching criminals, not bothering people like me. Are you going to call those people?"

"They're going to call back. Your daughter was worried about you. Why didn't you answer the phone, Mrs. Starr? Is it out of order?"

"I unplugged it. I didn't feel like going to the office. I wanted to make spaghetti today. That's not a crime."

"Did you make it?"

"What?"

"The spaghetti?"

"No." Kate sighed. "I drank wine instead. I drank too much and got sick. I made coffee, though," she said brightly. "You won't tell that to Gus, will you?" She started to cry and then to babble about Patrick, about Betsy, about being alone. "I can't possibly compete with Gennifer with a G. I'm almost fifty years old. She's got this fly-away hair and . . . she calls people 'love.' He fell for it, too."

The officers looked at one another before they led Kate back to the kitchen. Officer Archer poured fresh coffee for her before he settled her on the chair. "Tell me what to say to your daughter. She's worried about you. Think about that for a minute while I plug the phone in."

"If it rings, don't answer it! This is my house."

Archer held up his hand. "I hear you, Mrs. Starr, we won't answer the phone." He eyed the two wine bottles. "Did you drink both bottles, Mrs. Starr?"

"Yes, I did," Kate said stiffly. "I'm in my own house and can do whatever I damn well please. I can swear if I want to, too."

"What should we tell your daughter?"

"Tell her . . . tell her I screwed up. Tell her I'm sorry if she was worried. She can call the office. Don't . . . Tell her *not* to call Gus. What are you going to tell him if he calls you back?" Kate asked suspiciously. "Tell him the truth, tell him I wouldn't open the door."

"That's only half the truth," Archer said, not unkindly.

"He doesn't deserve the whole truth. I'm going to be embarrassed if I see you in town or on the street."

"Don't be, Mrs. Starr. We all have days when things crowd in on us. Alcohol doesn't make things better, but I think you already know that. Look, why don't we call your daughter from here, tell her you're all right. You're going to leave all the lights on and you're going to sleep this off. We'll check back later, come around back to make sure things are okay. We'd like it if you'd sleep on that couch over there so we'll be able to see you from the sliding doors. Will you do that, Mrs. Starr? Do you want the answering machine on?"

"Yes, and no to the answering machine. Turn the phone low."

"All right," Archer's partner said, leading

her to the couch. "Does your front door lock automatically?"

"Yes." Kate leaned back on the pillows the officer placed behind her head. She listened to the officer's voice as he spoke on the phone.

"Your mother is fine, Miss Starr. She's a little under the weather right now and is about to go to sleep. She had a bad day. . . . No, I don't think you should make the drive up here. We're going to look in on her later. She said you should call the office for her. She doesn't want anything said to the gentleman who called the station. The one you said called you also. She's quite adamant about that."

Kate fought the blanket of sleep that was about to engulf her. She had to remember what the officer was saying to Ellie. It was important because it was about Gus. She surrendered to sleep with Gus's name on her lips and in her thoughts.

Archer checked out the sliding door. "No wonder she couldn't open it, there's a rod in the track. It might be a good idea for us to take the key, return it tomorrow. She could sleep for hours or for twenty minutes. She looked pretty upset to me. You know who she is, don't you, Enright? Her husband is the one who was shot down over Vietnam and has never come back. She raised her girls on her own, started up a business, again, on her own. She got fed up with the government and the Air Force and buried her husband's things. It was in the paper a few years ago. If this is all she's ever done that wasn't on the straight and narrow I don't think we should judge her. This Gus person sounds like he's at the root of whatever it was that set her off today."

Enright grinned. "She's going to have one hell of a hangover tomorrow."

"Yeah, I don't think the lady ever had one before. Maybe we should leave her a note. 'Tomato juice with a squirt of Tabasco sauce. Drink this and it won't be so bad. Add three aspirins if the headache is unbearable.' "

Enright scrawled the note and propped it up against one of the wine bottles, then the two officers let themselves out of the house. They checked on Kate twice during the evening. She was sleeping peacefully at eleven o'clock when they went off duty. Their replacements checked on her at two in the morning and again at five-thirty. Their report to Archer and Enright was, "The lady is sleeping peacefully." By mutual consent the report they filed read, "Mrs. Starr's phone was disconnected. She was making spaghetti when we arrived. Mrs. Starr was fine when we left the house and said she would call her daughter to tell her she was all right."

Kate woke at seven the following morning with a pounding headache and a sour stomach that got worse the moment she walked into the kitchen. She ignored the softly buzzing phone as she headed for the bathroom off her bedroom. When she returned to the kitchen dressed in a vibrant purple robe, her hair wrapped in a bright orange towel, she saw the note and cringed but followed the instructions. She gagged twice, but the juice stayed down. She felt a little better an hour after she took the aspirins. She cleaned up the kitchen and the mess she'd left by the bathroom door, swearing at the same time never, ever, to drink wine again. She curled up on the couch and slept the better part of the day. When she woke at six o'clock, she played the messages on the machine. Eleven were from Gus, three from Ellie. The tape was full.

Kate made tea and called Gus at the office. Her voice sounded nasally and scratchy when she identified herself.

"What the hell happened?" he said. "I've been calling you all day and all last night. I thought something happened to you. I called Ellie and the police. Don't ever do that again, Kate. I tried calling you back the other night when I got in. Jesus, Kate, I've been sick with worry."

Kate smiled. "I'm sorry, Gus," she said happily. That meant there was no Gennifer with a G. "I don't know what got into me." Her headache was less intense, almost gone — in fact, she felt light-headed.

"I can't tell you the kinds of things I was thinking. God, an imagination, especially one like mine, is a killer."

"I know what you mean. Sometimes mine gets away from me, too," Kate said lightly.

They talked for an hour, then: "Listen, Kate, I'll call you tomorrow okay?"

"Sure. I'm going to make some spaghetti now."

Instead of making spaghetti, Kate stretched out on the couch, the portable phone at her elbow, closed her eyes and daydreamed. Her name was Cate with a C and she was forty-six years old. . . .

CHAPTER 16

Kate looked up at the garish sign over the shop in Tijuana, Mexico. Jesus Tobacco Shop. She stepped carefully on the rotted, wooden step. The shop seemed to sell everything. She'd expected displays of cigarettes and cigars but didn't see any. She did see a telephone. So this was where Della came to make the few calls she'd placed over the past year. "Señor," she said slowly, distinctly, "Can you send someone to fetch Señora Della Rafella?"

"Sí, but it will do you no good. Señora Della has gone to help her niece. It is miles. One day if you go in a car, two days if you are walking. Then two days coming back. She will stay one week to help. New babies take much care. Many pesos, señora."

"Oh no!" Damn, she hadn't counted on

this. So much for the surprise element. Four days. Her plane left for Hawaii tomorrow evening. She shook her head. "If I leave a note, will you see that Señora Della gets it when she returns?"

"Sí, señora."

Kate ripped a blank page from her address book. Thank God she didn't know anyone whose name started with an O. She handed the shopkeeper a ten-dollar bill along with the note.

"She is your friend?" the man said curiously.

"The best friend I ever had. I miss her very much. Do you know her well?"

"She does much good for her family, and for others, too. She is an American citizen," he said proudly, "and still she stays here with her people. She comes in often. Much sad eyes," he said, shaking his head. "Much like yours, señora."

"You won't forget to give her my note?" Kate said.

"No, señora, I will not forget. I do not get many American ladies here who want to leave notes. Is there anything you wish to buy?"

"Oh, yes, yes, there is. Cigarettes and . . . a lighter and these two key chains. I'll take that Bic pen and that notebook. This shoe polish and these mints and two boxes of that cherry Jell-O."

Thirty dollars changed hands. Kate knew she was being ripped off, but she didn't care. She accepted the greasy bag and left. Later she left the bag in a store she browsed through, buried beneath a pile of garish-looking shawls.

Back in her hotel in Chula Vista, Kate showered and watched television the rest of the day. She went to bed early and slept late, rising to order room service, shower, and go to church. She walked around town, had lunch, and returned to the hotel. She repacked her overnight bag, checked out, and arrived at the airport three hours ahead of schedule. She ate again and read several magazines as she waited for the tour director to arrive.

"I'm going to strangle you, Ellie," she muttered when the tour director, a giddy young girl of nineteen or so, arrived, her charges trailing behind her. All of them, Kate noticed, were retirees with white hair. At a glance she knew there wasn't one of them under seventy years of age. She would just have to make the best of it.

An hour later when the director herded them onto the plane, Kate drew her aside and said, "Why are you patronizing these people? And do you have to yell at the top of your lungs? I'm not deaf, and neither is anyone else. I don't see any reason for you to hold up those ridiculous signs, either. I'm embarrassed for them. Think about that, Miss Tour Director. I won't be joining you once I get to Hawaii. The agency that booked me on this tour obviously didn't have my best interests at heart. Was it really necessary to have each of us stand and expound on our backgrounds? We aren't children, and I resent it. I have half a mind to cancel this tour and go off on my own right now."

"Are you saying I'm overdoing it? You have to be careful with older people. They want things explained, they wear hearing aids and bifocals."

"Which makes them see and hear better, so you don't need the signs and don't need to shout. You embarrassed all of us."

"All right," the director said stiffly. "What are you, some kind of mentor, watchdog or something? *Company spy?*"

Kate just smiled. "Or something," she said, thinking of Della and Donald. "Just because you're old doesn't mean you're a fool, and it doesn't give *you* the right to humiliate people."

Taking her seat in the smoking section at the back of the plane, Kate wondered what had gotten into her to make her speak up that way. In twenty years I'll have white hair like them and I'll be taking a trip like this, that's why, she answered herself. When she was seventy Gus would be fifty-six. She'd be doddering and he'd be pushing her along with a spring in his step. She shuddered. God, why had she allowed Ellie to talk her into this? Christmas should be spent at home with loved ones. But the few loved ones she did have had other plans. No one wanted to spend Christmas with her. She'd be with strangers who had no one, either.

At the small airport in Kona, Kate parted company with the tour. She collected her bags, rented a car, and received a map showing her the way to Kona Village. "Just watch for the little hut on the side of the road," the rental agent said. "Make a left and it will take you to the village."

Kate missed the hut and had to drive five miles before she could turn around and make her way back. "She should have told me it was set back in from the road," she muttered as she whipped the open Jeep around the corner. For miles all she could see was black lava. Where was all the greenery and bright flowers? The word *devastation* came to her mind as she drove the rutted dusty road. "I am going to kill you, Ellie, with my bare hands, when I get hold of you." Where in the damn hell was civilization?

Finally a speck of green caught her eye. A palm tree. Thank God. And water; she could smell the ocean. Kate continued to drive. At last she came to the village. She sucked in her breath: here there were flowers and greenery. People. A slice of paradise. She looked back over her shoulder but couldn't see the fields of black lava.

Kate smiled when a woman dressed in native costume came out to the car to place a fragrant lei around her neck. "Welcome to Kona Village. And you are . . . ?"

"Kate Starr. I was with the Cromwell tour, but I won't be staying with them. I understand I have my own quarters. I'd also like to make my own eating arrangements."

"There won't be a problem, Mrs. Starr. Come with me, please." The woman smiled and led the way to the office, settling Kate behind a tiny teakwood desk. "It will be just a moment until I get registration forms. In the meantime, enjoy this fresh pineapple juice," she said, offering Kate a small, frosted glass before leaving her alone.

Kate settled back and looked at the brochure on the desk. The world's most prized hideaway . . . 125 thatched *hales*. She flipped over the brochure. Happy Hour at the Bora Bora Bar from five to six P.M. On Tuesday there would be a General Manager's Cocktail and Pupu Party, whatever that was. Sailing and snorkeling. Tennis. Sport fishing. Helicopter flightseeing. Therapeutic body massage. "Ah," Kate said, sipping the pineapple juice. Shiatsu, Swedish Massage. Reflexology, hand and foot massage. Hawaiian lomi lomi, electric methods of massage, local style. She made a note to sign up for one of each. Two dining rooms. Hale Moana for breakfast, lunch or dinner, and the Hale Somoa for dinner, no ties and jackets. Thong sandles were acceptable. Make dinner reservations at breakfast time. No phones, no radios, no televisions, no air-conditioning. Do not feed the wildlife. Kate closed the brochure packet.

"Did you like what you read?" the smiling woman asked, returning.

"Very much. It seems so quiet and restful here. I was surprised, though, that guests aren't given keys."

"I'm sure we can find a key if it would make you feel better."

"No, it's all right."

"I hope you brought a lot of reading material. We have a gift store with a nice selection of paperback books, and the newspapers are flown in every day. There is a phone around the corner from where we're sitting. Each *hale* has a mailbox. Should you receive messages, they will be placed there. Sign here, Mrs. Starr. Your bags have been taken to your *hale* and your car parked in the lot behind the swimming pool. Come with me now and I'll take you to your quarters."

The *hales* were thatched huts. Everything was magnificent. The lagoon was peaceful. "Is that a *black* swan?" Kate asked in amazement.

"Yes, there are several. As you can see, you have neighbors, but not too close. This is your *hale,* Mrs. Starr. If you need anything, come up to the office. There is a small map inside for walking about. Enjoy your stay with us."

"I'm sure I will," Kate said, in awe as she took in her new home.

The room was parrot bright, with a colorful spread over the bed. Two rattan chairs and a table completed the front room. A desk and a second bed/couch made up the second room. The bathroom vanity held a coffeepot with attached grinder along with a container of Kona coffee. A small refrigerator held soft drinks. Other than the shower and toilet, there was nothing else to see. She had a front porch with two chairs, the thatched fronds hanging down the sides to ward off the sun.

So far Kate hadn't heard a sound. Kona Village was certainly peaceful and quiet, but she'd have to work on the deluxe part. She bounced on the bed, checked the sliding glass door, and was relieved to see that it could lock from the inside. She turned on the paddle fan overhead. It whirred softly to life.

"I think I could get real depressed here," Kate muttered as she turned on a low-wattage lamp that did little to lighten the dim, cool room. "I do not like this!" she said aloud. "In fact, I think I hate it! I am not a sun person, I am not a beach person. I do not like living in dim, dark rooms." She kicked out at her suitcase and then yelped in pain.

"Is that a damsel-in-despair cry I just heard?" a voice called from the porch.

"Gus? . . . *Gus!* My God, *Gus,* it can't be you! I'm dreaming. I have dreams like this all the time. I cannot believe that you would show up and be staying in a grass hut the way I am. I hate this place. Do you hate it? Don't answer that. You aren't supposed to talk in dreams."

"Pinch me," Gus said, opening the screen door. Kate pinched his bare arm. He said, "Ouch. See? It's not a dream."

"But how, you said . . . When did you get here? Do you like this place?"

"I got here yesterday. It's great, Kate. The food is out of this world. I look at it and gain weight. I had banana pecan pancakes for breakfast. I ordered seconds. The coffee is the best I've ever tasted. Both pools are super. It's a great place. For lovers," he said, winking at her. "It gets a little rowdy toward morning with different birds scratching on the roof. I got up early and had coffee on the porch. You should have seen the guests who came to call. There were twenty different birds out there, but I had nothing to feed them, and we aren't supposed to feed them anyway. God, Kate, it's good to see you. What say we shuck this place and you move in with me?"

Kate sucked in her breath. Was she ready for that? Damn right she was, she thought smartly. Well, almost ready. Sort of ready. *Absolutely not*. "Yes," she said.

"You mean it!"

"Gus, I'm forty-six years old. You're fourteen years younger than me. You're more suitable for Ellie. When I'm seventy you'll only be fifty-six."

"I want to marry you, Kate. I can make you happy. I'll love you forever. I can't picture my life without you in it."

"That's how I feel, but I don't know . . . marriage is . . . There's Patrick. . . ."

"There is no Patrick, Kate. You buried him, remember?"

"His things, Gus. Not his body."

"Do you love me?" He held his breath waiting for her reply. When it came, it *swooshed* out of him like a pricked balloon.

"Yes," she said without a moment's hesitation.

"Jesus. I never thought I'd hear you say that."

"Do you love me?"

"Do birds fly? Of course I love you. Why do you think I'm here? I cooked this up with Ellie. I want us to start the new year together. Guess that makes me one of those hopeless romantics. Ellie approves of me. She'll give us her blessing. My mother will like you."

"Your brothers and sisters?"

"Hey, they're coming around, just like you said. One of my sisters cashed her check. She has two kids in college. She's talking to me. It's a start."

"Are you going to kiss me?" Kate asked breathlessly.

"D'ya think I'm easy?" Gus grinned. "Not till I carry you over the threshold. We're moving in together, Kate. Grab one of those bags and let's get a move on."

He carried her over the threshold. Nothing in her life prepared Kate for the depth of emotion that swept through her. She loved this man, truly loved him, with every breath in her body. She said so.

"My God, I feel giddy," Gus said.

"I do, too," Kate said.

"We're going to do this right," Gus said nervously.

"Yes. If it isn't right, it won't work," Kate said. "What's right?"

"Jesus, I don't know, I had this all planned, I was going to . . . ravage you, have my way with you, make you want me, make you want me so bad you'd kill for me."

Kate laughed shakily. "It sounds good."

"Which part?" Gus asked hoarsely.

"All of it."

His voice came out in a squeak. "All of it?"

"Uh-huh."

"I had this plan, you see. . . . What it was . . . is . . . was, I was going . . . how many 'was' was that? Whatever, I was going to kiss you, get you all fired up, and then I was going to cool it and say, 'Let's go for a walk so I can show you this place.' We need to get that out of the way. Then I thought we'd come back here, mess around a little, clean up, maybe shower together, drive us both to the brink, and then we'd go to dinner. I signed you up this morning for six o'clock. We'd eat, drink a little, come back here and . . . and *do it*. What'ya think?"

"I think it all sounds like a wonderful plan. So, kiss me and let's get started."

It wasn't just a kiss, it was an event, Kate thought wildly as Gus's lips devoured hers. She moaned softly, opening her lips, felt his tongue spear into the silky recesses of her mouth and was rewarded with a deep animal sound that ground through her being. Their tongues meshed, wrapped around each other, until Kate drew away, gasping for breath. They gazed into each other's eyes. The only sound in the quiet hut was their breathing. Kate felt something primal about the way they were staring at one another. She wanted more, said so brazenly.

"About that walk and the rest of the plan . . ."

Kate's breath sighed in his ears when she said, "My feet hurt. Plans are meant to be broken. You're all the food I need."

"Brazen hussy," Gus said, ripping at his clothes. She ripped at hers.

Gus pulled down the parrot-colored spread that was identical to the one in Kate's hut. The sheets were crisp and white, unwrinkled. Pristine. Just the way I feel, Kate thought. The instant her head met the pillow, his body covered hers. There was a wild mating possessiveness to his embrace when he gathered her in his arms.

She felt a head rush, and then a small speck of alarm riveted through her, as if she were about to sail across an uncharted sea. She loosed a long, shuddering sigh as Gus's lips found and licked at the pulse in her neck. She curled into him so his lips could trail down to her breasts. She snuggled deeper, her fingers curling in the wiry furring on his chest, felt his involuntary tremor. She shivered in ecstasy when his tongue slid into the warm nectar of her mouth.

"Let go all the way, Kate," Gus whispered as his fingers skated up and down her spine, searching for the secret place between her thighs.

She could feel her body jerk to total awareness. She wanted more, much more, and said so. She was in a place now she'd never visited before, a place where she *wanted* to be, *needed* to be. She moved then, her hands cupping his face, smothering his mouth and chin with kisses before she explored his mouth with her hungry tongue.

"Oh, yeah, yeah. Don't stop," Gus groaned.

She felt powerful suddenly with his words, and proceeded to take the initiative, sliding smoothly on top of him. She smiled when she heard him groan again. The heat of his body mingled with hers, set off a banked fire she'd been holding in reserve all these years.

She teased him then, nibbling at his earlobes, whispering wondrous things in his ear while she explored the wet, slick length of him.

Before she knew what was happening, she was on her back, Gus over her, staring down at her. "You're so beautiful," he murmured. His hot breath seared her skin, making it impossible to think. All she wanted now, at this moment in time, was to feel, to taste, to *live*.

Her body was warm honey, her mouth a raging volcano he sought to conquer. "Do you like this?" he moaned.

"Oh, yes, yes, I do," Kate moaned in return. Hungrily she brought his lips to her again. She felt his knee part her legs. "Not yet," she purred, grinding her body upward against his. She felt him shudder, drawing her up, up, until they were locked together in a sitting position, their bodies slick with sweat, grinding and rocking to the beat of some unheard music.

His hands moved, sliding up and down the sides of her body. Needing the closeness of her, he drew her hard against him as she moaned, arching her back. He kissed her eyes, her lips, fiery kisses that trailed along her jaw, down to the valley between her breasts.

The burning heat from his body transferred itself to her, scorching her skin. She was a brushfire gone wild, a raging forest fire that only Gus could extinguish. His summer-blue eyes were burning, the only bright color she could see in the dim room.

"Now," he whispered fiercely.

"Yes," Kate whispered in return.

Her body was exquisite, her responses delicious, but it was the expression on her face, the rapture and pleasure he saw there, that drove him forward. He read total joy and a hint of disbelief in her clear gaze, saw a lone tear in the little hollow under her eye. When relief came to both of them, her name exploded from him like a gunshot in the quiet room.

Kate lay still, her breathing matching his in hard little spurts. She should say something, she thought, or he should say something. Anything. What? God, she hadn't known sex could be this perfect, this wonderful. "I *liked* that," she gasped.

"You did, huh?" Gus said, smooching her cheek. "Well, guess what? I liked it, too. Hell, I goddamn *loved* it! What took us so long to get around to doing this?"

"My stupidity. On the other hand, maybe you weren't aggressive enough," she teased.

"You want aggressive? I'll give you aggressive" — Gus laughed — "but later. You wore me out, lady. I need a breather." Jesus, he was happy. He couldn't ever remember being this happy. She was his now. "You are, aren't you?" he said anxiously.

"Are what?" Kate sighed.

"Mine."

"All yours, forever and ever," she said happily. "I've never been this happy. In the whole of my life no one ever treated me the way you do. No one ever seemed to care about me the way you do. I was so afraid of this . . . afraid I wouldn't — couldn't — that you would be disappointed. Patrick was always disappointed in me. I think I was afraid of what I would see in your eyes."

"What did you see in my eyes, Kate?" Gus asked.

"Love," she said shyly.

"Kate, you will never see anything but love in my eyes. You've made my life complete. I've been trying to tell you that for so long. Do you realize what we've been missing? When are we going to get married?"

Kate's stomach lurched. "Gus, don't rush me. I have other . . . demons to set aside. Our age difference is no small thing to me. I have to work that out in my mind. Legally . . . am I a widow? I don't know. Do I get a divorce? I never . . . there wasn't any need. . . . I don't want to leave California. You live in New York. You have a good job, I have a business. Can we, for now, just enjoy what we have, and work at the rest of it?"

"Only on one condition, that this time next year we're married. We should be able to resolve everything in twelve months. Say it, Kate. I need to hear you say you want to marry me twelve months from now. We can come back here and do it. Say it, Kate," he said fiercely.

"In one year we'll come back here and get married. I do want that, Gus, more than anything. Waking up with you next to me every morning will be wonderful. Cooking for you, making love with you, doing your laundry. I want to say nice things to you and mean them, and I want to hear you say nice things to me and mean them, too. I want to be with you to watch the sun come up, and I want to be with you when that sun sets at the end of the day. I do love you, more than I ever thought I could love a man."

Gus sighed happily. "Okay, I accept that."

They talked for hours, about everything and anything. When the torchlights were lit outside on the path, Gus said, "It's dark!"

"Now that's a brilliant deduction if I ever heard one." Kate giggled.

"I think we missed dinner," Gus said.

Kate snorted, a very unladylike sound. "Eat me," she gurgled. *God in heaven, did I say that?* "Let's go *ballistic* this time!"

Gus threw back his head and roared with laughter. He'd wakened a sleeping tiger. He obeyed the lady to the letter.

Kate stirred sleepily at three o'clock. She knew instantly where she was and what had transpired earlier. All the proof she needed was lying next to her. She smiled to herself in the darkness as she listened to Gus's lusty snores. A shout of happiness birthed in her belly, stretched upward, and was about to explode from her mouth when Gus's arms snaked out to draw her close. "Was I snoring?" he asked sleepily.

"Ohhh, you feel so good," Kate murmured, snuggling against him. "Yes, you snore, like a bull, but I like the sound. We made love four times," she said, her voice full of awe.

"You were counting?" Gus teased.

"Only after the third time. I'm wide-awake. I'm hungry. Actually I'm starved. I feel like . . . oh, I don't know."

"All charged up."

"Exactly."

"Want to go for a walk?" he asked. "We could get up, shower, go for a walk, come back to our front porch and watch the sun come up. And," he drawled, "I'm the guy who has two Hershey bars and a pack of *double* Oreo cookies in his flight bag. Plus . . . plus four bags of United Airlines peanuts and one banana. A veritable feast."

"Come on, come on," Kate said, bounding from the bed. A moment later she realized she was naked. She turned slowly to face Gus in the dim lamplight. "I want you to look at me in the light, Gus. I'm forty-six years old. I have stretch marks, a bit of a potbelly, and my butt is starting to droop. This is what I am. I need to hear you tell me it does or doesn't make a difference. I need to hear it now. I'm tired of sucking in my gut, tired of wearing control-top panties, tired of trying to cover up my . . . my imperfections."

"You want to compare bodies?" Gus said, swinging his legs over the side of the bed. He stood up. "So look and tell me you like tall skinny guys covered with hair from top to bottom. I look like a goddamn grizzly bear, and my hair is thinning on top, in case you didn't notice. It is also receding. My legs are skinny and go all the way up to my chest. But to answer your question, it doesn't matter, and you would be doing me a personal favor if you didn't suck in your gut anymore. I love you just the way you are. Get it through your head. Okay, it's your turn now," he said uneasily.

"Uh, your dick looks kind of wilted." Kate whooped and ran for the bathroom. God, did she really say that? Ellie would say something like that, not a forty-six-year-old mother. She turned on the shower full blast.

"Son of a fucking bitch!" He ran after her, yanked open the shower door and said, "You forgot to mention that you also need glasses. I'll accept your apology *now*."

She gave it, one hundred percent.

Later they walked barefoot up and down and around the trails, peering at the different huts, stopping to smell the hibiscus. Gus plucked one and slid it behind her ear. She picked one for him; he stuck it in the pocket of his T-shirt. His arms around her, they threaded their way past the dining room, the open-air bar, the gift store, and up to the beach.

"This is as near perfect as anything I ever experienced," Kate said, gentle waves lapping at her feet. "Everything just feels so right. It's hard to believe there's a world we have to go back to that is so ordinary. I wonder what it would be like to live here."

"It would probably get boring after a while. Places like this are just little slots of time God allows us to experience from time to time so we can exist in the real world. It occurs to me that we both have enough money to buy a house or condo over here if we want to. We could check out Maui. I hear it's lush and vibrant. We could get a boat. Maybe a Sunfish. Snorkeling gear. A jet ski. An open-air Jeep like the one you rented. We could be beach bums a couple of times a year."

"It sounds wonderful. Let's do that after . . . later on."

"Okay."

Hand in hand they walked back to their hut and watched the sun come up. They forgot about the peanuts, the banana, cookies, and candy.

For ten days they frolicked, always to return to their hut to make love for hours on end. When it was time to pack and leave, Kate cried. "I don't want to leave. I don't want to go back to an empty house. I don't want to have to worry about what Betsy is going to do next. I don't want to go into the office and work. I want to be with you. I don't want to give this up."

Gus started to unpack his bag, a wry grin on his face.

"I know we have to go back."

He started to repack.

"I could stay the rest of the month if I call Ellie and the office."

He started to unpack.

"But that's not fair to the office staff. If we stay, it won't be the same. You're right, we were allotted these ten days."

He started to repack.

"Don't you have something to say?"

"Are we going or not?"

"Yes, we are going, but I don't want to."

"Neither do I. It's going to be cold back home. Did you notice something, Kate? There's no air-conditioning in these huts."

"I know, which just goes to prove I'm more astute than you are. Did you know there are no keys?"

"Yep." Gus snapped the lock on his suitcase. He turned, placed his hands on Kate's shoulders. "These last ten days have been the most wonderful of my life. I would not trade them for anything. I love you so much it hurts me. I keep thinking I'm dreaming and when I wake up I'll know it was a dream. God, I love you, Kate. A year is too long to wait to get married. Can we move it up? I don't want you getting away from me. I'm serious, can we move it up?"

"To when?" Kate asked shakily.

"Next week. Hell, I'm ready now. I feel like dragging you back to the mainland and the nearest justice of the peace. Just soon. Will you consider it?"

"Of course." Maybe June, Kate thought. Or September. No, not June, she'd married Patrick in June, had been a June bride. August was a nice month.

They would part in San Francisco, Gus to fly on to New York and Kate to fly into LAX, where Ellie would pick her up, drive her home, and spend the weekend with her.

"I'll miss you," Kate said at the gate.

"I'll call you in the morning."

"Okay," Kate said in a choked voice. " 'Bye, Gus."

" 'Bye, Kate. I love you."

"I love you, too."

A moment later he was gone. She'd never felt so alone in her life. She was still wearing the lei he had placed around her neck. She thought she could smell his after-shave. In her hand she had a lei in a bubble box that she'd bought for Ellie. God, it was wonderful to be loved. To love someone and have that love returned tenfold.

With an hour to kill before her plane left, Kate walked into the lounge and ordered a Diet Pepsi. She fished around in her flight bag for a pen and paper to write Della a letter. She ended up with seven pages. Four lines concerned Kona Village, the rest was about Gus and his proposal. She ended the letter with, "I want you at my wedding. If

I have to, I'll come and get you. You must be here when I march down the aisle or march up the steps to the justice of the peace. I miss you terribly, Della. You are always in my thoughts, and you know there is a place in my heart reserved just for you. I send my love. Please call or write." She signed her name, licked a stamp. She spotted a mailbox outside one of the gift stores, dropped in the letter, sighed, and walked over to the gate, her ticket in hand.

It was unseasonably cold in Los Angeles when Kate got off the plane. She shivered in her cotton dress.

Heart soaring, Ellie handed her mother a heavy sweater. She'd never seen her look so happy, so full of life. She smiled from ear to ear and kept on smiling when her mother blushed. "Right now, right here, I want to know," she said.

"Ell-ieeee!" her mother admonished her.

"I don't care." She yanked her mother out of the way of the other travelers. "I played Cupid, I feel like Cupid, and I deserve to know. Was it great? Was it everything you thought it would be? — and I know you thought about it a lot. I don't want details, but I want to know that. God, you look so damn happy. Oh, Mom, I'm so happy for you. You deserve the best, and for you the best is Gus. I believe that in my heart, I really do."

"He asked me to marry him. It was wonderful, Ellie. And you're right, I have never, ever, been this happy. I said yes. My God, I really did say yes. He . . . he doesn't care that I'm forty-six. He doesn't care that my behind looks like cottage cheese. He loves *me*. I'm still a little hung up on the numbers, but I think I can handle it. I take it you approve of . . . all this."

"You got that right! You should have heard him that day you didn't answer the phone. He was wild, absolutely wild. He thought you'd been in an accident or something. He actually called several hospitals, and then of course the police. He truly loves you. By the way, what *was* that all about, anyway? You never did tell me."

Kate told her, in the middle of the moving walkway. Ellie doubled over laughing, and so did Kate. People turned to look at mother and daughter with amusement. "Did you tell that to Gus?" Ellie gurgled.

Kate nodded. "He fell off the chair laughing. Actually, I pushed him off."

"Is he a good lover, Mom?"

"The best," Kate said. "On a scale from one to ten, I'd give him a . . ."

"Yes, yes, what?" Ellie demanded.

"A nine and a half. No one is a ten," Kate said glibly.

Ellie hooted and she yanked at her mother's arm as they neared the end of the walkway.

Kate spent the weekend with her daughter, cooking and hanging out in the hot tub. At night they rented videos, all horror flicks to which Ellie was addicted. On Monday morning when Ellie left, Kate hugged her. "Thank you for going with your instincts and . . . and for arranging everything. I don't know if I could have done it on my own. I needed that push."

"It was all Gus's idea. I just went along with it."

"Ellie, does Betsy know about Gus?"

"Not from me she doesn't. If she knew, she'd be making all kinds of noise. If you want some advice, and I hate to say this, I don't think I'd mention it until it's a done deed. I keep hoping that one of these days she's going to get all her ducks in a row and come back to whatever is normal for Betsy."

"I think I'll take that advice, Ellie. Thanks for picking me up at the airport, and thanks for spending the weekend with me. I'm really glad you like your prospective in-laws. I knew they'd love you. Happy New Year, honey!"

"Same to you, Mom," Ellie said, hugging her mother.

The new year started out in a legal mode, with Kate paying visits to the Mancuso law office on a weekly basis. She wanted the Air Force to issue a death certificate, which they were reluctant to do. "I'm not going to fight or argue," Kate said after the sixth visit, in late May. "File for a divorce. I want it done quickly, and if it can't be done quickly, I'll go someplace else, like Nevada or Mexico. I want this behind me. I'm getting married, and I don't want any surprises along the way. I want everything legal."

Mancuso shrugged. "I'll do my best. I did manage to get you a clear title to the house in New Jersey. Anytime you want, you can sell it. Do you have a buyer?"

"As a matter of fact I do. I'm going to divide the money between Betsy and Ellie. Mr. Stewart is buying the house for his mother. I imagine he's going to put the deed in her name. It's a cash sale. He'll be sending all the papers to you. You have Ellie's address, so you can send all the papers to her. She does my taxes and the taxes for the corporation. This sale isn't going to come back and haunt me later on, is it?"

"I don't see how it could, Kate. Everything

is legal. Don't worry about anything. Go home and plan your wedding. By the way, when is it?"

"I was hoping for August or September, but it looks more like December at this point. I can't wait," she said, a girlish ring to her voice.

"I hope you'll be very happy."

"I don't just hope. I *know* I will be. Thanks for all your help, Nick. I never would have gotten this far if not for you."

"Kate, about Betsy. Do you have any idea of the kind of money she's been spending on all these searches she's been doing over the years?"

"A lot. She's dedicated her life to finding her father. It makes me sad when I hear she's begging for money on the streets to finance . . . whatever it is she does. Every lead fizzles, and still she keeps at it."

"Do you give her money?"

"When she asks, which isn't often," Kate said, then added nervously, "She doesn't know I'm planning on getting married."

"I see," Mancuso said, which meant he didn't see at all.

"I hope so. Keep in touch, Nick."

"Good luck, Kate," Nick said, extending his hand.

Would she need luck? She wasn't sure.

What's more, she didn't care.

Three days before Labor Day, Gus called, his voice full of excitement. "Kate, how would you like to go to Costa Rica with me for a week? Can you get away? I won this crazy trip and the tickets just arrived. I took my mother to this senior citizen thing and they were raffling off this prize and I goddamn won. Of course I bought all the tickets, so it was only natural that I would win. Pack your duds. I'll meet you at LAX."

"You bought all the tickets!"

"No one else wanted to buy them. The raffle was my mother's idea. I was with her when she was considering the prize. I had a feeling no one would want to buy them so I held out for Costa Rica. She wanted Disney World. Write this down. We're going to live in the bush, so don't bring any fancy clothes. You game, Kate?"

"I'll be there," she said breathlessly. "Did you really buy all the tickets? How much?"

"Ten grand's worth. The group had to make a profit. They're taking a bus trip to Atlantic City. I'm giving each of them twenty-five bucks for the slots and lunch and dinner at Resorts. I love you, Kate Starr, soon to be Kate Stewart."

"I love you, too, Gus Stewart."

"You have a passport, don't you?"

"Yep."

"Thank God. Now write."

Kate stuck the paper in her purse, stood, straightened the hem of her tailored jacket, looked around the office and said, "I'll be leaving now. I'm not sure when I'll be back. I have things to do and places to go. Carry on, ladies and gentleman."

From home she called Ellie, who squealed in delight. "In the bush! I love it. Go for it, Mom. When are you leaving?"

"Tomorrow."

She was light-headed, giddy, as she packed her bag and searched for her passport. She was going to see Gus again. "I'm blessed, truly blessed. Thank you, God, for sending him to me."

CHAPTER 17

Komsomolets Island, Russia

"Captain Starr, there is someone here who wishes to talk with you. Mr. Gorbachev himself has sent this visitor," a Russian guard said in broken English.

Patrick's heart leaped. He had a visitor. "What does it mean?" he said in Russian to his guard. They were friends now, teaching each other English and Russian.

"I do not know. Perhaps something to do with the American inspection of the missile sites. We are scheduled to destruct the launchers and ancillary equipment. The Americans are to supervise. Perhaps they want your opinion," he said slyly.

"And your ass goes in a sling when they see me. How are you guys going to explain keeping me here all these years? The shit is going to hit the fan. Finally. Come on, Sergi, is my visitor an American or Russian?"

"Both," Sergi said.

"You shittin' me?"

"That means what?"

"That means are you lying to me, you asshole?"

"Ah, yes, asshole I understand. Two visitors, one American, one Russian. They look important. Maybe American Express."

"You mean American embassy. You are stupid, Sergi. Well, let's go."

"First you shave, comb hair, wear clean shirt. Asshole!"

"Up yours," Patrick said, excitement rushing through him. It must mean something. It had to mean something. He cried when he shaved and combed his hair. He wiped at his tears with the back of his hand when he put on a clean shirt. He was shaking so badly he could hardly button his shirt. "Please God, let this be what I want it to be."

"It is time, asshole," Sergi said from the open doorway.

"No, no, I call *you* 'asshole,' not the other way around. Say you're sorry, Sergi."

"I'm sorry, what do I call you?"

"Try Captain Patrick Starr. I like the way that sounds."

The guard spit on the bare floor. "Move," he said sharply.

Patrick squared his shoulders and followed Sergi to a cold room with a table and four chairs. Seated at the table was one obviously Russian-looking man and an American who was thirty or so years of age — a good-looking young man with sandy hair and warm brown eyes that were now filling with moisture. His voice was husky and filled with emotion when he said, "Captain Starr?"

"God, yes. Yes, I'm Patrick Starr, United States Air Force. You found me!"

"Yes sir, we did. You're going to make your family very happy, sir."

The Russian held up his hand. "We talk first."

"I'm David Peterson, this is Vladimir Suidnetzy. Sit down, Captain Starr. We have things to discuss."

Patrick sat down, his breathing shallow. Why weren't they just taking him out of here? Now that they knew he was here, he should be walking away with this David Peterson, who was as old as he was when he bailed out over Vietnam twenty years ago. He felt frightened and tried not to huddle on his chair. He blanked everything out, moved himself to Westfield, New Jersey. He was a kid again, riding his bicycle up and down the street, waiting for the guys to come out and play stickball, one ear tuned to his father's call. Out of the corner of his eye he could see Kate Anders carrying a bag of trash to the curb. He sidled down the street, his feet propelling the Schwinn bike. "Whatcha doin', Kate? Need any help?"

God, she was pretty, probably the prettiest girl in school. He liked her smile and the thick blond braids that were always tied with colored ribbons to match her dress. She had on the same dress she'd worn at school, red-and-white checks with some kind of X-ing around the hem. "You going to the picnic on Saturday? They're gonna have all kinds of food and races and stuff. Huh?"

Kate's saddle shoes scuffed at the cracked concrete walk. He noticed they were polished, the white part real shiny and the laces just as white as the tips of her shoes. "If you go, I kind of thought we could walk around together. I have two dollars I've been saving. I bet I could win you something."

Kate blushed and continued digging at the crack. If she didn't watch it, she was going to scuff the leather off the tip of her shoe. "Maybe. If I get my chores done. I don't have any money, though. What could you win for me?" she asked shyly.

Maybe was almost as good as a yes. "You

know, one of those things on a stick. Maybe a monkey, maybe a bear. Something like that. Jack's mother is working at the hot dog stand. He said she'll give us all hot dogs."

"For free?" Kate asked in amazement.

"Well, sure. Will you try to go? I can meet you by the gate. Maybe you can get up early and do all your chores. I could even come by and ride you out to the picnic on my handlebars."

"What if my dress blows up?" Kate asked anxiously.

"Well heck, Kate, hold it down. I don't think there's going to be any wind. I've been paying attention to the weather reports. They always give 'em in advance when it gets close to the date of the picnic. There's gonna be an air show late in the afternoon. You're the prettiest girl in school," he blurted.

Kate turned beet-red. "You're good-looking, too. All the girls make goo-goo eyes at you. Janie Chalmers wants you to kiss her."

"Well, I'm not going to kiss her or anyone else. I'd kiss you, though, if you'd let me. Will you let me?"

"On the lips? I don't know about that. I'm only thirteen. My mother says I can't date or kiss boys until I'm eighteen."

"That's five years from now. Don't tell her. Kisses are nice."

"How do you know?" Kate asked suspiciously. "Who else did you kiss? I didn't think you were that type. You know, going around kissing girls. Who'd you kiss?"

"Swear you won't tell."

"I swear I won't tell," Kate said solemnly.

"Nancy Eggers."

"Nancy Eggers! Nancy Eggers! She's older than you and she has pimples. Why'd you kiss Nancy?"

" 'Cause she's the only one would let me. I wanted to see what it was like. I liked it. You'll like it, too. I'll show you how to pucker up. Don't wear lipstick."

Kate inched closer to the curb. "I'm not allowed to wear lipstick. C'mere . . ." She motioned him closer to the curb, leaned over, and planted a wet kiss on his lips. Then she jumped backward and ran into the house.

"Oooheeee, we saw that, Pat!" his friends hooted from across the street, where they'd been concealed behind the hedges. "Pat has a girl, Pat has a girl. Pat loves Kate. You love Kate, don't you?"

"Shut up, Danny, or I'll punch you in the mouth. Now, you want to play stickball or not?"

"Patrick . . ."

"Captain Starr, are you listening to me?"

"What?" Patrick said, returning from his

youth to the room he was in and the two men sitting across the table from him.

"Listen to me very carefully," David Peterson said.

"We should be walking out of here. Now. We shouldn't be sitting here talking. I'm a United States citizen and an Air Force officer shot down in the line of duty, and you want to fucking talk to me. Get me the fuck out of here!" Patrick said belligerently.

"I'm going to get you out of here, but first we have to talk."

"Why can't we talk on the way out?" Patrick snarled.

"Because we can't, and that's the best answer you're going to get at the moment. Now I want you to tell me what happened from 1971 until 1973 when you were brought here. We think you were sent here in 'seventy-four because that's when we lost track of you."

"How's my family? Do they think I'm dead? Do you have pictures of them? I want to see my family."

David Peterson opened his briefcase and withdrew several photographs. "Your daughters' graduation pictures. Their faces are circled. Your daughter Betsy has a doctorate degree. Your daughter Ellie is a CPA. This is a picture of your wife taken at your younger daughter's graduation."

Patrick's eyes filled with tears as he brought the pictures up close to his eyes. "I need glasses," he said. "My teeth are rotten and need to be fixed."

"That will all be taken care of. Now tell us what happened."

"Do you know any of it?"

"No, Captain Starr, I don't. I guess you could say I was sent here because I was in the U.S. embassy in Moscow when the call came in. I was the one who could get here the fastest. We don't want you here one minute longer than necessary. Please, the sooner you get on with it, the sooner we can get you out."

"During my first tour I was flying Thuds. You probably know them as F-105 Thunderchiefs. I shot down four North Vietnamese aircraft, one shy of making me an ace. On this tour I was flying an F-4E Phantom 11 fighter-bomber. I'd only been flying bombing and flak/missile suppression missions, so I didn't get a chance to get my fifth MiG to win ace status. That ate at me.

"The F-4E was a real honey of an aircraft — she could drop bombs on a dime in support of ground troops, *and* handle recon, radar/flak/missile suppression, and MiG hunting. I was carrying eight tons of ammunition, bombs, air-to-ground missiles, napalm, and a combination of fuel tanks. I also had a Vulcan — that's a twenty-millimeter cannon to you — that fired six thousand rounds a minute. God, I loved that plane.

"I was flying out of Ubon Air Base, Thailand, on this tour, as a member of the 547th Tactical Fighter squadron, part of the Eighth Tactical Fighter Wing. It was December fifth, 1970, and we were fragged, that is, scheduled to hit targets in North Vietnam. My primary target was the Radio Hanoi AM transmitter site — the NVA main propaganda and communication network. We were never able to put it out of commission.

"I was the leader of Romeo Flight. There were four F-4s, each of us equipped with two 'smart bombs' — two-thousand-pound laser-guided bombs. Our mission was to take out Radio Hanoi.

"The site was surrounded by a twenty-foot-high wall. I put every one of the fucking bombs right into the target area. At one P.M. Hanoi time, right in the middle of a vicious anti-American broadcast beamed in English to our troops in South Vietnam, I cut off their transmission.

"I zoom off at five hundred knots. My weapon-system officer reports the bombs smacked in the middle of the transmitter compound . . . when suddenly a surface-to-air missile detonates very close by with a hell of a flash and bang. Exploding fragments killed my WSO. My aircraft had serious damage to the hydraulic system. Christ, I had holes in my wings. I tried for as much altitude as I could get. I knew I'd never make it back to Thailand. The best I could hope for was to get out over open water where the U.S. Navy could pick me up. The others in the squadron who dropped their bombs warned me I was on fire. My cockpit filled with smoke and the F-4 started to yaw to the right, wanting to go into a roll. I knew then I couldn't control it. My wingman is yelling for me to punch out before the F-4 explodes.

"I knew my WSO was dead, he wasn't answering my calls, so I released my canopy and fired the ejection charges. I was dazed with the force of the ejection explosion, but I was okay. I'm swinging underneath this parachute. I activated my survival radio in my vest in case any rescue aircraft can locate my position once I'm on the ground. I didn't think there would be any rescue, but I hoped. I prayed all the way down. I landed in a rice paddy swarming with Vietnamese.

"Man, I literally fell into the arms of my captors. They immediately stripped me of everything but my flight suit. They didn't hurt me then. The next thing I knew, I was in a truck and driven blindfolded into Hanoi.

"I guess I was treated to the standard North Vietnamese routine for the first three days. I was yanked into the commandant's office at the end of the third day. He told me I was the lead aircraft that bombed the Hanoi transmitter site —" Patrick's voice faltered and broke. "It seems his fiancée was the one doing the broadcasting when I pulverized her. He was in such a fucking rage I thought he was going to kill me. They threw me in isolation and beat me senseless. There wasn't anything they didn't do to me. They told me they broke me. I have to believe they did, but I have no memory of it. The commandant got a kick out of repeating the things I told him.

"There were other Americans there. I heard them talking, but I was so bad off, I couldn't talk. They left me alone to rot in my cell for a week, maybe it was longer, I don't remember. I tried to scratch my name in the wall, but I don't know if I did. Maybe I thought I did it.

"More time passed. Maybe weeks. Maybe months." Patrick shrugged. "Anyway, one morning — it was still dark outside — my guards took me to the commandant's office, where he served me up this speech. He said he'd informed the Russians that I was a highly skilled pilot and someone they would like to talk to. It was his revenge, he said. He said I would never see my country again or my family. Then I was brought here to this missile base.

"At first the KGB was all over me, questioning and testing me, demanding long technical descriptions of various American fighter aircraft and aerial weapons and electronics gear. They wanted to know it all. I resisted at first, but they wore me down with drugs. One of the guards told me I was like a vegetable for a long time. I don't know how long. That was the end of it. The guards told me that over the years they forgot about me. They'd go off on a furlough and come back, and after a while we almost became friends. Once or twice they even brought me a woman. I never had enough to eat, was never warm enough. Sometimes they gave me aspirin. Once, one of the guards took pity on me and pulled out a molar that was decayed. With pliers.

"I was passed from one commandant to another. I guess you could say I was their mascot. Life was tolerable. I was alive, but that was all. I never gave up hope I would be found.

"I learned Russian, and I tried to teach

two of the guards English. We managed to communicate. Sergi told me about the Strategic Arms Treaty and said maybe I'd be sent home. I hung on to that. I've been counting the days, just waiting for the American inspection of this missile site. I figured they'd hide me when that happened, so I've been working on Sergi, hoping he'd let something slip or outright tell the Americans I was here. I told him if I got out, I'd take him back to America with me. The jerk wants to meet Jane Fonda.

"That's my story, Mr. Peterson. Now, how did you find me? Who told you I was here? There hasn't been an inspection."

"Gorbachev has taken over and he's initiated glasnost," Peterson said. "You know about START. They called. On the telephone. The White House. They offered to return you if you agree to keep your mouth shut until Gorbachev's government reforms are securely in place. The question now is, will you keep your mouth shut? If you agree, sign on the dotted line, you walk. That means no parade. No interviews with the press. No nothing. We move you home, you join your family. We say, if necessary, you are a cousin of Patrick Starr. The government will compensate you. You have to understand you will not go home to a hero's welcome. Unfair,

I grant you, but that's the way it is."

He was back in Westfield at his high school graduation, decked out in his cap and gown. He was valedictorian of his graduating class, his speech firmly in mind. He was going to locate Kate and speak directly to her so he wouldn't get nervous. She'd curled her hair and was wearing pink lipstick.

It was all planned; they were going to run away together after graduation. He had $700 and Kate had $290. They'd get other gifts of money at graduation, enough for them to pack up his clunker and head out to Texas, where he'd been accepted at Texas A&M. He was going for his B.S. in engineering. He was going to join ROTC and get his commission in the USAF. From there he'd go on to get his M.S. in aerospace engineering. If he was lucky, with Kate at his side, he'd try for the U.S. Test Pilot School at Edwards AFB, California.

Kate was confident she could make a home for them cheaply, baby-sit children for extra money. He'd work part-time. Kate said they could do it. He believed her.

Off we go, into the wild blue yonder . . .

"Captain Starr, I'm waiting for your answer."

"Does my family know?"

"Not yet. No one is jumping the gun here.

We take you home, quietly, if you agree to the terms."

"I only survived because of Kate. All I did was think about her, about the girls. I always knew I'd get home. Do you pray, Mr. Peterson?"

"Yes."

"I didn't, not for a long time. I thought God forgot about me. Of course I wasn't thinking clearly. Why is it when things are the hardest, when it can't get any worse, people turn to God? It's almost an afterthought. I thought God wiped me out of the picture, but I knew Kate would never forget me. Kate loved me, loves me," he said, his voice breaking. "I'll sign your damn paper, but only because I want to see my wife and children. You'll have to read it to me since I can't make out the print."

Patrick listened to Peterson's flat, emotionless voice. "I guess you know I'm signing this under duress. I have no lawyer here to advise me. I want that understood. You're fucking me over. You know it, I know it, and this asshole sitting next to you knows it." He signed his name, an illegible scrawl. Later he would tell the truth. For now all he wanted was to get back to Kate, to smell her heavenly vanilla-lemon-scented hair. He wondered if she'd bake a chocolate cake for him. Would it be sitting in the middle of the kitchen table?

"If you talk, we say you defected," Peterson said coolly.

He was crying when he walked out of the bare, cold room in his coarse shirt and baggy wool trousers that hadn't been washed in a long time. His boots had holes in the soles and were stuffed with rags.

Jesus Christ! He was going home!

CHAPTER 18

"Can you believe we've been here a whole week?" Gus asked from the shade of a lush tree.

Kate finished the banana she was eating. "Time has whizzed by. You know, I never thought I would ever see a rain forest. I'm so happy we came here. It's a beautiful country, but I wouldn't want to live here. There's no place like the good old U.S. of A.," she said, snuggling in the crook of his arm.

"What I like best is there are no phones, no newspapers, no radios. I feel so insulated. The word *safe* comes to mind, but it isn't the one I'm searching for. I'll say one thing, though, I'm probably never going to eat another banana."

"And give up all this wonderful potassium?"

"Uh-huh. Have you come up with a date, Kate?"

"I feel guilty going off and getting married in a strange place. I'd like my girls to be there. At least Ellie. I doubt if Betsy would come. And I want Della, and the girls from the office. We could still get married by the J.P. if you want."

Gus cuddled her close. "I don't care either way. I just want us to be married. Period. I can deal with anything as long as that's the outcome. Women like that stuff. Men don't care. A date? I need to hear a date."

"What about a candlelight service at a Unitarian church and a small party at the house afterward? We can fly out that night from LAX and be in Hawaii the following morning. Or we can have a dinner party at least, in a hotel in Los Angeles. I haven't found a dress yet," Kate fretted.

"Burlap will do nicely. A date. I'm not hearing a date."

"How about Saturday, December fifteenth?"

"God, you actually set a date," Gus said in awe. "I've been thinking you'd switch up on me or change your mind. It's a given, then?"

"It's a given," Kate said quietly.

"Kate, we've never really talked about Patrick. Maybe we should. I don't want . . . what I mean is, I don't think I could handle it if you made comparisons. I don't want a third person living with us even if he's a memory. You have let go, haven't you?"

"Of course. Many years ago. Time, my darling, heals just about everything. It's sad to say, but I can hardly remember what Patrick looked like. I could never compare you to him. You are so totally different, so warm, so caring, so giving. Patrick wasn't like that. I loved him, though, very much. He was the father of my children. There will be no ghosts between us. I packed up all his pictures and the few things I kept in a drawer that belonged to him. I cried my tears then. Part of me will always wonder what happened to him. I think that's natural and normal. If I think about him from time to time, I'll tell you about it. There won't be any secrets between us."

"I love you very much, Kate Starr. I can't wait to call you Mrs. Kate Stewart. Do you think you'll have trouble adjusting to your name?"

Kate laughed, a joyous sound. "Hardly. I practice writing it every chance I get. I guess we're going to have to get a his and hers checking account. Speaking of checks, when do you think your other brothers and sisters will cash their checks?"

"I'm hoping by Christmas, so I can wrap up that chapter in my life. I can't sell that damn estate, though. Seems like no one wants to pay eight mil for it. I dropped the price five hundred thousand and had no takers. Until some moneybags comes along, it's just going to sit there. The siblings want no part of it. So they say."

"Did you keep your share of the money? You should, you know."

"Yeah, it's in an investment account at Merrill Lynch. I got a real savvy broker named Gary Kaplan. Mike Bernstein, the CPA I hired, is just as savvy. They take care of everything. Jeez, I forgot Ed Grueberger, the estate planner I hired. You need to know all this, Kate, in case anything happens to me."

Kate went rigid in his arms. "Do not *ever* use those words to me again. I don't want to know, don't want to hear about wills and junk like that. I can't go through all that. Swear to me, Gus," she said vehemently.

"I swear. Okay, okay, relax. Come on, let's go skinny-dipping before you get your knickers in a twist."

Kate was peeling off her clothes as she ran to the water. She dived in, her rump in the air. Gus whooped his delight and followed her, overtaking her with five sure, deft strokes. "Want to make love?"

"We've done that for seven straight days. Why do you think I tricked you into the pool?" Kate gurgled.

A long time later she said, "That was delicious."

Gus hugged her. "Speaking of delicious, what are we having for dinner?"

"Bananas, crackers, and Hershey bars. It was your idea, Mr. Stewart, for us to go off on our own. We'll live off the land, you said. The only thing growing on this land as far as I can see is bananas. Take it or leave it. Tomorrow when we get to the airport we can eat real food. Maybe a steak or a chunk of chicken with stuffing and gravy. God, I could eat a whole cow right now," Kate muttered.

"Cows give milk. Steers are for meat," Gus said, nibbling on her ear playfully. "So it wasn't one of my better ideas. I thought there would be other fruit. I really don't care what we eat as long as we eat it together. Still, a steak would be nice."

"It's been a wonderful vacation, but I don't think I want to come back here, do you?"

"Nah, it's too primitive. At least we know what we like and what we don't like. I'm really looking forward to our trip to Hawaii — our honeymoon. As Mr. and Mrs. Gustav Stewart. I didn't think it would ever happen."

"I didn't either," Kate said softly. "I love you so much, I ache sometimes just thinking about you. I'm afraid something will go awry, that you'll meet one of those Gennifer types and not want me. I worry about that. Those numbers won't go away."

"I can't change the numbers, Kate. But they don't mean anything to me. They shouldn't mean anything to you, either. We're getting married and will spend the rest of our lives keeping each other happy. That's all that matters to me."

"You are the dearest man, Gus Stewart. When I'm seventy years old and drooling, I'm going to remind you of those words. I'd like to make love again, if you don't mind."

"Whatever you want, lady," Gus said, smothering her face with kisses. "Whatever you want.

"I want," Kate purred.

The following evening, while Gus checked their baggage, Kate presented her tickets to the agent behind the counter along with both passports.

"Mrs. Starr, there's a cablegram here for you. One moment while I fetch it."

Kate's heart leaped in her chest. She looked around for Gus and immediately panicked when she didn't see him. Something must have happened to Ellie or Betsy. "Oh, God, no, please, let them be all right," she murmured. He was coming toward her, in silhouette, the sun from the doors at his back. She felt herself sway, heard the ticket agent call her name.

"What's wrong?" Gus asked, his face masked in worry.

"Mrs. Starr, I have your cable."

She saw Gus reach for it and then felt him lead her away to a quiet area. He fingered the yellow square gingerly. "We have to open it," he said nervously.

"I know, but I'm afraid. I just know something's happened to the girls. Maybe they were in a car accident. I wasn't there for them. I was off in the damn jungle fucking my brains out. I'm their mother. How long have they had that cable?"

"I don't know," Gus said quietly. He felt something between his shoulders he'd never felt before.

"Ask. I'm not opening this until I know," Kate cried. "God, what if they're dead?" She was talking to herself; Gus was at the ticket counter.

"Five days."

"Five days!" Kate cried in anguish. "Five days!"

"That's what she said. Do you want me to open it, or will you do it?"

"You do it," Kate said, burying her face in her hands. "Which one? Please, God, don't make this be serious, whatever it is. Please, God. I'll do anything. Let my girls be all right."

"Kate."

Kate looked up, her heart in her eyes. Her shoulders slumped when she saw Gus's white face. "Which one?"

"Neither. Your daughters are fine."

Kate jumped up, her arms waving wildly. "Thank you, God, thank you! Did the office burn down, what is it? I can handle anything as long as I know the girls are okay. Della! It's Della, isn't it?"

"No, Kate, it isn't Della. The office didn't burn down, either. It's your husband. He's on his way home. The telegram reads, 'Dear Mom, a Mr. Peterson called to say he's bringing Dad home. He wants us all at the house for his arrival.' It's signed 'Ellie.' "

Kate slid to the floor in a dead faint. Gus dropped to his knees to gather her close to him. "Kate, Kate, snap out of it! Come on, we're going to the bar. We need to talk this over . . . we need to call your daughter.

Kate, please snap out of it." Lightly he whisked his fingers back and forth across her cheek.

"I don't believe this," Kate said when she came out of it and struggled to a sitting position.

A crowd was gathering. Gus waved them away.

"This can't be happening," she said in the bar as she gulped at the fiery brandy. "It must be a mistake. I don't know a David Peterson. It's a mix-up. Twenty years is too long. I'm sure it's a mistake. We have to call. You do it, Gus. I can't . . . I don't . . . please," she begged. Her eyes rolled back in her head. Gus reached for her, his heart pounding like a triphammer in his chest.

"Kate," he said harshly, "get it together. I know this is a shock, but I can't have you going off the deep end here. We'll deal with this." Yeah, sure, he thought, that's got to be the understatement of the decade.

Kate shook her head. "It has to be a cruel joke. Something Betsy would do. Gus," she said frantically, "see if there's an American newspaper in one of the shops. If what that cable says is true, there will be something in the paper."

Kate watched as Gus sprinted off. Watched

and waited. A group of college students loaded down with camping gear and backpacks straggled past her, their boombox blasting. She kneaded her thighs and knew she was going to be bruised.

At last she raised her eyes to see Gus loping toward her, his face white beneath his tan. She wondered how white her own face was. She felt herself start to grieve. "There's nothing in this paper," he said, holding up a three-day-old copy of the *Wall Street Journal*. "Some woman had a copy of the *New York Times* she'd brought with her yesterday. I asked if I could look at it. There was nothing in it, either."

"I told you, it's a cruel joke of some kind. Who would do such a terrible thing?"

"The telegram has Ellie's name on it. She wouldn't play a joke on you. We have to call her, Kate. As it is, I think we're going to miss the plane. I have no idea how this telephone system works down here. Then there's the time difference." He waited for Kate's response. His heart and gut told him it was not a cruel joke. And why the hell should anything go his way? All along he'd known it was too good to be true. He'd lived in fear that Kate would change her mind about him, but the one thing, the only thing, he'd never factored into his fear was Patrick Starr's return.

"I don't know what to do," Kate whimpered. She held up both hands. "I'm not going home. I can't deal with that. I wouldn't be able to hold up to all the publicity, living in a fishbowl. They can't make me go back. Gus, what's going to happen to us?"

"You filed for a divorce," Gus said desperately, knowing it made absolutely no difference. Kate's first loyalty, her *only* loyalty, was to her husband, and that left him out in left field without a mitt. He felt like crying. He didn't want to say it, but the words trembled from his lips, driven by a force he couldn't control. "You have to go back, Kate. If all this is true, I can't even begin to comprehend what your husband must be feeling. He deserves . . . to have you and his daughters. I could never fight that."

Kate cried softly into a wad of tissues. "I can't even remember what Patrick looks like. He won't be the same person. He can't be the same person. *I'm* not the same person. Why is this happening to me? I know why," she said, jumping to her feet. "Because I've been unfaithful. God is punishing me."

"Kate, honey, you can't look at it like that. God doesn't punish his children. He's sending Patrick home after . . . God, after nearly twenty years. That itself is a miracle in my eyes. How it affects us isn't important."

"My God, Gus, you sound like you're on his side," Kate cried desperately. "What about us? What about all the plans we made?"

Gus dropped to his knees as the loudspeaker called their flight. "Kate, my feelings for you will never change. You have to know that and believe it as well. Because I love you with all my heart and my soul I can . . . try to step aside. Let's call your daughter now and find what's going on. That was the last boarding call, so we have time now. We've had our shock and we're going to deal with it."

Kate followed him in a trance, her gait stiff-legged. She watched as Gus fished out his calling card, placed the call, and then handed her the phone. She shook her head violently.

It was an hour before they were able to reach Ellie. Their hands clasped together, Gus and Kate sat on hard plastic seats, eyes glued to the telephone three feet away. When it finally rang, they went to answer it with their hands still locked together. His voice was rough, sounding raspy when he said, "Ellie, did you send the telegram?"

"Yes, I did, Gus. Can I talk to Mom?"

"Then it's real. There wasn't anything in the papers," Gus said, as though that fact alone would make it all unreal. "We're still at the airport, we missed our flight. Ellie, your mother is in shock. She asked me to call. She's standing right here. Now, tell me what happened." He sucked in his breath as he listened. Kate stared off into space.

"The day after you left, a man named David Peterson called me, and then someone else came to my apartment. They had Betsy with them, so they told us together. Dad's been in Russia all this time. The Vietnam government turned him over to them after he was captured. He's here in the United States — Washington, I think. They didn't tell us. All they said was he was in a holding area. They won't bring him home until Mom gets here. It's all hush-hush. Betsy claims to know what's going on, and she won't share her information until Mom gets here. She's like an angry hornet right now. I wouldn't tell her where Mom was, only that she was on vacation and I'd try and get in touch."

Gus's shoulders slumped. "Why wasn't anything in the papers? I would think the world would want to know. I'm a reporter, for Christ's sake! I know about stuff like that."

"They know all about you, Gus. Not from me, so don't think I spilled my guts. Betsy doesn't know but *they* know. They want to talk to you, too, when you get back. But separately. Someone is going to be at LAX at customs. I don't know who *they* are. Important people from the government, I guess. How's Mom taking this, Gus?"

"She's in shock, like I said." They wanted to talk to him. His reporter's antennae went up and his nose started to twitch. "As I told you, we missed our flight. The next one out is around nine tonight. Can you meet your mother?"

"Yes. I'm supposed to call Mr. Peterson."

"Is this call being monitored?" Gus asked suspiciously.

"I wouldn't be a bit surprised," Ellie said quietly. "These people are . . . very cold. They made me feel like I did something wrong. They don't smile. Look, tell Mom I love her. I love you, too, you big schmuck. Take care of her. She loves *you,* and don't you ever for one minute forget it."

"All right. See you later."

"Well?" Kate said hoarsely, when Gus had hung up.

He repeated his conversation. "I don't know what it means. If I were to assume — and a good reporter never assumes — I'd say they're waiting for you to get home and then they'll spring this wonderful, joyous homecoming. I'm sure there's an avalanche of accusations, denials, and all kinds of shit hitting the fan. How the hell did he get to Russia, and why? Somebody is going to have to come up with some answers. Ellie said it's all hush-hush, so I assume the parties concerned are busy trying to cover their asses."

"It's true, then."

"Yes, Kate, it's true," Gus said quietly.

"I buried him . . . his things. But I also buried him in my mind. I really believed he was dead. Ellie believed, too, because of me. Betsy was the only believer. God, I wish I were dead," Kate moaned.

"Don't say that," Gus said, his arms about her shoulders. He led her back to the hard plastic chair. "Something's not right about all of this," he muttered. "Ellie told them where you were. They could have found us in a heartbeat if they really wanted to. Listen, can I have your permission to call my paper and ask a few questions?"

"Of course. No one told us not to ask questions. I'll wait here for you."

Kate watched him walk away. What would she say to Patrick? Hi, how are you? I've missed you. Gee, it's good to have you back. By the way, I'm in love and I'm getting married in two months. You understand, don't you? No, I don't have feelings for you anymore. I buried you. I sold your father's house to Gus and gave the money to Ellie and Betsy. I thought you were dead, never coming back. I have a life, too. I put it on hold for twenty years. What about me? What about me?

She cried harder, sniffling and blowing her nose every few seconds. "Damn you, Patrick! Damn you for ruining my life a second time."

Forty-five minutes later Gus took his seat next to her. "No one knows anything. *Nada.* I had my chief call the foreign chiefs, and there've been no leaks of any kind. Everyone is going to be sniffing now. I might have stirred something up."

"So what?" Kate said belligerently. "I can't let his coming back ruin my life. Again."

"Kate, don't think like that. This is something you have to do. You owe it to your husband. The selfish part of me doesn't want you to go back. While I was waiting for news at the phone, I thought about all the money at Chase and the estate. I thought about running off with you, but that's not what you and I are all about. We're decent, normal human beings who had the good fortune to fall in love with one another. I'm telling you, you have to go back, face your husband, and do whatever is best for the two of you. It is the decent, human thing to do. And you know it."

"What about us?"

"I have this feeling that when we land at LAX, there won't be any 'us.' I might not have the chance to tell you later, but I understand. I will always love you, that's never going to change. Whatever you decide to do, I'll accept."

"I can't picture my life without you in it," Kate said quietly. "I've been unfaithful to Patrick."

"Not knowingly," Gus said.

"It doesn't matter. I broke my marriage vows. That's a sin in the eyes of God."

There was nothing for Gus to say, so he remained quiet. He reached for her hand.

"I feel like smashing something," Kate said a long time later.

"I could probably destroy this entire airport single-handedly," Gus said an hour or so before their flight was scheduled to leave. "Let's go get a drink. I think we deserve one."

In the bar, Kate held her glass of beer aloft, her eyes blazing angrily. "I want to drink to the would-haves, the should-haves, the could-haves."

Gus chomped down on his lower lip before he clinked his glass against hers.

"Will we stay in touch? Can we still call each other?"

Gus nodded. "Anytime you want. I'll always be here for you. Listen to me, Kate.

I have this feeling . . . my reporter's instinct, that all is not what it seems. I want you to promise me something. When we get back, listen to what people have to say. Don't agree to anything. Don't disagree with anything. The most I want you to say to anything, is, 'I'll think about it.' Then call me, but not from home. Call me from a phone both and at the office. Can you promise me that?"

"Yes. Yes, of course. You sound so . . . dramatic, so . . . What is it you're trying to say?"

"I think I'm remembering the way my story got squelched and that 'keep quiet policy' they bound all you wives to. Government agencies have power you wouldn't believe. They use power against people like you, and they try to use it against big papers like mine and reporters like me. Don't make promises you'll regret later. It's important, otherwise I wouldn't ask it of you."

"I think you just scared me, Gus."

"Good. Keep it that way."

"Will you call me?" Kate asked wistfully, in a small voice.

"I don't think that will be a good idea. What if Patrick picks up the phone? Your office probably isn't a good idea, either. It'll be best if you call, when you can, from outside. Tell Ellie the same thing. Betsy is sharp, she probably already figured all of this out, whatever *this* turns out to be."

"There's something fishy here, isn't there, Gus?"

"The newshound in me says yes. Kate, I . . ."

"I know," Kate said softly.

The four-and-half-hour flight was made in virtual silence. They held hands, their knees touching, each of them busy thinking. When the plane landed, they were the last to leave, postponing the inevitable as long as they could. When they walked through the door, two men stepped forward. They had a twin look about them, a government look, Kate thought. One called her by name and one called Gus by name. They spoke at the same moment: "Come with me, Mr. Stewart."

"Come with me, Mrs. Starr."

Kate felt a hand at her elbow and flinched away. "Take your hands off me right now," she said viciously. "If you don't, I'll scream my head off."

"Easy does it, Mrs. Starr, I'm here to help you. Don't do anything foolish." His voice was the same as Bill Percy's, her old case-worker. They must have all studied under the same elocution teacher, she decided.

"Where are we going?" Kate demanded.

"To a private room where we can talk. Your daughters are there waiting for you."

"Then why was Mr. Stewart taken separately? What's going on?"

"Shouldn't you be asking questions about your husband?" the man said coldly.

"Don't tell me what I should and shouldn't do. I asked you questions and you asked one in return. I'm going to ask you again, and if you don't answer, be advised my lungs are strong." She stopped short, slamming up against the agent to make her point. Those long-ago days of bullying and intimidation were gone.

The man at her side stared at his charge, correctly interpreting her state of mind. This was one woman who'd make good on her threat. "Mr. Stewart is a reporter," he said curtly.

"What does that have to do with anything?" Kate demanded, her feet rooted to the carpet.

"In matters of national security we have a certain protocol to follow. Your daughters are waiting. They've been waiting for hours. You weren't on your scheduled flight," he said coldly.

"So what!" Kate snapped.

"So you've kept everyone waiting. I suggest you move along here, Mrs. Starr."

"And if I don't?" Kate said belligerently.

"Then I'll have to resort to other measures."

"You can't talk to me like this. Maybe once because I was dumb and thought I had to take it. Not now, Mr. whatever the hell your name is. You — you're kidnaping me!"

"I'm *not* kidnaping you, and my name is Eric Spindler. I work for the State Department."

"You say you work for the State Department. How do I know that? You didn't show me any identification." But even as he reached into his suit coat pocket for his wallet she said, "I've changed my mind. I'm not going anywhere with you. Now what are you going to do?" she asked him. "You're invading my privacy and . . . and you can't make me do anything unless you're arresting me. I want a lawyer and I want one now!"

"You're being unreasonable, Mrs. Starr," he said, managing to flex open his wallet as they walked, revealing his badge. "All I want to do is talk to you in private with your daughters in attendance. Thirty minutes at the most and then you're free to go."

"I'm free to go now, isn't that right, Mr. Spindler? I have rights, and you are stepping on those rights. I want a lawyer present when we talk."

"For every minute you delay this, that's

another minute Captain Starr is being detained. Do you have any idea how those minutes count to him? Put yourself in his place, Mrs. Starr. Look, I understand how this must seem to you. I have orders, I follow them. You have every right to an attorney, and you're also right, I cannot make you go with me. I told you the truth — all I want to do is talk to you and your daughters."

"Mr. Stewart?"

"Mr. Frazer is talking to Mr. Stewart. Same deal. No one is going to be held against their will. It's been a long night, Mrs. Starr, for everyone concerned. Please cooperate."

"I'm going to hold you to that thirty minutes, Mr. Spindler."

"Fine. This is it," Spindler said, holding the door open to a small cluttered room with three desks and four chairs and stacks and stacks of baggage tickets. The room was airless, with no windows, and smelled like garlic and peppers. Four suitcases rested one on top of the other. Kate wondered if they would fall over if one moved the wrong way.

"Mom!" Ellie and Betsy said in unison, rushing to her. The suitcases toppled. No one picked them up. Kate held out her arms to them, tears dripping down her cheeks.

"All right, Mr. Spindler, you have thirty minutes. The clock is ticking," Kate said, looking at her watch.

"Your husband is safe and sound. He's in a . . . what we call a holding area, going through a process of debriefing and medical testing. As a matter of national security, your husband must be returned to you and your family as . . . Harry Mitchell. Captain Starr has agreed to this. It was one of the terms of his release by the Russians. Now do you understand why Mr. Stewart is not involved? His first loyalty is to the paper he works for." Kate and her daughters said nothing.

"Your husband will join you tomorrow. He'll leave Washington in the morning and arrive on your doorstep at approximately three o'clock in the afternoon. We need the same assurance from you, in writing, that we got from Captain Starr, that you will not divulge to anyone that he is indeed your husband."

"What he's saying, Mom," Betsy said, "is our side screwed up and we pay for it. Dad is denied a hero's welcome. He gave twenty years for his country, and his country now wants to deny his very existence. The end does not justify the fucking means, Mr. Spindler," Betsy snarled.

"There are no choices here, no options, ladies," Eric Spindler said coolly.

"He's right, Mom. If we don't sign his

damn paper, if we don't do whatever he says, they'll stick Dad somewhere else for another twenty years. He has us all right where he wants us."

"Is that true?" Kate demanded, knowing her daughter spoke the truth. "How did this happen?"

"I'll tell you how. No one wanted to listen to me," Betsy spat. "I believe, and can just about prove, that the Defense Intelligence Agency and the CIA had a pretty good idea at least one American was being held in the USSR who was reported MIA in Vietnam, but nobody in the White House wanted to act on the information because they were afraid of both domestic and overseas reactions to such information. So to avoid embarrassment at home and to ensure friendly talks with the Russians, the information was buried. Dad is the loser. Tell me I'm wrong, Mr. Spindler," Betsy said tightly.

She's right on the money, Kate thought as she stared at the expression on Eric Spindler's face. She hated him the way she'd come to hate Bill Percy. So many lies. Everything was a lie.

"What's more," Betsy said, "we'll all be under surveillance from now on. Our phones will probably be bugged, our mail gone through. Someone will always be watching us. One false move and we're all history. People die every day. People disappear. I'm not saying it will happen, but it is a possibility. Ellie and I talked about this all night, and she agrees. Sign the paper and let's go home, but I think we should rent a car. At least we'll know it isn't bugged. Our life as we knew it is gone, and we can only imagine what it must have been like for Dad."

Gus, Kate thought. He wasn't overreacting. He'd told her to watch and listen, but not commit herself to anything. "For how long?" she asked coldly.

"Until we tell you otherwise," Spindler said.

"That means forever. Otherwise you'll be considered a traitor to your country. Don't waste your time reading it, it's all bullshit," Betsy said, taking a fountain pen from her purse. She scrawled her name and shoved the paper toward her sister along with the fountain pen. She had no other options. Patrick was the only thing that mattered now. Kate had to borrow it from Ellie to sign her name.

"I don't suppose we get a copy of this?" Betsy snapped.

Spindler's face registered disgust.

"Is this the same agreement my husband signed?" Kate asked.

"I can't tell you that." He folded the papers and placed them in his briefcase. "Customs has been taken care of. Your baggage is alongside Carousel Three. You're free to go."

"Dickhead," Betsy spat as she shouldered past Spindler to get to the door.

"Fuckface," Ellie snarled.

"Asshole," Kate snapped. But, that wasn't true, an asshole served a purpose.

"This is not a happy time," Betsy said bitterly. "I thought there would be a parade, the President would shake Dad's hand, the whole nine yards."

"It's sneaky. They're making your father sound like he did something wrong. Knowing him, I'm surprised he didn't spit in their faces and refuse to sign the paper. We should have read it," Kate said.

"I'm going to get a rental," Betsy said. "I'll meet you right in front."

"Is all this necessary?" Kate asked Ellie, her face puckered with worry. "Did you tell her about Gus?"

"No, but fuckface did. I think she knew. She didn't say a word. Mom, it'd blow your mind to know what she knows. All those groups, all those organizations she belongs to. She says there are still men in Vietnam. She can prove it, too. No one will listen, no one will help. All these years . . . and she was right. I gotta tell you, when Donald died, she went to mass — she converted, you know. She had mass said and she went to the cemetery a few days . . . after. She's the one who put the flowers there. She'll go up against anybody, like she did to that guy back there, go to the wall and not think twice, but she couldn't handle Donald's death. She's got guts, Mom. More than I'll ever have. She's going to apologize. If we want her back in the family, we have to take her as she is."

Kate nodded. "I thought she was going to . . . to punch out his lights back there."

"Me too. Mom, how did Gus take all this? You must be devastated. You can handle it, can't you?"

"I hope so. I'm numb right now. Gus was . . . was . . . He said he understood. I think he does. He's a good, kind man."

"I know that. It's you I'm worried about. Can you handle this?"

"I think so. I don't see that I have choices or options at this point. Whatever is best for your father, I'll do. Without reservations. What about you, honey?"

Ellie shrugged. "I'll be meeting a stranger. I really don't remember Dad. I'm open to a father-daughter relationship. I can stay a few days if you think it advisable. Betsy is, too. He's going to be like a stranger, even to you, isn't he?"

"I'm afraid so. It's been twenty years since I've seen your father, give or take a few months. Betsy . . ."

"Has a mouth on her. Guess she gets it from all the people she hangs out with. I still can't believe she has her doctorate. When did she do it, in her sleep? Who does she get her brains from?"

"From her father. You do too. I was the slow-witted one. I always felt so inferior to him, like I could never measure up."

"He's going to be real proud of you now. You have a degree and a successful business with three offices. That's not shabby."

Kate felt pleased with her daughter's compliment. "Do you think Betsy is overreacting? That bit about the CIA and that other organization . . . is that possible?"

"Betsy says it is. I believe her."

"Is she right about the surveillance? Gus more or less said the same thing. He made me promise not to agree with anything, and what do I do? I do the exact thing he warned me not to do."

"We didn't have a choice, Mom. Anything else would have been cruel to Dad. We did the right thing. We'll live with it."

"I don't have a good feeling about this,

Ellie, and it has nothing to do with Gus. That's my bag, the one with the flowers. It has wheels."

On the walk to the sliding doors where Betsy would be waiting, Kate said to Ellie, "I just came in from a foreign country and didn't go through customs. There's no stamp on my passport. Officially Gus and I are still in Costa Rica. I thought you *had* to go through customs."

"This is what Betsy was talking about. The power. He whisked you two right off the ramp. Nobody said boo."

"It's scary," Kate said, shivering.

"I swear, Mom, you're losing your tan just standing here."

"Fear will do that to you," Kate muttered. "Here's Betsy," she said, moving to the curb. "In a Lincoln Town Car, no less. Where does she get her money?"

"She gives speeches and she tutors. She's not hurting. She charges thirty-five dollars an hour to tutor and gets a grand a speech. She knows her stuff. I feel bad we missed so many years. We talked all night. I kind of like her. I think she liked me. We agreed to work on this sisterly thing."

"What about the mother-daughter thing?" Kate asked quietly.

"I don't know how to open the trunk,"

Betsy called out, "so slide your bag on the backseat. Do you have enough room?"

"Plenty," Kate said, sliding onto the seat.

Four hours later Kate and her two daughters were soaking in the hot tub, glasses of wine in hand. The portable phone rested on the ledge. "The bottom line here is if we open our mouths and admit Dad is back, we become an embarrassment to the government and endanger national security," Betsy said over the rim of her glass.

"If your father agreed, if he can handle it, so can we," Kate said.

"Mom, if you were in Dad's position, you would have signed anything to get out of there. He was coerced, threatened. We all have to remember that. Duress. But try and prove it. They'll call him a defector."

"We don't know that, Betsy," Kate said.

"Well, what do you think happened to us at the airport? Weren't we threatened and coerced? It opens up all kinds of cans of worms. How many others are there? Where are they? Why hasn't something been done? The press, of which your friend Mr. Stewart is a member, would have a field day. It would rock this country, and the government would have egg on its face. Listen, let's talk about something else for a little while. What are we wearing tomorrow for the big moment?"

"I don't have anything with me," Ellie groaned.

"Me either," Betsy said.

"We'll get up early and go shopping," Kate said. "Mr. Spindler said your father won't arrive till three or so. We can have lunch together like we used to. We also have to think about dinner. For the life of me I can't remember what your father likes to eat. I should remember, but I don't. I don't remember what he looks like, either," Kate said, crying softly.

"It doesn't matter, Mom," Ellie said gently. "He won't look like he did back then. It doesn't matter if you don't remember."

"You must be very happy, Betsy."

"Is this where I get to say I told you so?" Betsy said, pouring more wine.

"Only if you want to," Kate replied. "How am I going to explain that . . . burial?"

"Mom, you don't have to make explanations. You have nothing to hide. You did what you had to do. That's the end of it."

"Your grandfather's house. I sold it."

"So what?" Betsy said. "Dad isn't Dad anymore. He's Harry now, a long-lost cousin. The house went to you rightfully. I'm all for not even mentioning it unless Dad does, and then you tell him straight. Boy, is he going to be surprised when he sees this house. I almost fell out of the car when I saw it. Pretty pricey, Mom."

"I bought it with Donald and Della's help. It's paid for now. I made a will a few years ago, girls. In it I left half of everything to Della's family. There are so many of them. I hope that's all right with you."

Both girls nodded.

CHAPTER 19

Time passed, as they knew it would, but slowly. They slept curled on the recliners in the large glass-walled family room, rose, ate, hot-tubbed again, ate some more, slept, and woke to what Ellie called "the day."

They canceled the shopping trip by mutual consent, the girls preferring to wear Kate's clothes with a few minor adjustments. The decision not to shop for new outfits allowed them time to stew and fret, to dither and wring their hands in anticipation of Patrick's return.

It was barely light out when Kate plugged in the coffee maker. Her chest felt heavy, her eyes heavier still. The girls seemed to vacillate between a state of euphoria and total despair. Kate just felt numb. She dreaded the upcoming meeting, but some part of her couldn't wait for Patrick to see and comment on her success. *Dear God,* she prayed at the kitchen table, *don't let this be the nightmare I think it's going to be. Please help us all to get through what I know is going to be a traumatic reunion.*

Reunion. A happy time. Laughter, hugs, kisses, talking about old times. Happiness.

"The early bird gets the worm, is that it, Mom?" Ellie said, coming up from behind to plant a kiss on her mother's cheek.

"This early bird is shaking in her slippers," Kate said quickly.

"That's natural," Ellie said. "We're all going to do our best. I'm sure Dad is going through the same thing. I can't even begin to imagine what he must be thinking and feeling. No one said a word about his mental state. I wish one of us thought to ask."

"Ask what?" Betsy said, yawning elaborately from the kitchen doorway.

"What your father's mental state is," Kate said.

"Shaky at best," Betsy said.

"Do we wait for his move, or do we . . . I don't . . . what I'm trying to say is, do we react to what he says or does? What if he doesn't like the way we turned out?" Kate fretted.

"What's not to like?" Ellie muttered. She

smeared three inches of jam on a piece of toast, looked at it, and pushed it aside.

"Change is never easy to accept. For anyone," Kate said quietly. "I don't think I'm being overly melodramatic when I say our lives as we know them are not going to be the same. That frightens me."

"I feel the same way," Ellie said.

"This may surprise you, but I do too," Betsy said. "All these years it was so easy to say I'll do this or that, I can't wait to show, tell, and now it seems . . . I think what I'm trying to say is I more or less thought we'd carry the ball, but that's not the way it's going to be. Mom's right, we're going to do whatever we do based on what Dad does or says. We are *incidental.*"

How sad her voice is, how tortured she must be feeling, Kate thought.

"Have you spoken to your fiancé?" Betsy asked.

"Last night. Why?" Ellie asked fearfully.

"These government guys seem pretty thorough. They have to know you're planning on getting married. They aren't going to overlook him. They're going to want assurance he doesn't talk. Can he hold up to what we're all going to be going through?"

"I don't know," Ellie said.

Gus's cautionary words rang in Kate's ears.

"We sound like we've done something wrong and . . . we're going to be under government scrutiny night and day."

"We are, Mom. Try, just try, to picture newspaper headlines, newscasts, talk shows, all of it. You . . . we simply cannot embarrass the government. We cannot endanger national security. I'm sure Dad will be able to tell us more. We're beating a dead horse here. Until we talk to Dad, we have to accept everything. We signed away any rights we have. I don't know if that would hold up in a court of law or if we could get a lawyer to defend us if we decided to go public. My best advice for all of us is we go with the flow and take a wait-and-see attitude."

"Your father was never known for his patience," Kate said.

"Dad is an officer in the United States Air Force. He's not going to go back on his word. It's that 'do or die, defend your country' thing." At her mother's worried look she said, "I have an idea. It's a beautiful day, so let's go to work on the flower garden. It looked a bit straggly to me yesterday. You guys did a real good job on it, it really does look like a rainbow."

"We did it for Donald," Kate said.

"I know," Betsy said, staring out the window.

"What are you making for dinner?" Ellie asked.

"I have everything defrosting. I thought I'd wait to see what your father wants. Besides, I'm all thumbs."

"Sounds good to me. I'll clean the pool, you guys do the gardening. I hate getting dirt under my fingernails." Betsy hooted. Then they were off, racing down the hallway the way they used to do when they were younger. At least one good thing had come of this, Kate thought. Her daughters were friends again. And she had Betsy back. For that she would be eternally grateful. She remembered the promise she'd made to God at the airport. *Don't let anything be wrong with Betsy and Ellie. I'll do anything. Anything.* One did not break a promise made to God. Ever. She started to cry, silent tears of anguish.

"Promise me tomorrow," she whimpered. Patrick was keeping the promise he'd made so many years ago. Where had her faith gone? Why hadn't she believed? Why hadn't she trusted her husband to make good on his promise? Why? *Why?*

Kate squeezed her eyes shut to stop her tears. All she could see was years of counseling ahead of her. Even when she was in a rocking chair on the deck, she'd be trying to explain, trying to understand where she went wrong.

Abruptly, she slapped her hands, palms down, on the table. "You're going to do your best, and you aren't going to look back. Yesterday is gone, tomorrow isn't here yet, and today is all that counts. So there." She slapped at the table again for emphasis. She didn't feel one damn bit better, but she wasn't going to think about that. She was going to get dressed and work in the garden. With her daughters.

It occurred to Kate later as she was pulling on her gardening gloves that they were almost a family again. She wondered why the thought didn't give her any comfort, since *family* was her most favorite word in the English language.

"Hey, guys, it's one o'clock. Shouldn't we be breaking for lunch and showering up?" Ellie called. "Three o'clock is going to get here real fast." She propped the skimmer against the Sunrise fence. "Hey, it looks good. Tidy. Looks like you trimmed with a scalpel. Real good job."

"God, it's a nice day, isn't it?" Kate said. "Anytime the sun shines it's a nice day." She looked around at the garden, at the empty cottage in the back and the flowers bordering the little front porch. A cluster of birds sat sentinel on the rail on the deck. Waiting. She'd forgotten to put out the seed this morning. How patient her feathered friends were. Maybe that was the key to life: patience. The birdbaths were empty, too. She looked up at the lower limbs of the Joshua tree, where birdhouses hung.

The huge redwood-and-glass house stared down at her. An architect's delight. She'd done a rendering of it that hung over the fireplace. She loved it, felt as if it were her first real home. Shortly there would be an intruder, a stranger, living here.

"Who's doing lunch?" Ellie asked. "What are we having?"

"You girls make it. Tuna or grilled cheese is fine with me," Kate called from the toolshed. "I have to feed the birds and fill the birdbaths."

She saw her daughters running for the deck, their bare legs flashing in the sun. The pool sparkled, the hot tub bubbled, the birds waited.

"How do we look?" Kate asked nervously at 2:45.

"We look beautiful," Ellie said. "We look like we belong together. You know, cut from the same mold or whatever it is people say about families."

There it was, that word again, *family*.

"You look great, Mom," Betsy said.

"I'm not overdone, am I?" Kate asked nervously.

"You mean the gold hoops in your ears? Nope," Ellie said.

Her dress was electric-blue, designed by Donna Karan to expertly disguise her thickening waist. It stopped two inches above her knees and reeked with chic.

"I don't want to know how much that dress cost," Ellie said.

"Good, because I'm not about to tell you," Kate said. "Does my hair look okay? I had the gray colored before I went to Costa Rica. I used to have this long . . . *ponytail.*" She was about to say Gus loved her new Princess Di style, but she bit down on her lower lip to squelch the words. It was simple, wash and wear, and fit her needs perfectly. The fact that it looked good on her was a plus. Having a natural wave to her hair helped.

"I remember the buttons and bows you used to deck us out in. God, we looked like dimity orphans." Betsy giggled. "Even our socks had ribbons and bows on them."

"You looked adorable," Kate said defensively.

"Mom, we looked like dorks. Everyone else was wearing blue jeans and tie-dyed shirts, and there we were in our rick-rack and trailing ribbons. It's funny now, but it wasn't then."

"I'm sorry," Kate said.

"The boys liked our outfits, though," Ellie said.

"Yeah, they did, come to think of it. God, is that a car I hear?"

"Yes, it is," Kate said, swallowing hard.

"Are we going to go to the door or stand here? Nobody said what we were supposed to do," Ellie said.

Kate looked at Betsy, whose eyes were glazed. "The screen door is open. He can just walk in. I . . . I don't think I can walk all the way to the front door."

"We're going to stand here and wait, is that it?" Ellie demanded.

"Yes," Kate floundered. "We look like . . . like —"

"Half of a family who's waiting for the other half to make it complete," Betsy said softly. "The screen door is opening."

Kate's heart thumped in her chest. What was she supposed to do? Run to her husband, throw her arms around him? Wait to see what he did? Go with her feelings? *I don't have any feelings.* She was so tense, she felt brittle. Ellie, on her right, felt stiff; Betsy appeared to be loose, but her facial features were tense, expectant. *Please God, make this right for her. She's waited so long.*

He appeared, the sun from the open front door at his back. Kate fought with her tongue and lips. He was drawn, his face pasty white. The clothes he wore were big on him, almost baggy; he'd lost a lot of weight. Somehow she'd expected him to appear in uniform, but then he wasn't Captain Patrick Starr anymore. He was Harry something or other. She had to say something — or was it Patrick who had to say something? He advanced farther into the room, shuffling, his shoes squeaking on the oak floors. How shiny his shoes were, she thought; they must be new. This couldn't be her husband, not this terribly old-looking man. Where was the dashing fighter pilot she'd married? God in heaven, what had they done to him?

He was in the room now, staring about intently. He spoke in a voice that sounded strange, unused. With a Russian accent. Kate felt tears burn her eyes.

"Kate? I know I look like ten miles of used road, but I'm here. I kept my promise."

"Welcome home, Patrick," Kate said.

The girls ran to him while Kate stayed rooted to the floor. She watched as her husband stared at Betsy, then at Ellie. "My eyesight is bad. I need to see you up close. You're beautiful, just the way I knew you'd look. I won't always look like this. Some good food, a little sun, some exercise, and I might pass for something human."

God, Kate prayed, *please let me feel something. Please.*

His arms around his daughters, Patrick advanced into the room. Kate stepped forward. "It's good to have you home, Patrick." The girls stepped aside until she couldn't see them in her peripheral vision. She felt his arms go around her, tentatively at first, as though afraid she would vanish. She smelled his foul breath, noticed the white film over his left eye, the scars around his neck and forehead. He was trembling, about to cry. *Please God, let me feel something. I want to. Please.* She hugged him, tears streaming down her cheeks.

Patrick pushed her away, held her at arm's length. He stared at her. "What did you do to your hair? You have on too much makeup," he said critically. "I don't like your hair. You smell different. For years I'd close my eyes and bring you to mind. You always looked the same. You smelled the same, like vanilla and lemon. I don't like the way you smell. Is that real gold in your ears? How much did they cost? You all look so well off," he said, peering at the hemline on his wife's dress and then down at her high-heeled shoes. "You never wore high heels before."

The sisters exchanged glances. Kate stammered, "I — I'm sorry, Patrick. I wanted to look nice for you. We dressed up for your homecoming."

"I don't like it." He moved around the huge family room, peering at everything, touching the things he wanted to see better. "Whose house is this? How much rent do you pay here?"

"It — It's my house, Patrick. I don't pay . . . rent. I own it outright."

He was shuffling again, yanking at the sliding glass doors. "Why don't you let those goddamn birds out here? Don't tell me you feed them. If you feed them, they never go away. I hate birds. Get rid of them," he said forcefully. "Where did you get the money to buy a house like this?"

"I — I worked for it. Friends . . . friends helped," Kate said in a choked voice.

"And what did you have to give those *friends* in return?" Patrick demanded. He made the question sound obscene.

"Just our love," Ellie said hoarsely.

"I didn't ask you, I asked your mother." He was moving again, shuffling his way out to the kitchen. "Well?" he called over his shoulder.

"Ellie told you, just our love. Nothing more." Her eyes were wild when they focused on her daughters huddled close together.

"I don't smell anything. Didn't you make a welcome-home meal? The prodigal returns, that kind of thing. I don't smell anything. I expected smells. I expected . . . I guess my return caught you all by surprise. Well, Kate, aren't you going to make something?"

"What — What would you like, Patrick?"

"You know what I like. Or did you forget? I want stuffed chicken, pork chops, steak, lobster. You must be able to afford that, living in this rich house. Where did you say you got the money?"

"I said I worked for it." Kate began to get food out of the refrigerator.

"You could never make enough money to buy a house like this. It must cost sixty or seventy thousand dollars."

"Try half a million, Dad," Ellie said coolly.

Patrick grabbed Kate by the arm. "Just what kind of work do you do?"

"Mom has her own business," Betsy said, coming up close to where her father was standing. Ellie took up her position on the other side of her mother.

"Do you sell Avon products? You don't know how to do anything."

He must be laughing. That sound *must* be laughter, Kate thought wildly. She dropped the chicken she was holding.

"Mom went to college and got her degree," Ellie said, her face a tight mask. "She does architectural renderings. She has three offices," she added proudly. "She's been written up in magazines. She's a professional woman. They call her a 'woman of the nineties.' "

The chicken was in the sink, Kate's tears splashing on the plump breast. Her children were defending her. To their father. It wasn't right. She whirled about in time to hear her husband say, "You won't be doing that anymore. I'll take it over. You belong here at home taking care of me the way you used to. You aren't going back to work."

"No!" The single word was like a gunshot. "No, you will not take over my business. No, I will not stay home taking care of you. Listen to me, Patrick. We must all make adjustments here, and I am prepared to make my share. It is my business, I worked at it twelve, fourteen, sometimes sixteen hours a day. I was the one who went out and knocked on doors, I was the one who did without when I could barely make the rent, and I will not turn it over to you. If you want to work with me, that's fine. I can teach you the business, but I will not turn it over to you. I will not stay home. I've become a career woman out of necessity. I will take time off if you need me. If we work together . . . together we might be able to pull all this together." She was shaking so badly, her daughters closed in protectively.

"You just said no to me, Kate," Patrick said. He glanced into the sink at the chicken. "I can't eat this stuff." He pulled back his lips to show a row of rotten stubs. Kate winced. "Make me something soft that smells good. Meat loaf. You don't have to worry about my not knowing how to run your business right. I know how to make money. I can probably show you a profit of fifty thousand in the first two years."

A devil perched itself on Kate's shoulders. "My net last year was three-quarters of a million dollars," she said proudly.

"When did you become such a liar?"

"She's not lying, she's telling you the truth," Ellie said. "I'm a CPA. I do her books. Betsy has her doctorate. Do we sound like we don't know what we're talking about?" Her voice was icy. She did not like this man who claimed to be her father. It didn't look like Betsy liked him much, either.

Kate dumped chopped meat into a bowl. She was searching for an onion when Patrick said, "I don't feel like meat loaf. Make some chicken soup. Where are the bedrooms?"

"The meat loaf is down the hall — I mean, the bedrooms are down the hall. Your room is the one at the end. It's blue, your favorite color."

"Where's your room?" Patrick said.

"It doesn't matter where my room is. *Your* room is down the hall. It is the blue room. Until we go through this period of . . . of adjustment, you will be sleeping there."

"Atta girl, Mom," Ellie whispered.

"Oh, God," Betsy said.

Patrick was back a moment later. "I don't see my pictures anywhere in the house. Why is that?"

"I thought you were dead, Patrick. I put them all away. I had to. I had to get on with my life."

"Don't you feel stupid now?" he said belligerently.

"In a manner of speaking."

"There's nothing in this house that belongs to me. It's your house. Whose name is on the deed? I want my name on the deed. This is California. I own half of what you own. The Air Force told me my trunks were sent to you. Where are they?"

Kate felt herself wilt. "I buried them in the cemetery. I held a service for you. Then I had them dug up and buried in the plot next to your mother and father back in Westfield. I'm — I was going to say I'm sorry, but I'm not sorry, Patrick. I had to make sense of my life. I had no stability, no hope of your ever returning. I didn't think I had choices. I did what I felt was right."

He slapped her in a rage, and would have slapped her again if Betsy and Ellie hadn't grabbed his arm. He was no match for his young, athletic daughters. Kate wept into her dish towel.

Patrick thundered out of the room.

"Mom, forget this damn dinner business," Ellie said. "Please make us some coffee, and we'll all sit down on the deck, in the sun where it's warm, and talk. I'm not leaving you here . . . alone with *him,* until I feel . . . comfortable."

"I agree," Betsy said.

"All right," Kate said through clenched teeth. The last thing in the world she wanted was to drink coffee and talk. *Who was this person?* There was nothing even remotely resembling Patrick in this stranger.

The stranger — that's how she thought of him — didn't seem to have much of an attention span. What was being done for him? Surely the military and the government wouldn't just turn him loose like this — wash their hands of him, cast him aside, and dump him in her lap. Kate measured coffee into the basket, filled the pot with cold water, plugged it in. The reality was, they'd done exactly that. Now what was she supposed to do? Pity for her husband she'd lost so long ago welled up in her.

Kate sighed. What was going to happen when the girls left for Los Angeles and she was alone with Patrick? She didn't think twice; she reached for her address book and flipped through it till she found the tobacco store in Mexico. When she heard the familiar voice of the man she'd handed the note to over a year ago, she identified herself.

"Please, you must get a message to Señora Della Rafella Abbott. Tell her Kate needs her immediately. Tell her Captain Starr has returned and to come as soon as possible." A sob escaped her. "Can you get this message to Señora Della?"

"Sí, señora. Señora Della will be in my shop shortly. I saw her go by an hour ago. I will tell her."

"Thank you, thank you very much."

The coffee was done. Kate heaved a mighty sigh. With Della here, she might survive what she knew was coming. She filled the tray and carried it out to the deck. She went back for the coffeepot.

In the bright sunlight, Patrick looked even

more ghastly. "I don't want you wearing clothes like that anymore. I like the old things you used to wear."

Should she humor him or talk straight from the shoulder? Was it too soon to set down the rules? Someone should have told them how to act, how to deal with Patrick. But no one cared; it was that simple. "I go to work, I have to dress appropriately. I'm sorry you don't like my dress. It happens to be a fine dress. I think I look good in it. I deal with businesspeople. I have to look professional. I don't make my clothes anymore, Patrick. I don't have to. This is the style. I like it. We'll have to think about taking you shopping, too. I didn't see any bags. Didn't they give you anything?"

"A change of underwear, some shaving gear and a toothbrush. I left the bag by the front steps. If you hadn't thrown my things away, I wouldn't have to go shopping."

"The things wouldn't fit you now anyway. I can't imagine you not wanting new clothes. You have to fit in, to look like —"

"Harry. You have to start calling me by name."

"All right, Harry," Kate said, sitting down on the redwood chair. She wished she could fall asleep and never wake up.

"I'm glad to be home even if I never saw

this house before," Patrick said quietly. "I know I look like ten miles of bad road. I said that before when I first got here, didn't I? I expected . . . thought I would see revulsion on your face. All those years I never had a mirror. You used to say I was handsomer than any movie star. Star, get it?" He made that strange sound that had to be laughter.

Kate told him about Betsy's rainbow and pointed to the border around the house. "She thought you would fly overhead and be able to find the little house we used to live in. We believed for so long that you would come back. We hoped. We prayed. I wrote to the President six or seven times, and anyone else I could think of. Anytime we even got close to finding out something, it would be squelched. What did you sign, Patrick?"

Patrick slurped at his coffee. Some of it dribbled down his chin. Ellie handed him a napkin. "I agreed to what they wanted so I could come home. They don't want me to tell anyone where I was or what happened to me. I asked them how long I had to remain quiet, and they said until they told me otherwise. I might never be Patrick Starr again. I might have to be this Harry fellow for the rest of my life."

"You'll always be Patrick to us," Kate said,

her voice sounding desperate.

"We had to sign a paper, too," Betsy said.

"Do you regret it?"

"No," they chorused.

"When are you going to get rid of the birds, Kate?"

"I'm not going to. I love waking up and hearing them chirp. They depend on me for their food. I would think you'd like having them around. You used to fly. You told me once you could fly better than any bird and they were doing what came naturally. I don't mean to sound nasty or overbearing, but you are going to have to make some adjustments. The birds are God's creatures."

"I don't want them here. They remind me of my flying days. I'll get rid of them myself."

Ellie and Betsy both fidgeted on their chairs. Kate was off hers in the blink of an eye. She dropped to her knees, keeping her distance from her husband. "Patrick, listen to me. You are not to touch the birds. Not now, not ever. If you do, I will have to . . . have to . . . think about having you live somewhere else until we can adjust to this situation. I'm going to try very hard to get . . . to get to know you again." She saw the kick coming and leaped backward in time.

"Don't you tell me what to do! For nineteen and a half years people told me what to do.

I'm a free man and I don't have to do anything I don't want to do," Patrick snarled.

"In my house you do," Kate said quietly. "Do not ever, ever lash out at me again. You will be out of here so fast your head will spin." Her husband sneered at her. She didn't back down.

Kate turned to her daughters and with a slight nod of her head indicated they should go into the house. She mouthed the word *cook*. Both girls seemed reluctant to leave but did as their mother wanted.

Kate pulled her chair around so she could face her husband, but far enough away so he couldn't kick out or lunge at her. She settled herself, the skirt of her dress hiking up to mid-thigh. She tugged at it. She'd taken this dress with her to Hawaii last year, had worn it to dinner with Gus. He liked it, said she looked like a rare flower and that the color became her. She in turn said it matched his eyes perfectly. How happy she'd been then. She tugged at the skirt again.

"Patrick," she said gently, "we need to talk. I think we should start over. We're different people now, both of us. We can't go back to nineteen seventy. That time in our lives is gone. We have a tremendous adjustment to make, both of us. I'm more than willing to seek out a therapist, and I know the girls will agree. I don't know what you went through, and if you tell me, I probably couldn't begin to imagine your pain and suffering. I'm sorry for that, but you can't take your anger out on me and the girls. I simply will not allow it."

"I was never warm, never comfortable. I was always hungry. All I thought about was you and the girls. That's what kept me going," Patrick said, staring across the garden.

"And we thought of you. For years. When I finally gave up, Betsy didn't. She worked tirelessly. My heart ached for you. I dreamed of the day you would walk through the door. For so long I lived in a fantasy world, hoping, dreaming of your return. You're angry, and justifiably so, but your anger is directed at the wrong people. We aren't the enemy. I thought you would be so proud of the girls, of me. You . . . you shot us down. We wanted to share, and you didn't want to hear. You haven't smiled once since you've been here. With skilled help, you can be whole again. We have the patience and the resources to help you. Don't take your anger out on us. We've lived in our own hell for a lot of years."

"Nothing is the same," Patrick said flatly.

"Time doesn't stand still, Patrick. Surely you knew things would be different," Kate said gently.

"I wanted it to be the same. I wanted to see that small apartment, trip over those damn ducks. In my dreams I could smell you. I could see the girls with the little bows on their socks and in their hair. They're grown up, and I missed all that. I always knew I would come home someday. I'd swagger in, be the conquering hero, sweep all of you off your feet. I dreamed about the hugs and the kisses, the big welcoming dinner. I expected a ticker tape parade, meeting the President, being invited to go on television and give interviews. None of that happened."

"Oh, Patrick, I'm so sorry," Kate said in a choked voice. "It's not right for your country to deny you, to pretend you're dead. You deserve much more. If there was a way for me to give you all of what you deserve, I'd move heaven and earth to do it. A man named Spindler made us sign papers, too. I hated doing it, but he said if we didn't you would be kept someplace. Betsy said they could do that. She said we should sign."

"They meant it," Patrick said. "Do you know how I kept my sanity all those years?"

"You said you thought about us."

"Besides that. When things were bad, I retreated into my mind, back to Westfield. I went door to door. I'd knock, and when someone opened the door, I'd say 'Hi, I'm

Patrick Starr. I used to live here.' I'd pet their dog or cat, and they'd ask me to come back again. I knocked on every door in Westfield. I visited every single store. As the years wore on, I paid a second and third visit. I saw the dogs and cats die, got invited to weddings. Hell, I went to two of them. In my mind. Both of them were held in the VFW hall. I went to a couple of funerals, was even a pallbearer. One person even asked me my opinion on choosing wallpaper for the kitchen. I told her she should get green and white, the kind you had in our kitchen. You know, so it would look like summer in the winter. The woman said it was a good idea. When I was really cold in the winter, I'd visit this one house where an older couple lived. They had a fluffy white dog that liked to lie in front of the fire. I'd carry wood in for them, and they let me sit by the fire. The lady made hot cocoa, and we toasted marshmallows. The dog liked them, got the sticky stuff all over his whiskers. They were nice people. No one had names, though, but they all knew mine. Isn't that strange?" Tears were streaming down his cheeks.

Kate moved her chair closer and reached for her husband's hands.

"This isn't going to be easy, Kate. I think I must be a terrible person. It's like I can't control myself. I'm not going to be easy to live with."

"I know. You're disappointed in me, aren't you? I wanted you to be proud of the success I've made of myself."

"I didn't think you had enough brains to go to college."

Stricken with her husband's words, Kate murmured, "I guess no one can ever know everything about another person."

"You turned your doodling into a business. It must really be a crazy world."

"One of my renderings hangs in the White House, Patrick. I don't exactly doodle."

Patrick's eyebrows shot upward. He seemed to cringe into himself. "I don't want you working. Wives shouldn't work. I want you home."

"Cooking, cleaning, and working my fingers to the bone? You want me making crafts again, the crafts you once hated. I can't do that, Patrick. We can't go backward. We can't recapture the past. We have to move forward, adjust to what we have and deal with the here and now. If your mind is still working on that California property split of fifty-fifty, you're going to have to readjust your thinking. You are no longer Patrick Starr, and since you are no longer Patrick Starr, you cannot claim anything. You are not my husband any longer. You're Harry. Don't threaten me, Patrick, I won't stand for it."

"You're full of piss and vinegar, aren't you?" Instead of waiting for her response, he rushed on. "I can make your life miserable."

"And I can boot your ass right out of here. I don't have to take you back. I cannot believe we're having this conversation. We're actually threatening each other. And to what end?"

"I'm the man of the house. You used to accept that. You never had a thought in your head. All you wanted to do was use that damn glue gun you had and make things. Now all of a sudden you're an authority on everything."

"I'm sorry you see it that way. I've had to survive, and I did it the best way I knew how. Please don't punish me for that. I made myself into an extension of you. You should never have allowed me to do that. I believed you when you said I couldn't do anything but keep house and have babies. I had nothing to compare it to. When you were shot down, I couldn't cope. I didn't know how to do anything but keep house. By the sheerest accident I met up with a wonderful woman in the park, and together we both managed to survive, helping one another. I was so ashamed that I was thirty years old and didn't know the first thing about *living*. Without her and Donald, our kids would have been put in foster homes and I would have been carted off to the loony farm."

Patrick stared at his wife as though she were a stranger. The sun was dropping. Soon it would be twilight and the end of the day. He hated the darkness. "Do you have lights out here?"

"Yes. Lots of them. Why?" Kate asked, confused.

"I don't like the dark. What you say you went through was no more than a pimple on your ass. You don't know the meaning of misery. I'm not going to be able to fly again. I always felt good in the air. They're taking that away from me, too. I hate them. I'm not even sure I like you, Kate."

"I'm not sure I like you, either," Kate said quietly. "You can fly if you want to. We can even buy a plane, if that will make you happy. You can get your pilot's license under your new name. That shouldn't be a problem. I wish everything would be as easy for you. A good dental surgeon will take care of your mouth. An eye specialist will take care of your cataracts and fit you with glasses. You're alive, Patrick. Be grateful for that. Good food, warmth, and fresh air will aid your progress."

"You left out the vitamins, the orange juice, and a weekly laxative," Patrick said nastily. "It's getting dark."

Kate walked over to the outdoor switch and turned on the floodlights. Artificial light bathed the yard in a warm, bright glow.

"What's that little house?"

"That's Della's cottage," Kate said.

"Maybe I should move in there."

"Maybe you shouldn't be alone. Maybe you should think about that. You've been alone too long."

"Are you telling me what to do?"

"It was a suggestion. The cottage belongs to Della. You would need her permission."

"Where is she?"

"Mexico," Kate said, her heart thumping in her chest.

"She's Mexican? She owns a cottage on your property? No, that isn't going to work. If you have all the money you say you have, buy it from her. I've had enough foreigners to last me the rest of my life."

"I'm sorry, I can't do that. I *won't* do that."

"Yes, you will. I'm your husband and I'm telling you to do it."

"The government says you aren't my husband. I'm not doing it, Patrick. You cannot make me do anything."

Patrick lunged at her, reached for Kate's hair and dragged her off the chair. His rancid breath swept past her fear-filled face. Her daughters barreled through the door and were on their father within seconds. They dragged him backward, each pinning one arm. Kate coughed and sputtered as she fought for breath.

"Mom, what —"

"I gave your mother a direct order and she refused to obey it," Patrick said, trying to jerk his arms free.

"This isn't the Air Force, Dad," Betsy said. "What was the order?"

"I told her I didn't want any foreigners here. Your mother said a Mexican owns that little cottage. I told her to buy it back and she said no. Let go of me!"

The girls dropped their father's arms at the same moment and then joined their mother on the deck. "Della will be here tomorrow," Kate told them in a low voice. "I called her before."

Patrick shrugged his shirt down over his shoulders and stomped into the house.

"He's like an animal," Betsy said wildly. "Mom, you can't stay here with him. He could have killed you. What's going to happen when we leave?"

"Della will be here. She'll come, I know

she will. Your father has been through a lot. He needs a few days to adjust. I think he feels betrayed, and rightly so."

"That has nothing to do with us," Betsy said, hanging on to her mother for dear life. "I didn't know . . . I had no idea . . . what did they do to him?"

"Every terrible thing you could think of, I imagine. If things get bad or if I think I can't handle it, I'll call that man . . . what's his name?"

"Do you have his phone number?" Ellie asked in disgust.

"Don't you have it?"

"No. Betsy doesn't have it, either. They didn't hand out cards. They contacted us, remember?"

"This is unreal," Kate muttered. "All we have to do is something they told us not to do and they'll be all over us. I think we can get help if we need it. He doesn't like us, me especially," Kate said.

"He's disappointed in us," Ellie said. "He wants yesterday."

Betsy sat down on the deck and hugged her knees. "Would it be wrong if we tried to give it to him? I didn't think it would be like this. I knew he'd changed, but I thought . . . hoped, he'd still be the father who went away."

"Yes, honey, it would be wrong to try and go back. All we can do is be here for him. He's going to have to work real hard, but then so are we."

"What's going to happen when Della gets here?" Ellie asked fearfully.

"I don't know. Your father suggested moving into the cottage. I feel that would be a mistake, though. He needs to be around people and learn how to interact again. All of this is going to take time."

"I'm not leaving here till he settles down." Ellie said. "You don't think he'll do anything to us when we're sleeping, do you?" she asked, her eyes wide with fear.

Kate had been wondering the same thing. So had Betsy, from the look on her face. "I think we can all sleep in my room this evening. It will be a slumber party. My God, did I just say that? I did, didn't I?"

"We started dinner," Ellie said nervously.

"What did you make?"

Betsy giggled hysterically. "We took all the meat and dumped it in the Crockpot with some vegetables. It's kind of soupy, so maybe he won't know the difference. Ellie poured a lot of spices and stuff in it. It even smells kind of good. Mom, did he say even one nice thing? Did he say he missed us, loved us?"

"In his own way he did. He feels those things, but I think he's afraid it's all going to be taken away from him again. He turned in one set of fears and accepted another set. It's not fair, what they're asking him to do. It's not fair to any of us. I just don't understand any of this," Kate muttered.

Through the open window they could hear the phone ringing. As one they moved to enter the house in time to hear the phone picked up in the middle of the third ring. From the kitchen they heard Patrick's voice say, "Don't call here again."

Kate bristled. "Patrick, who was that?"

"She said her name was Della, that foreigner you said owns the little house."

"And you hung up on her?" Kate sputtered. "Don't you ever do that again! You don't hang up on people I know or do business with."

Patrick's response was to yank the yellow phone from the wall. He threw it across the table. Carrots and string beans flew in every direction. The phone bounced twice before it skittered across the black slate floor. "Now we don't have to worry about any more foreigners calling here," he said, smacking his hands together. "I need some money."

The women stared at him speechlessly.

"Mom, let's get in the car right now and

get the hell out of here," Ellie said tightly.

"I'm all for that." Betsy pulled her mother toward the front door.

"What do you need money for, Patrick?"

"You *said* you have all the money. I don't have any, so you should give me some. The government gave me a check and it's been deposited, but they said it won't clear for seven to ten days. It's hush money."

"What do you want money for? The stores are closed now."

"You never used to ask questions, Kate. Now you ask too damn many." He was rummaging along the counter, pushing and shoving everything in his way till he found the Betty Crocker cookbook. "You used to keep money in the back. I bet you thought I forgot about that. Well, I didn't forget anything, Mrs. College Student with her degree."

"Does that intimidate you?" Kate said quietly.

"Why should it? I have a master's. Do you have one of those?"

"No, but I have a doctorate," Betsy said, stepping forward. "Does that intimidate *you*, Dad? Don't put Mom down. I did enough of that over the years. She doesn't deserve it."

"You raised a disrespectful snot here, Kate," Patrick said, lifting the lid of the

Crockpot. A rush of steam surged upward. He jerked backward, swinging wildly.

"Oh, God," Ellie wailed as vegetables and meat sailed up and out.

Kate raised her eyes to see a chunk of celery on the ceiling. When it dropped, it landed on the tip of her shoe. She wanted to bellow her outrage, to call Gus and tell him to come and get her out of this nightmare. "Why don't we change our clothes, clean the kitchen, and order a pizza," she said calmly.

In her bedroom, with the door closed and locked, mother and daughters clung to one another. I'm supposed to be the strong one, she thought, the guide, the one who leads her daughters in the right direction. She wanted to scream, run, run as fast as she could and not look back.

"He's a tormented soul," she said.

"He's nuts, Mom. He should be in a hospital with trained people to help him," Ellie said tightly. "He could seriously hurt one of us. You better start thinking about what's going to happen when Della gets here."

Kate looked at Betsy. "I think he needs intensive therapy, but I don't know if he'll agree to it. What if . . . *they* don't want him in a . . . place like that? He could say something that would . . . blow it all away. How can he have therapy when he isn't allowed to talk about his past?" The horror of what she'd just said hit Kate full force, her daughters, too.

"They took him out knowing there would be problems, made him swear to secrecy, us too, and now they expect him and us to survive? What kind of people are they?" Betsy demanded.

"Does that mean we scratch any kind of therapy?"

"Yes, I'm afraid that's exactly what it means," Kate said quietly.

"What do you suppose he wanted money for?" Betsy asked.

"Men need to have money in their pockets. It's right he should have money. I'll give him whatever he wants," Kate said.

"He wants to buy a gun so he can shoot the birds," Ellie blurted. "Don't let him buy a gun, Mom."

"I won't. Let's change now. I don't think we should leave him too long."

They scrambled into jeans, shirts, and sneakers, and they looked like triplets when they walked out to the kitchen. Kate pulled up short. The table was set, most of the mess cleaned up. The contents of the Crockpot were in a big bowl in the center of the table. Patrick was sitting at the head of the table.

"I'm used to eating things off the floor,"

he said. "My guards used to throw my food at me. Sometimes it had rat hairs on it, but I ate it anyway. We shouldn't waste food. I didn't think you would eat it, so I made you jelly bread sandwiches. Is that okay, Kate?"

Kate burst into tears. She shook her head. "I don't think the food is done, Patrick. I can fry you some eggs or open some soup."

"No, this is fine. I ate raw meat. This is a luxury. Sometimes I just had fat and grease on bread. This is good. I like it," he said, trying to chew the food with his bad teeth.

"These are good sandwiches, Dad," Betsy said, her mouth full. "I remember you used to make them for us when you had a day off."

"I used to sprinkle sugar on the top and tell you not to tell your mother. Do you remember that?"

"Yeah, I remember," Betsy said, tears streaming down her cheeks.

"Don't cry," Patrick said.

"Okay." She wiped her eyes on the sleeve of her shirt.

"Kate, do you think I could get a dog? A big one. I think I'm going to need a friend, one who will tolerate me when I do something wrong. I think I need someone to love me. I thought . . . all this past week I thought

I could handle anything as long as I was home. I can't. It's like everything is rushing at me, smothering me, and I have to do something. React in some way. For many years I wasn't permitted to do or say anything. I used to whisper to myself so I wouldn't forget how to talk. They beat you if they heard you clear your throat. Did you say I could or couldn't get a dog, Kate?"

"Yes, of course. We can go tomorrow if you like." God, maybe this was going to work out after all. "Patrick, I have to talk to you about Della. I don't want to upset you. Will you please listen?"

"Yes."

Kate told him about Donald and Della, with the girls chiming in from time to time. "She took care of us, Patrick. She and Donald made us whole again. They wiped away our despair, made us want to live again. We wouldn't be here for you now if it wasn't for Donald and Della. Will you accept her and be kind to her?"

"Do you think I'm a monster, Kate?"

"No, of course not."

"If I say yes and you say yes to the dog, does that mean we are both working at" — he waved his arms about — "all of this?"

"Yes, it does."

"Should we vote?"

"Voting sounds good," Kate said.

"I vote yes," Betsy said.

"Me too," Ellie said.

"You always did that when you were little," Patrick said. "You have to say, I vote yes."

"I vote yes," Ellie said carefully.

"I vote yes, too," Kate said.

"I vote yes, too. No hot peppers."

"I'll tell Della."

"I think I'll go to bed now, unless you want me to finish cleaning up."

"No, we can do it, Patrick. Sleep well."

"I love you all," he said brokenly.

"Is he trying or is it a trick?" Ellie said when she heard his door close. A moment later the door opened. She heard her father say very loudly, "I don't like doors that are closed."

"Let's believe he's trying, and let's all try harder," Kate said, clearing the table.

"Maybe it will work out." Ellie sounded as though she didn't believe what she was saying.

"The Captain Patrick Starr I knew would never give up," Kate said staunchly. "He was the best of the best. He'll . . . make it. I know he will."

CHAPTER 20

"I think I know what happened," Kate said, wiping her eyes. "Your father has been locked up for so long, his thought processes can't be normal. He's got justifiable rage in him, and he lets it out the only way he knows how. He can't vent that rage on the people who freed him, so who's left? Us. The good part of him, the part they couldn't take away from him, came through. It's mixed up in his mind and tied to . . . how he must have lived, afraid of doing something wrong and being punished or tortured for it — for no reason, more often than not. He may have . . . thought, for just a little while, that we were his captors. That we would punish him for what he'd done. The good part, the Patrick part, cleaned up and tried to make it right with the jelly sandwiches.

Does that make sense?"

"It's as good as anything I can come up with," Ellie said, rinsing the dinner plates.

"None of us are qualified to offer therapy," Betsy said. "You're absolutely right, Mom, we can't take him to any kind of professional. He can't tell them where he's been all these years and what he's gone through. Those bastards really covered their asses on this," she said bitterly. "I always dreamed this would be such a happy time. Damn it, I wanted it to be happy. Think about how we feel, and then think about what he must be feeling. My God!"

"Della will . . ."

"Della will what, Mom? Clean up after him? Cook his meals? Wash his clothes? That's not what I'm talking about. *You're it.* You are Dad's only chance of surviving this. It's going to be a twenty-four-hour job. You're the only one who can make him whole and well again."

And when he's whole and well again and able to function in this big world we walk around in, then I can . . . then I can go to Gus. "How long do you think it will take?" Kate asked, hating the desperate tone in her voice. When her daughters shrugged, she sank onto a kitchen chair. The shrugs had to mean a year at the very least, maybe longer. Would

Gus wait for her to do her duty to her husband? How awful that sounded. How terribly selfish.

"Mom, this is probably going to sound . . . weird, but did you notice how Dad talked, how he moved? He said all these strange things, and some of them he repeated like he was trying to make a point. It didn't seem like he *heard* you. Do you think . . . is it possible he has a hearing problem, too? If they beat him, maybe they punched him in the head or something. I kept watching him. He heard us at the table because the table is small and we were close. What do you think?" Ellie said.

"We'll find out tomorrow. I'm taking your father for a complete physical, and from there to the best oral surgeon I can find. Hopefully the doctor who gives him a physical can recommend a good eye doctor. I think when they see his condition, they'll want to do everything they can for him as soon as possible. The question is, do I take him to L.A. or go local? People know us in town. Questions might be asked that I can't answer."

"I think you just answered yourself," Betsy said. "L.A. is your best bet."

"All right, that's what we'll do, then. I'll follow you girls back to the city. I know you want to stay and help and . . . protect me. However, I think I'll do better with your father one on one. Come up on the weekends, call, that sort of thing."

"What about your business?" asked the ever-practical Betsy.

"I was hoping you'd step in, Betsy, and take over for me. If I have to worry about the business, I won't be able to free my mind and give a hundred percent to your father. Besides, your drawings were always as good as my own."

"What about Gus?" Ellie blurted. She covered her mouth instantly, her face full of guilt.

"Oh, for heaven's sake, I know all about Gus Stewart," Betsy said sourly. "Nothing you two did escaped me. So I was an ass. Let's not go into all that old stuff. Well, Mom, what about Gus? Why don't we go outside on the deck or walk around the yard," she said suddenly.

Ellie's eyebrows scooted back almost to her hairline. Kate strode to the door and outside, her daughters right behind her. They sat down on the lounge chairs by the pool and whispered.

"None of us would make good spies," Kate said hoarsely.

"The point being we are ordinary people thrust into an extraordinary situation. What about Gus?"

"For now there is no Gus. It's that simple."

"You love him, don't you?" Betsy said.

"Very much. We were going to be married in December."

"And now?" Ellie said.

"And now we aren't."

"Do you love Dad at all?" Betsy asked.

Kate was tempted to lie, to wipe the miserable, hurt look off her daughter's face. "Not in the way you mean. Your father was my first love. One never forgets that. But it was never a healthy relationship. I idolized him, worshiped him to the exclusion of all else. I was like some kind of robot going through the day-to-day motions. I existed. I only came alive when your father came home. I did everything by rote. I had all these schedules that only an idiot like me could follow. All they did was allow me to exist until your father walked through the door. I came alive then. In the morning when he left, I went back to being a robot. I thought I was normal. That's why I couldn't function when your father was shot down. I simply didn't know how. All I ever wanted was his approval, a pat on the head, but he never gave it to me.

"During our therapy sessions — do you remember, when you were sixteen or so? — Dr. Tennison asked me if Patrick loved me, and I said, without a moment's hesitation, He doesn't even like me. Then he said it was possible for someone to love another person but not like them, and vice versa. I pretended I understood what he was saying, but I really didn't. I still don't know what he meant. I don't see how a person can love another person and not like them. Do you understand that?" Her daughters shook their heads. "So, I'm not so dumb after all," Kate said ruefully.

"In my stupidity, I would have made you two girls clones of myself. If your father hadn't been shot down, if I hadn't met Della and Donald, I might have ruined your lives. You shook me, Betsy, when you rebelled, but deep inside I cheered you. You forced both Ellie and me to change. So, some good did come of all this."

Kate's daughters wrapped her in their arms. They cried together for the past, the present, and the future.

A long time later Ellie said, "Do you think Dad will ever be okay?"

"I think so," Kate said, not knowing if it was the truth.

"I'll take over the business," Betsy said. "If I screw up, don't blame me."

"I'll be watching you, big sister. Just because you're the oldest doesn't mean you're the smartest," Ellie teased.

"Oh, yeah, who else do you know who got their doctorate at the age of twenty-six?" Betsy retorted.

They were needling one another. To Kate it sounded wonderful. This generation had such a strange way of communicating. For a few minutes she felt almost happy.

"Why don't you girls go in the hot tub. I have to make some phone calls to see if I can get some appointments tomorrow for your father. Bring the phone down with you and some soda pop. With all the lies I'll be telling, my throat is going to be dry."

They listened, the water bubbling and whirling about them as Kate called one person and then another until she got the promises she needed. "A distant cousin is here from Poland and needs extensive, immediate medical help. Can we schedule the appointments all for the same day? . . . Of course I'll do a rendering of your brother-in-law's house. It will be my pleasure. How about by Thanksgiving? . . . Sooner? Absolutely. I'll drop everything and do it right away. Call the office and give them the addresses. . . . Framed? I wouldn't have it any other way. Thank you, Stephen."

"What say we fake him out, Mom, and I do it," Betsy said, giggling. "I'm going to flatter you now, and tell you I've seen just about every one of your renderings in town. I even bought one that was hanging in the bank. What do you think of that?"

Kate laughed. "Tell me how much you paid for it." Betsy told her. She laughed again and said, "Guess I made a hundred and fifty percent profit on that one."

"Two years ago I had the flu and nothing to do, so I amused myself by trying to copy the rendering. I had it matted and framed, and except for my signature, you wouldn't be able to tell them apart."

"She said with no trace of modesty," Kate said, and smiled.

"If you got it, you got it. All I'm trying to say is I can do the renderings, and if you feel they're as good as yours, maybe you'll sign them for this guy. It'll make me feel like I've done my part in helping Dad."

"That's not very honest," Kate said.

Betsy's mood and tone of voice changed instantly. "I don't want to hear about honest right now. Just take a look at the position we're all in. Let's just forget that word right now."

Trying to head off something she didn't want to get involved in, Ellie said, "What about me? Do I carry your pencils or what?"

"You carry my pencils and add the numbers

in the ledgers. Maybe we can shame this guy into paying."

"Not a chance," Kate said. "You might give some thought to signing them with just 'Starr' and the date. The next ones I do I can sign the same way. It'll make it less dishonest."

"I'm ready for bed," Ellie said, climbing out of the tub. "This thing knocks you on your butt, but you sleep like a baby afterward."

There was anxiety in Kate's voice when she said, on her way to her bedroom, "Are we sleeping together?"

"Yes," both young women said at the same time, following her.

"Good. I guess we better leave all the lights on in case your father wakes up. We should check on him, too."

Kate stopped short as she peeked in on her husband. "Oh, my, he's sleeping on the floor. He must have six blankets wrapped around him."

"Maybe he thought he'd fall out of the bed. It is kind of high," Ellie said.

"Maybe he's used to sleeping on the floor," Betsy said. "Maybe he didn't have a bed. This carpet is thick enough to be a mattress."

"He looks so . . . alone," Kate murmured.

She advanced into the room and dropped to her knees. She was about to brush his hair back from his forehead when he woke, his eyes filled with total, complete terror. He huddled into himself and muttered something in Russian that Kate couldn't understand. "It's Kate, Patrick. It's all right," she crooned, patting his shoulder. "Nothing is going to happen to you. Not while I'm here."

"Kate? Kate?"

"Yes, Patrick, it's Kate. Go back to sleep. I'll stay here with you for a while." Her touch was gentle when she brushed at his hair. Because she couldn't remember any lullabies, she started to croon, "Mary had a little lamb, its fleece was —"

"White as snow, and everywhere —"

"Mary went, the lamb was sure to go."

"Sing it again, Kate."

Kate waved off her daughters. When she finished with Mary and her lamb, she started on Jack and Jill. There was a smile on her husband's face when he drifted back to sleep. Kate's heart swelled in her chest as her tears splashed on her husband's shirt-clad shoulder. Anger, hot and scorching, rushed through her. They hadn't even given him clothes. A change of underwear, he'd said, that was all. Because he wanted to be warm, he slept in his clothes. She wanted to kill someone for what they'd done to him. "I promise you, Patrick, your day is coming," she whispered.

In the morning, Kate handed Patrick an overlarge cable-knit sweater. "It's chilly out," she said. "We're going to Los Angeles. I made appointments for you. It's going to be a full day, Patrick. Are you up to it?"

"Yes, Kate," Patrick said quietly.

"Tomorrow we can get you some new clothes. Or the girls can follow us later. They can shop for you so the clothes will be here when you get back. Yes, that's a good idea. Do you agree?"

"Do you think it's a good idea?"

"Yes, I do, but what do you think?"

"I think I want my own things. I think I want to throw away these clothes. Not the sweater. You gave me the sweater. Yes, it's a good idea. Did I do that right, Kate? Did I make a decision? I'm not allowed — I wasn't allowed to talk or ask questions. I have not made . . . decisions."

"Well, you just made your first one. Today you are going to make more," Kate said gently.

"What if I make the wrong one?" Patrick asked. "What will happen?"

"Not a goddamn thing." The scorching anger ripped through her again at the nameless, faceless people who had done this to her husband. She tried to force a smile in her voice. "Sometimes it's fun to screw up because you get a second chance to make it right."

"I'll get two chances, then."

"You bet. More if you need them," Kate said, her voice breaking. Where did the anger, the rage and hostility, go? she wondered. Was he being submissive for a reason? Fear did strange things to people. She fought with her scorching anger. *Your day is coming, Patrick.*

"Who's going to make breakfast?" she asked cheerfully.

"I will," Betsy said.

"I'm going to shower. Patrick, did you shower?"

"I . . . it was too cold."

"You have to take a shower every day. And you have to shave and brush your teeth. I understand what you're saying about it being chilly. I'll show you how to work the fan in the bathroom. There's a blower. It will take five minutes for the room to warm up."

Patrick moved alongside Kate down the hall and into the bathroom. He watched her carefully and nodded to show he understood how to turn the blower and the fan on and off. "Don't close the door, Kate."

"I won't."

"Are we going to get the dog today?"

Good Lord, she'd forgotten. Well, the girls would have to help with that, too. "Yes, Patrick. Do you have a particular one in mind?"

"A man's dog," he said sprightly.

"A man's dog it is. You'll have to train it, you know. Do you promise to take responsibility for it?"

"Yes, I promise. They treated me like a dog. I would never treat a dog the way they treated me. I want to prove that. I have to prove that. No, let's not get it yet."

Kate's throat closed. Somehow she managed to say, "We're going to get you the best dog in the state of California. Not yet, though. You're going to be real buddies." Patrick smiled at her. *You son of a bitching bastards. I'm going to get you for this.* She rushed from the room to her own bathroom, where she showered and washed her hair, all in under five minutes. She was out, dressed, and in the kitchen in twelve minutes total.

"You look nice, Mom. I bet Dad approves of those slacks and sweater. Peridot is your color."

"Thanks. What's for breakfast?"

"Pancakes. They're soft. I melted the butter and warmed the syrup. Betsy squeezed the orange juice. The coffee's good, too."

"Girls, I have another job for you. If you have time, bake a chocolate cake with lots and lots of frosting. Pick up some ice cream."

"What kinds of clothes should we get? We need sizes," Betsy said, reaching for the notepad. "And what should we do if Della gets here while you're gone?"

"Hug her. Buy large. Casual. He doesn't need a suit yet. Loafers, maybe moccasins, size eleven. Real warm socks. Think warmth. His underwear is probably thirty-two. Flannel pajamas, a warm robe. Lots of sweaters. Warm trousers, a lined windbreaker. A wool hat and some gloves. Just go through the men's store and use your best judgment. Later on I'll pick up a flight jacket. I think he'd like that."

"If we have any time left over, do you want us to paint the house?" Ellie quipped.

"Don't forget to bake the cake," Kate said, lighting a cigarette from the stub of the old one.

"Hi, Dad. Sit down, I made pancakes," Betsy said proudly. She layered six onto his plate.

"They look very nice," Patrick said.

Betsy giggled. "They taste very nice, too."

Patrick ate everything on his plate, then finished his juice and coffee. "I never leave anything. If you left something, they didn't feed you the next time," he volunteered.

"You don't have to worry about that anymore," Kate said. "If you feel warm enough, we should be on our way. I'll call you this evening, girls. The credit card is with the money in the desk."

"Don't you use the cookbook anymore?" Patrick asked.

"Sometimes I do. But sometimes I forget and just stick it in the desk drawer. You said you wanted money, Patrick. I'll get it for you. How much do you want?" she asked, and saw Patrick's face fill with panic. "How does fifty dollars sound?" she added gently.

Patrick's face relaxed. "Fifty dollars sounds . . . okay." There was such relief in her husband's voice, Kate wanted to cry. To the girls she said, "Get a wallet, too." To Patrick she said, "You can keep the money in your pants pocket for now. We'll see you girls later on."

"We'll come up to see you on the weekend, Dad," Ellie said.

"Okay. Do you want me to kiss you goodbye?"

"Sure," Betsy said, her eyes wet.

Ellie hugged her father and said, "I wish I could remember you."

"I remember you. You used to pull my ears when I carried you on my shoulders.

Betsy pulled my hair. I remember everything. One time they told me you all died in a car crash. I knew that wasn't true because your mother was a good driver. I told them I believed them, but I didn't," Patrick said proudly. "I don't have much hair left," he said suddenly.

"You have enough," Kate said. He was so docile, so mellow. When would he erupt again, she wondered, or was yesterday's anger a one-shot deal?

"You never lied to me, Kate, so I believe you."

"No, Patrick, I never lied to you. I won't lie to you now, either."

They were on the highway, the heater blasting in the Mercedes, when Kate said, "Did you ever love me, Patrick?"

"I'm not sure. You were a good mother and you kept house good. We were happy, weren't we?"

"I thought I was. I loved you with all my heart and soul," she said quietly.

"That's a lot," Patrick said in amazement.

"Yes, it was. I'm not sure you even liked me. Why did you volunteer for that mission?"

"I wanted to get my ticket punched. It was the only way to make rank. It was a mistake. I didn't use to make mistakes, did I?"

"Not too many."

"I wanted everything to be like it was. I'm sorry about yesterday."

"I'm sorry, too. Did you really think I was dumb, that I needed you to think, that I never had a thought in my head?"

"Yes, but only because it was true."

Kate cringed. "You don't hear well, do you?"

"No, I don't. I guess I had too many blows to my head. One ear is good."

"Why didn't you say something?" Kate asked sadly.

"Because there were so many other things wrong with me. You couldn't see inside my ears."

Please God, help me get through this. Help me to be kind, to understand. "We'll get that taken care of today, too."

"When do you think I'll be normal, Kate?" Patrick asked.

"I don't know. We're all going to do our best for you, but you're going to have to work hard. I'll do whatever I can."

Kate almost laughed when Patrick said, "Because you love me heart and soul?" Almost. "You don't love me anymore, do you?" he asked, his tone conversational.

Kate thought about the question before she answered. "Part of me will always love you,

Patrick. But I'm not *in love* with you." Please, she prayed, don't let him ask me if I love someone else. Don't let him ask me that. "Do you love me?" she asked, hoping to forestall the question she felt was coming.

"I think I was in love with the idea of marriage. I needed a wife. You need a wife in the military or you don't get ahead. I liked you. Most of the time." It was said so matter-of-factly, Kate found herself half smiling. Maybe, she thought, it doesn't sound so bad because of the Russian accent; when things were quiet, when her head was together, she would think about what her husband had just said. That and the fact that suddenly, with Patrick's words, she could feel her guilt start to wash away.

"Today is going to be difficult, Patrick. Tell me something. I don't understand why you weren't given medical treatment. I don't understand how they could just . . . send you off in your condition. They're treating you like an animal," she blustered.

"It was my choice. They took me to someone, and I had a going-over, a quick one. My eyes and ears were scheduled for later. I also had to go through extensive debriefing. Once I told them how I spilled my guts, they more or less lost interest in me. I've had nineteen and a half years to think about all of this, and I know in my heart no human could have held out against the torture and the drugs. I wanted to come home. They said they would reimburse us for all the medical bills. They lie, Kate."

"I know that."

"If I get better and start to look normal, do you think we could go out to dinner? In a public place."

"Would you like that?"

"The thought is a goal. Right now. I'll pretty much have to learn to walk like everyone else. I shuffle, and sometimes, most of the time, I move in jerks. That's because I was scrunched up a lot."

"We'll work on that. We'll take walks, ride bicycles. Remember how you used to ride past my house on your bike? You always pretended you had a flat tire when you got to our driveway."

"You saw through that, huh?"

"Pretty much so."

"Are you really rich, Kate?"

"I'm comfortable. I don't think we'll have to worry about starving. I have an investment planner. Ellie oversees it all. You should be very proud of the girls. Betsy . . . Betsy understands all this business with the government. I don't pretend to understand how she . . . She takes after you, Patrick. When you're feeling up to it, you should talk to her. Ellie says she's an expert in international government affairs. I guess that means she knows how the system works or doesn't work."

"They're fucking me over, Kate, and there's nothing I can do about it."

"We aren't going to worry about that now, Patrick. For now we're going to defy them and get you on your feet. We're going to make you robust and . . . and we're going to work on your anger so we can all deal with this reasonably and logically. I don't believe that nothing can be done. I refuse to believe that."

"We're caught up in the system now." Kate heard the fear in his voice and reacted angrily.

"I don't want you quitting on me before we even get started. If we believe we can take on the system, we're halfway home. It's not always the winning that counts. What counts is calling them to accountability. When the time is right, Patrick. It all depends on you."

The rest of the trip was made in silence, the radio playing softly, the heater blasting.

At the hospital Kate was told to come back at four o'clock. Patrick would have his physical, visit the dentist and eye specialist. His hearing test was scheduled last. The doctor assured her that when she picked up her cousin Harry, he would have glasses and his hearing aid. If possible, dental work would be started.

With time on her hands, Kate treated herself to lunch and a long walk. She stopped for coffee in the middle of the afternoon so she could use the bathroom. The phone on the wall made her light-headed. If she was lucky, Gus would still be in the office. Generally he ate lunch in the office, unless he was out in the field working on a story. She counted her change. She had enough to make the call, but if Gus wanted to talk, he'd have to call her back.

The moment she heard his voice she started to cry. She was still crying when he told her to hang up and he would call her back. They talked for thirty minutes, about the weather, about Betsy and Ellie, and about how certain she was that Della would be at the house when she got back. "I miss you," she said. "I dreamed about you last night."

"Kate, I'm worried about you. Can you handle this?"

"One minute I think I can, but the next minute I think it's hopeless. I have to try. You said you understood."

"I do understand, but that isn't going to

stop me from worrying. Is there anything I can do?"

"How did it go with the man who picked you up?"

"Not well. They tend to work on intimidation. He thought he was intimidating the *New York Times*. I told him to go screw himself. I signed his damn paper, and underneath my signature I wrote, 'Under duress.' He tried to tell me I wouldn't be permitted to leave until I signed a second form. We looked at each other for five goddamn hours. He went out to make a phone call, and finally he let me go."

"I wish I'd had the guts to do that."

"You need to be in a position of strength to fight them. You had nothing going for you. You have your husband back. They played on that, the bastards. As long as I know you're okay, I can live with this. When can you call me again?"

"I'll try every few days. I'll try to work out some kind of schedule. A routine is going to be important to Patrick. I've been thinking about enrolling him at a gym. I can take him into town and wait. I can't give you anything more definite right now. I have to do this, Gus."

"Yes, you do. The poor bastard deserves the best. If there's anything I can do, let me know. I love you, Kate, more than life itself."

Kate squeezed her eyes shut. She wanted to tell him she loved him just as much, maybe more, but the words wouldn't come. She had no right to say them. Not now. Maybe never.

"Take care of yourself, Kate. You're in my thoughts every hour of the day."

"Don't eat too much fast food," Kate said, choking back a sob before she hung up.

When she took her place at the table to finish her cold coffee, she looked around. The few customers who had been there when she'd entered were gone. A man who absolutely reeked of suspicion, right down to the propped-up newspaper, stared at her. Kate stared back, her eyes defiant. She was chagrined, to say the least, when she went up to the cash register to pay her bill and the man said, "Mrs. Starr?"

"Yes?"

"I thought I recognized you. I'm Reverend Timmins. You did a rendering of our rectory several months ago. I've been meaning to write you a letter to tell you how many comments I received from my parishioners." His hands went to his tie. "Sorry, but today is not my collar day."

"We all need days like that," Kate said, offering a huge smile. She felt like a fool as she walked out into the afternoon sunshine.

At the hospital, Kate settled herself in the waiting room to wait for the doctor. He found her at ten minutes of five.

"Well, Mrs. Starr, I'm happy to report your cousin Harry is not as bad as we thought at first. His EKG is fine. His lungs are a little congested, but medication is going to relieve that. His kidneys are good, his bowels are okay, too, considering the strange diet he's been living on. Our resident dentist filled nine cavities and pulled six front teeth. A partial plate is being made up. It will be ready in three days. Soft diet, of course. His cataract is not ready yet to be removed. Laser surgery will take care of that, and he will have the use of his left eye. He's already got his new glasses and can see quite well out of his right eye. His hearing has been severely impaired, but he's now wearing the latest in hearing aids. He was quite fascinated with it. It goes behind the ear and is hardly noticeable. His entire mouth is numb and will stay that way for about six hours. The man is exhausted and is napping in one of our recovery rooms. Oh, yes, his preliminary blood and urine tests seem to be okay. We'll know more when you come back for his partial plate. You can take your cousin home, Mrs. Starr. But" — he wagged an invoice under her nose playfully

— "stop at the office and give them this."

"Thank you, Doctor," Kate said, and glanced at the bill in her hand. Two thousand, eight hundred dollars. A small price to pay for Patrick's health. She wrote out and signed the check with a flourish.

Back in the waiting room, she stood quietly as Patrick tottered toward her. "I feel like hell," he said around the packing in his mouth.

"You look like hell, too," she said cheerfully. "You can sleep on the ride home."

"I could hear every word you said," Patrick mumbled, his face full of amazement. "Every word. I can see you clearly, too. You're very pretty, Kate, but you're too fat around the middle."

Kate didn't know whether to laugh or cry when Patrick poked her playfully on the arm. "If I wanted to be nasty," she said, trying to hide her smile, "I could tell you you look like shit right now. So *there*." She dug her elbow into his arm. A sound escaped his mouth. He's laughing, Kate thought. He's really laughing. She grinned from ear to ear.

Patrick fell asleep the minute the car started to move, and he was still sleeping when Kate pulled into the driveway. The house was lit up like a Christmas tree. She was out of the car in a flash when she saw Della's plump figure outlined in the lighted doorway. They laughed and cried, hugged and kissed, and then they babbled like magpies. Patrick continued to snooze in the car while they walked around the garden.

"I really need you, Della, can you stay? Will you stay?"

"Of course. Now you need me. Before you didn't. Those girls left such a mess. It took me hours to clean up. The cake was such a disaster, the top slid off onto the table. Even the birds wouldn't eat it. I made another one. I made chicken soup and spaghetti and pudding and all kinds of things. It's all ready. I hung Captain Starr's clothes up. Your daughters have good taste, Kate. Betsy hugged me. She told me she loved me. We cried and cried. Everything is fine now. They did tell me that Captain Starr might not take to me because I'm Mexican. What should we do about that?"

"It's not that you're Mexican, but that you're not American. I settled all that. He might be a little standoffish for a while, but I know Patrick — he'll come to love you like we do. And stop calling him Captain Starr. Actually, we're supposed to call him Harry. 'Hey you' sounds better to me than Harry."

They were in the middle of the yard under

one of the many Joshua trees when Della said, "What about Gus?"

"I spoke to him today," Kate said softly. "I thought my heart would break. He told me how much he loves me. I wanted to tell him how much I loved him, but I couldn't. I don't have that right anymore. I don't know what's going to happen. Patrick told me on the ride to the city that when we got married, he was in love with the idea of marriage more than he was in love with me. He said he just *liked* me, 'most of the time.' *Liked* me! How could I not have known that, Della? Was I that big a fool? I would have died for him if he'd asked me to. Everything I thought was real, wasn't. I must have been the stupidest person in the world. A woman should know if her husband doesn't love her. But not me — I was so busy making chickens and ducks, bows and ruffles, that it never occurred to me. How am I supposed to know if Gus loves me? Patrick used to tell me he loved me."

Ever practical, Della said, "Ask him if he's in love with you."

"I can't do that," Kate faltered.

"Then I'll do it," Della said.

"No, you won't." Kate wrapped the older woman in her arms. "We have to get Patrick into the house and into bed. He's had a tough day."

"I see it's taking its toll on you, too, Kate. Well, I'm here now. Does he want to have sex with you?"

"Dellllllaaa!" Kate sputtered. "I think sex is the furthest thing from Patrick's mind right now."

"He's a man," Della said. "When it becomes in the front of his mind, what will you do?"

"I don't want to talk about this, Della."

"You're going to have to think about it sooner or later. Captain Starr is a man. He's not always going to be in such a *delicate* condition."

"Then I'll think about it later, but not now. Definitely not now." There was an edge to Kate's voice.

Della shrugged. "Life is never easy," she said philosophically.

Kate's heart leaped to her throat at the sight that met her eyes when they returned to the driveway, the floodlights glaring down on the candy-apple-red Mercedes. Patrick was cowering in the front seat, his hands scrunched around his head. The sounds he was making were those of a trapped animal. "It's the lights. He must think he's being interrogated. He doesn't like the dark. The girls must have turned the lights on before they left," Kate whispered.

"Patrick, it's me, Kate," she said soothingly as she approached the driver's side of the car. "We went to the hospital today. You fell asleep on the way home. I want you to get up now and climb out of the car. No one is going to hurt you. These are good lights, Patrick, they make the dark go away." She ran to the passenger side of the car and opened it.

"I thought it was a bad dream," Patrick said.

"It's all right now," Kate purred. "Della is here, Patrick. I want you to say hello. She's going to help us. She's also going to make a poultice for your gums. Come along now."

"The lights weren't this bright before, were they?"

"Yes, they were, but you can see better now with your glasses. "Della, this is my husband, Patrick, also known as Harry."

"I'm very pleased to meet you, Captain Starr. For years I heard about you from your wife and daughters. I feel like I know you."

Patrick stiffened. Kate exerted pressure on his arm. "Hello," he said, relaxing almost immediately.

Della fussed then, hustling them inside, where she immediately set about making a poultice of tea bags for Patrick.

When Patrick was settled for the night,

the wet tea bags clamped between his gums, Della said, "You have a long road ahead of you, Kate. The bottom line is, what happens when you get to the end of that long road?"

"Like Scarlett said, I'll worry about that tomorrow," Kate said wearily. "Della, will you sleep in my room with me?"

"That's where my things are. I think you should turn in, you look exhausted."

"Della, having you here means everything to me. I feel better just looking at you across this table. As usual, I'll never be able to thank you."

"And as usual, no thanks are needed. Are you sure you don't want anything to eat?"

"I'm positive. Besides, Patrick told me I was fat today. I guess I could lose a few pounds around my middle."

The following morning, Patrick's new routine began. To make it official, Kate carried a ruler. She wasn't sure why, and Patrick didn't ask. He was attired in gray Nike sweats, L.A. Gear sneakers, and a Mets baseball cap. He was still biting down on the wet tea bags. His tinted aviator glasses were in place, his hearing aid turned to full volume. He looked at Kate expectantly.

Kate waved the ruler and cleared her throat. "You ate a good breakfast, hot cereal, mashed banana, pudding and juice. Now we're going to . . . to do a few simple exercises. Simply because *I* probably can't handle anything more strenuous. Then we're going for a walk. A long walk. If we get tired, we'll rest, come back, eat lunch. Della has spaghetti, soup, and a lot of soft stuff, and you'll need to change your tea bags. You'll rest or nap an hour and then we'll do it all over again. If you're up to it, we'll go to town, maybe see about joining a health club. We'll stop by the drugstore and get some Grecian Formula to color your hair. Then we'll have high tea, cake and whatever else Della makes. We'll swim, soak in the hot tub, and I'm going to hire a masseur to give you daily body massages. Maybe me, too."

"You need it," Patrick mumbled.

"I heard that," Kate snapped. He made the funny sound she knew was laughter. From the kitchen window Della smiled.

On the third day, when they made the trip to the city for Patrick's partial plate, he didn't sleep at all. Kate giggled most of the way home as she watched him admire his new bridgework in the visor mirror. When she stopped for a light, he skinned back his gums and smiled, and then made the funny laughter sound.

"I know you're probably saying something profound," Kate said as they neared the exit for Bakersfield, "but I'll be damned if I know what it is. I guess it's because you aren't used to the bridge yet, and that Russian accent isn't helping. I think we should hire a tutor. One-on-one will be good for you. Don't worry, we'll fit it in somehow. What's another sixty minutes out of your life?" Patrick rolled his eyes, then patted her on the arm. Kate felt touched with his simple gesture.

"Why don't you freshen up now," she suggested as they pulled into the drive. "I'll make some iced tea and we can drink it out on the deck."

"Okay," Patrick said agreeably, and he trotted off to do as she'd ordered. She watched him shuffle down the hall, her eyes full of pity.

It was all too much. He felt trapped and free at the same time. His mind whirled. His room . . . He didn't like the sound of that: his room. *The* room didn't sound any better.

He'd wanted everything to be the same, had expected just that. He'd even allowed for the change in the girls, but not Kate. Kate was . . . Kate was . . . a slick chick. He used to call her that, but at the time it was just words. Kate had been plain, a comfortable person, a warm person with love shining in her eyes.

His eyes searched the room. It looked like a man's room, with the box-pleated, navy-blue bedspread and matching drapes. Even the pillows had special covers. He wondered why that was. Maybe they were afraid he had lice or dandruff. The room was too big, it had too many windows. He needed a smaller space, some place where he could huddle. All this openness confused him.

This was a stranger's room in a stranger's house. Was he ever going to belong here? He sniffed, hoping for some kind of familiar scent. Mothballs. The room hadn't been used. A guest room. He was in the guest room. He looked at the light blue walls, at the deep blue shag carpet that was one shade darker than the spread and drapes. He wondered if he could ask for yellow or maybe light green. Red would be good, even orange. He thought about orange then as he crunched into himself.

He saw it then. The closet. He hadn't gone near it. He wondered why. "Maybe I didn't see it," he muttered. He opened the door and a wave of cedar washed over him. He sniffed again and again before he decided he liked the smell. The closet was small, with a rod and one shelf he could reach if he wanted to. His hands were shaking when he stretched to remove the bar. The shelf came away easily. He placed both outside the door, then walked into the closet. His shaking stopped when he leaned into the corner, his thin arms wrapped around his chest. His hands crept upward. He beat at his face, his shoulders, yanked at his sparse hair. His shoulders started to shake as he slid down to the floor. His feet clawed at the fluffy shag carpet.

"I need you to help me, God. I can't do this myself. Please, help me. I can't bear the looks on my family's faces. I'm scaring them. I don't want to do that. Why am I in this closet? Why can't I stand in the middle of the room? Why do I need this dark, narrow space? Kate won't punish me. The girls won't whip me. Show me what to do. Show me how I'm supposed to act. I forgot. Somebody has to help me," he pleaded. "Give me a sign, something I can hang on to when it gets bad. Anything. My mind will recognize it. I want this so bad. Please, God, help me."

"Patrick?"

His sign. He struggled to get up.

She stared at him.

He stared back.

"Are you going to ask me why I'm in here?"

"I think I know why. You're comfortable there. All the rest of this kind of . . . scares you. It's going to take time," Kate said softly, a smile in her voice.

"Kate, can I ask a favor?"

"Of course."

"I don't like these colors."

"Oh. Well, we can change that. What color would you like?"

"Something . . . sprightly."

"Like . . ."

"Yellow. Maybe green. I like red."

"It's a done deed, Patrick. Tomorrow I'll have someone come out and do it over. How about a nice moss-green with daffodil yellow accents? That will look . . . sprightly."

"Yes, sprightly." Patrick grinned crookedly. Kate was his sign. Kate was going to make everything right. "Thank you, God," he murmured.

As the days and weeks passed, Patrick improved so rapidly, it boggled Kate's mind. By the time the new year rolled around, he'd gained fifteen pounds. Twenty more would put him in his proper weight class. His face had filled in and begun to fit the aviator glasses he loved. His movements were less jerky, and if he paid close attention, he could actually stride, and even at times glide, to Kate's amusement. He had color to him now, thanks to the tanning bed at the health club. "It's just temporary, Patrick, sun isn't good for you," she told him.

By St. Patrick's Day, when Della cooked a huge corned beef and two heads of cabbage along with small white potatoes, Patrick was walking five miles in the morning, working out with minimal weights at the gym, swimming, and then walking another five miles before dinner. Afterward he had his body massage and worked with the tutor.

Kate was exhausted and had lost only seven pounds.

In June Patrick passed his driving test and Kate bought him a Jeep Cherokee, a bright red one to match her Mercedes. He still carried the original fifty dollars in his pants pocket that Kate had given him on his arrival.

By the middle of August he'd gained another eighteen pounds and was constantly at the refrigerator. He ran and jogged, swam and continued to work out.

One bright, golden afternoon, Patrick sneaked away from the house while Kate was taking a shower. He drove to the pound, where he turned over his fifty dollars and bought a dog that had been picked up off the freeway. It was a mangy, unkempt, filthy mutt with huge sad eyes and half a tail. He licked Patrick's hand. "This one. Does he have a name?"

"We've been calling him Jake. Kind of fits him, if you know what I mean." Patrick didn't know and wasn't about to ask.

Jake smelled so bad, Patrick had to roll down the windows for the drive home. "We're going to catch hell when we get home, Jake. I'm not supposed to go anywhere on my own." This last was said with barely a trace of his former Russian accent. "You know what, Jake? You look like I did when I got here. You know what else? My wife is okay. She's putting her life on hold for me. I want to say something to her, but I don't think the time is right. She doesn't like me too much."

He rambled on, from time to time looking at the dog as though expecting him to answer.

"She's not what I expected. Nothing like I expected. She has *opinions*. Before I left, she didn't even know what an opinion was. Now, look at her! I guess I'm jealous. I wanted it all to be the same, and it isn't. I want to love her. I think she expects me to love her. I think she's waiting for me to . . . *do something*. You know, get horny or drag her out to the bushes. She's being so good to me, trying to help and all. She should, she owes it to me. I want to feel something besides gratitude, and even the gratitude eats at me. Why is that, do you suppose, Jake?

"You know, back then I had to get away from her. She was smothering me, and then when I got captured, she was all I could think about. I care about her. I cared about her back then. She was almost perfect in a . . . smothering kind of way. For a wife. You take me, now, I was the perfect pilot, everyone said so. And what did that get me? Twenty fucking years out of my life, that's what.

"Kate has a secret. I can see it in her eyes. The girls know what it is, but they aren't talking about it." He laughed, a strange sound that made Jake's ears go flat against his head.

"The thing of it is, Jake, I've intruded in her life. She doesn't want me around, and she feels guilty for the way she feels. See, I know this woman.

"If someone came up to me now, this very minute, and said, 'Come on, Patrick, I'm going to let you fly again,' I'd be out of here so fast, I'd leave scorch marks on Kate's fluffy carpet. That's all I want, Jake, to fly again. Kate and the girls, they have their own lives. I wish I loved her, really loved her. I wish there was a chance for us, but there isn't. Kate doesn't know that yet. She's the world's best fixer-upper. She thinks she can make me over, make our marriage work. Yesterday is gone, Jake. She keeps saying that all the time. She thinks my brain is gone. Now she's trying to make me an extension of her. That's what got us into trouble in the first place. Back then she made herself an extension of me. But I'm smarter; I'm not going to let that happen. No, sir, I'm not going to let that happen.

"Well, we're here, Jake. This is where I live these days. It's temporary. Kate thinks she's here for the long haul, but I can read her like a book. What she's doing, Jake, is her duty. Okay, let's get out so I can show you what a really good life you're going to have."

When he climbed from the Cherokee, Jake stayed in the back and refused to get out. He's afraid, Patrick thought. "This is freedom, Jake. We're gonna give you a steak, the biggest one you ever had, and we're *throwing away that bone.*" If the dog had been a cat, he would have purred at Patrick's gentle touch. "Come on, boy, I'm going to clean you up. You can sleep in my room, and if *she* says anything, we'll tell her how it is."

A minute later he came back outside to Jake, a sheepish expression on his face. He could hear his wife still screeching his name from the deck. "She's pissed," he said. "I'll tell you how I know she's pissed, Jake. When she calls me Harry, she's mad. When she calls me Patrick, it's okay. We are in deep shit this time."

Kate burst through the front door, eyes flashing fire. "You know the rules, Patrick. I was worried sick! Why didn't you at least *say* something? . . . Well? What do you have to say for yourself?" she snapped.

"Meet Jake. I drove to the pound. I used the fifty dollars and bought him on the spot. He smells a little. Kind of the way I did when I got here. I guess nobody wanted him."

"What fifty dollars?" Kate demanded.

"The fifty dollars you gave me when I got here," Patrick said patiently. "I have change."

"I thought you said you weren't ready for a dog."

"Then, I wasn't. Now I am. This is my kind of dog. When I spruce him up, he'll be okay. Don'tcha think, Kate?"

It was the first time Patrick had taken the initiative to do anything on his own. She'd forgotten about the fifty dollars. He looked so anxious, and the dog looked . . . petrified. Despite herself, she stooped down and scratched him behind the ears. "He's going to need *a lot* of sprucing up."

"That's what I thought. I think we should feed him. I told him we'd give him a steak and throw away the bone. I think that's good, don't you?"

"Yes. On the grill or under the broiler?" she asked.

"The grill. I'll do it."

"Did you have any trouble finding the pound?"

"No. I asked for directions. I saw a mailman and he told me. I was . . . very anxious. But I was careful. I wore my seat belt."

"I would have taken you. All you had to do was ask."

"I needed to do this myself. I think you're getting tired of me. You need time to be by yourself. Jake can go with me on the walks or when I run. I don't want you to start to hate me, Kate." He shuffled his feet at the bottom of the deck stairs. "In a few weeks I'll be home a year. A year is a very long time."

"I don't mind. Betsy is running the business better than I did. I made a commitment to you and to myself. I could never hate you. I don't want to hear you talk like that."

"Okay, Kate. My motor skills are good now."

"Yes, they are. I'm very proud of you."

Patrick beamed.

In the kitchen, Kate sat down at the table. She could see Patrick turn on the grill and flop the steak on it, Jake at his side. "Why do I feel so funny all of a sudden?" she asked Della.

"Pretty soon he isn't going to need you. It's hard to believe he's the same man I saw when I first got here. The biggest hurdle, at least to me, was when he started sleeping *in* the bed. I might be wrong, but I think by next year he's going to be ready to go off on his own. Legally, that leaves you in limbo more or less, but you will be free to go to Gus."

"Shhh," Kate whispered.

"He wants to fly again," Della said.

"I know. I don't think he's ready for that yet. On the other hand, maybe that's the last thing he needs to make him whole again. I'm going to talk to him about it. Just last week he told me the amount of money the government gave him — two hundred thousand. I never asked him how much it was, and he never mentioned it. He seems to be doing a lot of thinking, and he's not talking about whatever he's thinking about." She sighed. "Christ, I have to start getting ready for the Chamber of Commerce meeting tonight. I picked up the videos he asked me to get. I don't know if it's good or not for him to watch all those Vietnam movies."

"It's one way for him to find out what

went on while he was in Russia. He read all the material you and Betsy gave him. He soaks it up like a sponge and then grows quiet for a day or so. Your husband carries many demons, Kate."

"He needs professional help for that. I'm certainly not qualified. Every time I ask him something, he changes the subject. I wish I didn't get so irritated when he takes so much time to think and act before he does anything. It's been almost a year. I think he should have lost some of his fear by now. He hasn't had a bad dream in a long time."

"Perhaps he is afraid of you," Della said softly.

"Me! Why in the world would he be afraid of me? All I've done is help him."

"I think you intimidate him. Perhaps the way he used to intimidate you. The mind is a curious instrument, Kate. He was looking for your approval when he came home with the dog, but I saw the fear in his eyes, too. I was watching from the kitchen window. He did wrong, but he did right too. He wasn't sure which way you would react. I think you handled it just fine."

Kate sniffed as she marched into her room to get dressed. She would not go to the Chamber of Commerce meeting, she decided. She would find a phone booth in a restaurant, call Gus and talk to him for an hour. Then she'd get something to eat and come home. She was being sneaky and devious. In the beginning Patrick had questioned her about the meetings, but he didn't do that anymore. He was content to settle himself in front of the fifty-six-inch television with a bowl of popcorn for hours on end. Tonight was what Kate called a free evening, which meant no tutoring, no anything, just relaxation.

She flicked at the hangers in the closet with impatient fingers. She always wore a suit to the Chamber dinner meeting, so she had to play the part. A wave of guilt washed over when she picked out a dove-gray suit and bright crimson blouse with a bow at the throat. It was what she called her neat, tidy look. Her hair, long now, was pulled back into a chignon. She slipped into a pair of Ferragamo heels and stood back to assess her image in the free-standing pier glass. All she needed to do was add the double teardrops to her ears and spritz on some perfume.

She was ready to talk to Gus. She felt good, looked good.

It was all she had.

She was in the hall, wondering where she'd left her car keys, when a whirlwind of soap suds slammed her up against the wall. Stunned, she let out a shriek and saw Patrick stop short, his hands flying into the air.

"What . . . what happened?"

Patrick was backing up, his face drained of all color, his hands in the air. From down the hall she could hear Della shouting at the dog. So that was what it was. Some internal instinct warned Kate that this was do-or-die stuff for Patrick.

"Oh, well," she said cheerfully, forcing laughter into her voice. "I didn't want to go to that damn meeting anyway." *I'm sorry, Gus, I'll have to call you later in the week.* How long would he wait at the paper for her call? All night, she answered herself.

"I think," she said, kicking off her heels and yanking at her suit jacket, "we should rethink this bath business. Now mind you, I've never had a dog, but on television they always jump out of the tub. What you have to do is close the door, and one person stands ready to catch the dog if he bolts while the other person scrubs him down. Now, the way I see it, since we can't close the door, Della will stand guard at the door and I'll help you. Between the two of us I think we can get Jake here squeaky clean. I'm ready if you are." She rolled up the sleeves of her crimson blouse.

Della led a bedraggled Jake into the bathroom, and between the two of them, they managed to wrestle the dog into the tub. "This was not a good idea, was it, Kate?" Patrick said.

"It was a great idea," she replied. "We just didn't count on Jake being so frisky. He's a nice-looking dog. I think we can put some cream rinse on him so his coat will be easy to brush when he's dry. I bet we could blow-dry him, too. That way he can sit on the couch with you while you watch your movie."

"He smells like a wet dog. Lord, when did he have a bath last?" Della grumbled.

"Probably never," Patrick said with an edge in his voice.

"That would explain why he's so afraid. I can feel his heart beating. You remember what that was like, don't you, Patrick?" Kate met her husband's gaze.

"You aren't upset that you can't go to the meeting? Your clothes are all wet."

Something was brewing here, something she didn't understand. "That's trivial, Patrick. You have to learn what's important and what isn't. In the scheme of things, this would go down as a big zero."

"It's two mistakes in one day," Patrick said.

Kate could sense the tightness in her husband's shoulders, and the set of his jaw bothered her. Was he going to fly into a rage? "You didn't make a mistake getting the dog.

All I said was you should have told me you were going. I was worried about you, but it wasn't a mistake. If you don't want to tell me something, you can leave me a note."

"You look sad, Kate."

She wanted to say, I am sad, I looked forward all week to calling Gus tonight; I have the right to be sad. But she didn't. Instead she said, "I'm sad because this poor dog is beside himself at what's happening to him. We need to rinse him. Della, would you fetch something from the kitchen so we can end his misery? No, no, that . . . it was a poor choice of words, Patrick. What I meant was we have to get him out of the tub and dried so he can go back to being a dog. We agreed you weren't going to take everything I said so literally."

"I'll try harder," Patrick said, his shoulders relaxing slightly, but not enough to reassure Kate trouble wasn't brewing.

Jake suffered through his blow-drying better than Patrick did. It looked to Kate as though he were relating somehow to the dog. She'd found over the past months that Patrick talked when he wanted to talk and not one minute before. But then he'd always been like that. She was more or less pleased that he'd retained one of his original traits.

Their evening began the way it usually did.

They had dinner, and Jake begged at the table, even though he'd had a three-pound T-bone steak. Patrick's voice sounded sharp when he told the dog to lie down. Jake's tail wagged, his sad eyes imploring when he sat up on his haunches, his tongue lolling out of the side of his mouth.

Kate saw it all in slow motion, saw Patrick's face contort, saw him raise his arm, saw Jake, eyes trusting, trying to lick the hand that was about to strike him, saw Della's swift movement, saw Patrick literally pulled from his chair onto the floor, Della standing over him, her chest heaving. Jake thought it was a game and proceeded to lick Patrick's face. Patrick rolled over on the slate floor and beat at it with his clenched fist.

"I thought you loved Jake? You fed him, bathed him, gave him a name," Kate said hoarsely. "He trusts you, and you were going to strike him. If you had done that, the dog might have turned on you and gone after you, and it would have been your own fault. What is it, Patrick?"

"I think I'll take Jake for a long walk," Della said. "Don't worry about the dishes, I'll clean up later when I make the brownies I promised . . . Harry."

"I understand, Patrick," Kate said, brushing his hair back from his forehead. Her voice was low, soothing, almost a croon. "In your mind it's all mixed up. You were treated like a dog, and you fed the dog and he was still begging, much the way I imagine you had to beg for food. You've come a long way, Patrick. These flashes . . . whatever they are, they're getting to be fewer and fewer. It's over now and Jake is okay. He thought it was all a game."

Patrick sat up and wrapped his arms around his knees. "I could have hurt him, turned him against me. When . . . when I told . . . said something about giving Jake a bath, Della said maybe we should just turn the hose on him, but then she said it was too chilly and he might catch a cold. That . . . that one word, hose, triggered all this. The V.C. turned a hose on me once. Who the hell even thought they knew what a hose was? It was like one of those fire hoses where the water comes out a hundred miles an hour. It drove me against the wall and then into a rack of bamboo spikes. That's what all those scars on my back are from. I thought I was going to drown. They laughed and laughed, poking sticks at me to force me back into the stream of water when I'd try to crawl away. That was probably the only real bath I ever had. Without soap." He grimaced.

Dear God in heaven. "Come on, Patrick,

we don't sit on the floor in this house. It's over; everything is okay now."

"You're wrong, Kate, it's never going to be okay. I can't ever get those years back. I won't ever be able to forget. I'm not permitted to talk about this to anyone but you and the girls. How can I put it behind me if I can't get it out in the open and deal with it? You said writing down everything in those stupid journals would be a start. I did it because you said it would help me. Well, guess what? You were wrong, it's worse now than it was when I first got back. It's almost a year — a whole goddamn year — and I was ready to kill that poor dog," Patrick said miserably.

"But you didn't, and that's what's important. You won't ever do anything to Jake. You'll always be aware, and you have control now," Kate said quietly.

"Do you realize it's been a year and no one has been in touch with us? No one has called to see how I'm doing. No one has checked up on me. Once I signed that paper, I became a nonperson. Patrick Starr doesn't exist anymore. I'm goddamn sick and tired of being honorable. Honorable should work both ways. All this past year you've talked me up when things were bad. You were always there. You never got mad, you never fought with me even when I was at my worst. And you don't even love me," he said, his voice full of awe. "I always know when you're pissed off, though. You call me Harry."

Kate laughed. "Yeah, I guess I do. So, now what? I can tell you've been doing a lot of thinking. It would be nice if you'd share your thoughts with me."

"Well," Patrick said thoughtfully, "I thought I'd stick around to participate in that one-year anniversary party you and the girls are planning for me. I overheard you talking," he said sheepishly. "I can hear a pin drop with this hearing aid." He laughed at the look on Kate's face. It was a nice laugh, full of amusement at his wife's embarrassment.

"And then?" Kate said anxiously.

"Then I thought I'd go back home and start a new life. Maybe I can buy my dad's old house in Westfield. I guess if you have enough money, you can buy almost anything."

"Not always. And after you do that?"

"Maybe sign up for some flying lessons, using the Harry name. Maybe I can even get a job at the Linden airport. I can try Newark, too. If there's one thing I know about, it's planes. I'll have Jake. I'll get a bike and pedal past your old house. If I have any money left, I might buy yours, too. This way Jake and I can pedal by and sit on your front porch and pretend you're going to come out and chase us away."

Kate bit down on her lower lip so hard she could taste her own blood. She wanted to cry. "That was one of your dreams. I don't understand. You said you weren't in love with me. Why would you want to sit on my old front porch?"

"It's one of the nicest memories. Back then things were simple. We were kids and pretty damn innocent. I don't think it's ever going to get any better than that. If you give me that old Betty Crocker cookbook of yours, the one with the pocket in the back, I'll be okay."

She did cry then, great hacking, gulping sobs. Patrick put his arm around her, pushing the button on the VCR at the same time. "I think you're going to miss me, Kate. Who are you going to miss, me or Harry?"

"Shut up, Patrick. Just shut up, do you hear me?"

"With this hearing aid I can hear —"

"Go to hell!" Kate cried, jerking free of his arms. She stomped her way down the hall to the bedroom. She slammed the door and locked it. Howling like a banshee, she threw herself on the bed. When she'd exhausted her tears, she rolled over on the bed and reached for the phone. Not caring who was listening, not caring about *anything,* she punched out Gus's private number at the *New York Times.* "Hi," she said, "I'm calling from home." The word *home* would set the tone for the balance of the conversation. "How are you doing with your Pulitzer?" It was a standing joke with them. She forced a chuckle into her voice she didn't feel.

"How's Harry?" Gus asked.

"Harry had a bad day today, but he also had a good day. He went out and bought a dog. He calls it Jake. Ellie is going to be married in February. Romantic that she is, she wants the wedding on Valentine's Day. Betsy is doing so well running the business that I don't bother calling in anymore. I'm thinking of taking up ceramics."

"God!" Gus said.

"Maybe I'll hook rugs."

"God," Gus said again. "You sound nasally, are you catching cold?"

"I think so," Kate lied. "I'm thinking about buying an airplane."

"Do you plan on flying it, or are you just going to look at it?" Gus asked.

"Look at it. More or less. I have this fear of heights."

"Me too. I mean I have a fear of heights, too. We have a lot in common, don't you think?"

"I always thought so. It's been almost a year since . . . since Harry came back. The girls are planning an anniversary party. Streamers, balloons, that kind of thing."

"Sounds like . . . fun."

"Depending on your point of view, it could be, I guess."

"Kate —"

"Well, I think I've taken up enough of your time. I've been thinking about you all day, and when I do that, I have to make sure my friends are okay. Go back to your Pulitzer writing."

"Kate —"

"Good-bye, Gus. I'll call again."

Kate waited until he broke the connection, then stayed on the phone a few seconds longer. She cleared her throat. "Whoever you are, you son of a bitch, I hope you go straight to hell." Then she put her finger between her lips and whistled the way Patrick had taught her when they were kids back in Westfield. "I hope your eardrum is ruptured!" she cried before she slammed the receiver back into the cradle. There were times, like now, when she wondered if she was paranoid. Patrick assured her she wasn't, that there really was some faceless man sequestered somewhere listening every time the phone was picked up. He believed it, so she believed it.

Kate threw her suit skirt and the crimson blouse in the corner and donned a pair of sweats and sneakers. Maybe she could snitch a couple of brownies if Della hadn't given up on the idea of baking them. She did love her sweets.

The movie playing on the VCR was *Private Benjamin.* Patrick was laughing while he fondled Jake's ears. Della, she could see at a glance, was removing the brownies from the tray. She snitched one, then dropped it immediately when she burned her fingers.

"Serves you right," Della snapped. "Load the dishwasher."

"What are we cooking for Patrick's party?" Kate asked.

"Don't you mean banquet? Your daughters have a two-page list. If you look at it carefully, you'll see the desserts are first. Four-layer chocolate cake, homemade pineapple ice cream, ambrosia, cherry cobbler. Shrimp cocktail, lobster bisque, roast capon, prime rib, candied sweet potatoes, string beans and almonds, garden salad, homemade dinner rolls, and there's a question mark next to the creamed corn. I have no idea what that means. Betsy wants pickled beets and eggs with lots of onions in the juice. Be sure to use balsamic vinegar, she writes. What would *you* like?"

"An Italian hot dog. Coleslaw and a slice of that four-tier chocolate cake. How about you?"

"A taco would be nice."

"How long do you think it will take us to make all this?" Kate asked curiously.

"It depends on how long it takes us to blow up the balloons," Della grumbled.

"Oh, shit," Kate said. "Della, I want to thank —"

"Kate, take these brownies in to Patrick. Two of them are for Jake. You better hand-feed him so he doesn't get it on the carpet."

Patrick smiled at her she handed him the plate of brownies. She started to break one apart for Jake. "I'll do that, Kate. I want him to know I'm the one who feeds him. You don't mind, do you?" he said, fondling Jake's ears.

"No, of course not." But she did mind, and she wondered why that was. She watched man and dog for another minute before she got up and went to her room.

Kate rose early the day of the party. For days she and Della had cooked and cleaned.

The girls would come up together around five. She made coffee and carried it out to the deck. A year ago today she'd thought her world had come to an end. She felt proud of herself. She'd had the same feeling the day she received her college diploma. Well done, Kate Starr. She patted her shoulder, tears burning her eyes.

"The early bird gets the worm," Patrick said quietly. "Listen, you were right — it's a wonderful, happy sound. And I wanted to shoot them. I don't know too many sounds that are as pleasing as the chirp of a bird. I want to thank you for not letting me . . . and last night, too. Jake woke me up in the middle of the night to let him out. He's a quick learner, better than I was."

Kate smiled. "But you started out with a tremendous handicap. I'm very proud of you, Patrick."

"That means a lot to me, because I know you mean it."

"I bought you a present," Kate said, suddenly shy with her husband's compliment. "If you wait here, I'll get it."

"I have something for you, too," Patrick said. Like kids they raced into the house to get their presents for one another. Kate returned to the deck first and handed hers over when Patrick came out.

"It's kind of silly," she said.

"A giant Slurpee cup. For my drive cross-country. This is great, Kate."

"Are you going to come back, Patrick?"

"Nah, me and Jake . . . we're gonna be nomads." It was a lie, but Kate didn't know that. "I really didn't know what to give you. It would be pretty stupid of me to buy you something with your money, since I haven't made the effort to work out that account I have." From under his Izod pullover he withdrew four spiral-bound notebooks. He handed them over as though he were offering her a priceless gift. And it was a priceless gift, it was twenty years of his life he was giving to his wife, who could never be his wife again.

"It's all there, Kate. Every single minute of my life for the last twenty years. You were right, I needed to write it down. It . . . it's right to the minute, right up to the part where I pull out of the driveway at dawn tomorrow. It's all I have to give you."

"Thank you," Kate said, tears streaming down her cheeks. "I'll . . . take good care of it."

"You don't have to read it," Patrick said. "It might upset you."

"I want to."

"Okay, but you don't have to. Thanks to

you, I'm going to be okay."

"I know that, Patrick. I always knew that. I thought you knew that I knew that," she babbled.

"You're repeating yourself," he said, smiling. "I thought you said you went to college."

"Hey, you win some and you lose some. Want to go for a walk?"

"Yeah, I'd like that. Jake likes that Gucci collar and leash you got him."

"He deserves it. He'll be the only dog in Westfield with a Gucci collar and leash."

"Hell, I know that, but will anyone in Westfield even know who Gucci is? By the way, who is he?"

"Some guy who makes shoes and pocketbooks. I think he's in jail." Patrick let out a loud guffaw. "I'll be with you in a minute. I want to put your . . . gift in my room."

"If we're walking five miles, make sure you go to the bathroom. I get embarrassed when you pee in the bushes."

"Nag, nag, nag," Patrick said.

Kate finished reading Patrick's journal at quarter to five in the morning. She'd read straight through the night once the party was over and everyone had gone to bed. She closed the last one, her cheeks wet with tears, and carried the book to her desk. She took a three-minute shower, dressed in clean sweats, and marched out to the kitchen. She opened Della's door, tiptoed inside, and bent over to whisper in the older woman's ear.

In the kitchen she turned on the percolator and then raced back to her room. She could hear both showers running, which meant Patrick and the girls were up. She sat down at the desk, drew paper and pen from the drawer. She bit down on her lower lip, wrote steadily for five minutes.

"Guess it's time for me to be on my way," Patrick said with a catch in his voice. "I didn't think it was going to be so hard to say goodbye. Maybe I shouldn't say it."

"Maybe you shouldn't," Betsy said. "I'm going with you."

"Me too," Ellie said.

Patrick walked over to his wife, took the bag out of her hand, and handed it to Della. "No, Kate, you can't come. A month from now, maybe a year from now, you'd hate me. It wasn't meant to be. Look, I like you. I even love you. But . . . you don't fit into my life anymore. I can't fit into yours. It's nobody's fault. It's the way it is. It was your job to get me to this place in time. I can handle it now. If I falter, I'll give you a call and you can pep-talk me. Jake here will get me over the rough spots. Don't cry, Kate, you look ugly when you cry.

"I'm not taking the girls away from you. We're going to get really acquainted. I need to spend time with them, to get to know them. I promise to send them back."

"Oh, Patrick, this isn't right," Kate wailed. "I want to go with you. We're a family again. Why are you doing this?"

"Because *you* don't have the guts to do it. Yes, right now, this minute, you want to go with me, but it won't work. We're two different people. I'm not the old Patrick anymore. I'm Harry what's his name and you're Kate. You grew wings, Kate, and you need to fly. Call that guy and tell him you're on your way. Life's too short for this crap. Hey, I have things to do and places to go. I'm going to do it all. My way. Me and Jake here."

"Oh, Patrick . . . you're breaking my heart," Kate cried.

"Come on now, give us a send-off," Patrick said cheerfully.

"Go to hell, Patrick," Kate cried.

"If I were you, Kate, I'd shed ten pounds before you show up on that guy's doorstep." Patrick laughed as he settled himself on the driver's seat. He waved airily. Jake barked. The girls blew kisses as the Cherokee sailed down the driveway.

"Why did you lie to her like that?" Betsy demanded.

"She wanted to come. We would have been a family again," Ellie cried.

Patrick looked at his daughters. "Didn't either one of you learn anything in those fancy colleges you went to? Your mother loves someone else. She was willing to give that up. For me. I almost let her do that. Right up to the very last second I was going to. . . . I'm a taker. Your mother is a giver. You need to know that. If there's one thing I know, your mother is going to make all of this right. You see, we both made promises. We kept them, and now it's time for each of us to live our lives.

"Okay, troops, let's hear it! *Off we go, into the wild blue yonder . . .*"

EPILOGUE

Gus Stewart sat in his office, chair tilted back, feet propped on the desktop, his thoughts miles away in California. Work was piled up all around him, but he saw none of it. Very little mattered these days. Not his job, not his investments, not the white elephant in Connecticut he couldn't sell, not even the family shindig his siblings had invited him to for the upcoming weekend.

Kate was lost to him; he'd known that from the get-go, but he'd hung on, hoping something would work out in his favor. But when she'd called in July, crying and sobbing so hard he couldn't make sense of what she was saying, he'd known it was hopeless. Before she'd hung up, he'd heard her mutter something that sounded like "To have and to hold, for richer or poorer, in sickness and in health." He remembered how his stomach had heaved, how his eyes had burned.

That very night he'd swept everything on his desk onto the floor and taken off on a three-day drunk capped off with Chinese food that left him so sick it had taken two weeks to recover. He choked now, remembering. He hadn't been able to eat any Chinese food since.

"Yo, Gus," a copyboy shouted, "package for you. Plain brown wrapper. Only your name on the front. Bet it's spy stuff," the kid said as he sailed the hefty envelope toward Gus from the open doorway.

"Yeah, the Arabs are in the lobby and we're going to be held hostage," Gus muttered as he grabbed the package. The moment he recognized Kate's handwriting, his heart thumped in his chest, once, twice, three times, before it resumed its natural beat.

He weighed the package, trying to guess the contents. It must be the album she'd said she was going to make for him with all the pictures they'd taken in Hawaii and Costa Rica. There had to be at least six yards of see-through tape on the package. A nerve jangled and then another, until his feet hit the floor with a loud thump. He rummaged for scissors in his middle drawer, finally yanking them free of a wad of rubber bands and paper clips stuck to the bands. One of the bands snapped, snicking his finger. "Son of a bitch!" It took him a full two minutes to cut through the thick tape. Before he withdrew the contents, he swept his desk clear, everything flying in all directions. The wrapping sailed through the air and landed by the door. He thought it made a noise, but he wasn't sure. His breath exploded in a loud *swoosh.*

Four spiral-bound notebooks, one yellow, one blue, one red, and one a marbleized black and white. A letter with something paper-clipped underneath. His hands were trembling. It was a letter from Kate. He read it, his eyes burning.

My Dearest Gus,

I'm sure I don't have to tell you what it is you're holding in your hands. With Patrick's permission I am giving you your Pulitzer prize. All of us are placing our lives in your hands. If that sounds exaggerated, I apologize, but it's how we all feel. We're going back on our word, and that means you have to go back on yours, too.

I personally dropped off this package to ensure it wouldn't fall into other hands. Attached to this letter is all the proof you need. Betsy, in her rebellious period, when she thought she could single-handedly rescue her father, bought a fountain pen that doubled as a camera from one of the ads in *Soldier of Fortune* magazine.

I didn't even know there was such a gadget, but she knew, and I guess that's all that's important. What you have are three photographs of the document Betsy, Ellie, and I signed at LAX a year ago. Betsy developed them herself. Real cloak-and-dagger stuff.

We're all going to try to get on with our lives. I'm asking you to help. I hope I'm not being melodramatic. On the other hand, I remember the look on Mr. Spindler's face that day.

I need you to do one last thing. When you lock this in your safe, take the elevator to the lobby. Someone will be waiting for you. I'm thanking you in advance because I know you'll do as I ask.

Love and affection,
Kate

His eyes blurred with tears, Gus unhooked the black pen attached to the red cover of the spiral notebook.

It was all here, but at what price? He flipped through the red notebook, took in the strange scrawl, the awful words. Kate was right. It was a Pulitzer prize.

Take the elevator to the lobby, the note said. He locked the books in his office safe. He blew his nose lustily.

He was blowing his nose a second time, not caring about the tears in his eyes, when the elevator slid open.

She was directly in his line of vision, a hot dog in each hand. "Hey, I promised you dinner, and I always keep my promises. What took you so long?"

Gus's fist shot in the air. "Hell, I always was a slow mover."

"Well, I'm not." Kate smiled. "Marry me, Gus Stewart. In my right-hand pocket I have a lab slip for our blood tests. Maybe we can rush it."

"Let's eat on the way. This is a hell of a prewedding supper."

Kate grinned. "It doesn't get any better than this."

"No, lady, it doesn't."

The employees of THORNDIKE PRESS hope you have enjoyed this Large Print book. All our Large Print books are designed for easy reading — and they're made to last.

Other Thorndike Large Print books are available at your library, through selected bookstores, or directly from us. Suggestions for books you would like to see in Large Print are always welcome.

For more information about current and upcoming titles, please call or mail your name and address to:

THORNDIKE PRESS
PO Box 159
Thorndike, Maine 04986
800/223-6121
207/948-2962